HOLIDAY
MYSTERY

DATE DUE   DEC 1 0 2016

WITHDRAWN

Fields Where They Lay

Books by Timothy Hallinan

The Poke Rafferty Series
A Nail Through the Heart
The Fourth Watcher
Breathing Water
The Queen of Patpong
The Fear Artist
For the Dead
The Hot Countries

The Junior Bender Series
Crashed
Little Elvises
The Fame Thief
Herbie's Game
King Maybe

The Simeon Grist Series
The Four Last Things
Everything but the Squeal
Skin Deep
Incinerator
The Man With No Time
The Bone Polisher

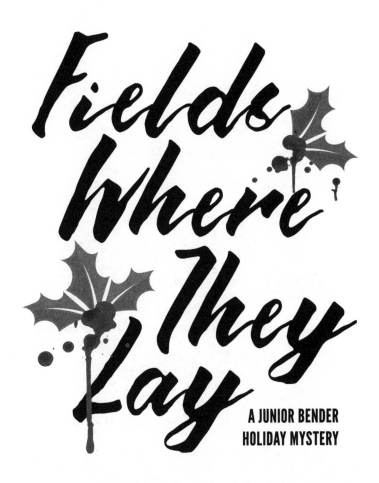

Fields Where They Lay

**A JUNIOR BENDER
HOLIDAY MYSTERY**

TIMOTHY HALLINAN

SOHO
CRIME

Published by Soho Press, Inc.
853 Broadway
New York, NY 10003

Library of Congress Cataloging-in-Publication Data

Hallinan, Timothy.
Fields where they lay: a Junior Bender mystery / Timothy Hallinan.

ISBN 978-1-61695-746-9
eISBN 978-1-61695-747-6

I. Title
PS3558.A3923 F54 2016 813'.54—dc23   2016017076

Interior design by Janine Agro, Soho Press, Inc.

Printed in the United States of America

10 9 8 7 6 5 4 3 2 1

To the star on top of my personal Christmas tree.

She knows who she is.

PART ONE

SHEPHERDS ABIDING IN THE FIELD

1
Two Santas

The astringent December sunlight looked, as always at this time of year, like it had been ladled into the smog with a teaspoon, like vinegar. The watery light and the goop in the air had softened shadows so that the whole composition seemed as flat as a painting, perhaps titled "Field with Lump and Cars." The lump, a hulking, windowless, three-story ellipse with a flat roof and stains shaped like dirt icicles running down its outer walls, was in the center of a field where herds of sheep or cattle might once have grazed but which was now covered in flat black asphalt, marked in white diagonal parking lines to create an enormous herringbone pattern.

The pattern was visible because there weren't very many cars, and the ones that had arrived were scattered around the lot as though the visitors wanted to avoid each other, perhaps out of embarrassment for being there at all. Later, I would realize that the outlying cars belonged to employees, dutifully obeying a rule that was intended to free up closer spaces for customers who probably weren't coming.

A huge electric sign on a concrete pillar that stretched higher than the top of the building was blinking its sales pitch in red and green. It read:

EDGERTON MALL PRESENTS
TWO SANTAS!!!!!!
HO! HO! HOOO!

Two Santas.

And I was going to be stuck here until Christmas.

Only one thing came to mind, so I said it. "Bah," I said. "Humbug."

Santa Number One, if you were reading left to right on the top row of security monitors, was a lot thinner than Santa Number Two, with a sharp, bony face and a ropy neck that plunged unconvincingly into his yards of scarlet padding before blossoming into Santa's expected bulk, something like the way the narrow shaft of an onion flares abruptly into a bulb. His belly may have been bogus but his merriness was almost authentic, at least at times. Santa Number Two had the requisite girth and the rosy cheeks of yore, but his *Ho! Ho! Ho!* rang hollow, and if his eyes had been the barrels of *Star Trek* phasers, there would have been a pile of fine ash at the foot of his plush red-and-green throne. Several perceptive kids had gotten a glimpse of those eyes and backed away fast, feeling behind them one-handed for Mom.

"Two Santas in one mall," I said. "Says a lot for the critical-thinking skills of American retailers."

"You got no idea," said Wally Durskee. Wally, who was occupying the chair next to mine, was a short, serious security guy in a tight green polo shirt that was stretched over so much muscle he looked almost cubic. His carrot-colored hair was in rapid and premature retreat, and he'd developed a nervous habit of fingering a bit hopefully the newly vacant acreage above his forehead. He had the moist fish-white complexion of someone who never gets outside when the sun is shining; a spatter of freckles as a genetic accessory to the red hair; and small, deep-set black eyes, as reflective as raisins, that tended to jump from place to place, a tic he'd undoubtedly developed from a great many days trying to watch thirty-two surveillance screens all at once, as we were at that moment. The jumpy eyes created an impression of unreliability, although he seemed straight enough. "You shoulda been here four days ago," he said. "Line out the front door, kids screaming, mothers having anxiety attacks. Cleaning crew swept up a couple handfuls of tranquilizers next morning, and not all legal, neither. They got into a fistfight over them. One-hour, ninety-minute wait to get to Sanny Claus's damn lap. Kids peeing in line. Some limp washcloth emailed cell phone pitchers to Channel Four and they sent a news crew. On TV it looked like the Syrians trying to get through the checkpoints into Germany."

I said something that must have sounded sympathetic, because Wally said, "And the only Sanny we had then was Dwayne down there, and kids'd scream to get up to him, take one look, and then scream to get away from him."

"Dwayne is the fat one?"

"Yeah. Dwayne Wix. Even I can't stand him, and I like everybody."

"Fire him."

"Sure, right," Wally said. He blocked the headline with his hands: "SHOPPING MALL FIRES SANNY CLAUS. Anyway, he's not our employee. We hire a contractor for all this stuff."

"Yeah? What's it called?"

"Ho-Ho-Holidays," he said. "Sounds like a stammer, don't it?"

"It do."

He lobbed a suspicious glance at me but resumed his narrative anyway. Wally was a guy with a lot of narrative and no one to resume it for. "So the contractor threw in Shlomo there at the other end, half price, because it was their job to make crowd estimates and stuff."

I said, "Shlomo?"

"Shlomo Stempel," Wally said. "The skinny one. Kids like *him*. Better than Dwayne anyways."

I said, "Okay."

"Why, you got a problem?"

"No, why do you—"

"What do you think, there's a tonload of unemployed Sanny Clauses this time of year? You can't put an ad in the paper says, *Christians only.*"

"No," I said. "I just don't hear the name Shlomo all that much. You know, it's not like Aidan or Max or Justin or whatever all the kids are called these days."

Wally was regarding me as though he thought I was likely to charge him at any moment. "You think Sanny Claus would object?" It was apparently a serious question.

"No," I said. "I think Sanny Claus would be thrilled to be impersonated by Shlomo Stempel."

"Great guy, Shlomo," Wally said. He started to say something else but picked at his eyetooth with a fingernail instead. "So anyways, that's why there's two of them."

"At opposite ends of the mall."

"It's a long mall," Wally said. He smoothed the miniature desert on his head, which was already smooth. "Seventh longest mall west of the Mississippi."

"Really."

"Wouldn't kid you. Not my style. Long story short, the

place is so long there's probably some kids, they only see one Sanny Claus." He looked back at the screens, and doubt furrowed his brow. "If they're really little."

"Well," I said, "that's good. Kids today have enough problems without worrying about whether Santa Claus is a committee." I stood up. The two of us were occupying creaking wheeled office chairs behind a scratched-up console, sticky with ancient spilled drinks, in a dark, cold, windowless room on the third floor, the low-rent floor, of Edgerton Mall. From time to time Wally toyed with one of the controls in front of him, making one of the cameras in some store somewhere in the mall swoop sickeningly left or right or zoom in and out.

"Where you going?" Wally said.

"Just getting up. So, yesterday someone added up the shoplifting reports from all the stores and discovered that it was way out of line."

"Fridays," Wally said. "This is Saturday," he added, making sure we were on the same page. "Stores submit their weekly reports on Friday and the security company, the guys I work for, plugged them into a spreadsheet overnight, and it spiked like Pike's Peak. You been to Pike's Peak?"

"Yes," I said, and Wally's face fell. He undoubtedly had a lot of narrative about Pike's Peak, all bottled up and ready to pop. "It's a whole week's worth of losses, right?"

"Right." He made one of the cameras pan and then zoom dramatically but his heart wasn't in it.

"How out of line is it?"

"Like Pike's Peak. Maybe a hundred, hundred and twenty percent gain. Or loss, I guess. You know, a gain in the *loss*." He sketched an acute angle, point up, in the air. "Pike's frigging Peak."

"Does the software break the data out on a day-by-day basis?"

"No. We get a one-week dump of numbers from each store, and that's what gets fed in."

"Why does it come to you?"

"Lookit my shirt. What does it say?"

He was waiting, so I said, "Sec—"

"Security," he said over me. "We get the data 'cause it's our asses when it goes kerflooey like this. Look, I'm not really sure who you are."

"And you haven't seen anything odd from up here."

"If I *had*," he said in a tone that suggested he'd taken most of the blame that had been ladled out during his lifetime and he was continually on the lookout for more, "you wouldn't be here, would you? And I'm still not sure who you—"

"But you were told to help me out, right?"

He replayed the question mentally, squinting at the wall behind me. When he'd finished combing it for ambiguity and trick clauses and, I don't know, the Oxford comma, he said, "Right. But who *are* you?"

"I'm a theft expert," I said.

I could hear him swallow.

I don't want to spring this on you too suddenly, but things are not always what they seem. One way we often perceive human artifacts—you know, the world of airplanes and washing machines and books and office buildings and shopping malls and easily available facial quality tissue—is to see them all as different things, things that exist independently of each other, brought into existence by separate processes and for different reasons. And that's certainly one way to look at it, and if it makes you happy, skip to page eleven.

But *another* way to look at the man-made world is to see it as an extension of or even a parallel to the so-called "natural" world, in which thousands of seemingly different plants and animals and rocks and things seem for some reason to cluster thickly in certain places and more sparsely—or not at all—in others. And if you ask yourself why this pattern of uneven distribution arises—what the connective tissue could be—the answer that's certain to come to you sooner or later is *water*. Water is, in a sense, the chord, albeit inaudible, that produces and supports all those individual tones: water shapes the landscape; water erodes the rocks and distributes the minerals; water is the vital force behind the oldest redwood, the laciest flower, the man-eating tiger. You're probably already ahead of me, but I'll say it anyway: The "water" of the man-made world is money.

The underground river of money, kept thoughtfully out of sight by those who manipulate it, is the unifying element that ties the man-made world together, that supplies the necessary vitality to produce everything from a fancy doorknob to a five-way traffic light, from a one-room shack to a roadside grapefruit stand to the New York Stock Exchange. Without the flow of money, these artificial landmarks could not spring up to decorate or desecrate the landscape and to impinge on our lives. And with money, as with water, you have *no idea* where it's been.

The clear liquid in the almost comically sanitary bottle of *aqua pura* you buy at the grocer's has probably passed through both business ends of multiple living organisms, a couple of sewage plants, and a poisoned river before evaporating to fall as pristine snow mass on some picturesque Colorado mountain and from there to melt into the stream or fill the aquifer tapped by the bottling plant. There's no way to tell. Just as there's no way to tell in a glittery mall full of gift wrap, candy canes, bright ribbons, sugar-stimulated children, and the repetitive racket of seasonal music where the money that waters that mall has come from.

If it's a big enough project, there's a pretty good chance—in fact, I'd say it's just shy of a certainty—that some if not all of that money is dirty. And in the case of the Edgerton Mall—the name of a nonexistent neighborhood chosen to conjure up visions of graceful, trailing willows, kids on bicycles, picket fences, and an overwhelmingly Caucasian population—the money flowing beneath *that* temple to Mammon, currently in the million-dollar throes of celebrating a millennia-old birth into poverty so abject that the child was delivered in a stable . . . well, the river of money down there was *filthy*.

2
No Vowels

I couldn't give Wally much detail about why I was in the Edgerton Mall because I was pretty sure it could have gotten me—or him, or both of us—killed.

Much earlier that day—just *three days before Christmas,* as my daughter, Rina, had reminded me in the half-octave-up tone that designated spoken italics—I'd had a wakeup call, literally, from a woman named Trey Annunziato, whose control over an ambitiously brutal San Fernando Valley crime family was increasingly tenuous and who felt I owed her a favor. I disagreed, but I kept my argument to myself, what with discretion being the better part of a possibly violent death—a fate that befell, much more frequently than the statistical norm, those who didn't do what Trey wanted them to do. Hastily dressed and largely uncombed, I showed up at Trey's walled-in Chinese fantasy compound down near Northridge at the appointed time. (Trey had once shot someone in the knee for tardiness, which is the kind of thing that sticks in the memory.) A grim thirty minutes later I'd driven back out of the compound with a very bad taste in my mouth.

I had an hour and some change to spare before I was scheduled to show up for the meeting Trey was sending me to at the cumbersomely named Wrightwood Greens Golf and Country Club. So I called Louie the Lost and asked his voice mail whether he could drop whatever he was doing and meet me at the Du-par's coffee shop in Studio City he and I occasionally frequented. There was nothing special about the place except that it was convenient to both of us and it was where my mentor, Herbie Mott, had taken me after my first professional burglary at the age of seventeen.

Du-par's had a lot of sentimental value.

As I pulled into the parking lot, my phone rang. Louie.

"Can't do it," he said. "I got no wheels. Tell you what. Get me two pieces of cherry pie—no, one cherry and one apple—and come down Ventura a mile, mile and a half to Pete's Putt-Putt Hut. You know it?"

"Sure," I said. Pete was a so-so mechanic whose lack of skill was offset by a profound lack of interest in who actually owned the cars he worked on.

Louie said, "Think they got punkin?"

"It's after Thanksgiving and before Christmas," I said. "Any coffee shop that doesn't have pumpkin loses its pie license."

"You think? Huh. Okay, then. Punkin."

"Instead of what?"

"Why you gotta confuse everything? Gimme some punkin and one of them other ones."

"Fine." I hung up and went in and got what was certain to be the wrong pie.

Sure enough, about six minutes later Louie said, "No apple?"

I opened the back door of my white Toyota and took out a piece of apple.

"Kid's learning, Pete," Louie called to a pair of shoes protruding from beneath a car. The shoes contributed a grunt of nonlinguistic agreement. The car Pete was buried under was a black Lincoln Town Car, Louie's favorite personal ride and also his go-to when someone needed a legitimate-looking limo. I'd driven it myself not so long ago. It brought back some really rotten memories, so I said, "Can we go in the office or something?"

"Sure. You remember the coffee?"

"You didn't ask for coffee."

"Do I gotta do everything?" he said. "Okay, but that means the pie's on you."

"You have coffee, Pete?" I asked.

"You don't want to drink it," the shoes said.

I followed Louie into an office that looked like it had recently been waxed with used motor oil and then buffed with a uniform coat of grease until everything was a restful, if shiny, sort of Confederate grey. Many large glossy calendars with pictures of tires on them had been hung randomly on the walls. "Jesus," I said as my feet almost slipped out from under me. "Should have brought my ice skates."

"Yeah, yeah, yeah. So? What's the emergency?" Louie swept aside some sparkly Christmas cards, heavily accented with black fingerprints, to make room on Pete's desk for the pumpkin pie. One of the cards fell over and emitted a few tremulous notes of "God Rest Ye Merry, Gentlemen" before lapsing into an embarrassed silence, like the kid in a choir who accidentally sings out on the upbeat.

"So," I said, "I've got to go talk to a guy named Tip Poindexter."

Louie was sliding his feet experimentally across the grease on the floor. "Tell you what," he said without looking up. "Here's my best suggestion. Go get your passport. Go get *all* your passports. Then go to Pakistan with a lot of plane changes and double-backs and new names along the way. And stay there. Hey, you know anyone looks just like you?"

"No."

"Too bad. You could use a double." He sat in what I guessed was Pete's chair, the only one in the room, and swiveled it silently back and forth a couple of times. Pete kept it well oiled, but then I figured Pete's primary purpose in life was to keep everything well oiled. I put the second piece of pie, the apple, next to the pumpkin. "This is the kind of situation," Louie said, "a guy who's like your twin or something, would come in really handy. And you should make yourself the beneficiary on his life insurance. In fact, tell you something: except for the double, I got someone who could *arrange* all that. She's a nice girl, too. Disappear you so good you'd be looking for yourself."

"So Tip Poindexter, despite having a name that would look good on a butterfly, is not actually—"

"It's a made-up name," Louie said. "When he first got here from Russia he had a kind of brainy American girlfriend, brainy by his standards anyway. She taught him to play Scrabble to improve his English, and she spelled out *tipping point*—"

"That's two words," I said.

Louie waggled his head from side to side. "He was an immigrant then, so what did he know? Lotta Scrabble points in 'tipping point.' She won the game. For all I know, a couple years later he figured out she cheated and had her thrown out of a helicopter, but at the time, when he needed a name with some vowels in it, he came up with Tip Poindexter."

"What was his original name?"

"With no vowels, who can pronounce it?" Louie said. He pulled out the plastic fork I'd stuck vertically in the pumpkin and dropped it into a wastebasket full of wadded, greasy paper towels. Then he picked up the piece of pumpkin pie, minus the paper plate.

"Russians have vowels," he said. "They may be short on some stuff, but vowels they've got." Louie took a bite out of the filling and tucked it in his cheek. "He comes from a place near Sochi, you know, where the Russians put on those weird Winter Olympics with all the fake snow, but his name was from some old language, whole alphabet only had a couple of vowels. It was like that TV show where they're always trying to buy a vowel, except for them the answer was always no. For hundreds of years."

"Ubykh," I said. "Last person who spoke it died twenty, twenty-five years ago."

"Musta been a lonely guy," he said around a mouthful of pie.

"Thousands of great, vowel-free puns lost forever."

"From what I know about the place, they probably talked mostly about goats and snow." He took another bite of filling.

Louie was the closest thing to a friend I had in the crook world, although, since his commodity was information, our relationship stopped a few feet short of full and open. He'd been a getaway driver until a wrong turn after a diamond heist went mildly disastrous and word got out that he could barely find his way out of his own driveway. After sitting around for months like Norma Desmond waiting for the phone to ring with the next job, he packed it in and went into business as a telegraph, with a sideline in unregistered and often souped-up cars as a sort of nod to his past as a driver. What he lacked in his sense of direction he made up in memory; if he'd ever heard something, he remembered it, and he made sure he heard pretty much everything.

He licked one of the craters he'd made in the pumpkin pie and said, "If you're going to do business with Tip Poindexter, maybe you oughta pay me in advance. Five hundred."

"After all these years?" I said, reaching for my wallet.

"Long time ago I heard something Irwin Dressler was supposed to have said."

I stopped counting and listened. Irwin Dressler was in his nineties now but still the King of Shade, the mobster who had done more than any other to shape modern Los Angeles. I said, "Yeah? What?"

"He said, back in the old days when someone who was operating at the B or C level all of a sudden went after someone in the A level, they'd say, 'Kid's got a lot of spirit.'"

I said, "That's the most boring thing you've ever told me."

He held up the hand with the pie in it. "And later, when the B-level guy showed up with a couple hundred bullets in him, they'd add a clause on. 'Kid had a lot of spirit,' they'd say, 'but not much judgment.'"

"So what are you suggesting?"

"Well, if you're gonna pass on Pakistan or the girl I got who can make you disappear, I'd suggest that Trey, with the personnel problems she's been having lately, is a kiss under the mistletoe compared to Tip Poindexter. If you're gonna piss anyone off, I'd pick Trey. Just don't show up for the meeting."

"So what does he do?"

"You got your Christmas shopping done?"

"No," I said. "I do it all on Christmas Eve."

Louie sat almost upright. My Christmas shopping habits seemed to engage him more than my imminent death. "What? You kidding me?"

"Give me a reason," I said, "even a bad one, for me to kid you about Christmas shopping."

"Junior." He swiveled from side to side in the chair, apparently organizing his thoughts. "I seen you *diagram a burglary.* You drive home like you got the Shadow tailing you two cars back. I ask you, you think it's gonna rain, you check your phone. This is not, like actors always say, consistent with your character."

"I have issues," I said.

"With Christmas."

"Look," I said, feeling my face heat up, "shrinks spend half their time prying out their patients' issues with their *mothers.* If I have a—a few—issues with Christmas, well, *there we are.* It's my problem, not yours, okay? Are we still friends?"

"Sheesh," he said.

"So, yes, I do my Christmas shopping on Christmas Eve. And?"

"And you might want to change that," he said. "Get it done early, like before you meet Tip. Wrap it, too. Write the cards. Get them all ready and then give them to someone to hand out for you, just in case. Tip is, ummm . . ." He finished eating the pumpkin off the pie crust and tossed the crust in among the oil-sodden paper towels. "You know," he said, "to me, punkin pie is the taste of the holidays. The smell is pine but the taste—"

"Tell it to Hallmark. What *about* Tip? I mean, what does he do?"

"Well, *now* he's a big-time money guy. Backs housing developments, fancy hotels, apartment complexes. Got a shopping mall, even. And since money needs a little muscle from time to time, he supplies that, too. Few years back he cleared all the houses in a straight line about four miles long to make room for one of those toll roads, all on the force of his personality. I mean, people sold in a *hurry*. But when he first got here, he was an importer."

"Importing what?"

"Girls from Eastern Europe. Fly them into Mexico, pay coyotes to walk them over the border, and I'm talking in groups of thirty, forty at a time. Haul them from Arizona to Los Angeles, make his mark on them—"

"His mark."

"Well, first it was three knife cuts in a row way high on the outside of the arm, just above where a short-sleeve blouse would end. Like a sergeant's chevron, you know, but straight, not those upside-down *V*s. Three lines, parallel, just deep enough to scar. Anywhere they went for the rest of their lives, he could get someone to make them roll up their sleeves, and *hey there*: identification. Then later he got himself a dog, and some asshole dog doctor told him about the chip, you know? The chip they put in so the dog can be identified anywhere? So he started putting those in, paid the vet extra to handle it, and told the girls that they were like transmitters, right? Said he had a gizmo he could turn on any time and see where everybody was."

I said, "This is a hell of a Christmas story."

"You wanted to know who he is, well, this is who he is. And the girls, they got trafficked off to massage parlors, cat houses, outcall operations, traveling house trailers—like the Good Humor Man, but with, you know. All over the country. Hundreds and hundreds of them. He owned part of the businesses, he got part of the girls' cut. The only recession-proof industry, money coming out of his ears. And then, after eight, nine years, he hooked up with some of the other

Russky mafiosos who got on one of Putin's wrong sides and had to haul ass out of the mother country, and they put him into other businesses. Legit businesses, even. Now he hosts fund-raisers for political candidates and plays golf and polo and gets his picture in the *Times* and is married to something you'd have to look at five or six times to appreciate fully."

"Get up," I said.

"Why?"

"Because it's my turn to sit is why."

"Jeez," Louie said, picking up the piece of apple pie. "I'm older than you." But he got up.

"Much better," I said. The chair had one haunch higher than the other so I was at a slight angle off the vertical, but with my knees feeling so weak it was hard to care.

"Why's he want you?" Louie was using his fingers to peel the top crust off the pie.

"I don't know. Trey said he needed an expert."

"Like I said, get your shopping done. You got a will?" He dropped the triangle of crust, which he'd managed to remove intact, into the trash. "On a diet," he volunteered. "Promised Alice I'd look out for my carbohydrates." Louie had a big, round Mediterranean face, the kind of face that it was easy to envision peering down into a jumbo bowl of pasta or singing opera, perhaps at the same time, and slightly curly, almost pretty, hair that he'd fought with for years until he finally just grew enough of it to pull it into a tight ponytail. I'd gotten to know that face very well, and looking at it now, I had a pang at the thought that if Tip Poindexter killed me, I'd never see it again.

"Would you miss me if I got killed?" I asked.

"Sure I would," he said. "So would Rina. So would Ronnie.

Even Kathy." Rina, as I've said, was my daughter, Ronnie my relatively new and impermeably mysterious girlfriend, and Kathy was my ex, Rina's mom.

"That's not many people," I said.

"Yeah?" he said, taking a bite out of the apple filling. "Well, listen, I'll send extra flowers."

3
The Fried Egg Effect

Around noon I'd obeyed Trey's command by driving up into the expensive hills south of Ventura Boulevard. I was following a street with a new name—not the name it had when I was growing up a few miles away—winding between ostentatious new houses and the occasional gated community, the products of the rampant gentrification that's making so much of the San Fernando Valley—hell, California in general—so much shinier and so much worse.

Say what you will about the past, it's rarely an improvement to bulldoze it wholesale. Even in Los Angeles, if you go back far enough, you'll encounter two or three periods when people briefly displayed good taste, and some of those structures should be preserved, if only for variety. Neighborhoods like the one I was driving through—all the houses architectural second cousins, built right next to each other only a month or two apart—always make me think of a very white, very new, very unconvincing set of false teeth.

The problem is that there isn't enough of California to accommodate all the people who want to live here. There seems to be literally no limit to what people will pay for their idea of the right house in their idea of the right place, and that means there's almost nowhere that's safe from developers.

Los Angeles has oil under it, but the *real* oil here has always been land, and that was never as true as it is today. Poor communities get bulldozed to make room for middle-class communities, middle-class communities get bulldozed to make room for upper-class communities, and upper-class communities get bulldozed to make room for rich communities. And the bulldozers sweep the poor into uglier and more remote areas.

The Wrightwood Greens Golf and Country Club to which I'd been summoned was one of the Valley's shiny new gathering places for people whose money was recently acquired and whose manners hadn't yet been sanded down into the smooth indifference that marks multiple generations of wealth. This concept of golf as aspiration is traditional in Los Angeles because golf clubs were actually the *first* LA status symbol. Stung by the East Coast's indifference to their financial success, in 1919 some of the newly crowned kings of the orange groves (that were even then being plowed under at an alarming rate) decided to prove that they, too, were high-class folks. They did it by kick-starting the Wilshire Country Club with an ostentatious Spanish-style clubhouse, a golf course that opened a year later, and of course by building a fence to keep out all those people who were simply not good enough to be admitted.

And whom did the excluded include? Primarily Jews.

Jews were not in short supply in early Los Angeles, nor were they without clout. In 1920, setting some sort of record for construction and landscaping, the Hillcrest Country Club opened across the street from Fox Studios, but the term "open" applied to Jews only. Thus, people who did business together on a daily basis were essentially prohibited from playing golf together. The rivalry was immediate, deep, and one-sided: Wilshire was as boring as a dietician's shopping list while Hillcrest, probably benefiting from a statistically improbable number of comedians and writers, was the liveliest place in town. The Monday morning jokes that circulated through the studios were all cracked originally at Hillcrest. Adding insult to injury, oil was discovered on Hillcrest's land, and all the members shared in the profits.

Hillcrest and Wilshire are pushing a hundred years old at this point, and they've settled into the landscape as though they'd been part of Creation. But Wrightwood, as perhaps befitted a club created for the Valley's new and shiny one, two, and three percent, still looked like an unhealed incision, cut into the land only three or four rains ago. The grass was a blinding nitrogen-overdose green and most of the trees leaned on stakes to keep them upright. The asphalt on the drives was as black and smooth as a velvet glove. But regardless of all its nouveau sheen, its fancy twelve-foot gates symbolized to those who entered that they'd been accepted into an elite that rejected most of their friends.

If I'd been in any danger of forgetting Poindexter's name, it would have been engraved in my memory by the time I set eyes on him. I had to give it to the guard at the gate, to the valet who hesitated in apparent revulsion before climbing into my little white Toyota, and to the guardian of the misleadingly named Welcome Desk, a woman whose hair was pulled back so tightly it looked like she was advertising her pain threshold. She passed me to a psychotically self-effacing maître d' who kept rubbing his palms together like someone who'd just shaken hands with Typhoid Mary.

I followed him into a long, airy room, the glass southern wall of which reluctantly admitted the grey, common-looking light of a cloudy December day. The room was set with round tables topped by brilliantly white cloth. In the center of each table was a precarious-looking circular arrangement of silver and blue Christmas tree ornaments threaded with tiny blue and white lights. In the room's far north corner, an enormous red sack bled elegantly wrapped packages across the wheat-colored carpet.

The time was just a couple of minutes after noon, and most of the tables were empty. At the table farthest from both the entry hall and the window, right in front of Santa's bag, sat a slender, fine-boned man with a high forehead fringed by dead-looking, oddly flossy blond hair, like an over-styled child's doll might have after her thirtieth perm. He pushed his chair back and rose, his pale eyes on me the moment I entered the room behind the hand-wringing maître d'.

The man to whom Trey Annunziato had recommended me was about my height, an inch or so over six feet, slender as a lost hope, not so much wearing as *draped in* a navy blazer that I estimated at $2,500 at first glance and $3,000 at second, and a pair of camel's-hair slacks so perfect I couldn't force myself to look at them. Gleaming on his left wrist was a discreetly slender circlet of gold, a carefully calibrated understatement of wealth. He epitomized the kind of guy Louie the Lost once described as "shit with a logo."

"How kind of you to come," he said, extending a hand just far enough to make me bend at the waist to shake it across the table. The words had only a hint of an accent, just that sense of being verbally on tiptoe you sometimes hear in people who are speaking a language they learned late in life. "Tip Poindexter."

He pronounced the *p*'s of the preposterous name independently, two little pops that sounded like automatic gunfire a long way off. "Junior Bender," I said, letting go of a very cold

hand as fast as I could. "Hap-py to meet you," I said, releas-
ing my own little barrage of popped *p*'s.

For a moment he looked straight through me, and then
he nodded. "Yes, I was told you were a merry soul," he said,
his smile baring a row of teeth big enough for clearing land.
"And you weren't misrepresented." There was just a hint of
roll on the *r* sounds. "Please. Sit."

I sat.

Up close, he wasn't so much slender as gaunt. His bone
structure was as clearly defined as it would have been in
an X-ray—high Asiatic cheekbones, a sharply squared
jaw, and a receding chin that robbed his face of some of
the authority it gained from the pale, steady eyes, which
were the color of dirty ice. Most of the people I'd come
across who were that thin lived primarily on rage, and I
saw nothing in front of me to suggest that rage wasn't a
good working thesis. "I assume you're going to join me for
lunch," he said. He tugged down at the crease in his slacks
as he resumed his seat.

"No, just something quick," I said. "I've got a lot to do
today."

He gave his full attention to shaking out his napkin and
placing it on his lap. Without looking up, he said, "Change
your plans."

"Christmas," I said. "You know?"

"I am aware of Christmas, certainly." He smoothed the
tablecloth with his palms. "Was that what you were asking?"

"I wasn't actually asking anything," I said. "The question
mark, used that way, is usually intended to soften a bald and
possibly rude statement of fact into the more polite form of a
rhetorical question. *N'est-ce pas?*"

Poindexter blinked so slowly I could have counted to

three. When he brought his eyes up to me, their near color-lessness had an unsettling effect, and he was obviously aware of it. "Whatever you have in mind," he said, "you will clear the decks, is that the way to put it?"

"It's one way."

"Do you have a shopping list?"

"No," I said. "I like to improvise."

"Then improvise. Here and now. At this table. *Make* a list. For someone as spontaneous as you like to appear to be, that shouldn't be too taxing. I will have everything bought and paid for by this evening."

I said, "That won't—"

"Wrapped, naturally. With cards. If you'll give me a sample of your handwriting and a list of pet names—" He paused, pursing his lips. "Pet names? This is correct for people?"

I didn't answer.

"Yes, it is," he said. "With your handwriting and the names of your favorite people, I'll have appropriate personal messages with a seasonal flair written in the cards."

"I don't think so."

"I am being very polite to you," he said. He put his fore-arms on the table and leaned toward me conspiratorially although no one was in earshot. "Trey says you are an asset worth cultivating."

"Not a very personal recommendation, is it?"

"Trey is not a very personal individual. Nor am I." He glanced down at his discreet bracelet and then used his other hand to buff it against his cuff. "But please. Let us do this in a friendly manner." Poindexter raised his head and gave me a small, cold smile. "I have invited you here," he said. "I am buying you lunch. I'm sure you'll agree that this is a much more pleasant way for me to proceed than by having someone collect your daughter when she gets out of her school in Tarzana at three and threaten to kill her."

It was my turn to look down at the table. The firestorm of fury his words had kindled would have been visible from across the room. My ears were ringing from the leap in my blood pressure, and I decided to use that as my timer. When they stopped ringing, I'd look at him again.

"Ahh," he said, "Lawrence," and I sensed the presence of someone at my elbow, giving off a whiff of stale cigarette smoke.

"Mr. Poindexter," the someone named, apparently, Lawrence, said. "Good to see you, sir. Happy holidays."

"We were just talking, my friend and I," Poindexter said, "about getting our shopping done."

"Best part of the year, sir," Lawrence said.

"I hope you've gotten some swell things for those beautiful children." The word *swell*, even in the absence of an accent, would have told me that English wasn't his original language.

"I try, sir. The membership's generous holiday bonus makes it easier for all of us. Can I bring you something to drink?"

"Mineral water, room temperature, no ice. Mr. Bender?"

I had to clear my throat. "Coffee. Black."

"Yes, sir." The waiter had barely shifted his weight, hadn't even lifted a foot yet, when Poindexter said, "*Wait*, Lawrence." The tone was polite and final at the same time, a whip wrapped in silk.

Lawrence waited.

"I'd like the trout with a small green salad, no dressing."

"Very good choice, sir. And you, sir?" he said, leaning in my direction.

"Just coffee."

"Mr. Bender," Poindexter said, "please take a moment to look at the menu."

A long, glossy piece of cardboard appeared on the table-cloth in front of me. I pushed it aside and said, "Coffee."

"But I am eating," he said. "Please. The kitchen here is very good."

"I'll do what you need me to do," I said, finally looking up at him and catching him in the stare of someone who is trying quite hard to read a muddled slop of tea leaves. He looked away instantly. "I'll talk to you as long as I have to. But there's no way in the whole wide fucking world I'll eat with you. *Coffee*, Lawrence," I repeated to the waiter, who had taken an involuntary step back. "Black."

He was making something of a production of eating his trout, which was apparently unusually bony, even for trout. After a brief conversational skirmish, which his side won, we sat in a stony silence broken only by repeated interjections of "Excuse me," as he extricated a tiny, sharp bone from his mouth and put it on the edge of his plate. I was occupying myself by taking apart the arrangement of ornaments on the table and putting them back in different configurations, currently the idiotic abstract of the "smiley," the happy face that has refused for decades to relinquish its stranglehold on the hearts of the easily pleased.

He said, "So we are clear? You will go to my mall, introduce yourself to the so-called security staff, and discover why I am suddenly being robbed blind." His Russian accent had found a crack in the wall and was asserting itself.

"Blind?" I said, turning the smiley into a frowny. "The kind of money you could lose through—what, *shoplifting*?—is small change to you. It's practically a cost of doing business."

His silence made me look up and then wish I hadn't. His eyes had taken on a sort of fried egg effect, whites clearly visible all the way around the pale iris, and they were actually *vibrating*, doing a tiny left-right-left, back-and-forth thing so fast it had to be involuntary.

"Nobody," he said, and stopped. He closed his eyes and pressed his fingertips to them and then opened them again. "*Nobody*. Steals. From. Me. *Nobody*."

"Got it."

"Everybody has stock in trade, *hmmm?*" The Russian accent had claimed control of his tongue. "You, maybe, I don't know, maybe you think is brains for you, you think you're so smart." He stopped and, with his mouth closed, swished air in and out between his teeth, making his lips protrude and recede quickly, the way mine might do when I use mouthwash. The eyes were now poached; some of the white was gone, but they were completely still. "For me, it is fear. Fear is what keeps me in business." Aside from pronouncing "keeps" as *kips*, his English was reclaiming lost territory. "Do you know history?"

"Bits and pieces," I said.

"The oh-so-civilized English, with the severed heads up on poles on the south entrance to London Bridge. Do you know about this?"

"Yes," I said. "Most thieves remember that bit."

"So did *everyone who was alive then*," he said. He was almost shouting, and a few heads turned in our direction from the newly occupied tables. He sat back in his chair, smoothing the front of his blazer, his eyes still fixed on me. "So what this means is, first you find out who's stealing from me and you tell me who it is, and second, until then you don't tell *anyone* I hired you. I don't want people even saying my

name and *stealing* in the same sentence. You were hired, if
you have to talk about it at all, by the Edgerton Partnership.
Are we clear?"

"Clear."

He blinked at last, and I had the sensation that I was on a
plane that had just taken a big dip. I sat back in my chair, too.

"And third," he said, "you *succeed*. Trey was very clear
about this. She recommended you, she thinks highly of you
in a minor way, but she doesn't care if she never sees you
again." He looked down at his plate and shook his head.
"Too many bones," he said. He gave me the small, well-
chilled smile again. "How was the coffee?"

4
Bric or Brac

Shoplifting was entirely outside my realm of my experience. I was completely disoriented. I felt large, I felt lumpen, I felt like I made noise every time I took a step inside the store I'd chosen as the scene of my impending crime. I felt like an *amateur*.

Over the last twenty years or so, I've probably stolen more things than most people own, but theft—the art of *skilled* theft, the kind of theft I'd trained for—is a solitary enterprise, carried out in the dark, in carefully chosen rooms, and silently, rather than under merciless fluorescents. Not to mention the incessant accompaniment of songs about snow and sleigh bells and merry old elves and being home for the holidays while I was stuck in this mall, two days away from the holiday in question, trying to learn a new way to steal.

I'd worked up my courage for the chore and surveyed the lay of the land by doing a circumnavigation of the mall on the second level. The circuit had taken me about twenty-one minutes. Most people take approximately that long to walk a mile, but I was weaving in and out of shoppers with their eyes on the bright windows and slowing frequently behind an adult or two with small children or groups of adolescent boys or girls (almost never together) who had lagged to appreciate the fine points of a gaggle of the opposite gender, so I wasn't doing my usual pace. My best guess, by the time I got back to the escalator I'd taken down from Wally's third-level surveillance room, was that the mall's internal loop was a little less than half a mile. With three levels, that meant a bit more than a mile's worth of storefront, given the commercial dead space lost to entrances, exits, eating areas, escalators, elevators, stairways, restrooms, and other unprofitable necessities.

The experience was mildly informative, but it was time to stop stalling. Feeling as big and as conspicuous as a lighthouse, I had made a hurried choice from the shops closest to me and gone into Bonnie's Bric-a-Brac.

The term *bric-a-brac* leaked into the English language in the nineteenth century as an approximation of a sixteenth-century French phrase, *à bric et à brac,* meaning something like *any old way, disordered, random. Random* certainly applied to the phrase as defined by Bonnie, who used it to encompass absolutely anything small, fey, bright, and useless. Little gnomes and leprechauns clustered on two shelves beneath a shelf full of oddly shaped coffee mugs, spice grinders, and fancy plates with pictures on them. Elsewhere I saw mummified-looking artificial flowers, little ceramic houses that seemed vaguely Dutch, shiny plaster toadstools, miniature wishing wells, trivets, and hand-embroidered potholders that said *Ssssssmokin'!* and *Hot Stuff!* Whole corners were devoted to purportedly collectable figurines of animals that, I supposed, were high on the list of animals that people collect figurines of: owls, turtles, dogs, the ever-popular black-and-white Holstein cows, and a great many pigs.

I'd chosen the store because the merchandise was small and theoretically easy to boost, and because the place was surprisingly full, more so than the stuff in the window suggested it would be. When I got inside, I saw one reason why there might have been so many customers. The entire back wall was given over to unusual Christmas wrapping paper, ribbons, and cards, and a huge sign that read BOXES FOR EVERYTHING. Some of the paper, especially large, flat sheets based on Japanese woodblock prints and magnified Impressionist brushstrokes, looked interesting, but I was there on business.

I wandered off into a relatively uncrowded area full of either bric or brac, in this case kaleidoscopes made in China, bulbous throw pillows, miniature wooden shoes (who *buys* this stuff?) and framed prints of avowedly comic scenes, dominated by several of the famous series of dogs playing poker. These were originally painted as advertisements by Cassius Marcellus Coolidge around the turn of the twentieth century, and about ten years ago, a pair of the originals sold at auction for almost $600,000, which had led me to revise my criteria for kitsch. Positioned in front of the prints, translating a bad idea into three dimensions, were little ceramic figurines of the dogs from the paintings. I looked around and found no one's eyes on me, so I picked up the nearest one, a bulldog with a cigar clutched in its teeth, and slipped it into my pocket.

Then it happened.

My nerve utterly failed me. *Me*—the consummately professional master thief, the never-arrested star protégé of the greatest burglar in San Fernando Valley history. Me, the guy who'd stolen the most expensive modern stamp on earth *from a professional killer*—you know, *that* me. Faced with shoplifting a discounted porcelain dog, I froze. I stood there, a charmless, worthless purloined china dog in my pocket, unable to force myself to take a step.

I scanned the store again for a slow count of ten, my fingers interlocked on top of my head, where they couldn't possibly be doing anything suspicious, the dog feeling bigger than a watermelon in my pocket. Then, eyes everywhere, I browsed several more shelves full of Bonnie's bric-a-brac for form's sake, inhaled deeply, and headed for the door.

Which set off an alarm. It went *dwoik, dwoik, dwoik* at a frequency that pierced eardrums like a red-hot wire, and through it I heard someone say, "Sir?" and turned to see, looking at me with the kind of disappointment I inspired so often as a child, an adorable, harmless, trusting, merry-faced little dumpling of a woman who wore gift wrap ribbon woven gaily into her hair and a green and white dress and whose name tag read BONNIE.

"We've only got one door," Bonnie said. We were sitting side by side in the back of the shop, sipping a hot mixture of gallon-bottle red wine, hard cider, cinnamon, and cloves, which tasted less ghastly than it sounds. "The bigger shops have two, and I probably shouldn't tell you this since you're pretending to be a thief—" She laughed merrily; she'd talked to Wally on the phone, and whatever he'd told her, I saw no reason to contradict it. "Not that you've got any talent at it." She laughed again, hit her wine again, pretty much emptying the cup, took the lid off a slow cooker plugged into the wall, and ladled herself some more. "Stay honest," she said. "You turn to a life of crime and you'll be on public assistance in no time. And listen, if you do want to try it again, don't do it upstairs in old Sam's." She checked the new level in the cup. It was her third cup since we'd sat down.

"Sam who?"

"Saddle store, no, *saddlery.* Sam's okay, but shoplifting

makes him crazy." She squinted like someone trying to find the trail she'd been following. "So," she said happily, "what was I saying?"

"Something you shouldn't tell me because I'm a thief."

"Yeah, *right*," she said, elbowing me. It might have been the first time I was actually elbowed. "So most of the bigger stores, the ones I was telling you about?" Her eyes narrowed and roamed the shop as though it were an unexpected cloud formation. "Bigger stores, bigger stores, *what* was it I was saying about them, the bigger stores?"

"They have two doors," I said.

"I knew that. Well, one of the alarm doodads is usually a dummy. Things cost the earth, so they buy one that works and one that's a phony, just a prop, you know?"

I said I had grasped the concept.

"And they set off the one that works every now and then to remind people what they're for."

"Saints alive," I said.

"And then there's the stores with *three* doors," she said, still warming to the topic. She pointed at her own door and said, "One," then pointed at the middle of her window and said, "two," and then at the opposite corner. "Three. Got it? You have to imagine them, the doors. Except for that one, I mean, the one that's really there. So." She closed her eyes and scratched the tip of her nose, evidently seeking the thread again, then opened her eyes and said, "So like I just said, entrance over *there*, takes you right into the merchandise, and then there's two exits, both near the cash registers. Come in, see the stuff, pay for the stuff, leave. The *merchant loop*, they call it. No one alarms their entrance, and remember, one of the two alarm doodads is a fake. So that's two doors without an alarm."

"And the really big stores? Boots to Suits and whatever used to be on the other end?"

"You'd think they'd have a million entrances, wouldn't you? But here's a s'prise. They've only got one—or maybe three or four, but they're all nexta each other, at the end that opens into the mall. They're not allowed to have private entrances, 'cause the whole *thing* about a mall is that you gotta pass other stores to get to the one you want. Hic."

I said, "Was that an actual hiccup?"

"What do you think, I'm practicing?" She knocked back what could be accurately described as a gulp. "You think anyone in the whole history of everyone has ever practiced a hiccup?"

"Not often," I conceded. I looked up, surprised to see that the crowd had thinned considerably in the short time we'd been talking. "Where is everybody?"

"They come, they go," she said. "It's like fishing. Gotta hook 'em while they're there. So the big stores like Boots to Suits and Gabriel's—"

"Gabriel's?"

"S'what useta be at the ghost town end of the mall, where the little booths are now. The bazaar, they call it. Although it's more of a swap meet. Anyway, the big stores, like I said, you could only go in and out in one place on each floor, where they had a whole buncha doors right next to each other and, see, they didn't want to put alarms there 'cause they kept getting the old *woo-woo-woo* when somebody walked in with something they stole in another store. And, you know, just 'cause someone swiped something someplace else, that doesn't mean they're not gonna buy something from *you*. Right?"

"You guys have to pay for the alarm system?"

"We buy the doodads," she said. "The thingies in the door. Mall pays the subscription or whatever it is to keep them working and up-to-date. And they also pay for the whatzit, the security staff, like that poor, dim little Wally. Jeez, I keep thinking we'll lose him to melanoma, especially with the way his hair's receding. It's like he leaves a trail of red hair behind him. The skin on top of the head is—"

"It's okay," I said, since she showed no signs of winding down. "He spends most of his time in the dark."

She squinted at me for a moment, trying to find her place. "An' they pay, the mall does, for the alarms on the big doors in and out of the building. Which don't work most of the time. I mean what do they care if we get ripped off a little? No skin off, *et cetera*. And the holiday stuff, tinsel and lights and Santas and witches and Easter eggs, they pay for somebody to supply those. And every now and then, like for Christmas, which is now, they buy some newspaper ads, like anyone reads a paper anymore." She took another hit on her cup. "This is what Mr. Pickwick drank," she said,

I said, "Really."

She shrugged. "I don't know. Maybe." She raised the cup and inhaled the fragrance and blinked a couple of times, fast. "Christmas always makes me think about Mr. Pickwick. Things were better when Mr. Pickwick was alive." She looked around the shop a bit mistily, it seemed to me. "Do you think Mr. Pickwick would have liked my store?"

"Sure," I said. "It's hard to imagine what he'd want that you don't have at least one of."

"It is a muddle, isn't it?" She leaned forward and looked into my cup. "You're an abstemious soul."

"Ah, but I'm a devil once I get started. Are you losing much to shoplifting this year?"

She extended a hand, palm up, and waved it in the general direction of the store. "Lookit these people," she said, although almost all the customers were gone. "They come in here alla, excuse me, *all the* time. I know their kids, some of them. We get hit a little harder in December than we do the rest of the year. I'm no math whiz, but I bet if you made a graph of the number of people who come through these doors, I mean *this door*, every month, with the number of people in one line on the graph and the amount of stuff that gets stolen in the other line, I bet the lines would move along like they were holding hands." She blinked, apparently reviewing the sentence, then nodded. "Yup, 'swhat I meant," she said. "Lose a little more 'cause we get more people this time of year, but nothing to cry about."

"What about the other stores?"

She shrugged. "Not my problem."

"You must hear things."

"Everybody complains, 'specially at Christmas. Hell, two days after Christmas last year, Gabriel's pulled out. In two days. They cheated everybody, even ducked the people returning ugly ties and stuff. Store was there and then it wasn't." She pushed out her lower lip and blew out, making her bangs fluff. "Everything's better at Christmas but everything's worse, too."

"That's the truest thing anybody ever said to me about Christmas."

She shook her head. "But I mean, look at this place. Not just my shop, the whole thing. Shoplifting isn't the big problem. The big problem is heart, I think. A loss of heart. *Entropy* is what my son says, but me, I think it's sadness. Malls are finished, you know? Nobody shops in them anymore. It's mos'ly kids hooking up and then it's Christmas, when people realize there's things they forgot to buy online and it's too late to get it delivered so they go to the mall. It's not what it used to be. Nothing is. Not even Christmas. *'Specially* not Christmas." She let the hand with the cup in it relax, slopping a little onto her lap, and some of the air seemed to go out of her. "I'm finished," she said. "This is our last year."

"Sorry to hear it."

"Me, too." She balanced the cup on her knee and gave the tinsel hanging from her left cuff an experimental tug. "Been a long time. I liked having a store called Bonnie's. I like the kind of junk I sell. I like the kind of people who used to buy it. But now, you know, it's just, everybody goes to *bricabrac.com* or some damn thing. Nothin's the same."

"I guess not."

She picked up the cup and studied it. "All gone," she said. "Like Mr. Pickwick. It's all gone."

5
Vlad the Impeller

Once out of Bonnie's Bric-a-Brac, toting the carefully rolled sheets of wrapping paper I'd bought and the cigar-smoking porcelain dog that she'd given me as a memento of my venture into crime, I began to eye the place more critically.

And that applied to my lethal Russian employer, too. It was absolutely impossible for me to think of him as Tip Poindexter, so I mentally renamed him Vlad the Impeller. Despite Vlad's thousands of dollars' worth of clothes, his discreet gold bracelet, his arduously cast-off accent, his aspirational name, and his country club membership, his shopping mall was a dump. The place was dotted with empty, mournfully dark store spaces, conspicuous as missing teeth—perhaps one in eight—and the shops that *were* open had a kind of off-flavor, a beyond-the-fringe, the-card-you-didn't-want-to-draw feeling, like Bonnie's had, but minus Bonnie's eccentricity and personal cheer. The Edgerton stores were a few steps down the scale from the retail outfits one associates with the upper middle class. The merchandise looked a lot alike. Except for a huge Boots to Suits discount outlet at one end of the ground floor, where there normally would have been a status department store—Neiman Marcus, Nordstrom, or even Macy's—the big chains had either never opened or, like Gabriel's, had fled. Rodeo Drive was in a galaxy far, far away.

Sure, the place was enormous. Sure, it was long and high, with a vaulted ceiling and a couple of low-pressure fountains playing in murky reflector pools at each end. Sure, it probably cost twenty-eight, thirty million to build, not counting the land. Didn't make any difference. There was an unmistakable sense of foolish money chasing merely unwise money.

All the tinseled Christmas foo-foo with its bright lights and *Ho! Ho! Ho!* glittered mainly on the first floor, where it would draw people in, an effect that made the second and third floors look dim and February-like by contrast. The place was pretty close to the "ethnically diverse"—read: "about half Latino"—middle-class town of Canoga Park, but it marketed itself, beginning with its WASP-magnet name, mainly to the newer, richer, and whiter areas of Chatsworth, Northridge, and even Simi Valley, which was white enough to house the Ronald Reagan Presidential Museum. Still, the patrons of the Edgerton Mall represented a more variegated racial mix than those three neighborhoods had been built to attract. At this point in its existence, Edgerton Mall was not an establishment that catered to those who could afford to spend in a carefree manner.

And it smelled damp.

But it would be misleading to stop on such a grim note. In spite of the melancholy of the dark shop windows and the inescapable impression of decline, the place hosted a *lot* of people at that moment, many of whom seemed to be celebrating, many of whom seemed to be with the folks they loved best in the world, and many of whom were small children. It's impossible for me to be melancholy around small children. They deserve the effort it takes us to do better.

About two-thirds of the adults were orbiting around one, two, or three kids, and a lot of those kids were at the stage when Christmas is the frosting on the year, the season when anything is possible, when wishes materialize beneath a tree. Or, minus the tree, on the living room floor; or even, minus the living room floor, at the foot of the bed.

These kids were *happy*. In fact, right in front of me at the moment I had that thought, a boy of seven or eight with a dark unibrow that suggested a blood relationship to Frida Kahlo tugged at his father's arm, his face gleaming, as he pointed at something in the window of the little electronics shop. He was the kind of happy adults forget having been.

It's too easy for an adult to sneer at Christmas, at the duet for sleigh bells and cash registers that provides the season's sound track, the shameless prices of the animated princesses dangled festively before children's eyes by a corporate entity with an estimated worth of a hundred billion cold-blooded dollars. It's impossible to connect all that modern spreadsheet calculation and cheap, icy glitter to the raw, unrestrained amazement in the faces of the shepherds who supposedly attended the birth on the straw. Whether you buy the Christmas story or not, there's a spontaneous combustion of pure spirit at its center, a sudden brightening of what it means to be human, and it changed the world, for better or for worse. And probably the only people who feel even a flicker of that wonder now are small children and possibly the stray adult like Bonnie, adults who have found a part of themselves where they can shelter the flame, maybe with an open book in front of it to shield it from the wind.

And as for me, well, I had my own complicated relationship with Christmas. It had renewed its claim on my affections when my daughter, Rina, was born, but like so many enthusiasms, my new attitude toward Christmas had faded over time.

I had mentally erased Vlad and his threats for the time being and was sitting on a bench not far from the good Santa, Shlomo, watching the faces of the smaller kids who were getting close to the front of the line to sit in the lap of the season. They mostly either glimmered with excitement or cried in terror, clinging for protection to the legs of their parents. And as happy or as frightened as those kids were about getting closer to Santa, most of them lit up a little once they'd been lifted up and he began to talk to them and tilted his right ear, big enough to have fought its way through all that hair, toward them so he could hear what they had to say. Even the criers went as bright as little lanterns. They didn't see the skinny, ropy neck, the yellowish skin, the teacup-handle ears and tired eyes. It didn't matter what Shlomo looked like. While those kids were talking to him, they were safe, and he was Santa Claus.

And I remembered as I sat there that the name *Shlomo*, despite its somewhat semi-comic Three Stooges sound, at least to the ears of uninformed Gentiles, was Hebrew for "peaceable," about as good a meaning as a name can have, and that it was one of several variations of the ancient name that's come down to us via the King James Bible as Solomon.

Shlomo and the kids had lifted my spirits to the point where I could get back to my exploring.

I was curious about the long-gone Gabriel's department store, a victim, apparently, of Christmas past, so I hoofed down to the far end of the mall to take a closer look at what was there in its place. The huge space had been gerrymandered into what Bonnie had called a bazaar, lines of booths made from cheap, crappy, thinly whitewashed sheetrock. Each booth had its name and number stenciled high on the stall's back wall. Vape and Vamp, selling an interesting mix of electronic cigarettes and lingerie, was next to Jenny's Knit & Purl, which was next to Boyland, selling boys' clothes, and a couple of stalls down from The Antique Geek, offering attic junk and sad old toys. The escalator to the second floor wasn't moving, blocked by a big Christmas ribbon with a bow in it. I did a quick circuit of the bazaar and then went back into the mall. I was most of the way through my second lap of the second floor, looking down at the ground floor with its dueling Santas and beginning to see something that seemed kind of odd about the way the crowd ebbed and flowed, when my phone rang and broke my train of thought.

"How's my favorite father in the world?"

Rina's voice made me feel like a kid who'd just climbed into Shlomo's lap. "If I see him, I'll ask. Hey, I know that Christmas isn't on your mind, but I happen to be holding a medium-size shopping bag that contains the very last thing you're expecting."

"Shopping bag? Where are you?"

I arrived at an escalator and got on. "In a mall."

"How 2010," she said.

"I hate to remind you of this, but in 2010 I was thirty-two years old."

"And?"

"Just, you know, it wasn't a whole geologic era ago."

"I was eight," she said.

"That's grim. So, take a guess."

"Does it plug in?"

"No."

She said, "Take it back."

I rode up to the third floor. "It's based on a famous work of art."

"Take it back."

"It's something no one you know, I guarantee, *no one*, has."

"Does it have Wi-Fi?"

"It has a cigar."

A pause. I heard a snatch of "The First Noel," the bit that goes, *in fields where they lay keeping their sheep,* and she said, "Okay, you're making me curious."

"No," I said. "Never mind. Skip it."

I stepped off the escalator and found myself facing one of the dark windows. Scraped off the glass, but still visible, was the word RECORDS.

"You know," Rina said, "Mom likes to say that your problem is that you're addicted to instant gratification, but look at you. You got her pregnant and then you waited all these years just so you could crazify me. What is it? What did you get?"

The only records I'd ever owned had been left behind by my father, along with my mother and me and a bunch of other stuff he hadn't wanted, when he abandoned us to move in with the woman my mother always called *his rental.* I'd only played a few of the albums before I sold them, but I suddenly felt like buying a record. I knew it was an anachronism, but it felt to me like Mr. Pickwick would have wanted to buy a record, too. "It's a small ceramic bulldog," I said, "holding a poker hand and smoking a cigar."

"How did you *know*?" she said, her pitch scaling up. "The one thing, the *only* thing that I wanted in the whole—"

"This is the trouble with being a liar." A pack of girls about her age cruised by, two of them smoking furtively, and I heaved a little sigh. "No one believes you when you tell the truth."

"Yeah, right. What are you getting Mom?"

"What does she want?"

"Are you kidding me? Do you know what *day* this—"

"I'd thought that maybe a small, ceramic bulldog holding a poker hand and smoking a cigar—"

"Have you thought about this at all?"

"I'm in a *mall*," I said.

"Which one?"

"Edgerton."

"Oh, good," she said. "They've probably got a special on mold." Then she said, "It's my dad," in the kind of tone she might use to say she was catching a cold.

"Not a top-of-the-line mall?" I asked.

"If you enjoy the idea of owning things made by exhausted child laborers in countries where insects are raised as protein, sure. Lot of great stuff to choose from."

"Who's that?"

"It's *me*," she said. "Your memory really *is* going."

"Who's with you? Who did you say, 'It's my dad' to?"

"Just Tyrone." In the background I heard Tyrone say, "Ain't no *just* about Tyrone."

"Put him on."

"Oh, sure. Stop talking to your only daughter and tell her to put someone else on. Whoops."

"Whoops what?"

"That was premature. I'm about to drop the phone. Whoops." The phone landed on something hard.

"Hey," Tyrone said.

"Hey yourself. What are you getting her?"

"Can't talk about that," he said, "with her sitting here with her ears hanging out. What about you?"

"What do *you* think I should I get her?"

"Up to you, Stu," he said, a little reproachfully.

"That's what I was afraid of."

Tyrone paused and let the silence take effect. "If you'll excuse me saying so, you're not taking this very seriously."

"I know, I know. And don't think it's something I like about myself. It's just that something . . . something . . ."

"Came up," Tyrone supplied. "That's lame."

"I'm aware. Listen, if you, um, if you think of anything great, call me."

"Sure," he said. "I'll call my girlfriend's father if I think of anything his daughter might want for Christmas."

"I already feel bad, Tyrone," I said, but he'd disconnected. I stood there, trying not to imagine the conversation in Rina's room. Trying not to collide with one of my *issues*, as I'd described it to Louie: my ever-lurking Christmas self-loathing as a failed father and husband who never felt further from the lives he had left behind than he did during the so-called happiest time of the year.

The girls who were sneaking smokes and their bubble of friends had stopped at the railing a few yards away, looking down at something or someone below. One of them shrieked a few high and unintelligible words and then jumped back and crouched down, out of sight, while her friends laughed. To my eyes, they wore too much makeup. To my eyes, they had no business smoking and hanging around some cheap mall and flagging down guys they might not even know. To my eyes, they were on the edge of trouble.

I probably would have had a negative thought or two about their parents, but I couldn't let myself go there. I admired my daughter helplessly, but I knew better than to take any credit for her.

6

The Christmases in the Wilderness

So the secret is out: one of my *issues* at this point in my life is that Christmas is my season for disliking myself.

You could, I suppose, tell an entire life story in Christmases, and for all I know it's been done a hundred times. The small child's Christmas, one wonder after another, beginning with the ordinary living room that's transformed overnight into Aladdin's cave by a brilliantly gleaming tree; the early adolescent's Christmas, the magic wearing thin at the elbows, the present you wanted either missing altogether or buried beneath the dreadful store-wrapped rectangles that might as well just blink *clothes you won't like* in neon; the late adolescent's Christmas, a seasonal obligation in a world that has turned rancid in its resolute failure to understand and acknowledge you, when Christmas is just the day when you total in your head how much the presents cost, hear the hollowness of the adults' laughter, and notice how quickly the eggnog and rum come out.

Then there are the first Christmases on your own, when you're the founder of the feast and the magic comes back, but *different*, as you buy something perfect for the boy or girl you love, who will miraculously wake up next to you on Christmas morning and give you the first smile of the holiday, the holy day, the day of your tiny, scraggly, glorious tree with its handmade chain of popcorn, its four strips of tinsel, and the two presents beneath it. Later the two of you can drop by your parents' places one after the other, comfortable in the gifts you've brought, generously tolerant of the ones you're given, and secure in your knowledge that the spirit in which you now celebrate the holiday—despite its relentless hucksterism and numbing music—is somehow new and original and self-created, and *massively* preferable to the way your parents celebrate it.

Finally, if you're truly fortunate, you get the *first* Christmas again, the infant's Christmas, but this time the infant is your child and you're Santa.

When you have a small child, you don't need to be religious to find the best in Christmas. From the time Rina was born until she was seven, I had the Christmases the carols celebrate. During those years the problem between Kathy and me, which was that she wanted me to be an insurance salesman in her father's office and I would have preferred to die slowly over a large barbecue, was forgotten at Christmastime because all that mattered was making the season magical for Rina and watching her face as she saw what we'd done. We were—and there's no reason to avoid the word—merry.

But the problem waited as unaddressed problems do, getting darker, hairier, and more impossible to negotiate, until Rina turned seven and Kathy and I could no longer find anything big enough to sweep the trouble under and began to talk seriously about splitting up. Once the decision was made, we took it in stages to minimize its effect on Rina, with me gone a couple of nights a week, then a week every month, and then *poof*, after Christmas, gone for good. Didn't matter how we tried to finesse it; the separation and the subsequent divorce devastated our daughter.

That was the beginning of what I think of as the Christmases in the Wilderness.

About the time Kathy and I began to treat the subject of our split as a genuine possibility, my life took a turn that made the relationship even more fragile and, possibly, endangered my wife and child: my occasional employment as a detective for crooks. It was a risky part-time job, but the extent of the potential risk didn't come home to me until the murder of Frankie Tongues.

Frankie was a walking short circuit, a guy who had been raised in an especially agitated Pentecostal church where the congregation frequently gave voice to prolonged utterances in no earthly language. This *glossolalia*, believers say, first occurred fifty days after the crucifixion, when the Disciples (minus Judas, obviously) gathered together and the Holy Spirit burst among them in a most dramatic fashion: *And suddenly there came a sound from heaven as of a rushing mighty wind, and it filled all the house where they were sitting . . . and they were all filled with the Holy Spirit, and began to speak in other languages, as the Spirit gave them utterance.* Frankie Tongues's congregation not only believed it, but sought ecstasy in reliving it. Loudly and, apparently, often.

This intermittently vivid upbringing left its mark on Frankie, whose nerves were agitated at the most placid of times. In moments of crisis he was likely to erupt into oratory loud enough to set off car alarms, in a language from beyond the solar system. Since Frankie made his living knocking over convenience stores, which has its inevitable tense moments, he left behind a long line of bewildered and terrified store

employees and an indelible impression on one and all. One
TV newscast had called him "The Jabber-Jabber Bandit,"
and when you're so memorable that the local news gives you
a nickname, you're in trouble.

Herbie Mott had attempted for years to get Frankie into
a more placid line of work, one where there weren't so many
people around who could hear, such as grand theft auto, late
at night. But Frankie *liked* to hit convenience stores. Truth be
told, he got off on going in broke and coming out a couple of
minutes later with a few hundred bucks and a week's worth
of Flaming Hot Cheetos, and he liked getting his toe stuck in
that spiritual socket and letting fly in the hair-raising tongue
of the angels. But everyone knew that sooner or later, if he
didn't either change his specialty or have his mouth sewed
shut, he was going down.

Everyone who hadn't met Frankie at the other end of a
gun liked him. He was sweet, generous, and amusing when
you could understand what he was saying. He was especially
prized in the regular poker games Herbie's circle of crooks
enjoyed because someone who looks down at a good hand
and spouts a train of syllables straight out of Little Richard
does give you an advantage.

So when someone shot Frankie Tongues while he was sitting in his car, getting himself all wired up to hit yet another
7-Eleven, I was hired to figure out who called up the hit.

And I did, but he turned out to be a guy with enormous
specific gravity who owned twenty-six convenience stores
and about the same number of betting joints (some of the
convenience stores also functioned as betting joints), and
when he caught wind of me, he pointed some very nasty
people on me, with intent to kill. I had to hire hitters to sit
outside Kathy's house until the threat was past.

So began the phase of my life in which I left my family's house, put my stuff in a bunch of storage units, and started hopping among the worst dumps in the Valley and in Hollywood, both of which have especially rich veins of dumps. There was, for example, The Elf's Village, where a truly demented woman who was only four feet tall had created an entire motel on a scale 30 percent smaller than normal, a sort of Motel Three and a Half where customers cracked their heads on the top of the doorway and hung out over both ends of the bed. Or Valentine Shmalentine, the world's only kosher love motel.

And I stayed away for longer periods of time from the house Kathy and I had bought when we were married. When I visited them I was often an hour late because I was dodging nonexistent tails, and so jumpy I made them turn off the living room lights and spent the evening peering through a crack in the curtains.

Not the best possible environment for Christmas.

This went on for several years, during which, with the grace that it seems to me is unique to women, Rina learned to laugh at all the drama, and Kathy learned to imitate laughing at it. Gradually we found a sort of balance that allowed me to participate, in fits and starts, in my daughter's life, even befriending her boyfriend, Tyrone, who had just a few moments ago chastised me for my laggardly approach to my daughter's Christmas and then hung up on me.

Then I bumped into Ronnie Bigelow and fell in love with her, and things changed again. To my great surprise, Ronnie and Kathy had become amicable, if not quite friends, and Rina had made it clear that she approved. We were a cautiously cheerful foursome.

Despite an immediate and frequently gratified physical

attraction, Ronnie and I had barely known each other when we had our first Christmas last year. It wasn't until later that I realized she'd been muted and restrained through the holiday season. I figured it meant she was missing something or someone she hadn't told me about. Ronnie treated her past as though it were classified information; if we had a major unresolved issue, to use a word that was coming up quite often, it was that I knew nothing at all about her years before I met her. This would be our first *real* Christmas together.

At a very recent point in our relationship, after Ronnie had saved my skin a couple of times, demonstrating interesting criminal chops as she did it, I invited her to live with me. We took up residence in the apartment I'd never shown to anyone, not even Kathy or Rina, the top secret hideaway where I had long planned to go to ground on the day when absolutely *everyone* wanted to kill me. I'd taken her into the most secret part of my life and invited her to share it with me, a gesture of trust that was as yet unreciprocated. She hadn't even told me where she was born. And yes, it disturbed me, but in a way it didn't matter. I knew she *cared* about me, and while I might have checked the calendar if she told me it was Friday, emotionally I trusted her entirely.

But.

But there was something about Christmas. Last year, when we were still getting to know each other, I'd written it off. This year it seemed to be serious.

Every time I tried to make plans or asked her what she wanted, she shut down. She defaulted to *whatever-you-want* mode, refusing to get drawn into conversation. I felt a little like a guy trying to sell a mirror to a vampire; every time I brought it up she changed rooms. Her energy dropped. A light somewhere inside her went out.

I asked what the problem was, and she said, "Nothing. I'm just not much for Christmas."

I said, "Why not?"

She said, "Oh, you know. Are you hungry?"

I said, "We just ate."

She looked at me for a slow count of three and said, "Then allow me to rephrase the question. Are you *still* hungry?"

What it looked like to me was that I should add Christmas to the list of things I wasn't supposed to ask her about.

So I had yet another issue with Christmas.

7

If People Have Touched It, It's Dirty

By 7 P.M., I felt like Edgerton Mall was the seventh level of hell and I'd already been there for the prescribed eternity. It had apparently started to rain outside because people had wet hair, there was a prevailing funk of damp cloth, and the floor, none too appealing to begin with, was slippery and streaked with mud, as were the previously snow-white paths to Santa's thrones. Other than those clues, for all I knew of the outside world, the Great Wave had finally crested the mountains and washed away everything on earth except the mall. And I'd only been there five hours. I couldn't fathom how people could work an eight-hour day in this place, locked away from everything that mattered in their lives, everything that wasn't valued in bills and coins.

As long as I was wandering in and out of stores anyway, I searched for solutions to the seasonal conundrum that Tyrone had brought home to me: What to buy? For Rina, I saw and rejected a "Dear Daughter" necklace, engraved with a sentiment that I found simultaneously cloying and embarrassingly accurate; a set of empowering refrigerator magnets about strong teenage girls who had their own refrigerators; and, most surprisingly, a collection of small stuffed toys based on human organs: putatively cute, smiling little livers and kidneys and bladders and hearts with weensy, creepy hands and feet. I actually almost bought those, but sanity prevailed. There's no point in giving a horrible gift unless you have a great one to follow it with. In one store, the inevitable thrift shop of off-brand, mid-level, mildly outdated tech (called, in this case, iShop), I found something I did buy, but it was a minor note in the hoped-for Christmas symphony of gifts, a collection of little Bluetooth tags that let you use your phone to find your keys or whatever else you've lost. After a moment's deliberation, I got one for Ronnie, too. Here we were, on the next-to-last night before Christmas, and I hadn't bought anything for her, either.

Acting on an afterthought, I pulled one of the sets from the bag and looked for directions. There weren't any. I asked the geek who'd waited on me, an ambiguously old-looking guy with the face of a dodgy teen and a halo of prematurely silvery hair, where the directions were, and he said in a tone that suggested that I'd already asked him that same question seven hundred times, "You DL the *app*. The instructions are in the app."

I thought about asking whether the app was free but I wasn't sure I could handle any more techno-scorn, so I just said thanks and wandered out of the place. Once I was on the safe side of the door, I looked at the sign and noticed, in a retro matrix printer font beneath the store's name, iSHOP, the words WINK SIMMONS, PROPRIETOR. I figured maybe he was just pissed off at being named Wink.

Earlier, during an hour or so that seemed to last forever, I'd talked to about a dozen store owners and managers, encountering an impressive uniformity of gloom. All was not well either in Edgerton or in bricks-and-mortar capitalism in general. Yes, they'd been stolen from, most of them; yes, they were suffering record losses; no, neither the mall's security systems nor their own employees had flagged many of the thieves. I tested that last assertion on my own and found it to be true: the success rate of my post-Bonnie's Bric-a-Brac shoplifting experience zoomed to about 65 percent. I'd also developed some theories about how to block one's actions from the prying eyes of the security cameras, unlikely as it was that Wally was watching the monitor I happened to be on as I bagged my swag, rather than one of the thirty-one others, or, for that matter, his iPhone.

Elementary-school easy, in other words. The question was probably why more stuff wasn't getting kiped.

I was standing once again on the third tier, looking down at the shoppers—the crowd thinner now that it was dinnertime— and trying to figure out what had caught my eye before about the way the crowd moved, when my phone rang again.

Unknown, it read. I punched in and said, "Yeah?"

"What have you learned?" Vlad said.

"I'll call you when I have something specific," I said, and hung up. It rang again immediately.

"Do not hang up on me," he said. "Never. And do not think you know what is specific or what matters."

"Okay, here's what I know so far. It's a good thing the world's nuclear secrets or the keys to the kingdom aren't kept here, because this place is a thief's theme park. Two-thirds of the doorways aren't alarmed, including the ones in and out of the mall—"

"How do you know this?"

"Because I filled a shopping bag with stolen merchandise from stores all over the place and went through one of your outside doors twice. *After* stealing all that stuff. Your alarms stink. Your surveillance cameras are old, low-res clunkers and you don't have enough people watching them. There are corners all over the place where you can stash stuff and recover it later. You name it, it's broken."

"This is what I mean," he said. "Nothing you have said matters."

"Then perhaps you could take a moment and provide me with a job description."

"I could have told you all of this at lunch today. Those have been the conditions for years. It was cheap to install and maintain, and until this month it held losses from theft to an acceptable level."

"Acceptable to whom?"

"I am the only one who matters," he said. "I will give you a small pat on the back for having learned all this, but it is something any cheap thief could spot. I was hoping for more."

"And you might have gotten it if you'd bothered to share some of this with me."

"Feh," he said. "I had no idea it would surprise you. There is no mall from which it is impossible to steal. *This* is the issue: shoplifting for the past six weeks is up *three hundred percent* from average—"

"Hundred and twenty is what your security guy—"

"Mr. Bender, tell me, do I give a shit what my security people think? Where do you think that idiot got his number?"

"Right," I said. I leaned over far enough to rest my forehead on the railing, hearing my mother say, *If people have touched it, it's dirty.*

Vlad was still talking. "And I gave him that number for a reason, and you don't tell him otherwise. Yes?"

"Fine." The railing was cool and smelled vaguely fudge-like.

"You had best pick up your feet a bit. Trot, if you will. Time is flying."

"Not here, it isn't."

"But it is for you."

I stood up. "I have to tell you, Vlad, I don't like the sound of that."

"I am not Vlad. Did you think this was a lifetime job? A what's the word?"

"Who cares?" I said.

"Sinecure," he said. "It is not. You have a deadline, and you should take that word seriously. Both syllables."

I ignored the threat for the moment, although it took an effort. "And would you like to *share* my deadline with me, or is that also something I'm supposed to figure out for myself?"

"Of course not," he said. "Christmas Eve."

"I take Christmas Eve off."

"Yes, Trey said you were difficult."

"And look how well *she's* doing."

"She is doing much better than you and your family will be if you do not—"

I wasn't hearing him anymore. There were black spots like burn-blossoms on film, expanding before my eyes. "You know *what*, you pretentious, overdressed Russky thug? Fuck you and your blue blazer, too. Everybody has to die sometime."

I hung up, almost gasping for breath, and a few seconds later, the phone buzzed to signal a text. Figuring that Tyrone had thought of something he didn't want to say in front of Rina, I brought it up.

It said: BUT OUR CHILDREN SHOULD NOT DIE FIRST.

8
The Good Thief

It took me the better part of ten minutes sitting in a toilet stall with a broken lock, the second stall I'd tried, pushing the door closed with my feet and clamping my tongue between my teeth, to get myself under control. A threat against me is sort of emotional junk mail; they've been delivered frequently enough that the novelty has worn off. A threat against Rina or Kathy, on the other hand—that opens the black area of my mind where murder is stored.

My immediate impulse was to have the son of a bitch hit, but I'd done that twice in the past few months and I didn't want it to become a habit. First, it's lazy, and second, it's inevitable that every time you do it, more people know about it—the hitter, the person through whom you contracted the hitter, the ever-widening circle of people *they* talk to, the people who put two and two together on their own. Sooner or later it reaches a critical mass, some mouth runs when it shouldn't, and you either get caught or you're tagged in some permanent fashion.

So I granted Vlad his life, for the time being anyway, and the fist that was squeezing my heart eased off a bit.

All he wanted me to do was find out what was going on— why the amount of theft had tripled and who was behind it.

My emotions aside, I figured I'd handled situations that were more complicated.

What Vlad would *do* to that responsible person, while undoubtedly operatic in scale, wasn't really on my side of the net.

So I got up from my porcelain seat and noted the lack of toilet paper. The bare cardboard tube seemed so totally symbolic of Edgerton Mall that it probably should have been on the logo.

It wasn't quite eight yet, so my little nervous breakdown had taken less time than I'd thought. I rode down to the second floor and took a hallway marked NO PUBLIC ACCESS to a big room behind the food court that had been set up to give employees a place where they could eat and say all the things they hadn't said to the customers. The doors to the right of the room, each labeled, led into the kitchen areas with the name of one of the food concessions. I went to the door marked TITO'S, opened it, and inhaled the fragrance of Tito's Tortilla Heaven, the best-smelling place at the mall. Getting an inquiring look from the woman whom I'd seen behind the counter, I said, "Whatever you've got with pork."

She smiled. "How many?"

"Two. And a Diet Coke."

"Have only Diet Pepsi."

"In that case," I said, "a glass of asphalt."

Her brow knitted and she said, "*¿Qué quieres?*"

"Just water, okay?"

"Two anything with pork *y agua*," she said with a smile broader than that menu warranted, and I gave her a thumbs-up and closed the door.

The big room was mostly empty. There was a trio of frazzled-looking saleswomen from Doris's Duds, one of the mall's bigger stores, down on the ground level. One of them was conspicuously pregnant and had told me that her first child would have a birthmark reading "Winter Wonderland" if she heard the song one more time. I nodded at her, got a wan, who-is-that-man smile, and headed for a table in the back, waving at Bonnie, who had her nose buried in a much-creased paperback edition of *The Pickwick Papers* and had no idea I was in her century, much less the room. Just beyond the station where we were supposed to get our utensils and napkins and minuscule packets of seasoning, I caught a glimpse of red, something that looked like a collapsed crimson blimp edged with white fur. I gave him a squint and saw that it was Shlomo Stempel.

He looked like he'd spent his day as a crash test dummy. His head was hanging down, his shoulders were slumped, and he was rubbing his face with both hands. I went over and said, "Mind if I sit down?"

"Long as it's not on my lap," he said. He looked up at me, clearly refocusing. Something had been on his mind that required most of his attention. "And you are?"

"Junior Bender," I said, pulling out a chair.

"Ouch," he said, raising a hand to wave the name away. "Terrible name, terrible."

"And hello to you, too." I sat. Up close, he was in his late sixties and feeling it. His skin was sallow, he had deep circles beneath his eyes, and his Adam's apple protruded from his narrow neck so sharply it looked like it was trying to signal for help. He could have blown me backward by wiggling his ears.

He nodded. "Yeah, well, names. I'm Shlomo Stempel, and when you're a kid with a name like Shlomo and there's not enough Jews in your school to make up a *minyan*, you get a little sensitive to names. You know that 'bender' is British slang for gay?"

"It's been brought to my attention."

"I bet," he said. "What's 'Junior' disguising?"

"Nothing. It's my name. As long as we're clearing things up, what's a *minyan*?"

"Ten people," he said. "The *quorum*—the number necessary for group worship. All ten have to be Jews, all over thirteen years old. The word *minyan* actually means 'number.'" He had a steaming cup of coffee with a little dusting of powdered creamer floating on it and a bowl of some kind of soup in front of him, chicken noodle, maybe. He'd picked up a spoon and was stirring the soup slowly without looking down at it. "So who are you, aside from being Junior Bender?"

"I'm a freelance consultant," I said. "I got hired here to evaluate things like shoplifting and make recommendations about it."

At the word *shoplifting* he dipped the spoon into the soup and brought it up full but rested it on the rim of the cup instead of raising it to his mouth, and it seemed to me he was searching for something to say. What he came up with was, "Kind of background does that take?"

I shrugged. "To catch a thief . . ."

He trained the tired-looking eyes on me. They contained a surprising amount of energy. "Well," he said, "that's candid."

"I watched you with the kids," I said. "*They* trusted you."

He nodded. "They pay me that honor, yes." He pushed his chair back an inch or two, hesitated, and said, "So tell me, you steal from the rich and give to the poor?"

"Once in a while. But mostly I steal from the rich and sell to my fence."

"But you *don't* steal from the poor."

"What have they got?" I said.

He grinned, baring teeth that looked like they'd been marinated in coffee. "Tough guy," he said. "You fancy yourself sort of like the good thief?"

"The good thief?"

"In your part of the Bible," he said. "You know whatever you believe about the Bible, it's an interesting book to have been written by a bunch of semiliterate late Iron Age tribesmen who hardly ever left an area about the size of New Jersey." He tasted the soup and cocked his head sideways, making up his mind, then dipped back in. "*Your* part was written later, of course."

"But who was the good thief?"

"Crucified with Jesus, right next to him. Thieves on either hand, the final irony of his life."

"Oh, yeah, I remember. One of them gave him a hard time and the other one said essentially, hang on, Jack, we're nailed up here because we stole stuff but this guy didn't do anything wrong."

"Good," Shlomo said. "And then he asked Jesus to put in a favorable word with his father when Jesus got, you know, *up there*." He dipped the spoon again. "And the thief hadn't been baptized."

"Yeah," I said, "but Jesus had clout."

"I don't think that's the meaning you're supposed to take away from it."

"What it means to me is that thieves can get a pass if they've got a good enough lawyer. Maybe not avoid crucifixion, but, you know, later and all. If you believe in later." I stretched, my hands balled into fists, to try to unknot some of the tension in my back. "Are you religious?"

Shlomo leaned forward and rested his chin on his free hand, the other still holding the spoonful of soup, which appeared to have slipped his mind. "I'm a good Jew in the sense that I pay attention to the Commandments, most of them anyway, give a little money to the right charities. I'm obviously not a zealot, or I wouldn't be wearing this outfit. But Jews, we don't think so much about what we'll be doing after we die. We think about what we should do while we're alive."

"Well, then, what *are* you doing? When you're not being St. Nick?"

"Nothing for money. I've got enough money. Not so much but enough. But I've been here three Christmases now. Just for the kids."

"The kids," I said. "They really like you."

"Yeah."

"You're good with them."

He smiled down at his spoon, which was brimming, and then put it into his mouth. When he'd swallowed he said, "All I do is listen. Kids don't get listened to much. Mostly, they're on the other end. When you see a parent and child and you hear the words, 'Now you listen to me,' it's a good bet it's not the kid talking."

"It might be, between my daughter and me."

He raised his eyebrows. "How old?"

"Fourteen." I sat back, struck by an idea. How often do you get to ask Santa for advice? "What do you think would be a good present for a fourteen-year-old girl?"

"Oh, boy," he said. "You haven't got anything *yet*?"

"Well," I said.

"If she was three or four, I could tell you what she wants. Even statistically, I could tell you. But fourteen-year-olds, they're not allowed to sit on my lap. Insurance company."

"What's with the Santa who wants to kill everybody?"

"Dwayne? Hung over. Every day, hung over. Guy's breath is forty proof. Some of the kids, getting off his lap, they wobble." He pushed the bowl away, having eaten almost none of it, studied the powdery surface of his coffee for a moment, and pushed that away, too. "So he comes across a little like the Japanese version, *Santa Kurohsu*, who's got eyes in the back of his head so he can spot the bad kids in all directions. No Ho! Ho! Ho! from *him*. But he's an okay guy, Dwayne, wouldn't hurt a kid, even though he scares them half to death."

"So you've been here for a few years. Anything different about this year?"

He gazed at me long enough to make me think he wasn't going to answer me, but then he looked down at the surface of the table and said, "More people. More kids. They got both of us, Dwayne and me, going nine hours a day this year. Year before last, it was eight hours, sometimes less. Last year it was only me."

"More people," I said, "even with this economy?"

"What can I tell you?"

"Anything else?"

"For example?" He was looking at his soup, not me.

"People who don't look like they should be here. Outside the normal kids and parents range."

"You mean like gang kids? Thugs in Lone Ranger masks?"

"I guess."

"Uh-uh. Just the usual, but more of them. Maybe twenty-five, thirty percent more."

"Kind of odd, don't you think, with all the talk about how malls are tanking?"

He shrugged. "Hadn't thought about it. Yeah, I suppose it's odd that business dropped off last year and this year they had to put both of us out there. They didn't even think they needed me the first day this year, got a panic call about four P.M., *Get in here.* Maybe it's just that the place is cheap. Times aren't great unless you're in the one percent, you know."

"Could be." I looked over at the door to Tito's Tortilla Heaven, wondering where my food was.

"Listen," Shlomo said. He was leaning forward to stir the cold soup he'd rejected, and he was giving it all his attention. "What it sounds like to me is that you really *are* the good thief, in a manner of speaking. You're kind of a crook, but you also play detective sometimes."

I weighed it for a moment. "I guess."

"Well, suppose I'd had something stolen . . ." He watched the spoon make circles in the soup.

"How long ago?"

"I don't know. I noticed it wasn't where it was supposed to be three days ago, but it could have been gone for months. It's not something I look at all the time."

"Stolen from where?"

"Mmmmm," he said.

"Let me guess. Your home."

He nodded. Then he cleared his throat and said, "Yes."

"Anything else taken?"

"Not that I can see."

"Valuable?"

"To me. Not worth a nickel to anybody else."

"Was it in plain sight?"

He closed his eyes. "Not even close."

"So," I said, "someone takes from your house something hidden that was important to you but that's not worth any money, and nothing else."

"That's it," he said. He looked back over at me. "Think you can figure it out?"

"Depends on how afraid you are of learning who did it."

"Yeah," he said. He swallowed, and the big Adam's apple took a little bow. "Sort of has to be . . ."

"Someone in the family."

In the silence that followed, the door opened and the counter woman from Tito's came in with two big plates. She waved me to sit back so she could put it all down.

"I have to think about it," Shlomo said.

"Hot sauce," the waitress said, pointing at one of two identical little paper cups. She indicated the other. "Sissy sauce," she added gaily. "I'll be checking out your choice." She gave me a wide smile and headed for the door.

Watching her go, Shlomo said, "You get much of that?"

"Not as much as I used to. My charm is pretty much limited to waitresses."

"What're you, thirty-five?"

"Thirty-eight."

"A baby, you're a baby. She really is watching."

I looked up, and the door closed quickly. "Thanks for the warning. I'd hate to disappoint her." I poured the mild sauce over the carnitas and then switched the two cups so she wouldn't know. "What is it? The thing that was stolen?"

"A set of dog tags," Shlomo said. "*Soldier* dog tags. From World War II. Belonged to my father."

"You were close to him?"

"At times," Shlomo said. "He wasn't always an easy man. I'll tell you, though, since it's Christmas, I'll tell you. We haven't had a lot of miracles in our family, okay? But those tags were part of a miracle, so I kept them. And you know, I'll bet the people who owned the water jars on the day when

Jesus turned all that water into wine, I'll bet they hung onto those jars. Didn't sell them on eBay or anything."

"No," I said. The door was open again, so I pointed down at the carnitas and waved my hand at my mouth as though to cool it. The door closed again.

Shlomo said, "Gonna ask her out?"

"No. I'm taken. I just wanted her to feel like somebody was showing off for her at the end of her day." I took a big bite. The sissy sauce was pretty hot, too. "A miracle, huh?"

"You bet," he said. "The shadow of death and everything." He tugged on the sleeve of his Santa suit and said, "Christmas, too. It was a Christmas miracle. For a Jew." He got up, leaving his food mostly uneaten. "Last hour of the workday," he said. "Tell you the story if we get some time."

9

The 1812 Overture, Rescored for Automobile Horns

"I need to know who the members of the Edgerton Partnership are." My cell phone was in my lap and on speaker, thereby turning it into a hands-free device. LA cops, who are feeling left out as the violent crime rate drops, absolutely salivate at the sight of someone holding a phone while at the wheel.

"People who built the mall?" Louie said.

"Yes, and if there's any talk about silent partners, those are probably the names I need most." I accelerated to change lanes.

"Why?"

"I just want to know who besides Poindexter is going to want to kill me by Christmas."

"Not going so great, huh?"

"No, no, why would you think that? Hang on." I was heading toward downtown on the 101 with the Cahuenga Pass and Hollywood behind me. Low, heavy clouds reflected the city's extra holiday wattage in a dull red glow that made them look as though they were being heated from above. Little Armenia and Thai Town were opening up to my right, disorientingly bright in the blaze of several million Christmas lights. Without thinking about it, I'd been waiting for the darkness of these usually dimmer environs, and I was unprepared to see the Melrose/Normandie exit coming up so fast. It took a little advanced weaving across a couple of lanes to get to it. I heard honking, but it sounded a few cars back.

"Hey," Louie said, "just out of curiosity, how much is Poindexter paying you?"

"He's allowing me to continue to inhale and exhale, and he was nice enough to extend that courtesy to my family if I'm a good little spaniel."

"No carrot?"

"He's not a carrots kind of guy." I did a little maneuver to put me onto Ardmore.

"That's what I heard."

"And I want his real name."

"That I can get easy. I even know his first name, but I'm not gonna try to pronounce it. It's Y-E-V-G-E-N-I-Y."

"Yevgeniy," I said. "Essentially, Eugene. How do you know that?"

"I guess I don't really, not with a, a thingamabob, a certificate of authenticity. Boy, that'd be a thing to forge, huh? Certificates of authenticity? But Yev . . . Yev—that's what people called him until about seven, eight years ago. Yev."

"Right," I said. "It could actually be anything."

"Why do you care?"

"This guy didn't change his name because he wanted to join a golf club. He changed it because someone, a lot of someones, wanted to kill him. Having met him, I can say that it's literally impossible that there aren't people all over the place who want to kill him. At some point I might want to get their phone numbers." I passed a furniture store with a green-and-red Christmas sign in Korean.

"Okay," Louie said, "the Edgerton investors, Poindexter's real name."

"That's it." I made a left on a residential street that would take me to Western Boulevard.

"You and Ronnie want to come eat Christmas dinner with Alice and me?"

I was startled. As long as I'd known Louie, I'd never been invited to dinner. "Let me check with Ronnie," I said. "For all I know, she's expected for Christmas at the White House."

"Awwww, come on," Louie said. "So she fibs a little."

"It's not so much that she fibs," I said. "She just refuses to talk about anything that happened before she came to California. But to hear her tell it, she was born in three cities."

"Little mystery," he said, "it's a good thing in a woman."

"Maybe. I'm not being very gracious about your invitation, am I?"

"Nope, but what else is new? Come on, think about it. Alice and me, we really do Christmas. Cook from scratch and everything. I told her about your attitude problem, she said I talk too much, I could never *talk* you into liking Christmas. She said it'd be like trying to talk someone into voting different and you know how that always comes out. What we should do, Alice said, is *show* you Christmas."

"Wow," I said. I'd never seen this particular Louie before. "I'll talk to Ronnie and get back to you. And thanks for the invitation."

"Hey," he said. "It's overdue." He disconnected, and I suddenly felt lonelier.

Western was coming up, and just as I went to signal for a turn, an icicle drove its way into my solar plexus. I had left the Edgerton Mall and gone straight to within a mile from where I lived with Ronnie, and I'd barely glanced in the rear-view mirror.

And I suddenly remembered the horns two or three cars

back when I made my diagonal charge for the off-ramp. That should have been enough all by itself: I'd been dragging someone behind, someone who knew how to tail. And I was about four minutes away from taking him home with me.

The apartment I shared with Ronnie was the deepest secret I had. It had come my way during a tense three or four minutes when a friend of mine, a Korean confidence woman named Winnie Park, had faced the worst possible outcome of having transferred a huge sum of money to her own account from one owned by a corrupt and heavily armed LA cop. Somehow I'd persuaded the cop to give Winnie seventy-two hours to round up the money, plus 20 percent interest, and Winnie had used the time to get herself to Singapore and to pay me off with an unwritten and completely illegal sublease on an apartment.

And what an apartment. It was in one of three radically dilapidated adjoining buildings built in the 1920s and bought entirely for cash by an anonymous Korean syndicate who had restored the units inside to their art deco glory while completely ignoring the exterior conditions. The result was like wrapping the first class decks on the Queen Mary inside a facade that said *Rats check in here but they never check out,* creating the perfect shelter for those with large amounts of unreportable income and people who might as well have been wearing OKAY TO KILL signs on their chests.

Nobody except for Ronnie and me knew about it, and here I was, on the verge of hanging out the neon. And oh, yeah, Irwin Dressler, the legendary king of Los Angeles crime, now in his nineties, but Irwin and I were getting along. For the moment.

I signaled for the right onto Western, which was reasonably busy, dropped south a couple of blocks, watched the follower make the turn a few car lengths back, and took an aimless right onto a quiet street of apartment houses, all gleaming with seasonal cheer. I slowed as though looking for an address. In my side mirror I saw one pair of headlights, and then another, make the turn behind me. And realized I'd gone wet beneath the arms.

Moving at a crawl, I pulled as close to the parked cars as I could, and the driver two cars back swerved left and passed. It kept going, so scratch one. But the other one stayed back there.

A parking spot came up—a gift, in that neighborhood, rare enough to have come from the jolly old elf himself—and I stopped and put the car into reverse, brightening my taillights, and waited politely for the car behind me to go by so I wouldn't come too close to it when I backed up. After a moment, undoubtedly swearing beneath his breath, the driver passed me.

Whoever he was, he was big enough for his squarish head to brush the inside of the car's roof.

As he moved slowly down the block, I began the pantomime of backing up. I intended to make four or five hapless passes to get into the spot in the hope that the giant tail would realize he couldn't just sit around without attracting attention and would take a turn around the block so he could come up from behind me again.

I pushed the button that would call Louie back and said, "You got anybody in Koreatown?" By *anybody*, I meant anyone who had rented one of Louie's legally clean cars to do something nefarious.

"I ain't got trackers on them." There was a pause while he did something. "I got four out but no idea where. Lemme get off the phone so I can call. Is this dangerous?"

"What do you think?"

"Okay. Hang on."

The tail made the first right, which gave me a minute or two.

I had only two choices that I could see: One, pull away from the curb as fast as I could, hoping either to get out of sight before the follower made it all the way around the block or two, get out of the car and try to hoof it back to Western and maybe duck into a restaurant or something. I wasted twenty or thirty seconds trying to decide and then I figured, the hell with it, grabbed a third choice that had just presented itself, cut the wheel, and gunned it. Plan three was to follow my pursuer around the block, come up behind him with my brights on, and worry *him* for a while, during which he would ideally not turn and shoot me.

Three, despite what everybody says, is not always the charm. As I began the right-hand turn, I registered the car sitting there facing me, diagonally blocking the street, headlights out. And then, just when I squinted at it like a complete duffer, he hit the high beams and blinded me completely. Seeing nothing but the ghosts of his headlights, I hauled the wheel left to get out of the turn and back onto the straightaway, scraped some chrome and paint off the car parked at the corner, and accelerated to what I figured was the safest speed for a guy who felt like he'd just been caught staring at a supernova. Meanwhile the follower screeched around the turn behind me and bumped me, ever so gently, on the tail of the Toyota.

This was unexpected. I'd been assuming the objective was to tail me home and see where I lived in case Vlad eventually decided he needed to come after me. But it appeared that logic hadn't been the best tool for the situation. Either the guy had been sent to do damage or he simply had a tenuous relationship with his masculinity and was unable to accept the fact that things hadn't gone his way. He bumped me again as I tried desperately to clear his high beams from my retinas and get a look at the street in front of me.

It wasn't going to happen soon enough. So moving at a decorous pace, I got a couple of car lengths in front of him, braked suddenly, dropped it into reverse with the clutch down, redlined the engine, popped the clutch, and slammed backward into him.

We both shot back a couple of feet, me bouncing around beneath my seat belt, and his horn began to blare. My vision was returning, so I threw it into first and hauled ass as fast as I could. His left headlight was out, which would make it easier for me to spot him if he was stupid enough, or steroidal enough, to follow.

And here he came, one eye blazing, dragging the noise of his horn behind him. My inoffensive-looking little Toyota has a giant Detroit engine shoehorned under its hood by Louie the Lost, via Pete at Pete's Putt-Putt Hut, so I accelerated like I'd been launched out of a slingshot, but it didn't leave him anywhere *near* far enough behind to give me confidence. And the question occurred to me: I mean, hadn't Detroit gone *bankrupt?* Why did I have all this faith in—

And then two things happened at the same time. My phone rang, and a bullet punched a hole in my rear window, whistled past my head, and spiderwebbed my front window.

I thumbed the phone frantically and shouted, "Hold on," then took the right coming up.

I was going so fast I left part of my tires scrawled over the pavement like charcoal. It was a relief to see the cyclops unable to make the turn until he was five or six car lengths back, but then he began to close the gap fast. I grabbed the right coming up, heading back toward Western, just barely avoiding some law-abiding Korean carefully turning her Lexus left into her driveway and then nearly sideswiping the car that had been a couple of lengths behind her. Somehow I threaded the needle and then I blew through the stop sign at Western and powered right, joining the southbound stream of traffic.

"What?" I said into the phone as the car with the single headlight narrowly avoided hitting a car as he made his own turn. His horn was still braying.

"Where you at?" Louie said.

"Western heading south, half a mile north of Wilshire."

"Got one on Wilshire, going East, at—what cross street did you say?"

I said, "I didn't," and Louie said to me, "Not you, shut up, I'm listening here."

Behind me, the cyclops's horn finally cut out. The traffic in the lane to my left was going faster than I was, so I angled into it, watching One-Eye try to follow, only to be greeted by someone flicking his high beams several times at remarkable speed, and Louie said, "Car's at Lucerne."

"Strapped or not?"

"You're shitting me."

"Is this the kind of joke I make? Would you put up with me if this was the kind—"

"Hang on." The cyclops made it into the left lane, and I went back into the right as I heard Louie say, "He wants to know, are you strapped." Then to me he said, "Strapped it is."

"Okay. I'm going to drag myself along on the right until I cross Wilshire. He should be there a minute or so later and he should make the right onto Western. He'll spot me because once I'm across and I know he's behind me, I'll turn on my hazard lights and drop to about fifteen miles an hour."

"What do you want?"

"I want a bullet through this asshole's back window, not to hit him because I don't want to make that kind of trouble for your person. I just want this clown to think I'm on a team."

"You do realize that sticking a gun out the window and firing that shot on a crowded street during the Christmas shopping season isn't a great plan."

"Okay, hang on, Wilshire coming up. As soon as he or she sees my hazard lights he should flick his brights once and I'll turn into a side street as soon as I can. Your guy can come up behind him then and take the shot when no one's behind him or out on the sidewalk."

Louie grunted, said, "Hold on," and repeated what I'd said. In the meantime, the light at Wilshire went red, the person coming up behind me hit the horn, and the cyclops sandwiched itself diagonally in front of him, blocking both my lane and the one to the left. Then, in case I hadn't noticed him, he bumped me again, just hard enough to push me into the crosswalk, which had a lot of Christmas pedestrians in it.

By the width of a couple of shirt buttons I missed a young Korean couple. The guy, who had made something of a production of snatching his honey out of harm's way when she'd already done it herself, started shouting at me. I put down my window and called, "Get out of here. Guy behind me has a gun," and the crosswalk cleared as though by magic. I sat there with both feet on my brake pedal in case he decided to knock me into the oncoming traffic on Wilshire.

"Still there?" Louie asked.

"Stuck at the light," I said. "I think he's going to try to push me—"

At that moment, the cyclops's engine emitted a roar, I felt a jolt, and then I was pushed out, my wheels locked and motionless, onto Wilshire Boulevard, one of the busiest streets in the entire city. Tires squealed all over the place, and I heard one car slam into another, but I cut my wheel so tight, turning my front wheels almost perpendicular to the rear ones, that my car started to turn right rather than be shoved farther forward. My phone slid off my knee and onto the floor, ending my contact with Louie. The moment I felt the cyclops ease off, I spun the wheel left and accelerated between cars—traffic had essentially stopped—across Wilshire and headed south.

By now the cross traffic on Wilshire, in my rearview mirror, might as well have been the Petrified Forest for all the movement that was going on. What sounded like the 1812 Overture, rescored for automobile horns, was filling the night. Traffic on Western wasn't exactly zipping either, so I was able to see the cyclops nose its way through and start to gain on me. I slowed down, popped my hazard lights, and drifted along at the approximate speed of a parade float.

The problem with my plan, I reflected as he bumped me again, was that Louie's person, like everyone else, was jammed into that stationary welter of cars on Wilshire. Surely, I thought, this clown isn't dumb enough to keep ramming a car that's doing twelve miles an hour on a major north-south street and blinking like a portable Christmas display.

Then he hit me again. Harder.

The first cross street, Ingraham, came up and I glided a little faster, half-aware of the car waiting there to turn right behind us as the tail bounced off my rear bumper again. I had barely passed Ingraham when I registered that the car waiting there had hit its high beams for a second, and I swear that the melody to "Joy to the World" bloomed in my ears. Then, in time to the music like a star soloist in some vehicular

Christmas dance, the new player turned onto Western right behind the cyclops. I sped up some more, cut the hazard lights, skipped Seventh, which was too commercial and too busy, in this season, for bang-bang, and made a right onto Eighth. Eighth was crowded, too, but I knew these blocks and I increased my speed again and made a right onto South Manhattan Place, which was perfect: ugly 1980s apartment houses on the right and, just ahead on the left, a long, blind stretch of windowless wall, apparently blocking something even uglier. I made that wall home base and drove toward it at an indolent pace until he was close enough to hit me again, and then I slowed further, which seemed to surprise him because I saw his brake lights flare, even as the other car practically drove up his exhaust pipe, and I had the sense to duck down just as a second bullet punched holes in both my windshields.

But this time it wasn't his bullet. It took a quick count of two or three for him to figure it out, and then he surged around me on the left and took off toward Seventh like he was trying for a sonic boom, the jagged edges of the bullet hole in his back window catching the streetlights like a spar-kler. I slowed and stopped and watched almost neutrally as he shot past the stop sign and into the now-moving traffic and was clobbered from the left, in a satisfying explosion of breaking glass, by an LAPD black-and-white.

10
Zero to Fifty

Almost before the noise of the collision had come to an end, the driver of the car behind me and I, in perfect unison, turned off our headlights in case the sound had drawn eyes. There was no parking on the left side of the street, so I swung as far right as I could and then crimped the wheel left. I hit the left curb and hopped it, finishing the U-turn with two wheels on the grass, but without any brake or backup lights. The car behind me pulled to its right as I went slowly by and then made its own slow, lights-free turn.

At the corner of Eighth I put my arm out and signaled left. When I had a nice, big gap in traffic, I turned on my lights and headed east on Eighth. Traffic was light, and I was able to slow in the right lane without setting off anyone's anger management issues until I knew I was being followed, and then I led us eight or nine blocks to Catalina, where I signaled, turned right, parked, and waited. When the other car was behind me at the curb, I opened my door, put both hands out, and followed them into the street. My palms were toward the waiting car, my fingers spread wide. I was the picture of harmless; I'd done everything but roll up my sleeves.

"Skip it," said a voice from the car, a clear, musical

contralto, not precisely the kind of voice I'd expected. "Louie says you're okay."

The driver's window slid up and the door opened, and a woman unfolded herself out of the car: nearly as tall as I was, slim as a thread of smoke, with skin of the color you might get if you mixed a creamy Thai iced coffee with a lot of cinnamon: a smooth, sweet-looking brown with a lively spark of something almost reddish underneath it. She had cheekbones as symmetrical as parentheses, a lavish lower lip, and bone structure that would have sent a sculptor fumbling for his clay. She was draped from shoulders to ankles in a gleaming black leather coat.

I said, "Um." Then I said, "I owe you."

"You do," she said. There was a little something in her speech, not in the pronunciation so much as the intonation. "But I'm patient. When I need it back, I'll expect it with interest."

"I'm Junior Bender."

"I know," she said. She stuck out a hand almost as big as mine but a lot better shaped. "Francie DuBois."

We shook, and eventually I let go. I said, "Do you eat Korean food?"

"Put some in front of me and see."

"Okay," I said. "Just hold on a minute. I really need to take care of this."

I scrolled down the recent calls on my phone and hit the one I needed. When he answered, I said, "Listen to me, you jumped-up *pirozhki*, you just broke it and you can't fix it. You try to get near my family and you'll walk into the St. Valentine's Massacre—"

"Wait," he said, "wait."

"And you can't find me because that golem you sent lost it and took a shot at me, and—"

"You are knowing—" he began, bits of the thin husk of Tip Poindexter flaking off with each syllable, "you are not making the sense. I nid—I mean, I *need* you—"

"And I'm not going to wait for you to come looking. I know where you chase your tiny little balls around outdoors all day, and in that window in the dining room, you might as well be standing in front of the fucking Hollywood sign. So look for me, because if you don't see me first—"

"You are not—" he said and I hung up.

"He'll call back," I said to Francie DuBois. "This isn't really a restaurant conversation."

"It's rare these days," she said, "to find a man who's so considerate," and my phone rang.

"What?" I said into the mouthpiece.

"You must letting me finish," he said. "This man, he is garbage. I send him, yes, to see where you live because is Christmas and I, I, I, I want, I want to send you, for, for Christmas . . ."

He trailed off, and then he laughed, and I laughed, too. It was too stupid not to laugh. Francie DuBois's eyebrows went up.

"Where is he?" Vlad asked.

"Downtown cops got him. He ran a stop sign and collided with a patrol car while he was carrying a gun and driving a car with bullet holes in it. They're going to want to chat with him for a while. Who knows, maybe he'll lead them to you."

"Peh," he said. "He knows nothing." And then, sounding more like Tip Poindexter, he said, "It would seem to me that you came off quite well."

"No thanks to you."

"So you are downtown?"

"Downtown is a big place. Oh, and find somebody else

to protect your mall. Right out of the Great Depression, by the way."

"I am actually glad this happened," he said. "I have been rethinking our arrangement. Threats are so primitive. And a man like you, I should have a *relationship* with a man like—"

"Fifty thousand dollars," I said. I felt Francie DuBois's eyes on me, and when I looked over, she nodded approval. "And I want twenty-five tomorrow, no bills bigger than a twenty, and twenty-five more the same way when I give you the name or names."

"You are getting anywhere?"

"For free?" I said. "You must be kidding. Twenty-five tomorrow at the mall, twenty-five when I'm done."

A pause. For all I knew, he was taking his pulse. "Where at the mall?"

"Eleven A.M. Phone me when you're in the parking lot, and I'll tell you where to come."

"Trust is important in a business—"

I said, "Tell me about it. If I don't see you by ten after eleven, I'll be gone." I hung up and found Francie DuBois looking at me appraisingly.

She said, "Fastest I ever saw anyone go from zero to fifty."

"He'll still kill me if he gets the chance," I said. I'd just hung up on Louie, who had promised to find a shooter who was in between jobs and get him or her out to Kathy's block within an hour. In the morning, we'd set up a rotating schedule.

"Oh, well," she said. "It'll keep you on your toes. Men who are half-asleep have no magnetism." She was plowing through an enormous plate of *bibimbap*, an adventurous mix of rice, meat, and vegetables topped with a raw egg. I was digging into *kimchi* and had some sliced rib eye and bits of marinated chicken grilling on the charcoal burner in the center of the table, making a column of fragrant smoke that the smoke hood above us was doing it best to blow back down. She tugged at the front of her blouse, sniffed it, and said, "I was tired of this thing anyway."

I got busy tending to the meat for a moment or two, a little taken aback by how much I was enjoying myself. It had been a long time since I'd had dinner with an attractive woman I didn't already know, and it felt good. On the other hand, my conscience reminded me, there was a splendid woman, bright, funny, tough, and mysterious, waiting for me in Apartment 302 of the Wedgwood. So how good it felt made it also feel a little bit bad, if that makes sense.

"Well," I said, trying to keep things safely neutral, "how did you happen to be driving around Koreatown, strapped and loaded, in one of Louie's emergency cars?"

"I wish it were interesting," she said. "I was Christmas shopping and my car is in the shop, so I borrowed, or I suppose rented, one of his."

"Shopping for whom?"

She didn't let the smile get any lower than her eyes. "Acquaintances, people I know, people I owe. The milkman, the plumber, big Judd down at the service station. The usual mix."

"Ah," I said.

"Ah, indeed. The gun, which soothes me by its proximity, was in the trunk, where it's supposed to be if it's registered to me, which it is."

"You're registered to own a gun?"

She smiled more openly this time, not a hundred-watt smile, just a little glimmer of friendliness-plus. "One of me is," she said.

The meat was all turned over, so I had no alternative but to look at her, which was a pleasant thing to do. "How many of you are there?"

"Two really solid mes," she said, "by which I mean they might get past Homeland Security if they were having a bad day, and three so-so mes, good enough for the LAPD, like you've probably got half a dozen of yourself."

"You show me yours and I'll show you mine," I said. "We'll compare. Are you really Francie DuBois?"

"Of course not," she said.

"You have the advantage of me, then, since I really am Junior Bender."

"I'll take any advantage I can get," she said. She gave her attention to the grill. "Those things ready?"

I picked up the tongs and checked the beef, which was done, and the chicken, which needed a minute or two. "Who are you really, then?"

"Let's not get ahead of ourselves," she said.

"Right." I put some of the meat on a plate along with a few of the roasting cloves of garlic and handed it across the table.

Sprinkling and slathering various condiments over a leaf of romaine, she said, "Tell you one thing, though. Whatever you've done for Louie, you made a friend out of him. I mean, here I am, peacefully driving home with a bunch of presents in the back of the car, and he's suddenly on the phone, practically shouting, building a big case why I should drop everything, get my gun, and go get shot for some perfect stranger." She wrapped the lettuce and spices around the barbecued beef like an Asian taco.

"I'm not all that perfect," I said, dishing out some chicken.

"That was my first thought when I saw you." She took a bite, and her eyes drooped closed in what looked like ecstasy.

Women recover from ecstasy faster than men do, though, and a second later she was saying, "But I'll tell you." She cleared the food to one side of her mouth in order to talk. "You're close enough that if you were standing in a department store window, I'd probably go shopping."

I could feel myself blush. Blushing is a gigantic tell, but there was nothing I could do about it, so I said, "There's a reason Louie likes me. It's because a long time ago, I got his koala bear back for him."

She rested her chin on her hand. There was no wedding ring on it. "Do I want to hear this story?"

The curve of her hand beneath her chin made me wish I could draw. "I'm not even sure I want to tell it."

"Oh, well," she said. "We're here." And she dug into the food again.

"The guy who's my fence has a sideline in smuggling. He's got runners who come through customs wearing fake bellies and inside the bellies are diamonds or gold or exotic animals. Four or five guys on each flight or at each border checkpoint to reduce the odds, not exactly top-line talent because who'd volunteer for this in the first place, and also they've got to be guys you can replace because some of them are going to get caught." I paused.

"I actually am following you," she said, chewing. "I'll signal when I get overwhelmed."

"One month, Stinky had been bringing in precious stones, mostly jade but also a couple of emeralds from Myanmar via Australia, which is the usual route for jade, and he had his guys pick up some koala bears, since, uh—"

"Since Australia," she said.

"Yeah. So he found himself with a surplus of koala bears. Too many koala bears lowers the profit margins, not just due to supply and demand since the supply of koala bears rarely gets out of hand, but because they have to be fed and cared for, and some of them eventually die. I saw some of the leftovers up at my fence's place, and I told Louie about it, and he bought one. Got it at a good price because my fence was sick of it. He and his wife—Louie and his wife, I mean—went all ootsie pootsie about it—"

"Ootsie pootsie."

"You know, baby talk about how cute it was, how *iddy biddy widdy* it was, how they loved it more than candy, which is saying quite a lot for both of them. There was a week or so there when Louie was calling me up all the time with the latest lovable koala story. I guess this thing filled a gap or something. And then one day Alice came home, probably from a run to Pet Mart, and the bear was gone, cage and all."

"Heartbreaking," she said. "Could I get some more chicken?"

"Louie called me, since I was the only almost-detective he knew. Could I get it back, how long would it take, it was breaking Alice's heart—"

"Blame it on the woman," she said, putting together another Korean lettuce taco.

"Well, Louie's not gonna tell me he's having a nervous breakdown over a koala . . . you're right, blame the woman. Anyway, it wasn't exactly a brain-buster. It had to be someone who knew something about Louie's house because he either had a key or the right picks for the back door and there was no sign of a search, and he probably also knew Stinky."

"What a colorful name."

"My fence. His family invented the perfume strip. So it took me about thirty-six hours to locate the guy who took the bear, a cousin of Alice's, in a motel a couple of miles away. When I picked the lock, he was dead on the floor, and there had been a dim-witted attempt to roll him under the bed. But the *really* interesting thing was that every single horizontal surface in the apartment—floors, counters, the seats of chairs—had been covered with newspaper. And the newspaper had been well used by the koala bear."

"The koala ate something," she said. "Something it couldn't digest. And the muscle was waiting for whatever it was to reemerge into daylight."

I nodded. "The idiot with the false belly had also been carrying some of those Myanmar jewels, and like the dolt he was, he put them in a leather drawstring bag. The koala, with nothing to do during the flight—nobody sitting next to him, nothing to read, couldn't see the video—he chewed through the bag and swallowed a twelve-carat emerald, almost perfect."

"What's *almost*?" She rested her chin on her palm, leaning toward me slightly.

I settled back in my chair, putting more space between us. "Emeralds tend to have more inclusions, usually little gas bubbles, than diamonds and sapphires do. Most people who know jewels look for the inclusions to prove it's actually an emerald. So a 'perfect' emerald is one that has a teeny inclusion, just big enough to whisper, 'Hey, I'm real.' And that makes it hard to cut big stones because the bigger the stone the more inclusions you run into, so the per-carat price of a big, good emerald is a *lot* higher than the price of a small one. This stone was Triple-A rated, deep green, high transparency, and worth about a quarter of a million dollars. I went up to Stinky's place and got the koala bear back, but he kept the emerald."

"I didn't know emeralds came from Myanmar."

"They don't, not much, but it's a good place to get them cut without any embarrassing records being kept."

"Who killed the cousin?"

"Hired muscle. The cousin had fed the poor little thing laxatives on a hunch, and when he saw what finally came out, he tried to hold Stinky up, and Stinky, well, he protected his interests. Anyway, I took the bear back to Louie and Alice once it got control of its digestive system again, and we've been friends ever since."

"It's not often," she said, "that a charming stranger tells a girl a story with smuggling, fake bellies, emeralds, koala bears, and laxatives in it, all at once like that. Four of the five, sure, but all of them? How's the bear?"

"In the LA zoo," I said. "They got tired of him."

A waitress shaped roughly like the Rock of Gibraltar was suddenly beside our table, so perhaps I was a bit less alert than usual. Without a word she picked up the large brown bottle of OB beer in front of me, sighted through it, and said, "One more?"

"Sure," I said.

"Lady?" the waitress inquired, tossing her head in Francie's direction.

"Doesn't it show?" Francie said. "Oh, you mean my beer. No, I'm doing fine." She spoke the last three words to the air because the waitress had turned away at "no." "Efficient, isn't she?"

I finished the bottle. "Your turn. What do you do when you're not rescuing imperfect strangers?"

"I'm sort of a travel agent."

"*What* sort of a travel agent? How many kinds are there?"

"I specialize in invisible itineraries," she said. "Let's say that heavy you were yelling at on the phone decides to kill you—"

"That's about a fifty-fifty—"

She stopped me with a raised palm. "Don't jinx it. Anyway, I'm being hypothetical here. You might talk to Louie, and Louie might talk to me, and I might build for you a sort of wormhole, like the ones the *Enterprise* was always going through, but without the engineer saying 'She cannae take it, Cap'n.'" She shook her head. "How many thousand times do you think Scotty said that? And he was *never right*, not even once, but he retained his credibility because it was TV. On a real spaceship, the whole crew would be imitating his accent. Someone puts an extra potato on a plate and ten people would say in unison, '*She cannae take it, Cap'n.*'"

I said, "You've given this some thought."

Francie let her gaze drift down to her food. "Where was I?"

"Building me a wormhole."

"Right, scooting you out of peril. It would involve various modes of private and public transportation, odd departure times, a bunch of obscure places good only for passing through, several identities, some simple disguises, and possibly a visit to a plastic surgeon. Presto. When it was over, no one would be able to find you."

"Except for you, which is the weak spot in the operation."

"If they learn I made you disappear, they come to me and I resist bravely and they slap me around a little and maybe punch me, and then I cave in and reluctantly show them everything: your itinerary, your tickets, a picture of your fake passport and also your *other* fake passport, even the hotel you were reserved into in your final destination."

"And after they kill me you give me a refund."

"You must be quicker than that, or you wouldn't be alive. What they don't know is that after three days in that hotel you sat down with another person like me, who routed you onward with new passports. And I have *no idea* where he or she sent you. So they trace you to the hotel, and then, as far as they're concerned, you disappear again. If you have enough money, you can go through three travel agents. Then even the second one doesn't know where you are."

"Do I get to pick my destination?"

"That's the problem. You're going to wind up in some-place like Bulgaria or Greenland."

"Nothing is flawless," I said, studying her face.

"What?"

"I just realized that Louie mentioned you to me this morning. The woman who arranges escapes. But what I was *looking* at was the color of your eyes." I had a not entirely unpleasant tightness in my chest. "My daughter's boyfriend, a great kid named Tyrone, is African American, extremely dark, and he's got eyes the color of a very light autumn leaf, sort of halfway between brown and gold. I'd never seen eyes that color before, but yours are very close."

"You have a daughter," she said. "How old?"

"Fourteen."

She raised one eyebrow, and it didn't look like she knew she was doing it. "Look like her mother?"

"Like both of us, I think. That's what people say anyway. I don't actually see much of me in her."

"Just your wife?"

I changed my mind three times in the tenth of a second before I said, "Ex." And I didn't add anything. I didn't answer the question she hadn't quite asked.

When we came out, it was raining. I was wearing an untucked long-sleeved shirt, and she threw one side of her ankle-length leather coat over my shoulders, keeping me dry, and we walked, hip touching hip and her arm around me holding the coat in place, to my car. She smelled like some kind of light floral powder. When we got there, we shared an awkward but warm hip-to-hip silence as the rain drizzled down around us, surrounding the street lights with pale, luminous spheres, until I leaned forward and then back again, resisting the impulse to kiss the tip of her nose and said, "Thanks."

She took a step back. Her expression was both amused and inquiring. She said, "No problem," and turned toward her car.

I said, probably a little too loudly, "I had a good time."

"I know," she said, popping the lock. "See you."

Then she was inside and the door was closed and I was looking at the dazzle of rain on her windshield. The door opened again, and she said, "If you want a rematch, call Louie. He usually knows where I am. I'm not going to embarrass myself by asking if you want my number." The door closed, the lights went on, and she gave me a tiny blurt of her horn and pulled away. I watched her go, kicking myself for everything I'd done and hadn't done.

After Kathy and I split up, I lived like a monk—well, a burglar monk—for several years. I was still in love with Kathy, for one thing, and for another, I didn't want to be the absent father who shows up from time to time to introduce his daughter to the latest in a stream of women. I had a friend who did exactly that, and his kids made a point of addressing Thursday's girlfriend, so to speak, using the name of Wednesday's. Not easy to explain away if you're the embarrassed philanderer.

And anyway, I was never a philanderer, which is a word that's gone out of style for a good reason; it sounds kind of quaint and harmless, but there's nothing harmless about what it describes. Kathy had been my girlfriend in both junior high and high school, with a couple of brief breakups to maintain the drama level kids need, and it was always clear to me that eventually we'd be married. What hadn't been clear was that we'd fall apart, and that it would be my fault.

After several years of somewhat variable celibacy I'd met Ronnie Bigelow, whom I suspected of murdering her husband. We'd both misrepresented our motives for the first week or so, and we fell in love even though neither of us had any idea who the other actually was. I *still* had no idea who she was. I'd learned in the year and a bit since we met that Ronnie was a little like the joke Christmas gift that comes in a giant box with about twenty wrappings: every time you peel one off you find another. She had something fast and loose about her, a matched set of devious instincts and quick thought processes that said *crook*. Somewhere back there in Trenton or Albany or Ontario or Coeur d'Alene or wherever the hell she'd come from, there had been something dark and slippery, and apparently she had decided to take it to the grave unshared, at least with me.

So it was a little like living with someone who had an extra shadow, but somehow I trusted her more than almost anyone else in the world. If someone had taken spiritual X-rays of us, say, the previous afternoon, they'd have shown some tightly closed drawers where dodgy facts were neatly folded and tucked away out of sight, but the *trust* area would have been as clear as mountain water.

And look what I had just done.

Just to be on the safe side—and also to get a little more accustomed to my new discomfort with myself—I did circles, loops, and switchbacks for fifteen or twenty minutes until I knew no one was behind me, and then I drove to the

Wedgwood. When I opened the front door, Ronnie got up from the couch, where she was reading something about Eleanor of Aquitaine, wife to two kings, imprisoned by the second, mother to a third, and smarter than all of them put together. She hugged me, sniffed, said, "Korean, huh?" and went back to the couch.

"I had a little problem," I said. "The guy who hired me today to look into shoplifting in the mall he owns sent somebody to follow me and he got all upset and took a shot, and I called Louie to see whether there were reinforcements anywhere. There were, and I bought us both dinner. The, um, the other driver and me."

"What about the bad guy?"

"He collided with the cops."

"Virtue always triumphs," she said.

This was not a comfortable thesis. "Christmas is driving me crazy," I said. "Why don't you make it easy on me and just tell me what you want."

"Oh," she said. She looked past me as though she was thinking about fleeing the room. She closed the book, a finger marking her place. "I don't want to—I mean, there's plenty of time."

"Three days. Actually, two now. This is our first real Christmas together. I want it to be something you'll remember." I heard Francie DuBois say, "See you," and suddenly I could smell her scent on me, and I blushed.

"Just, just, I don't want anything, okay? I'm happy the way things are." She was so eager to escape the room she got up from the couch.

Determined to make up for whatever I'd just done, I said, "Whatever you want. I'll find a way to get you whatever you want."

"What I *want?*" she said, and there was a catch in her voice as though she was either angry or on the verge of tears. "Gee, I don't know." She shook her head. "A . . . a set of matching cheese graters? A pair of sweat socks? Who the hell cares?"

"Ronnie," I said. Her voice had scaled up a couple of tones.

"*Look* at this place," she said. "Look at *you*, look at that roomful of books in there. It's *all* Christmas." She wiped her cheeks with the heel of her hand, not gently. "You know what? *You're* Christmas. Leave me alone—no, no, that's wrong. *Skip* me, buy something extra nice for Rina, something special for Kathy. Get yourself a new front left tire, I don't like the way that one looks."

"A new front tire," I said.

She was crying. "Wrap a ribbon around it, show it to me first, I'll go, *Ooooooohhhhhh* and then you can get Louie's guy to put it on your car. I need to go to bed."

"Sure," I said. "I'll, uhhh, I'll be right in."

"No," she said, brushing past me. "Give yourself some time. Read something. I'd just, I'd just like to be alone for a little while. Okay? Just a little while."

"Fine," I said. I called out to her back, "I'll be in the library," but she was gone. I stood there in my beautiful 1920s living room with the Christmas lights of Los Angeles sparkling at me through the art deco windows, and then I went into the library and sat in my favorite chair and looked at my books without reading any of them and loathed myself until I figured she'd had time to stop crying and, maybe, fall asleep.

PART TWO

AND THEY WERE SORE AFRAID

11
Some Reins and a Bit

I'd told Francie I thought it was about 50/50 whether Vlad would eventually try to kill me, but privately I put it at closer to 20/80 in his favor. So after I'd spent most of the night stewing about what I'd done and said in the Korean restaurant, about the lies of omission I'd told both Francie and Ronnie, and most of all about my disinclination to clear it all up, I choked down two cups of coffee and got to the mall in time to be waiting at the employee entrance for Wally Durskee. I thought I might use Wally's magic room to get a look at the potential cast of assassins.

"The cameras are mostly inside the stores," he said as his surveillance screens flickered into life. "That's where the merchandise is, you know?"

"What are the black screens?" Two in the bottom row of eight were dark.

"Those are on the second and third floors where Gabriel's used to be."

"That's the store that split last Christmas, right?"

"Yeah, you know, used to be in what's now the bazaar area and the two floors above it. You can see the bazaar there." He indicated the last screen in the third row and the first two in the fourth. They were bright and I could see a few vendors moving around as they set up for the day. "The screens in Gabriel's aren't actually black," he said, indicating two that looked pretty black to me. "I mean, they're not dead, they're on, but there's no light. If you look at *this* one, see that pale area that's flat along the bottom? That's the escalator coming up from the bazaar."

"Got it."

"I've got cameras covering all the escalators," he said. "People like to fake accidents on the escalators and sue."

"What about the common areas? You know, the food courts, the ground floor, the perimeters on the second and third levels. Suppose a fight breaks out or—"

"Got it." He pointed to a line of screens that were relatively dim. "If something happens, I can use these and the ones on the escalators. Probably have to redefine the field of vision."

"As complicated as that sounds, I'll bet it's child's play to you."

He almost flexed. "I can make these babies do tricks, yeah."

"Let's make it a challenge," I said. "Suppose you wanted to find people who were looking for someone."

"Who?"

"It doesn't matter. The president. Where would somebody station himself to spot the president at the main doors, and, no, there won't be a bunch of TV lights trailing along, this is just an attempt to duck all that and shop in peace, buy the family some actual surprises that won't show up on the network news. So where would someone, or two or three someones, stand to spot the prez at the entrance to the mall?"

"*At the doors,*" Wally said. He smoothed the skin in front of his hair. "There are two of them. He'd wait there."

"Good. And to watch from farther away? Maybe some-place that's invisible from the entrance doors?"

"Second or third levels, about halfway on the east side 'cause both outer doors are on the west. But you can't watch both doors at once, you know, 'cause they're at opposite ends of—"

"And so?" I said, furrowing my brow.

"You'd need two guys."

"There we are," I said. "I knew you were the guy to ask."

"But I don't have cameras there. I mean, I couldn't look down."

"No problem. I don't want to look down at the doors. I want to look at the places those guys would be standing."

"Watching the *watchers*," he said with an air of total con-centration.

I mimed a little knockout punch. "That's exactly it."

"Lookit," he said. "Numbers fifteen and seventeen."

"Wait, wait, numbers . . ."

"Next-to-last screen on the right in the second row, first one on the left in the third," he said. As my eyes found those monitors, there was a dizzying zoom on both screens and we were looking at two dim rectangles, empty but for the railing at the edge and the mostly dark shops behind it. "Fifteen is the second floor and seventeen is the third."

"Perfect," I said. "Keep them focused there until we've been open for a while."

A look of cunning took charge of his face, as though he was trying to see something far, far away. "This about the shoplifting," he said. "You think somebody's giving signals or something."

"I do," I said, although I hadn't figured out how, and it wasn't what I was looking for right then anyway.

o o o

By ten-fifty I had a headache from lack of sleep, and the mall had been open for almost an hour. I said, "Zoom in. Number fifteen."

"Gonna get grainy."

"I can live with grainy." I blinked away the sand in my eyes and took a better look. The man standing at the second-floor railing, looking down toward the left-hand door, was medium-height, but if he'd been a mobile home he would have been a double-wide, and it was all muscle. He had a very short nose and a very long upper lip, which made it look like his mouth had been installed by someone with no previous experience. He was dressed like a juvenile delinquent from the fifties, an imitation Brando in a plain white T-shirt with the sleeves rolled up to expose biceps that had cost him a lot of pain, plus tight jeans with a thick black belt.

"Boy's been lifting," Wally said.

"Prison is a great gym," I said. I pulled out my phone, framed the long-lipped Brando fan on the monitor, and shot it. I got some parallel lines running through it, so I said, "Can you freeze that as a still image?"

"Ummmm," Wally said.

"I'm getting these lines."

"Those are moiré patterns," Wally said without even looking, instantly making me ashamed of myself. "Both the images, on the screen and on your phone, they're just dots, and the lines are overlapping patterns of dots."

I said, "Huh. Well, it's good enough."

Wally said, "Number seventeen."

"Thank you," I said, rubbing at my eyes. And there was another one, an over-sharp dresser, more in the Tip Poindexter mode: white sport coat, black shirt, slacks the color of camel's hair although probably a less expensive wool-something blend—a sartorial homage to the father of the feast but sufficiently down-market to avoid arousing envy in the original. He had a receding hairline, a nose sharp enough to pop a kid's balloon, and the abnormally small, deep eyes I associate with Vladimir Putin. As I watched, the one with the pointed nose shot an arm out to clear his cuff off his watch, a gesture so theatrical that just the sight of it made me want to go out there and tip him over the railing and onto the big Christmas tree two levels below. Movement on the other screen caught my eye. The double-wide was looking at his watch, too. I took a picture of Putin-eyes and said to Wally, "My phone is going to ring."

My phone rang.

"How'd you do that?" Wally said, and I wanted to hug him. I would have been *far* too cool to ask that question if our roles had been reversed.

Into the phone, I said, "Where are you?"

"Downstairs," Vlad said. I could see him on the first floor, in one of the top screens. "Where are you?"

"Closer than you think." Vlad brought his head up and did a quick scan of the upper levels. "Did you bring anyone with you?" I asked.

"No."

"So there's nobody on the upper levels looking for me?"

"We were on good terms when we hung up last night," he said. He was turning in a slow circle. "It would be wise for you to keep it that way."

"You just told me a lie. Goodbye."

He stopped moving. "I have a present for you. And your money. You don't want your money?"

"Not all that much," I said. "You can keep the present, too." I hung up.

"Who's that?" Wally looked worried.

I yawned, part exhaustion, part nerves. "Buddy of mine."

"You hung up on him."

"He gets off on it," I said. I looked up at the screens. "Our watchers are gone."

"The one in the T-shirt got a text or something while you were talking. Checked his phone and left."

"And the other one?"

"I don't know, but he's gone, too."

My phone rang. I picked it up and said, "Go to the food court. Wait in front of Tito's Tortilla Heaven." I looked up at the screens. "The tables should all be empty. Take a seat and wait. When you're there, I'll come meet you. Nobody with you, nobody even on the same level of the mall, or you won't see me." I hung up again.

"Mexican food," Wally said. "Gives me the gas."

"You want anything from one of the other places?"

"Coffee, black," he said. "From the Bottomless Cup. You get free refills, that's why they call it—"

"Got it," I said, and I took one more look at the screens before I opened the door.

In yet another economy move, the mall wasn't heated at night, and a damp chill was putting an unpleasantly gelatinous edge on the holiday spirit. I stepped out of Wally's eyrie and headed for the escalator at the northeast end of the building, which would be out of Vlad's field of vision if he was sitting at any of the tables in the food court one level below. I kept well back from the third-floor railing, as much out of the light as possible, and as I reached the escalator I spotted the double-wide Brando push his way through some incoming shoppers to exit via the northern outer door, probably on Vlad's orders. I didn't see the other one, Mini-me, but I figured that with one down, my odds had improved. On the ground floor a tall, skinny guy dressed as an elf began to ring a bell as the hungover Santa—Dwayne, Wally had said his name was, Dwayne Wix—settled into his crimson throne as though half of him expected a lethal jolt of electricity and the other half expected his head to fall off and shatter on the floor like a pumpkin.

Today Vlad sported a white turtleneck—a garment I didn't even know was still being manufactured—under a wool/silk beige blazer with gold nautical buttons shaped like tiny anchors and tobacco-colored slacks. His boots were very thin alligator with three-inch heels, and they zipped up. Taken as a whole, the outfit represented a style period that, so far as I knew, hadn't actually happened yet.

"*Here* you are," he said. This time he didn't stand to greet me.

"I guess I am." I sat and waved hello to my friend, the woman behind the counter, who looked behind her as though I'd mistaken her for someone else, which in fact I had. It was a different woman.

"Do not get used to thinking you can summon me and I will come."

"The last thing I want to do," I said "is summon you. *Especially* if you'll come."

The corners of his mouth went down, which meant he could control them in both directions, although I have to say that his scowl was more convincing than his smile. I said, "Do that too much and you'll look like the Queen of Hearts." I got up.

"Where are you going?"

"Coffee. You want anything?"

"No. And I am in—"

"Okay. Be right back."

"Wait," he said, and I kept going.

I could almost feel the steam pouring off him as I walked away. It gave me a stupid, junior-high surge of satisfaction, coupled with a sensation that my back was very large and unprotected. I also figured my rudeness made it a little more likely that he might someday prevail on someone to put a few holes in me. But I just hated every cubic inch of him, and I guess I let it show.

When I came back and sat, he said, "Who is the other one for?"

"Me," I said. "Do you have the money?"

"Of course." He reached inside the blazer, treating me to a brief twinkle from a big diamond on his pinky. My mother always says that a man who wears a ring on his pinkie has no character. Mom is big on character, and look at me. Vlad's hand came out of the jacket holding a standard number ten envelope, the ones I always think of as money size, and plopped it down with a nice *thwack*. It was pretty thick, but he reached in and took out a second. "Hundred-dollar bills, two hundred and fifty of them. The twenties you asked for would have been ridiculous, twelve hundred and fifty of them."

"Damn," I said. "I wanted to throw them around my room and burrow through them like Scrooge McDuck."

"When you will—excuse me, please, *when will you* give me my answer?"

"Tomorrow night. Christmas Eve," I said, picking it out of the air. "Seven-thirty. Here."

"I do not want to come back here."

"And I don't blame you." I put one envelope in each hip

pocket. "But if I'm going to take delivery of all that money from you, I want a lot of people around."

"Ah," he said, and his facial muscles did something that was probably supposed to make him look pleasant. "We will think of something else. Here, I almost forgot." He dipped into his blazer yet again and came out with what looked like a postcard, printed a dark chocolate brown on shiny coated stock. It said *Sam's Saddlery: Fine Leather Goods* on it, which I immediately registered as the shop Bonnie had told me not to swipe from, a small third-level store, shoved up against the dark hulk of Gabriel's, that didn't seem to do much business.

"Is a gift certificate," he said.

"For how much? It's been left blank."

"For as much as you need to get yourself a nice briefcase for all that money I just gave you."

"I'm not really a briefcase guy—"

"Then get yourself some reins and a bit. I don't give a fuck." He stood up.

"Is this my present?"

"No." He gave the part of the mall he could see a quick but careful look, and it seemed to me, just for a moment, that his assurance slipped and I saw a little fear hiding back there. "Your present is in the second envelope, the one in your left rear pocket. It should assure you of my sincerity in the matter of last night." He scanned the place again and then turned and headed for the escalator, and across the mall I saw Mini-me watching him go. He caught me looking at him and bared his teeth. He probably hissed, too, but I was too far away to catch it.

I waited until they were both out of sight and then changed seats so that I had my back to Wally's camera. For a second I considered the possibility that Vlad had chosen that chair for a purpose, and the thought sent a little, many-legged bug skittering up my spine—who was *Vlad* afraid of?—followed closely by another, possibly even scarier—why did he want video of my face?—but there was no way I could think about either of those questions right now, so I dismissed them and opened the envelope, being careful to keep my back between the envelope and the camera.

Money, money, money, photograph.

The photograph showed a car, shot at a diagonal that favored the front bumper on the driver's side. The bumper was punched in pretty decisively, and the headlight above it was an empty socket framed by broken glass. The driver's door stood wide open. Hanging out of the passenger compartment at a forty-five-degree angle, held in place only by a fully extended seat belt, dangled a very large man with a squarish head and half a lower jaw. The other half of the jaw was spattered across the surface of the car. The little white things on the ground were teeth.

Four or five minutes later I walked up to Santa, who was momentarily between children, and said, "I need to sit on your lap."

Santa said, "Can you fit under the sign?"

"If I go down on my hands and knees."

Shlomo shook his head. "I get lunch at twelve forty-five."

12
Average Yelp Rating 2.4 Stars

An hour later I'd made a couple of yawning loops on both the second and third floors, watching the customers trickle in and the kids line up for Shlomo. I'd also taken a brief and somewhat hair-raising break sitting in the bathroom stall I was beginning to think of as my office. I'd needed someplace private in which to review the photograph of the golem hanging out of his battered car.

It was *much* worse than I'd thought at first. I had assumed the lower jaw had been taken off by a close-range blast from a good-size gun. The jaw had grabbed my eyes and held them when I first pulled the picture out of the envelope. I hadn't noticed the actual message that went with the present.

It was a golf club, a driver, leaning casually against the chassis just behind the rear door. Probably taken right out of Vlad's own designer bag. His way of telling me first that he'd taken care of my little problem in person, and second, he'd been working on his drive just in case he and I ever got down to it.

It struck me for the second time as I sat there that he was afraid of something. Okay, he was a brutal mass-market pimp who'd risen to Advanced Thug level, where one wears blazers and sips tea and pretends not to enjoy it when the country club help licks his zippered boots, and guys like that

will do a lot to protect their status. But he already owned
me, or thought he did: we'd come through our little spat last
night without actually breaking up, and I'd put a price on my
soul, which he paid without a murmur of protest. This kind
of—excuse the term—*overkill* was unnecessary.

Unless he was scared half to death of something, and that
something was related to the shoplifting in this wretched
mall. And I was the one who was supposed to hand him the
map out of his problem.

And I asked myself again: Scared of whom?

Since I was behind a closed door and out of view of
Wally's cameras, I took off my belt and used the point on
its tongue to scratch large letters into the paint, which was
already a bulletin board for low achievers. It took me a
few minutes and I had to check my phone for the number I
needed, but by the time I got up with my belt back in place,
I'd gouged into the wall—in letters that looked big enough
to be seen from the air, like the *help* a castaway stomps into
the beach—FOR A GOOD TIME CALL TIPPY, followed
by Vlad's phone number. Beneath that, written left-handed
so it looked like a second opinion, was *Average Yelp rating
2.4 stars, but there's a short line.*

As I said earlier, junior high school, but my options were
limited.

By the time I came back out to the second-floor railing,
I could see that Dwayne was still in position, although he
seemed to be staring at his lap as though he wasn't sure it
belonged to him. There were eight or ten children waiting, a
few bored and a few looking fretful, but the majority staring
slack-jawed at the screens on their phones. Right in front of
them was Santa, in the deeply marinated flesh, and the kids
were fascinated by pixels. Down at the other end of the mall

I could see Shlomo with a kid on his lap and a much longer line of waiting children. Kids have pretty good instincts.

The crowd below me still wasn't big enough for me to begin trying to find anything unusual in the way it was behaving. A year or two earlier I'd become interested in the way large crowds of people tend to move, especially in the kinds of deviations from essentially random movement that often occur under certain circumstances, and what those certain circumstances tend to be. Obviously no single person actually moves at random—possibly barring the ones who had written the graffiti in my bathroom stall—but when a crowd achieves any of several specific ratios between density and the amount of space it's filling, certain group behaviors, too disorganized to call patterns, begin to emerge. You can *call* them random in that they seem to be driven by individual whim, in the absence of some kind of mass attractor that would draw a significant portion of the individuals in the crowd. Think of a large number of birds taking off in any old direction before they achieve flock formation.

What Edgerton Mall hosted at the moment was a relatively low concentration of shoppers, moving according to a few rules so ordinary that they wouldn't draw the attention of someone looking for deviations. Those of us who are educationally invested in the Western alphabet read from left to right, and since most Americans read ABCs, a predictable majority of us choose the left aisle in a movie theater or, the left door into a structure large enough to have two entrances, assuming the two doors are essentially equidistant to our parking space. On the other hand, groups in circular or oval spaces, like most malls, tend to move clockwise—in other words, to the right of the door they entered through. The fact that people are usually more comfortable moving *with* a crowd rather than against it multiplies these preferences and magnifies them. People are drawn to light much the same way moths are, and a brightly lit space in a relatively dim area will draw almost everyone in a crowd over time, and a statistically predictable percentage of the individuals in the group will usually be moving toward that light source at any given moment. The same holds for something in repetitive motion, an attracting effect often exploited at Christmastime by shops with blinking lights.

This may all sound theoretical and devoid of real-world value, but insights like these—plus factors such as proximity to escalators, to food, and to the outer doors, to name a few—were all integers in the hardheaded math that went into determining the rental value of virtually every square inch in a large retail structure like the one I was in.

I'd seen *something* that was off the previous day, but I hadn't watched long enough to know whether it was just a brief anomaly or something more interesting, and I couldn't conjure it up sharply enough to superimpose it on the sluggish group below me, so I gave it up and chatted with a few more shop employees and supervisors and shoplifted a couple of small items just to keep my hand in, although nothing as good as yesterday's poker-playing dog. I was sure one clerk had spotted me but it didn't rouse her from her torpor. *Yes,* most of the managers said when asked, they were losing considerably more to theft this Christmas season than they had in prior years. The few chain stores said that losses were up a bit, but nowhere near as sharply as in the little independent shops. Three more owners echoed Bonnie of Bonnie's Bric-a-Brac in saying that this was probably their final year in business.

Some of the stores I went into had a lot of customers and

some had none or few. Given their essential exterior same-
ness, I couldn't account for that using the little I knew of
crowd mechanics, but it gave me an idea, probably the first
of the day.

"Been watching you," Wally said when he opened the
door for me. Then he retreated back behind his console and
put his hands in his pockets, usually a sign of anxiety.

"Yeah?" I took a little yellow bathtub duck out of my
pocket. "Did you see me take this?"

He looked like I'd betrayed him. "No."

"Well, don't worry about it. This time through, the cameras were the only thing I was really thinking about."

He was having trouble with the entire concept. "I saw
you take those sunglasses, though. How many things have you
boosted?"

"Eleven or twelve, but I put them all back within an hour
or two."

"Not the duck."

"I will."

He said, "Honest?"

"Wally," I said moving the duck over imaginary waves,
"what am I going to do with this?"

It took him a moment, but he said, "Okay."

"You can watch me put it back if you want. You could
even come with me. Listen, how far back is the surveillance
video kept?"

"One month," he said. "On, for instance, December seventh,
the stuff from November seventh is erased and overwritten."

"Can you pull out certain material and save it longer?"

"You mean, like if somebody falls down or there's a fight
or something?"

"I suppose."

"All I gotta do is transfer it to a different storage system. In case we get sued. People sue all the time. Their car gets scratched in the lot, they sue."

"I don't see the parking lot on any of these things."

"We don't watch it, but here." He flipped six switches, and suddenly those screens were showing us the lot. "It's recorded, but the only time we check it is when somebody makes noise about it." He toggled back to the interior views of the stores.

"So you have all the video for the past month. Do you also have the weekly store spreadsheets—you know, profit and loss, shoplifting stats—for that period?"

"No."

"Can you get them?"

"Sure. I just need a reason."

"Tell them that the theft consultant wants to see them. If that doesn't do it, tell them to phone Mr. Poindexter's office."

"Okay," he said, straightening at the sound of Vlad's alias. "I'll give it a try."

"And here's what I want you to do. Fast-forward through the tapes for the month, looking for stores that are unusually crowded, and make a note of which day and which store. Then go to the weekly spreadsheets once you get them and see whether those crowded days fell during a week or weeks when those stores reported a significant level of theft."

He was looking at me as though he was waiting for the simultaneous translator to finish, but then he said, "You want graphs?"

"Graphs," I said, "would be peachy."

13

A Long, Steep Stairway of Fashionability

I chose several watching spots on the upper levels so I could observe the crowd resolutely refusing to do whatever had caught my eye the day before. They didn't do much of *anything*, actually, except wander slack-jawed, bump into each other, and manage their kids with varying degrees of effectiveness. After an hour of that I heard three of the season's most hellacious songs one after the other, "Jingle Bell Rock," "I Saw Mama Kissing Santa Claus," and "Rockin' Around the Christmas Tree," and realized I'd heard them in the same sequence the previous evening, more than once, and the wad of money in my pocket began to feel kind of light. I went down to one of the armed security guards and, after he cleared it through Wally, got him to let me borrow the keys to the unoccupied stores.

They were uniformly dirty and sad, but there had been beams of imagination shining on them at first: Bonnie assembling her bric-a-brac and seeing all the sparkle and none of the cheese. The guy who loved music so much he sank whatever he had into a record shop, a lifetime of enthusiasm colliding with a fading technology. Connie's Active Tots had sold exercise equipment for toddlers. The sign over the door said AN ACTIVE BABY IS A HEALTHY BABY. I thought I probably would have liked Connie. Two bookstores, shelves empty and echoing with all the words that had been lined up there, back when browsing meant actually holding a book in your hands, in a space that had been built for that purpose by and for people who loved books. I've never met a bookseller I didn't like, and now, as a species, they were as endangered as the honeybee.

So the empty stores were depressing, but there were no secret caches of boosted merchandise under their counters, no hidden rooms or locked doors or ancient, fading maps of the ventilation system. They were husks; whatever energy had once animated them, it was gone now.

The same thing could be said about malls themselves. The shopping mall was a gift to America from a Viennese architect named Victor Gruen, who looked at American cities and decided that they lacked what one sociologist called *third spaces*, areas that serve as a kind of social point that was neither *space one*, home, nor *space two*, work. As a third space—analogous to European town squares—Gruen envisioned a huge enclosed area with retail institutions, amusement venues, places to sit, people watch, meet friends, fall in love, eat something. There was a Utopian element in Gruen's design: he wanted his malls to serve as town squares, complete with libraries, childcare facilities, even areas offering health care.

He launched a new retail era when he opened the first one in 1956: Southdale Center, in Edina, Minnesota, chosen because it was a small enough town that the land was cheap and Gruen could be certain that the mall would be the area's chief attraction, and also because it was a short hop over a good road to and from the fat wallets of Minneapolis. Southdale set the mold for what was to follow, ever bigger commercial developments, free of rain, snow, and heat waves, sealed off from the outside world in the same way casinos are, with the same effect: people lose track of time. The libraries and other public-service centers, though, never materialized: as the malls multiplied, the sheer cost of building them took them out of the hands of Utopian architects and the occasional liberal city government and put them into the claws of venture capitalists.

At one point in the nineties, malls had grown so grandiose and so ubiquitous that an American historian suggested that archaeologists thousands of years from now, digging them up, would assume they had been places of worship. And I suppose they were. But like the Mithraic temples knocked down to provide building material for early cathedrals, the malls ultimately lost their worshipers to a new commercial religion. In the nineties, when the Internet began its wildfire growth, cracks started to appear in the foundations of the country's malls. The big department stores, the "magnet stores" that were the malls' most essential tenants, began falling off the *buy* lists of influential stockbrokers. A little startup named Napster appeared in 1999 and started to toll the bell for hard copy distribution of all kinds of essentially digital content: music, films, television; and the lights of the big record store chains and the little enthusiasts' shops like the one in Edgerton began to blink out.

Even before then, in 1994, an online shopping service called "Cadabra" had opened its virtual doors without making much of an impact. When one of the firm's lawyers misheard the name as "cadaver," it was changed to *Amazon*. As Amazon the company started with books; in its first week under that name, in 1995, it took in $20,000, and almost immediately began to diversify. Only five years later the "accidental" name became the basis of a logo in which a curved arrow beneath the word stretched from A to Z, implying an entire universe of products.

The image of the mall rapidly descended a long, steep stairway of fashionability: stale, retro, tarnished, passé, out-dated, embarrassing, shuttered. Malls declined all over the country, hundreds of them closing to shoppers and opening themselves to the slow decay of damp and mildew. Photographers broke in to document the ruin in ghoulish images of color and rot. The mall at the center of the teenage world, the Sherman Oaks Galleria, featured in the movie *Fast Times at Ridgemont High* and widely celebrated (and reviled) as the mecca of the "Valley Girls" phenomenon, shut its doors for "remodeling" in 1999, opened unremodeled in 2002, and limped into the sunset, only to lose its roof and return in diminished form as yet another open-air shopping area. In 2009, General Growth Properties, one of the largest mall owners in America, filed for bankruptcy.

The Edgerton Mall was surviving on fumes, offering a sad contrast to a very small number of developments in the LA area that had somehow flourished, like resilient elms that had dodged the blight. I didn't know exactly when during that long industry-wide slide to the skids Edgerton had been built, but it seemed unlikely to me that the business plan would have made exciting reading to anyone who knew what he was doing. And yet a bunch of high-level crooks who were at least nominally not stupid had apparently invested millions in it.

The sixth time a shop owner told me she didn't know whether she could survive this holiday season, I went out near the railing—I was on the third level at the time—put a finger in my free ear to block "Here Comes Santa Claus" and called Louie.

"Hey," he said, "so you liked our girl last night, huh?"

"*Your* girl," I said, feeling a body slam of guilt, "not my girl."

"Ooooookayyy," he said. "I ain't gonna doubt you."

"Good."

"Or her, either, for that matter."

"Well, thanks for digging her up," I said. "She was a big help."

He said nothing.

"What?" I said.

"Whadya mean, *what*? Nothing, nothing. Hey, you seen that Japanese movie?"

"Yes," I said, "and it has no bearing on—"

"You don't even know which movie—"

"*Rashomon*," I said, "and I know what you're—"

"Damnedest thing," he said. "Everybody's got a different version of what—"

"I *said* I've seen it."

"—happened, it's like you ask a bunch of crooks which one of them took something, and from the answers they give you, you'd think they was all in different states."

"Finished?"

"Hell of a movie."

"Finished?"

"I was beginning to wonder who you'd be bringing over on Christmas—"

"*Finished?*"

"Jeez. Nice girl, though, isn't she?"

"An outstanding member of the global sisterhood. Listen, about the partners in Edgerton—"

"Same Japanese movie," Louie said. "Everybody you talk to's got a different story. And they're all nervous. Fact is, I was going to call you, because I need a little—"

"How much?"

"Seventy-five hundred for the guy in the slammer, plus a promise I'll never say his name until he's dead and I am, too. And now that I've asked around, I need hazard pay for me. So the same for me. Figure fifteen, total."

"Thousand."

"Whadya think we're talking about, pecans?"

"You think your source actually knows something?"

"He was there," Louie said. "And he's scared enough."

"Where is he now?"

"US pen in Victorville. Got an appeal coming up and needs a little grease for his lawyer."

"That's not much grease, seventy-five hundred bucks."

"When he's out, he's got, like, the master key to Tiffany's, so the lawyer can get it on the come. But he's not letting anybody else open it up."

"I'll get it to you tonight."

"I can come get it. You're over at Edgerton, right?"

"I am."

"I can pick up the money—wait, you got it *on* you?"

"I do."

"Doing pretty good, aren't you? Okay, I can buy something for Alice when I'm there. What time?"

"I have to meet somebody for lunch," I said. "How about one-thirty?"

"Where at?"

"There's a big red throne at the south end of the building," I said. "I'll be coming down with Santa."

14
A Little Elevation of My Body Temperature

I said, "How long have you been married?"

"Forty-eight years." He was still wearing the padding under his red suit because he had only forty-five minutes for lunch. Sweat was trickling down his forehead.

"Does she work?"

"What is this, a job application? A therapy session?"

"No. Well, maybe yes, but if it is, I'm the patient."

"She did work," Shlomo said. "She was a pharmacist. We lived on my salary and saved hers. And we've both got pensions, so at least we don't lie awake worrying about money."

"And you were—"

"Teacher," he said. "Eighth grade."

"My daughter's in eighth grade. Kind of a difficult period."

He nodded. "I always thought of it as one of the last years you could catch them. They're still in the corral then, but they've become aware of the fence. The things adults build around them are protections until kids get to be about that age, and then they turn into fences, to be jumped over or crashed through or, if you're lucky, outgrown. You know what I mean; there are right and wrong ways to open the gates."

"For example?"

"Well, on the most basic level I suppose you can open them to go toward something or to run away from something. And even then, it depends on what they're running away from or toward. There are a lot of bad paths. Anyway, eighth grade, I figured you could still catch a few of them at that point. Before they did something they might not recover from. So that's the level I taught."

"You have kids?"

A heavyset guy in an apron came through one of the doors with a tray and set it in front of Shlomo. "Here you go, Shlo," he said. "Burger medium with pepper jack, fries burned."

"Hot sauce?"

"Oooy," the guy in the apron said. "Be right back."

"So," Shlomo said, poking the fries with his finger, "you asked me what?"

"Whether you've got kids."

"This is what you call sitting on my lap? You asking me about my problems?"

"Your kids are problems?"

Shlomo just stared at me.

"Okay, yeah, I'm stalling. I've done something, the kind of thing women would immediately talk to their friends about, but I'm, you know, a man."

Shlomo lowered his eyes to his plate. "Something that makes you, what, uneasy?"

"That's a good word."

"Then you were wrong," Shlomo said.

"Hell, I know that. If it was *that* easy—"

"But you don't know *how* wrong it was."

"Something like that."

"Here's the first thing. Don't do any more of it."

I said, "Well . . . "

"That's not a healthy reaction, but if that's what you need to talk about, I'll give you some time to work up to it. We've got three kids. *Kids*, I call them, they're older now than I was when I met their mother. And I'll tell you if this is a truth session, there are times when—" He sat back in his chair, eyes on a spot in the air that looked pretty much like the rest of the air to me, his lower lip pushing out and then retreating, After a couple of those, he said, "What kind of bird is it, leaves its eggs in other birds' nests?"

"Cuckoos, I think. And cowbirds. They call them brood parasites—"

"More than enough information, thanks. Our daughter, she's her mom all the way, but our sons, I hardly knew them even when they were babies, and I know them less every year. Like they got dropped down the wrong chimney." His hot sauce had arrived, but he didn't seem to notice. "Is this your way of getting to that other thing we were talking about, the dog tags?"

"No," I said. "Interesting you took it there, though."

"It's what I think about," he said. "Last week or two, it's what I think about."

"So how are they so different? Your sons, I mean."

"How do I put this? Their mom has a hobby, okay? She does ceramics. She and I, we're good solid clay all the way through. Not mud, clay, and good strong clay. Fired the slow way. We don't need much, we're happy living on our pensions and our nest egg. It gets a little smaller every year, the nest egg, but so does the time we've got left to spend it. We've lived in the same house for forty years. It's not much, but we like it. We earned it ourselves, we were happy there, mostly, and we can find our way through it with blindfolds on without tripping and breaking a hip. You'll be thinking about *your* hips, too, soon enough, just wait. So we're not fancy, okay? Good clay, fired right. Not glamorous but it looks all right. Lasts a long time."

He put up a hand to tell me he wasn't through and picked up the packet of hot sauce in his other hand. He ripped off a corner between his teeth and said, "Ooh, that's hot," took the bun off his burger, and squeezed the sauce onto it.

"But my sons?" he said to the plate. "It's like the first thing they decided to do when they figured out who they were was to get themselves gold-plated. Whatever we had, it wasn't good enough. Everything was about how things looked, and things had to look shiny and expensive. They drive cars they can't afford, they live in houses they can't afford. One of them has a wife he can't afford. Got more clothes than Bergdorf Goodman. Her idea of a vacation is plastic surgery, can't have a good time without an anesthetic. Half the time when she comes over my wife has to tell me who she is. Your wife got any of these problems?"

"No," I said. "I was most of the problem."

"Divorced?"

"Yes."

"Hard on the kid."

"She's an amazing kid." The room was filling up around us, and I scooted my chair a little closer so we could hear each other without shouting.

"Fourteen," he said. "You need to be around when she starts going for the fences."

"We have a good relationship, my ex-wife and me. At least, in that area. We're both there for her."

"That's better than nothing. Got anything to do with what you're feeling guilty about?"

"Not really."

"That's a lawyer's answer."

"Well, it's accurate."

"That's what I mean. One of my sons is a lawyer, the other's a real estate salesman. What they say is usually accurate, too. Problem is, they leave out the things that matter." He picked up some french fries and said around them, "You're not eating?"

"I couldn't eat if you put a gun to my head. But what's the problem? Your kids are grown up, out on their own. Suppose they have themselves dipped in platinum the first of every month, who cares at this point? They're not standing on street corners, selling heroin to schoolgirls."

Shlomo was dragging the empty sauce packet in circles on top of the patty, smoothing sauce that didn't need to be any smoother. He'd spilled some of the sauce on the table.

"Are they?" I said.

"'Course not. But there's a right way and a wrong way to live. My boys are on the take. It's all legal, but legal, my ass. Look at Congress. Those guys do scuzz all the time, sell out their supporters every day of their lives, but it's all *legal*. They get to wear their power ties and have their suits tailored to hide the fat around their middles. Hell, declaring *war* is legal."

"Do you really think one or both of your sons stole those tags from you?"

"They would in a minute," he said, "if they were worth anything to anybody else." He picked up the burger, glared at it, took a bite as though he hoped it would hurt, and chewed. Then he put it down and said, "Okay, you think you got problems? I think one of them stole the tags, maybe to pressure me into selling my house. Hell, maybe both of them, they're maybe in it together."

"Why do they care if you sell your house?"

"Cora and I have lived there, I already said this, for more than forty years. The kids grew up there. They learned to *walk* there. They learned to swim in the pool. I built them a tree house. There was a time when we were all happy there. You know what they call it?"

"No."

"A *teardown*," he said. "The house where these little gonifs were conceived. A teardown."

"It's a different world," I said.

"Our daughter, Shelley, she loves it, so don't give me that 'different world' shit."

"Where are you?"

"Tarzana, about a mile south of Ventura."

"Oh," I said.

"Yeah, *oh*. Used to be a nice little street. Trees, you know? Eucalyptus, orange, lemon. Lots of nice lawns. Now they're gone, either cut down or hidden behind high walls so the people who live there can pretend they're celebrities. Big empty houses with walls around them. Nobody knows anybody anymore because they're all pretending to be something else. They wear sunglasses when they go out to get the paper. House across the street sold for two and a half million last year."

"How much did you pay?"

"Seventy-three thousand."

"And you owe?"

An impatient shake of the head. "What do you think? Nothing."

"Right," I said. "What do your sons say you could get for the place?"

"More than a million six. It's a double lot." He finally took another bite of the burger. "I don't need a million six. I need to live in the house I love. I need to be left alone." He chewed for a few moments and said, "These kids here, they get up onto my lap and I find myself wondering who they'll turn into. Right now everything is wide eyes and bright lights and Mom and Dad, but sooner or later it'll be bucks, square feet, and a corner office."

"Not all of them. Look at your daughter."

"Yeah," he said, and his back got a little less rigid.

"And anyway, it's kind of nice that they want you to have all that money."

"I'm an old guy," he said. "Cora's old. What're we going to do, take a cruise? Buy cars when we don't like to drive anymore? You ever heard of *inheritance?*" He exhaled heavily, then glanced at his watch and broke off a piece of the burger with his fingers, popped it into his mouth. "Haven't got forever," he said with his mouth full. "I mean for lunch, though you can take it the other way, too. There's a lot of kids down there. I don't want to drive them all to Dwayne."

"Will you tell me the story behind the dog tags?"

"Sure, but not now. If I decide to take you up on your offer to, uhh, solve my case, I will. Jeez, get something to eat, would you? Or, if you'd rather, tell me what's nipping at your conscience."

I rubbed my face with both hands. It felt good, like it had needed rubbing for ages and I'd ignored it. "It's complicated."

"Here's a trick," Shlomo said. "Imagine you're with somebody who's got to get back to work real quick and has a bunch of kids waiting for him."

"Okay, okay. I'm in love with someone."

"Not your wife."

"Ex-wife. No, someone else, but she's met my ex. They like each other."

"Says a lot for your wife." He tore off a piece of the bun

and mopped up the hot sauce he'd spilled on the table, took a quick look around, and put it in his mouth. "So far I don't hear a problem."

"I have a lot of secrets," I said. "It goes with the way I live. This woman I'm in love with, I mean, I'm not always easy to get to know, but after a while I began to open up to her. I know how Huffington Post that sounds, *I began to open up to her*, but I mean, I told her pretty much everything. More than anybody ever, including some things that could put me in jail until the sun stops rising."

"Good for you. For telling, I mean."

"And she's told me nothing. Zero. I don't know anything about her past, I don't know where she was born or what she's done, except that she's got some pretty serious crook chops, so it wasn't all selling Girl Scout cookies."

"And this feeling is just now coming up? It never troubled you before?"

"No. It bothers me in waves, you know what I mean? Things are fine for a while, and then they're not and this big, cold wave of doubt washes over me. I keep coming up against the question, *If she loves me, why doesn't she trust me?*"

"The answer might say more about you than her. Are you someone people can trust?"

It stopped me cold. Ronnie had said pretty much the same thing not so long ago and I'd erased it from my mind. I had to think before I could find a sentence that was completely true. "I've never betrayed anyone I care about. Until maybe yesterday."

"The nub," he said, "and in the nick of time, too."

"I, um, I met someone last night. She may have saved my life. So I took her to dinner—it's not the way it sounds, I hadn't laid eyes on her when I led her to the restaurant—but when we were together, at the table, it felt—you know—it felt *like that*."

"Like what?"

"Like I was with someone I wanted to know much better. Like there was maybe a little elevation of my body temperature. Maybe the room seemed a little brighter."

He didn't respond, but I had all his attention, and that made the silence awkward. "Like I wanted to know her *differently*."

"That was all?"

"I almost kissed her on the nose."

He looked past me and then back at me. "So you're telling me you met somebody who woke your glands up, and you're using your current girlfriend's failure to tell you her secrets as a rationalization for feeling that way, and you're telling me it ended with an almost-kiss on the nose?"

"It did."

"It did not. Did you tell this woman you were taken?"

"No." I rubbed my face again.

"Did you tell your girlfriend about this woman?"

"No."

"Then it *didn't* end with an almost-kiss on the nose, did it?"

"Jesus," I said. "Are you this tough on the kids who sit in your lap?"

"I don't have to be," Shlomo said. "*They* know what they want."

15
Maybe You'll Get a Two-Wheeler

I was buzzing unpleasantly as I accompanied Shlomo down the escalator to his throne, as though low-voltage electricity were running through my body. I tried to attribute it to my lack of sleep, but I knew better.

It absorbed enough of my attention that I walked right past Louie. I didn't register him until he grabbed the long-sleeved shirt that hung open over my T-shirt. Wearing two shirts was my concession to the December weather.

"Hey," he said. "Too busy with your new friend to have time for me?"

It was probably exactly the wrong thing to say, although he couldn't have known it. I was so rattled I went on social automatic pilot. "Hey, Louie," I said. "Louie, this is—"

"Santa," Shlomo interrupted, and I registered all the kids standing around, staring at him.

"Right," I said. "It's Santa. And Santa, this is, um, Louie."

"I think we met before," Louie said. "I never forget a face."

A kid said to him, "That's *Santa Claus,* silly."

"Oof," Louie said, slapping his forehead. "I remember you. You brought me that bike."

"How'd he get it down the chimney?" I asked.

Louie stepped on my foot, hard. "You got things to do,

Santa," he said. "Lot of great-looking kids here." Louie was totally soft on kids.

Shlomo clapped him on the shoulder, laying it on a little thick, I thought, and said, "Be a good boy, Louie, and maybe some year you'll get a two-wheeler." He nodded to the thin, green-clad elf standing beside the throne, and the elf began to ring his brassy bell. I waved at Shlomo and tailed after Louie.

"The bell," he said over his shoulder. "Isn't that Salvation Army or something?"

"It's all Christmas, I guess," I said. "I am so sick of Christmas."

"*Listen* to you," Louie said. "You know what your problem is?"

"A Russian gangster? The fact that someone tried to kill me last night? Being stuck in this mall? That *music*?"

"You ain't bought anything for anybody yet. How can you enjoy Christmas if you're not thinking about giving people stuff?"

"People," I said.

"You know," he said, stopping, "there may be a limit to how long I can stand you, so why don't you give me my money?"

"Sure." We were on the ground floor, about halfway to part of the former Gabriel's that now doubled as a bazaar. In front of a deserted shop with a faded sign on the window reading THE TOT TOGGERY, I turned my back to the passing shoppers and took out the two envelopes Vlad had given me. "Your seventy-five," I said, handing him one, "and Rodion's." The remaining ten thousand sat fatly in my pocket.

"So," he said. The envelopes had disappeared, although I couldn't have told you how. "If you was gonna buy something, where would you go?"

"Beverly Hills."

"Well, you're not *in* Beverly Hills. I'm gonna give you one more chance to stop feeling sorry for yourself. Where?"

I reached into my shirt pocket and handed him the gift certificate. "Here," I said.

He looked at it, then turned it over. "No limit?"

"I'm special," I said.

Sam, the proprietor of Sam's Saddlery, had come a long way from Eastern Europe and had brought a lot of it with him. His shoulders were broad, his complexion was waxen, and his back was curved in a way that suggested hours hunched over a workbench. Scars as angular as graffiti—probably a gift of the tools used to cut leather—covered his hands, and he had a high, thoughtful, even professorial forehead beneath a fringe of short white hair that contrasted with dark, deep-set eyes and a noteworthy nose. He nodded when we came in but didn't get up from the unpainted wooden stool on which he was sitting, a book in his lap. The place was small and not well lit, just a single glass counter and a couple of tables with gloves, vests, and other merchandise on them. More stuff, mainly belts but also some handbags, hung on the wall. The room smelled like new shoes. A little curtain hung across a rear corner, probably masking a storage area.

"What are you reading?" I asked as Louie examined some supple-looking gloves.

He said, "Sienkiewicz. You know him?" There was a dare in his tone.

"No," I said. "I've heard the name, but—"

"Of course you have," he said, the sarcasm as thick as frosting. "Who has not?" He held the book up, eyebrows raised in a question. The title was in a language that might have been Polish. "May I continue?"

"Sure," I said. "We'll try not to bother you any more than necessary."

From one of the tables, Louie said, "Nice gloves."

"They're for a man," I said. Behind me, I heard Sam turn a page.

"I'm a man," Louie said. "Should be obvious after all this time."

"*Someone else*, you said, remember? The joy of buying something for someone else?"

"They will fit you good," Sam said. "They are kid."

"Kid gloves," Louie said. "Hear about it all the time, first ones I ever saw."

Sam said, "Nobel Prize."

I turned back to him. "Would you spell his name?"

"You cannot follow it. Is Polish name, very long, has many consonants."

"Oh, what the hell. Give it a try."

"S-I-E-N-K-I-E-W-I-C-Z." It was a challenge, pure and simple.

Louie said, "How much—" but I held up a hand and, uncharacteristically, he stopped.

I said, "Hendrick, something like that?"

Sam pulled his head back an inch or so, as though I'd swung at him. "Henryk."

"Sure," I said. "*Christmastime*. Um, Nero, the arena, gladiators, Peter and Paul . . ."

"Good," Sam said, nodding.

"*Quo Vadis*," I said. "Not exactly Christmas, but the aftermath. Martyrdom."

"And conversion. And forgiveness." He closed the book.

"I read it," I said, "but in translation. Tell me about this." I held out the gift certificate. "Do you get anything if I use this?"

"Maybe a small smile from the big man," he said. "An IOU. I could maybe use to patch the wall."

"Okay," I said, tearing it in half. "My friend there would like those gloves, and I'd like to buy them for him, and I want the best belt in the place."

"I have many good belts," he said.

Louie said, "You're giving them to me?"

"Sure. It's Christmas, right?"

"It's a miracle," Louie said. "You shoulda seen this guy fifteen minutes ago,"

Twenty minutes later, I'd paid for the gloves and the belt, and Louie had bought another pair of gloves and a nice suede jacket for Alice, and Sam was bagging the things and saying, "Is very different in Poland. Not all spending money and Ho! Ho! Ho! Is *waiting*, waiting for the miracle. Christmas Eve, we call *Wigilia*, you don't know this word, but it comes from Latin, same word as *vigilant*. You know, like keeping watch? So, waiting and keeping watch. Nobody eats until dinner, but all day long is cooking, so you are hungry, you are waiting. You remember what it is to be hungry and you remember that there are still hungry people in this rich, rich world." He finished wrapping Alice's gloves in tissue and slipped them carefully into the bag.

"So we are making the tree, putting the things on the table. Maybe straw in the corners so we think about the manger, the little king in the manger. When we finally sit, my father, he takes *oplatek*, a little cookie—no, not cookie but biscuit, thin, like at Communion . . ."

"A wafer," Louie said, and I remembered that Louie was Catholic.

"Wafer, yes, yes. The rich people have them in fancy box, with the baby on them, but in my house my mother make and she cannot draw, so they plain. And my father, he breaks it in many pieces, and the first piece he gives to my mother because the love between the husband and the wife . . ." He made a peak with the straight fingers of both hands. "It is the roof on the home, it protects everybody. The, the home . . ." He broke off and cleared his throat. "Roof protects the home, and the home protects the family, yes? Then the guests and the children get a little bit. It tastes like nothing, like nothing, but it tastes like heaven. It is for peace in the year to come, for to have enough to eat, for the family to have love. We had dogs and cats, and they got some, too." He neatly folded the tops of the bags and slid them across the counter to us. "Supposed to be, if the dog and the cat eat *oplatek* on Christmas Eve, then at midnight they will speak the language of people, but you can only hear if your spirit is clear and not dirty."

"Did you ever hear them?"

"Here I am," Sam said, spreading his scarred hands. "Do you think my spirit is clear?"

"Looks good to me," Louie said.

Sam raised his right hand in benediction and said, "*Wesolych Swiat*. Is 'Merry Christmas' in Polish."

Louie said to me, "You hear that?"

"I did."

"Can you say it?"

"No," I said. "But I may eventually mean it."

16
The Walnut Orchard

After an uninteresting half hour looking at the stores on the second floor, Louie and I got off the escalator on the first floor. "Old Sam," Louie said. "He could be my old man. Home, home, home, it's all he talked about. Food was better over there. Sky was bluer. Sun was brighter. My mother kept saying, *Life expectancy was shorter*. He didn't even hear it. All he ever wanted was to be back home."

"Where was this?"

"Sicily. The big guys were no one to mess around with. You're out walking and one comes by, you take off your hat, hold it in both hands and hope they don't shoot you."

"Sam's from Poland, Hungary, in there. Under the Russians in that part of Europe, there was no home except where they put you. The smart thing was to live on a border, like Voltaire."

We were nearing the bazaar, and there seemed to be a lot of people browsing the stalls.

"Why'd he live on a border?"

"So he could offend alternate kings."

"Why'd he offend kings?"

"Because he was Voltaire."

Louie looked around the bazaar. "What's in here?"

I said, "Oh, who knows? So tell me about the Edgerton Partnership."

"There were four of them plus Tip in the original group." I'd come to a stop in front of a stand called Kim's Kollectables that was presided over by a no-nonsense Korean woman. I'd missed the Kollectables on my earlier exploration. Judging by her merchandise, Ms. Kim had a good eye, or rather, two of them, and for the moment she was keeping them firmly on Louie and me. "But now one of them, the one you gave me the money for, is in jail. They got it for nickels, relatively speaking."

"How many nickels?" I reached out and touched a bracelet, and the back of my hand warmed as Ms. Kim's extremely sharp gaze homed in on it. "Where is this from?"

"Tibet," she said. She pursed her mouth, her eyes on the bracelet. "Maybe Nepal."

"When you buy a business," Louie said, "you usually pay for three things, right?" He leaned forward and examined the bracelet, which was made of polished, spherical pieces of turquoise the size of large peas and some filigreed beads, shaped in what looked like silver-and-crimson lacquer. "Very nice," he said. "You thinking Rina?"

"I am." To Ms. Kim, I said, "Old?"

"Not much," she said. "Maybe twenty, maybe thirty year. Not antique."

"So the three things," Louie said, helpfully touching a finger at each point to keep me oriented. "One, there's the physical plant, which includes the structure and the land it's on, okay? Then two, there's the stock—that's the merchandise—if you're buying like a store and you want to sell the same stuff they're selling, and then number three, there's the goodwill. You following?"

"It's only three things," I said. "I've gone that high before. May I pick this up?"

"Yes." A tiny crease of anxiety appeared between Ms. Kim's eyebrows.

"Place was originally built in eighty-eight," Louie said. "Land was cheap because it had been a little kind of amateur theme park for kids. *Cowboy Land,* it was called, if you can imagine anything dimmer. Swimming pool, miniature golf course, horsie rides, cruddy little Ferris wheel, like that. Designed for kids from like 1948, but by then they were all grown up. And it went bust when some kid fell off a horsie and the place got sued into dust. That thing really is pretty."

"Do you have a daughter?" I asked Ms. Kim.

"Have," she said, looking at me rather than the bracelet.

"Would she like this?"

"Don't know," she said. "She want crazy thing. Want metal in nose, want tattoo."

"How old?"

"Fourteen. Too crazy."

"Mine is fourteen, too."

Ms. Kim shook her head, the definitive headshake of an expert on the topic. "No good. Before, good girl. Now, crazy."

Louie said, "So the guys who built this place, they got the land in bankruptcy for bupkus, some kinda put-up deal, no other bidders, built the place for twenty-four million, cut some corners that caused trouble later on. Are you *interested* in this?"

"Sure, I am." To Ms. Kim, I said, "You know the guy who's Santa Claus, down at the other end? Not the drunk one up here, the other one."

"You got a drunk Santa?" Louie said. "That's no good."

"No," Ms. Kim said to me. "I don't know."

"He was a schoolteacher for forty years, eighth grade, fourteen-year-olds. He's taught more than a thousand of them and he's got a lot of ideas about how to handle them. You should go talk to him."

"Talk Santa Claus?" Ms. Kim said, a little carefully.

"To the man who's *dressed* as Santa here at the mall. The other end."

"Not fat," she said, nodding.

"Right. His name is Shlomo. When you go to dinner tonight, go see him. Tell him you talked to me, Junior. Talk to him about your daughter. He might be able to help." I turned the bracelet over in my hands. It wasn't just pretty, it was beautiful, and I'd never seen anything like it. "How much?"

"Fifty."

"Fine." I put down the bracelet and reached into my pocket.

"No," she said, waving both hands side to side, palms facing me. "You say forty."

"Why?"

"Just obey the lady," Louie said. "I got things to do."

"Forty," I said.

Ms. Kim said, "Forty-five."

I said, "Fine."

"Forty-two fifty," she said, wrapping the bracelet in baby-pink tissue. "See? You save money. I talk to Slo-Mo."

"She's gonna love it," Louie said.

I said, "I think she will," and as I slipped the bagged bracelet into my pocket and Louie and I turned away, Ms. Kim called out behind us, "Merry Christmas."

Now that Christmas was just two days off and the afternoon was wearing on, there were more shoppers. Almost all the

booths, even the one sad little one owned by the Antique
Geek, had a customer or two. A crowd of teenagers elbowed
each other in front of Vape and Vamp, picking up the slender boxes with the e-cigarettes in them, blowing imaginary
smoke rings, breaking into the mysteriously contagious teen
laughter that seems to be prompted by nothing and is really
saying, *I get the joke, I know why it's funny, I'm one of you.*
I saw a couple of e-cig boxes disappear into a jacket pocket,
and the next thing I knew, Louie had the kid by the arm.

"Put 'em back," he said.

The kid, whose face was flaming with embarrassment,
said, "Put *what*—" but Louie said over him, "Don't screw
with me. Put back the two you hooked."

"I don't know what you're—"

"*These*, asshole," Louie said, and before I even knew he'd
reached for the kid's pocket, Louie had both e-cigs in his
hand. He tossed them onto the counter in front of the guy
I supposed was the head Vape. "Listenna me, jerk-off, take
a couple hints. If you're gonna bag something, make sure
nobody's looking at you, okay? And steal something that's
worth something. Oh, yeah, and number three, don't *ever*
steal something that can kill you. Lookit this guy," Louie
said, thumbing toward me.

The kid looked at me.

"This guy, he don't look like much, but he's stolen ten
times more stuff in the last six months than your whole family has owned in the seventy, eighty years since it snuck into
the country. You wanna grow up to be a nick? Figure out the
how and the *what*. How to do it and what's worth taking.
You wanna wear a cute prison jumpsuit and get hammered
every night by some three-hundred-pound pedo with a mani-
cure, just keep doing like you're doing. Got it?"

"He's kidding," I said to everyone, since absolutely everyone within sight seemed to be listening. "About me, he's kidding."

"He's just modest," Louie said to the kid. To the Vape, he said, "Kid wasn't really trying to steal them. He was showing me a new pocketing move. He's an amateur magician." He slapped the back of the kid's head with an open hand and said, "Practice, stupid. *Practice*."

As we headed between the rows of booths, I said, "Tell me next time before you do that, would you?"

Louie, totally calm, was looking at merchandise. "Why?"

"So I can cross a state line."

"You know," he said, slowing at a stall that sold old china, the blue-and-white kind my mother always used, "I feel like we gotta, you and me and other people with talent, we gotta do something to raise the quality level of the next generation of crooks. You know, pay the criminal world back for the great lives it's given us."

"Louder," I said.

"We can't keep *taking* all the time. Sooner or later we gotta give something back. What'll it say for the tradition we leave behind, the tradition we *learned*, you from Herbie and me from my brother Arnold, if you got duffers like that kid running things? It'd be like magic would be if everybody forgot how to do the tricks, so you know, you can see the coin disappear or the guy always gets the card wrong. It'd be a disgrace to the memory of Herbie and Arnold and—and Robin Hood. A picnic for the cops. Don't you feel like you *owe* something?" He fingered a big, old-looking blue-and-white bowl. "What does Ronnie think about old china?"

"How would I know?" I said. "I don't even know which way she votes."

"I think she'd like this," Louie said.

"And *why* do you think she'd like this?"

"I got an eye for these things."

"Why not a catcher's mitt?" I said. "A collection of used fountain pens? You've barely met her."

The bowl Louie was putting his fingers all over, like all the other stuff on the counter, was decorated with versions of the Chinese willow pattern: the fringe of willow trees, the lovers, the bridge they escaped over, the birds they were eventually turned into for their final escape. I looked up at the sign hanging on the wall, which read WILL O' THE WISP. The shop's proprietor, a slender, blue-haired, chilly-eyed gentleman of sixty or so, wearing a very nice piece of amber that was actually too large to look good in a ring, was watching Louie through half-lidded eyed as though considering whether to call security.

"You know," Louie said, twirling the bowl around to look at all sides, "You've forgotten what a cloud of gnats you were when I got here, just glooming along with your hands in your pockets and sneering at the holiday spirit. And now you, you met old Max or whatever his name was—"

"Sam," I said.

"So you met old Sam, you got me them gloves, you did a nice turn for that Korean lady, you bought something great for Rina, and now you're turning into the Junior I know. 'Cause you're in the *spirit*. Come on, get this bowl for Ronnie. How much?" he asked the man behind the display.

A moment long enough for a count of three. "Three hundred and fifty dollars," he said without getting up. "It's chipped."

I didn't like his tone. I said, "How much if it wasn't?"

He lifted his head just enough to look down his nose at

me. "Quite a bit. It's a relatively rare bowl, not thrift shop junk." He looked past us at a substantial-looking lady bowed beneath the weight of shopping bags, who had been lured to the counter by the amazing blues. "Yes?" he said to the woman. "May I help you?"

I took the bowl from Louie and turned it over, then put it down, sharply enough to draw the proprietor's eyes. "Fake," I said. "Not Spode, despite the mark, not mid-nineteenth century. Junk, as you said, probably made around 1890 for sale to tourists at Brighton. Worth maybe twenty bucks."

"Oh, an *expert*," the dealer said, literally curling his lip, which looked like it had taken some practice. "Nothing beautiful is junk."

"On the contrary. *This* is beautiful, or at least pretty, and it's still junk. Why is it junk? Well, first, because it's fraudulent. It's been stamped with a fake maker's mark to drive up the price. Second, it's a stencil transfer—I mean, they all were—but this was *cheap* stencil transfer, and the stencil was torn. Here, this jagged line through the willow branches? That's a tear."

"Well," the woman said, taking a step back.

"Even the beautiful little legend," I said. "It's hogwash. The lovers, the birds, the whole thing. This pattern was invented in England by pottery makers who were impressed by the blue the Chinese got by using cobalt in their pottery, but being English, they wanted something original, something better, something *British*. So they put together bits and pieces of a bunch of second-rate Chinese pictures, and someone came up with the fairy story that went with it. A marketing gimmick. There's a poem from the period that tells you something about how the English felt about the Chinese: *My willowware plate has a story/Pictorial, painted in blue./From the land of tea and the tea plant/And the little brown man with a queue.* Another poem, used in an ad taken by one of the *four hundred* firms that cranked this stuff out like wool socks, described the Chinese as having *Little pig-eyes and large pigtails/and a diet of rats and dogs and snails.* Quaint from an 1850s perspective, I suppose. These days we'd be harsher."

The lady with the bags was two stalls away, briskly heading east. "So," I said to the dealer, "either you don't know anything about what you're selling or you're doing what the English did, peddling a bunch of racist gimcrackery when you could be running an honest business, pointing out how pretty this thing is and selling it at a fair price. By the way," I said, flicking a fingernail at the piece Louie had picked out, "this isn't a bowl, it's a tureen, and the chip is nothing compared to the fact that you don't have the matching lid. Twenty bucks would be high. Merry Christmas."

As we followed the lady with the bags, Louie said, "Mighta made you feel better, tearing him to microscopic pieces like that and spitting them around the room, but you still didn't get anything for Ronnie."

"It *did* make me feel better. I hate people like him. Incompetence makes me crazy." I stopped and took a look around. The bazaar, once the ground floor of the old department store, was enormous, even chopped into booths as it was. It was impressive enough to prompt a moment of admiration for the baronial retailers who had envisioned these vast emporiums and gambled their fortunes and their futures on the possibility that people would change the way they'd shopped for centuries and patronize what they called *department stores* to suggest that there were departments for many kinds of merchandise. They were the original malls, in a way; Hudson's in Detroit had been twenty-five stories high, four of them below the ground, the tallest store in the world at the time. But after more than half a century, the malls began to eat the department stores just as large galaxies swallow up smaller ones. And then the malls foundered, and now we were in the shell of a department store, housing the oldest form of capitalism, the bazaar.

Dead center in the echoing space rose the diagonal slash of the defunct escalator, the big red ribbon still closing it off. It was the double-wide kind, with one side going up and the other down. Across the way I spotted a stall beneath a nice vermilion sign reading REMEMBRANCE OF THINGS PAST. It offered a potpourri of items from various decades, and I steered Louie toward it. The best way to get a bargain is to know what you're looking at, and I was good at that with this kind of stuff.

"Okay," I said as we walked. "The little amusement park went bankrupt, somebody fixed the bankruptcy sale so the original builders of this place could pick it up for nothing, and when they built it they economized unwisely. Was that where we were?"

"Yeah. They called it The Walnut Orchard. And because they used crappy materials it started to leak, the foundation cracked some, and the place got mold. Over five, six years, it turned into a loss leader. And then in 1994, *bang*, the Northridge earthquake. Every pane of glass in the place broke and the pipes for the sprinkler systems crimped and snapped and started to spray water. One of the pairs of outside doors, I forget which, was knocked off the vertical about an inch and the grate couldn't be lowered all the way. Anybody could get in. Within a few days, the place was empty, just cleaned out by people getting the five-finger discount, and then the homeless started to move in."

"Dead end," I said.

"Yeah. About a year later, the place was bought by the Edgerton Partnership, LLC. Your boy Tip, then calling himself Yevgeniy, plus an Anatoly, a Lavrenty, a Rodion, which sounds like a radioactive mineral but is the guy in the pen up in Victorville, and an Igor. Gotta have an Igor. All former Russky mafiosos."

"How did you get all this?"

"Some of it from Rodion, with more to come when I give him your money. He's the one who tried to warn me off. The rest of it I paid for, mostly someone combing through real estate transactions and property records."

"Okay. Sorry to interrupt."

"Anyways, after the earthquake the bureaucrats were tearing their hair out. Whole blocks flattened, big apartment houses knocked cockeyed, bridges down, gas and water lines out all over the place. A million people looking for help from local government, and nobody to give it. So the Edgerton Partnership slipped in sideways and bought the place for, like, a handful of apples. Remember the one-two-three? *One*, property and building, worth zip at that point. *Two*, stock—merchandise—zero because it had all been boosted or turned to mildew. *Three*, goodwill, you gotta be kidding me. So they grabbed the place for a short song and then gave the bureaucrats a quick look at a renovation plan from a big-time structural engineering outfit, complete to code, with a codicil committing them to do more renovations if the code changed in the next thirty-six months. All wrapped up with a bow."

"Very impressive for a bunch of thugs."

"Except it was all bogus. Even the stationery from the engineering company. Printed special. What with the quake, they figured nobody would have the time to double-check, and no one did. So the whole place cost them, including fixing it up—guess how much it cost."

"How much for the land?"

"Less than two hundred K."

"Boy. Okay, I'm going to say about twelve million."

Louie's mouth did a disappointed shift to the left. "Pretty close."

"Most of it for getting things back to vertical, probably."

"So they got it open again in 1997," Louie said. He sounded a little sulky that I'd deprived him of his big finish.

I stopped in front of the booth that had caught my eye from across the room and picked up an oval object, the color of cream with a little lemon in it, about four inches long and two and a half wide. "How old?"

The young woman in the booth had a cascade of copper-colored hair pouring out of a knit cap and freckles that reminded me of Wally's, up in the surveillance center. "Made about 1890," she said. "Brought into the country in the 1940s, so it's legal on both counts."

"*What* counts?" Louie said. "And what is it?"

"It's ivory," I said. "It's against the law to buy or sell anything made out of Asian elephant ivory that's less than a hundred years old or that was brought into the country later than about 1980. This could be what they call marine ivory, taken from a walrus tusk, but you still want to be careful. What it *is,* is a small carving called a *netsuke,* made either by a professional artist or a fisherman."

"What it looks like," Louie said, "is a clam. With a string around it."

"Look." Before I opened it, I said to the woman, "Obviously, the cord isn't original."

"No, but it's handwoven, from the period. More or less.

I get them from a woman who sells antique kimonos. It's strong enough, if that's what you're thinking about."

"So look," I said again to Louie, and I opened the shell. Carved inside was a tiny palace, stairways and doorways and minute windows. "Not a fisherman," I said. "They mainly did seascapes, underwater scenes."

"Wow," Louie said. "It's so weensy."

"How much?"

"Four hundred fifty," the woman said. "I've got a certificate saying that it's more than a century old, but it's in Japanese."

"That's okay. I'll trust you. Can you bag it up?"

"Sure."

I passed five hundreds across to her and said, "Keep the change, and merry Christmas."

Louie said, "Who's it for?"

"Ronnie," I said. "It's perfect. It's beautiful, it's rare, and if there's one thing in the world Ronnie Bigelow knows how to do, it's clam up." I'd said it without thinking, and as I heard it aloud, I felt a little cramp of guilt.

"It was all Tip," Louie said.

"Call him Vlad," I said. "Tip is just too silly." We were heading for the doors leading into the central area of the mall. I had a good start on my Christmas in my bags.

"He scouted the deal, according to Rodion, he found the property, he sold it to this little band of gangsters, talked them into the whole thing. He handled the fake docs, hired the shyster lawyers, did the incorporation, all of it."

"Were they eager?" A stand with some nice-looking books caught my eye and I slowed.

"Not so much. Rodion says a couple of them felt like it

was too far out of their yards, if you know what I mean. Kind of a stretch from breaking thumbs and shipping women all over the place. And a couple of them had heard somewhere that malls were on the fade. But Vlad kept banging away at it, saying how it would position them to get at big, legit money in the long run. Kept saying it would 'open the vaults at Bank of America,' kept reminding them that they never would have put that toll road in if he hadn't scared the shit out of everybody who lived there. When they were building the road, Rodion said Tip actually turned up a couple times with bulldozers, started knocking down the houses next door, the ones they already bought, to prove they meant business. Cut down every tree on the street once."

I picked up a nice hardcover copy of Peter Matthiessen's *At Play in the Fields of the Lord* and opened it to find it was a first edition. In pencil it had been priced at $3.00. "They must have made a bundle on the road."

"MCI," Louie said, "Money Coming In. And in, and in. So much they didn't know what to do with it. And Tip—sorry, Vlad—kept hammering at *respectability*, backing political candidates, owning mayors and stuff."

To the kid behind the counter, who was reading a comic book, I said, "This is a first. Did you know that?"

"A first what?" he said.

"Where did you get it?"

"My gramps. He died and left thousands of the things. We don't want them, and we can't sell his house until we clear it out."

"Tell you what. I'll give you twenty for this if you'll promise to email me and let me come look through the books before you cart them all away. Maybe I can take a bunch off your hands."

"*Twenty?* You got it."

I wrote down my email address and gave him the twenty. I put the book into the bag with Rina's bracelet. "Present for me," I said to Louie.

"Twenty," he said as we walked away. "Generous guy."

"Used first edition usually runs fifty to seventy-five, a hundred in fine condition, maybe three-fifty to four hundred signed. This one is very nice and it's signed. If his gramps has a house full of these, I'll either make a fortune or get a lot of nice books, or both. Okay, to get back to the story, Vlad talked them into it."

"Yeah, it was all on him. He was where the whole thing came to a point, you know, like how a woman in spiked heels weighs more than an elephant?"

"No," I said. "I don't know."

"You know, down at the point, the tip of the heel, whatever the hell you call it. She's putting more, uhhh, pressure on the floor, per square inch, I mean, than an elephant." He spread curved hands to suggest the existence of something large between them. "With big, flat feet."

"Got it."

"So the point of their pressure, these guys' pressure, was aimed between Vlad's eyes. He had his, you know, his credibility riding on it. And when you lose your credibility with these guys, it's not like you're in for an unkind word. And I mean, look around, you can see it's not turning out so good."

"He got his country club and his fancy name."

"Yeah, but Rodion says he's walking on eggs. If this place isn't doing good, and how *could* it be, he might be in line for open-heart surgery, maybe in some car someplace. Which leads me to the other thing I learned from Rodion, who says Vlad is the reason he's in jail, that he was sold to the cops to keep him from bringing the whole partnership down. Rodion was trying to force a sellout even then, more than a year ago. He says most of the partners want out. Seventeen, eighteen years now, with no real payoff, they want to unload the place as soon as Christmas is over, and that Vlad's pissing blood about it. Says that even considering how cheap they got it, they'll barely break even, if they can sell it at all." He looked around. "Which is a good question."

"That's interesting, I said, because—" I broke it off, staring. Mini-me, still in his ventriloquist dummy's outfit. He was obviously following me, but something to his right had snagged his attention. Maybe he felt my stare because he turned, caught me looking, froze, and then wheeled around and started to walk away. I said to Louie, "I'm going this way," and began to follow him. For a few yards, Mini-me dawdled along as though unaware I was back there, but then he turned his head, caught sight of me, and picked up the pace.

"I need to talk to this guy," I said. "Hold these, okay?" I shoved my packages at Louie and shouted, "Hey!" at Mini-me, and he responded by breaking into a run, dodging between the people in the aisles. I had figured he'd head toward the entryway into the mall, where he might be able to lose himself in one of the stores, but instead he was pushing his way in the opposite direction. I said, "Stay here" to Louie, who'd chased after me with the bags, and took off after him.

It was as though I'd reached out and tapped him on the shoulder. His head swiveled back again, and this time I saw panic in his face. He stretched an arm to his right, grabbed the inside edge of a table full of glassware, and tilted it into the aisle. The table tottered and toppled forward, its cloth sliding off and taking the glassware with it. The merchandise hit the floor with a musical crash, sending up a sparkling cloud of glass fragments. By the time I'd cleared the fallen table with a leap and shoved my way through the people who had turned to gape at it, Mini-me had sprinted straight through the big red ribbon, leaving it dangling like a torn flag, and was charging up the motionless escalator.

17
PAH-rum-pum-pum-pum

Louie was right behind me, bags hanging off him everywhere. I said, "Stay down here."

He said, "Hell with that."

"I don't know what's up there."

"Me, neither," he said. "We're a perfect team."

"I don't want anything to happen to my presents."

"Oh," he said. "Well, if you put it *that* way."

"Meet you in the food court in a few minutes. If I'm not there in twenty, go find a uniformed security guy and tell him you saw someone break through the ribbon and go up to the second floor of the department store."

"I can handle that." He licked his lips, shifted his weight from foot to foot a couple of times, clearly conflicted. "If you're sure."

"I am. See you soon."

He trudged off, glancing back once, and when I was sure he wasn't going to reverse direction and come after me, I turned back to the escalator.

The big ribbon, which had been cut from thick red paper, had torn unevenly as Mini-me rushed through it. A hubbub of voices drew my attention back down the aisle where the glass had hit the floor, where a few helpful people were *very* carefully picking up the pieces. Eyes were beginning to turn my way. I pointed up the escalator to remind them that someone else had caused the damage and started to climb, experiencing the uncoordinated feeling I always have when every step is a different height; motionless escalators are real ankle-breakers. Before I fell flat on my face, I paused and looked up at my destination.

It wasn't a welcoming prospect. It was so dark up there that even halfway up the escalator I still couldn't see the ceiling. Only the light filtering up from the bazaar area seemed to thin the darkness.

I took a quick look around the bazaar below, just orienting myself. The deserted department store was at the north end of the mall, a space that was more or less rectangular, wider from east to west than it was from north to south. The north wall was curved, paralleling the structure's curving exterior. The ceiling down here was about fourteen, sixteen feet from the floor, and I saw no reason to think the dimensions of the space would be any different in the floors above; the mall was pretty much an architectural layer cake with all the layers the same thickness.

Okay, so it wasn't much information, but it was more than I'd had a moment ago.

I felt eyes on me and turned to see Louie, almost all the way to Kim's Kollectables, looking back at me as though for the last time. I gave him a grin that was high on muscle and low on cheer, and continued up the stairs, keeping an eye on their height.

The noise from below dropped away as I emerged slowly into the huge, dark space of the second floor. There was just enough light coming from below to see it hadn't been cleared to the walls the way the bazaar had. There were barriers to both sound and vision: carpeting, barren counters, glass display cases, shelving units, half-walls, all the architectural tricks designers use to break up a big space into a bunch of smaller retail neighborhoods, the "departments," each designed to entice and slow the seeker of some specific type of product. Each area limited the shopper's close-up sightlines to that single kind of merchandise without any distractions, while the occasional, strategically placed gap offered hints of vistas to come. All those surfaces would also absorb sound.

It was, in other words, a nightmare, either to search or to survive, assuming that something potentially dangerous was waiting for me. I could dither around in the dark, banging into things, while Mini-me waited quietly, either looking to dodge me forever or hunched behind something, holding his breath, his gun, and his garrote or straight razor, while I stumbled within reach.

It was that kind of a space, a space that suggested garrotes. If Victor Hugo were alive, he would have immediately begun writing *The Phantom of the Abandoned Department Store*.

To make things even grimmer, the one thing they *hadn't* turned off on this floor was the speaker system, which probably had a single set of controls for all three levels, so I was alone in a very dark, very irregularly shaped space jammed from wall to wall with spider holes, points of ambush, and Mini-me, and I was being force-fed "The Little Drummer Boy."

So *why* was I doing this again?

Because Herbie had taught me—and he'd been right, as I'd learned the hard way over the years—that when you turn and bite a real Type A to reclaim some space for yourself, which was what I'd done on the phone to Vlad the previous evening, their reaction is to keep pushing back *into* that space, mapping your resistance and planting tiny flags until they can reclaim it all, and if they do, the credibility of your threats is gone forever. They'll never again believe you're truly dangerous, all the way up to the actual moment when one of you has to kill the other.

I'd told Vlad I wouldn't be followed. And now he was having me followed again. I could either handle this now or start looking under the bed every night, since eventually someone *would* succeed in trailing me to the Wedgwood.

Where Ronnie was. Hiding from Christmas.

Gabriel's had been a *big* department store. It was hard to get a sense of the size up here, with the space all fragmented, but I retroactively estimated the first floor, where the bazaar was, at about 30,000 square feet. If I assumed that this floor was the same size and the footage on the third level was smaller, as it generally is, then this place had once claimed 85,000 or so square feet. And more than half of it was dark.

PAH-rum-pum-pum-pum.

I had to try to listen *past* the music, to be aware of any sound that wasn't "The Little Drummer Boy," while I moved quietly to my right, away from the diffusion of light around the escalator. I could see the ceiling now, maybe fifteen feet high, so I could also see the underside of the escalator directly above me, rising toward the third floor. Nothing would be simpler, I thought, than for him to get up here and double back behind the escalator, and then follow me after I got off. So I kept shifting to my left, away from the light, until I felt like it wouldn't be so easy to see/shoot/knife/brain/strangle me, and then I slowly revolved 180 degrees to make sure he wasn't directly behind me.

If he was, I couldn't see him. There were hip-high glass counters to my left, and the air was scented with the kind of fragrance molecules that Stinky's family sold. This had probably been the makeup and perfume area. Walking on the balls of my feet and breathing silently in the way Herbie had taught me, lips open and tongue touching the roof of the mouth, I trailed my fingertips over the edge of the dusty countertop to my left, using it as a guide to keep me on a straight path, and moved parallel to the escalator, which was on my right now, half-expecting to see him scurry off into the gloom.

But he wasn't there. And when I'd gotten all the way to the bottom of the escalator leading to the third floor and looked up, I learned that I didn't actually know what dark meant. The motionless steel stairway more or less vanished about two-thirds of the way up, and I had to put my hands over my eyes and count to ten to widen my pupils all the way before I could even make out the deeper blackness where the ceiling of the second floor had been cut away to create the space for the escalator.

With a kind of decisiveness I rarely demonstrate, I resolved that I would not be searching the third floor.

And far ahead of me and to my left, something moved.

He'd bumped something or other and it had gone over. Nothing big. A wastebasket, possibly. It was unlikely that there would be a wastebasket in the aisles, so he was behind a counter somewhere, probably moving bent over. That meant he thought I might spot him out in the open, and *that* meant that he saw in the dark a lot better than I did.

PAH-rum-pum-pum-pum.

The noises had come from my left, I reminded myself. So he was moving in the direction of the rest of the mall.

Maybe, I thought, the doors leading into the mall's second level were only locked from the outside. Maybe they opened from the inside, maybe it was possible to get out through them, just shove them open. I stood there, motionless, not breathing, pushing "The Little Drummer Boy" out of my ears and hoping to hear a door open, to see a slice of light sweep across the store so I could make a beeline for it and chase him out there in the light.

Sure. Absolutely. And even as I stood there, Santa was wrapping my personal presents up at the snowy North Pole. Writing my name on all the tags, making up for the Christmases after my father left us.

Angling away to the left of the escalator, I found a long, straight counter to guide me and began to move forward. It was pretty dark where I was, but where the escalator surfaced from the bazaar there was a sort of loose, formless cloud of light, and while part of me welcomed it, I also knew that I was going to have to move in front of it and that I'd be visible from probably 75 percent of the floor when I did.

My foot crunched on something, as loud in my ear as someone eating popcorn. I stopped.

The kid kept singing about his damn drum. Who the hell bangs a drum around a newborn baby?

The wad beneath my foot was a crumpled piece of paper.

I had no way of knowing whether he'd heard the paper crackle, but he didn't seem to be on the move, either toward me or away from me, unless he moved more quietly than the last of the Mohicans. I had my eyes trained to the left of where it seemed to me he'd kicked the wastebasket, holding completely still and trying to find in my peripheral vision any mottling of the darkness that might represent movement. Nothing.

"The Little Drummer Boy" is the longest song in the world.

The counter beneath my fingers ended. I stepped left,

sliding my shoes over the department store carpeting, into an aisle that would take me away from the bloom of light at the top of the escalator. I was happy with how silently I was moving, so I picked up my pace, stopping every eight or ten steps to listen. When I came to the next intersection of aisles I turned right so I'd once again be moving across the store with the escalator behind me.

A sudden solidifying of the darkness in front of me immediately took on the form I least wanted to see, and it was only *inches* away: a human silhouette. Instantaneous recognition of the human form is instinctive and complex, which is why camouflage is usually a pattern of colored patches to draw attention away from the outline. In the absence of such distraction, however, someone whose nerves are sufficiently keyed up can not only separate the human form from all other shapes by sheer instinct, but can even identify many characteristic poses. In the half-instant between seeing that dark outline only a foot or two from me, and *almost* registering the pose, I screamed.

It was a loud, panicked, embarrassingly shrill scream that was choked off quickly as I realized that the form had its hands on its hips.

In the standard threat ranking of human positions, hands on hips comes in very low, probably just a notch or two above kneeling with the palms pressed together in prayer. But I was still in instinct mode, and the heel of my hand shot out at throat level and destroyed the voice box of the figure in front of me before the shape registered as *female.*

My hand hit something hard and she went down as stiffly as a tree and, uhhh, *clattered* on the carpet. Whatever I'd hit, it hadn't yielded like a voice box or any other kind of living tissue. In fact, my hand stung.

A flare of light from somewhere to my right and a *thput*, and something sang past my head and shattered several sheets of glass in rapid sequence, probably passing through two or three display cases. Before the noise had stopped, I was down on my hands and knees on the carpet, inches from my victim. The nude display mannequin's hands were still on her hips, jaunty even in decapitation, and her bald head had rolled about ten feet.

I crawled quickly behind a counter as the reverberation in my ears gradually died away. I squeezed my eyes shut, opened my mouth as widely as I could, shook my head, relaxed the muscles of my face, and put one hundred percent of my conscious energy into *listening*.

And heard *PAH-rum-pum-pum-pum*.

Fuck it, I thought, self-preservation overcome, as it occasionally is, by pure, incandescent fury. I grabbed two heavy objects that were on the floor beside me—judging from their shapes and weights, a hand mirror and a stapler—stood, screamed as loudly as I could, threw the things at the cases near me, and was off and running in the opposite direction, to the accompaniment of a short composition for breaking glass and two more pistol shots, which triggered more breaking glass, but the glass had broken well behind me. Figuring he was even deafer than I was for the moment, I scooped up the mannequin's head and tucked it under my arm like a football, then zigzagged between aisles, bent low, in the general direction of the two muzzle flashes. I stopped, dropped to my knees, and breathed with my mouth very wide to keep my gasps inaudible.

The little sod with his drum had finally canned it, a blessing that was immediately eradicated by some bright sleigh bells and the news that Santa Claus was coming to town.

I was far enough from the relatively light area around the escalator that I couldn't really see much of anything. I counted to twenty, stood, and threw the mannequin's head as far as I could, along a line that would put it close to the place where the gun had been fired, and waited.

I was reminded by the singers to check my list twice, and the message seemed almost cosmically appropriate. After what felt like an immensely elastic moment, I heard the mannequin's head hit something that toppled and clattered— maybe another mannequin—in a rewardingly distracting way. I backed rapidly away from the spot where I'd been standing, going through an opening between two counters, until the bare back of my neck hit what felt like the world's biggest, thickest spiderweb.

I froze, then reflexively jumped forward. Given a choice between facing either a Russian lunatic with a gun or a four-pound spider, I'll take the lunatic every time. I also seem to have said, "Gaaahhhh" or something, because he snapped off another shot, and this time the bullet nearly gave me a dueling scar: I could feel its heat on my left cheek. The guy may have dressed like Fred Astaire's understudy, but he could shoot. I scurried backward and sideways behind the counters again and felt the web hit the back of my shirt and *not break*, and a part of me relaxed. While there are Amazonian spiders that build webs strong enough to catch birds, they have so far been kind enough to remain in the region of the Amazon, and it seemed unlikely that I'd find them lurking in a bird-free abandoned department store in a relatively northern latitude. I grabbed the web and found it fringed with something soft, which was why it had felt so spidery. A *garland*. A Christmas garland. I remembered Bonnie saying that Gabriel's had closed right after Christmas the previous year.

Something over where he was fell to the carpet, not terrifically loudly, but loudly enough to triple my pulse rate.

With nothing else at hand, I took the garland in both hands and gave it a tug. Pretty strong. Probably not strong *enough*, although I had a vision, about half a second long, of tying Mini-me hand and foot in a glittering Christmas garland and driving a stake of holly through his heart, Ebenezer Scrooge-fashion. Instead, listening for any other sound of movement, I followed it hand over hand until I came to the point where one end was fastened to the wall, and pulled it free. I folded into sections about two feet long as I tracked it to the other end, quite a distance away. Call it fifteen feet, but the thing had hung in a graceful drape, so it was actually twenty-four, twenty-five feet long. I pulled the other end free and tested the garland's strength folded into four equal segments. It was unyielding.

So.

So *what*?

He chose that moment to move.

There was a *thump*, followed by a grunt loud enough to be heard over the endless and somehow ominous news of Santa's arrival, so he'd probably jumped down from something reasonably high, perhaps one of those two- or three-foot pedestals that had supported chic mannequins with one or both hands on their hips. The grunt had come from in front of me, maybe thirty-five, forty feet away, and to the right. Then he tripped on something, not much of a trip, not a nice, useful pratfall or anything, but a big enough trip to be audible, and his surprised gasp gave me the information I needed. He was moving to my left.

One of the things Herbie always said came to mind: *When you're in a hurry, slow down*. Check the environment: The lane that ran between the glass display counters was about five feet wide, and as far as I could tell, it stretched absolutely straight from the back of the store all the way to the doors that opened out into the mall, now behind me. I was in between him and the way out of here. *I* wanted to get out of here. Wouldn't *he*?

I dropped to my knees behind the counter and began a little frantically to feel my way around. The glass cabinets had sliding doors, also glass, allowing the salespeople to get at the merchandise without giving the customers equal access, thus delivering them from temptation. I slid the door open, and it moved noiselessly.

The lane separating this line of counters from the next one was the route he would probably take as the most direct path to the doors to the mall.

Maybe I could *make* him take it.

With the garland folded into thirds, it was a little more than seven feet long. Just enough. Maybe.

He shouted, "Hey." So he wasn't afraid of drawing fire. He'd figured I hadn't packed a gun to go Christmas shopping.

Moving as fast as I could, I slipped out of my shoes and wound an end of the triple-thick garland around one of them, tied a knot, and put the shoe on the lowest shelf of the counter, maybe eight inches above the carpet. I pulled the sliding door closed and tugged on the garland to jam the shoe up against the glass I tugged again, and the toe of the shoe pushed its way out. Working very deliberately, because if I hurried I knew I'd panic, I repositioned the shoe, slid the door closed, and tugged again. There was a tiny creak of complaint, but it was firm.

With the garland in my right hand and my other shoe in my left, I did the Chuck Berry duck walk across the lane between the counters, staying as low as I could. Once behind the counter, I tied the garland around the other shoe and put the shoe on the lowest shelf of *that* counter, but the garland drooped to the floor so I wrapped it two more times around the shoe and felt it go tight. Sweat ran down into my eyes, stinging them. I slid the door closed with the shoe inside, right against the glass. The garland was taut enough to strum.

I needed the goddamn mannequin.

Using the counters for guidance, I scurried to the place where I'd beheaded her, picked her up, tucked her under one arm, and toted her as fast as I could back to Booby Trap Lane. Then I took off my long-sleeved shirt, draped it over the mannequin, grabbed a long, long breath, and then yelled, "Ow!" loudly enough to waken the lightly sleeping dead, pulled my cell phone out of my pocket, and hauled the mannequin at a dead run down the lane toward the door, banging against everything I could. Another shot, wider this time, and then I made an *Uhhhhhhh* sound, let the mannequin fall, and went down with a grunt as I flicked on the flashlight on my cell phone and pitched it ahead of me. I abandoned the shirt-clad model prone on the carpet and scrabbled on hands and knees back behind the counters.

From where I was, it looked pretty good: I'd tossed the phone so it landed flat, bulb on the upper side, beaming directly up, like a lighthouse for spaceships, and between it and me, silhouetted against the cell phone's pillar of light, was the mannequin, supine, with my shirt over it.

I heard nothing. I realized I was holding my breath.

He either thought he'd hit me or he didn't. There wasn't anything more I could do.

I almost jumped out of my skin as my cell phone rang. And rang.

It seemed to be the cue he needed, because I heard him immediately, racketing toward me down the aisle, and just as he entered the circle of light emitted by my ringing phone, his foot hit the tripled garland. It was as though he'd been scythed at the ankles: his feet stopped but his body kept moving until his center of gravity was so far off the vertical that he simply slammed onto his face with an explosion of breath that must have left him hollow.

And I went straight up and over the counter and landed on his back with my knees.

He made a strange grating sound, the last few cubic inches of air being forced over his vocal cords, and then he did the thing I should have expected him to do. He inadvertently fired the gun in his right hand, a black, nasty, silenced automatic that I instantly recognized as a Glock 42.

The display case beside me exploded in a cloud of slivered glass, some of which was driven into my bare arms and the right side of my face. I went for the gun but instead brought my palm down on a large shard of glass that was tilted upward from where it rested against his forearm, and the cut made me instinctively yank my hand back. At the same moment, he flexed his knees and brought his heels up into the center of my back.

I saw little flares. Silhouetted against my cell phone light, his arm came up and his hand swiveled around, and then I was rolling away as the gun went off, sending a shell through the space I'd been occupying a second before, and he rose up onto his knees, lots of little cuts bleeding from the right side of his face. He parted his lips to give me a complete view of his front teeth, pointed the gun at me, and pulled the trigger.

But the slide had locked back on the final shot in the magazine. He glared at it, a man betrayed, and swung his left leg out to snap a fast circular kick at the right side of my face, knocking me cockeyed into the aisle. Then he was up and running, and in only a few seconds he was banging through the doors and into the light and life of Edgerton Mall.

My phone stopped ringing. I worked my way to my hands and knees, my head seeming to expand and contract with every heartbeat, and as I crawled to the phone, I heard something that sounded like a kitten mewing, a tiny, high, windy sound, ephemeral as a finger squeaking on clean glass, that stopped as the carol on the speakers ended. But then the sound came back, and this time it tapered into a transparent, barely audible cough and a long, loose sigh that raised the hair on my arms. I'd heard that sound once before, and there was no mistaking it.

Someone had just died.

As I tried to fix in my mind the direction from which the sound had come, an unaccompanied choir burst forth with:

We wish you a merry Christmas
We wish you a merry Christmas

The mewing sound had been close, or I wouldn't have heard it at all. And I was almost certain it had come from behind me, on the right. I turned around, so it was now on my left.

Immediately to my left was the pair of glass counters I'd used to anchor one end of the trip line.

We wish you a merry Christmas
And a happy new year.

I stepped behind the counter again. Holding the phone in front of me for light, I slowly paced the distance between the counter and the wall. The phone vibrated in my hand and started to ring again. Six or seven feet ahead, the counter took a ninety-degree turn to the left, where the cash registers would have been. The light was dancing a bit more than the vibration would have caused it to, which was how I knew that my hands were shaking.

Good tidings we bring
To you and your kin

The wall behind the counter was practically papered with Christmas decorations: bows, cards, bright paper wreaths, cut-outs of poinsettias, and photos of groups of the women who had worked here, all of them wearing soft-looking reindeer antlers, two with the bright red nose that Rudolph brought on the scene. For people who were about to have their jobs yanked out from under them, they looked pretty happy.

At the corner. A shoe.

With a foot in it.

Good tidings for Christmas
And a happy new year.

As I neared the corner, more of the body came into view. I saw bare legs, a hemline that seemed to be seasonal colors—red and green—and then a hand, the fingers curved restfully inward. Something glittered, pooled in the open palm. Tinsel. The strands hung down from the sleeve. I put the light on her face, but I already knew it was Bonnie. Bonnie of Bonnie's Bric-a-Brac, Bonnie of the hot spiced wine. Bonnie, who would have been happier in the world of Mr. Pickwick.

I rejected the call, which was from Louie, and dialed Wally. When he answered, I said, "Get a guard and come to the second floor of Gabriel's. Now."

18
They Want Everyone to Be Guilty

The room was a small, windowless cube with white walls that had been given almost twenty years to get dirty and had succeeded admirably, becoming an abstract mixed-media painting of hair oil spots, the muzzy ghosts of handprints, black smears from the heels of shoes left by guys with a foot up, and cumulus clouds of grunge around the light switches. The cheap linoleum flooring was a bilious avocado green, the ceiling felt head-bumpingly low, and a rusty fan stood in one corner to move the air around. The fan was unplugged. The place smelled of mildew and unshowered men, in approximately equal measure, and was barely big enough to hold the desk and three chairs that had been jammed into it. This was the office where the mall's uniformed security guards convened, and no commercial establishment anywhere has ever wasted a moment's thought on making things a little nicer for its security guards.

I had been put in the chair behind the desk, farthest from the door. Facing me were a lean, high-strung cop named Cranmer and Wally Durskee, who'd been brought in because he'd seen bits and pieces of what had happened on his screens.

"So," Cranmer said, glancing down at his pocket notebook, "you say you were shopping."

"I not only *say* I was shopping," I said, "I actually *was* shopping." It was probably a little snippier than it needed to be, but my feet had been swept out from under me by the sight of Bonnie, whom I'd liked quite a lot. And over and above my personal sense of loss and the sheer amount of violence that had been done to her, I was also nervous, not so much about Cranmer or my story—Wally and I had kept Vlad's name out of the conversation—but because I had no idea who else was going to float through that door. I'd never been charged with a crime, or even arrested, but there were a few cops in Cranmer's division who would have loved to change all that. If one of them came in and recognized me, things could get very sticky, which is a wishy-washy way of saying that I would immediately become a *serious* suspect instead of what I was now: a temporarily convenient suspect.

"And you'd bought stuff."

"That is the *goal* of shopping, as I understand it."

Wally said, "I *saw* him shopping," a sentence that worried me more than it reassured me because it sounded so defensive. And also, Wally was such a bad liar that he gave it away even when all he had to do was stand there and listen to someone else tell the lie. His eyes were all over the place, as though he was tracking a mosquito.

Cranmer literally waved my unpleasantness aside. "And you gave this stuff to a friend of yours to hold. Why again?"

"Because I realized instinctively that it would be easier to run without a bunch of bags in my hands."

Cranmer's eyes were already narrow, but he narrowed them further. "Careful, bub."

I said, "Bub?"

"I meant to say Mr. Bender," Cranmer said. "*Bub* is a relic of my upbringing."

I revised upward my estimate of Cranmer's intelligence and sat up a little bit. "No problem."

"And your friend is no longer among us."

"Well, when you say *that*—"

"Among those of us who are at this here mall."

"He had things to do."

"Don't we all." He flipped through the notebook.

"You know how it happened," I said. "You saw the tape that, uh, this gentleman showed you. This guy in the silly clothes pulled the table over and ran."

Wally blushed scarlet.

Cranmer said, "Because you saw him take an object off the table."

"Yeah. And I shouted *hey* or something and he took off."

"Reason I ask"—he made a show of flipping some more pages—"is the people who run the booth say nothing was stolen."

"Really," I said. "So they've finished gluing all the pieces back together?"

Cranmer leaned back in his chair and gave me the narrow eyes again.

I said, "Mr., um, Durskee here can tell you again what he saw. What you saw, *too*, since his cameras recorded it."

"This guy," Wally said, his eyes on a point near where the wall met the ceiling, "was shopping with his friend, and the other guy, the one he chased, he, uh, he took, I mean, he pulled the table over and ran—"

"We didn't see him take anything off the table," Cranmer said.

"Neither did the people *behind* the table," I said. "I had a better angle. Listen, if he hadn't swiped something, or at least *tried* to swipe something, why would he run?"

"I'm asking the questions," Cranmer said.

"Well, if you asked me that one, I'd say I have no idea why he ran. If he hadn't *stolen* something, that is. And then you saw him run away and break through that, that thing—"

"The bow," Wally said. "It was there because the insurance company—"

"—and then run up the escalator to the second floor. And *then* you saw me go up the escalator after him."

Cranmer thought for a second, trying to see where I was going. "Because what? Because you're like on a crusade about shoplifters?"

"Because it's *Christmas*," I said. "Because Christmas is about giving, not taking."

Cranmer looked at his notes, but it was a dodge. Whatever answer he'd expected, that wasn't it.

"And then people heard shooting, right?" I said. "People have told you they heard shooting. No one else came up or down the escalator. A few minutes after people heard the shooting, the guy who pulled the table over bursts through the second-floor doors out of the store, into the mall—"

"That wasn't on camera."

"No," I said, "but *I* saw it from inside, and you have him running along the second level with his back to the store." This had been captured by one of the cameras Wally had set up to find the watchers Vlad had deployed, which he'd never returned to their usual vistas. "And then you have him shoving his way down an escalator, bouncing off a rather large guy and then into Santa, knocking Santa's throne over, and then running out through the north door and probably across the parking lot to a car."

Wally cleared his throat, and Cranmer looked from Wally to me and from me to Wally.

I said, "And while he's doing all that, you have me *staying* up there with a cut hand, bullet holes and broken glass all over the place, and a dead woman behind a counter. Then you have me calling security so they can call *you*. Come on, nobody but an imbecile would go up that escalator to kill someone when every single person within fifty yards is watching him. And with all that, given that I'm the one who stayed and called it in and he's the one who didn't, which of us behaved more like he was guilty?"

"Nobody said you were guilty."

"Yeah, well, he wasn't either. He was up there only about twenty seconds before I got there, and he was way the hell at the other end of the store."

Cranmer gave me a smile he probably thought looked patient, but there were too many muscles in his lean face for anything to look patient. It all looked like heavy lifting.

I shrugged. "Or maybe I watch too much TV."

"What does your friend do? The one who left with your bags?"

"He's a gentleman of leisure. Call him, you got his number off my phone." It had been Louie who'd rung me after Mini-me ran away, and I'd called him back immediately after I talked to Wally so we could settle on how I'd describe him to the police.

"I already called him."

"What did he say?"

Cranmer closed his notebook and looked slowly up at me. "That he was a gentleman of leisure."

"Well," I said, kicking myself under the table, "there you are."

"Yeah," he said. He pushed back his chair and gave me the narrow eyes, which I guess were supposed to have bored into me. I tried to look like someone who was being bored into. "Listen," he said, "don't go anywhere, okay? You just stay right here in LA."

"Where would I go?" I said. "It's Christmas."

"You really handled him," Wally said admiringly. We were in his dark little room, looking at Cranmer on one of the screens as he talked to Dwayne Wix, who had needed three or four tries to regain his throne after Mini-me knocked him off it. I saw Cranmer lean in as though sniffing Dwayne's breath and then take a big step back and fan in front of his face with his notebook.

"The thing to understand about cops," I said, "is that you can't take it personally. They want everybody to be guilty. That way, they can wrap things up and go get a donut. What you've got to do is hand them what they need so they can give up on you and move on to the next person."

"And who's that going to be?"

"Yeah," I said. "That's the problem. Thanks for keeping my secret."

"If Mr. Poindexter doesn't want people to know about the shoplifting, it's not my job to think I know better."

"That was a really nice woman," I said.

"Bonnie?" he said, and then he sighed. "She was a real peach."

"So who killed her?"

He looked startled. "Who—"

"Killed her," I said. "It obviously wasn't Mini-me—sorry, I mean the guy I chased—because he was nowhere near her when I got to the top of the escalator. Anyway, same argument. Nobody breaks through a barrier and charges up a busted escalator in front of half the people in his zip code so he can kill someone. Whoever it was, he did it only a few minutes before we got there."

"How?"

I was wondering who knew that the doors to Gabriel's could be opened from the inside. I was wondering about other ways to get in there. I was wondering why Bonnie had been up there. What I said was, "How what?"

"How did he, ummmmm, how did he kill her?"

"A knife," I said. "At the bottom of the rib cage, probably angled up. My guess is that he meant to put it through her heart but the knife was too short and it punctured a lung. She, uh, she whistled when she breathed."

Wally said, "Oh, no." Then he said, "Hey. Lookit."

We watched on a monitor as four people in gloves, masks, and crime-scene PJs went up the escalator from the bazaar. It had been turned on, so they glided up effortlessly.

"Wally," I said. "The lights are on up there now, right?"

"What? Oh, sure."

"Bring it up on the monitors."

"Not gonna see much," he said, flipping some switches. "We only had two cameras up there, mostly for fire. The big department stores had their own surveillance system, cameras all over the place."

"They took their cameras out?"

"Yeah." He rocked back and forth in his creaky chair. "It was about the only things they got. They paid me on the Q.T. to help them, on account of I know all the wiring in the place, right? And they didn't want to get electrocuted and I didn't want them to short-circuit the whole building. Which they would have done on purpose."

"Why?"

Two of the darker screens were now coming back to life.

"Management was pissed. Gabriel's didn't give six months' notice like they were supposed to, and they'd fell behind in their rent. See, the big stores pay six, eight months in advance so if they close down, that money is like an extra deposit and the mall keeps it. But they got four months behind, Gabriel's did, and then told us they were pulling the plug right after Christmas. This was in November, when they told us. So after Christmas was over, the mall said the hell with them and locked down the freight elevators, changed the locks to the loading dock so that no merchandise could come in and nothing they wanted could go out that way, you know, where they could pull trucks right up and stuff, and we made them get everything out in two nights after the place closed. We even shut down the escalators. Put on extra guards who weren't allowed to pick up *nothing*. Couldn't help at all. They had to carry everything down, and we wouldn't let them take their counters and stuff. That's why they left such a mess."

The image of Bonnie, the tinsel gleaming in her open hand, kept claiming my field of vision, and I have to admit I hadn't been paying much attention to what Wally was saying, but then I registered movement on one of the screens. "Ah," I said. "There they are." The four who had ridden up the escalator came into view from an overhead camera that was looking straight down from the ceiling through a fishbowl wide-angle lens. The place was dim; it would have been hard to see them if their outfits weren't relatively pale. I said, "Can you zoom in?"

"No. The point with these was just to see as much of the floor as possible, to look out for fire."

The group, bunched together in the center of the aisle, was preceded by little cones of illumination, which I recognized as the beams of flashlights. "Not very bright, is it?"

"We been raiding those fixtures every time anything burned out in one of the active areas. Why waste them, you know? Not many left now." He stood up to watch them, shifting from foot to foot with his mouth slightly open. "You think they'll figure out who did it?"

"It's their job."

"Yeah, well, Washington is supposed to run the country, too."

"I don't know whether they will or not," I said. "But that was a nice, sweet, good-spirited woman. If they don't get him, I will."

There was a knock at the door. Wally threw a switch at his console and a little screen just above the door, which I hadn't noticed before, shimmered into life. "How I knew it was you," Wally said. "Whoops. It's that cop."

On the screen Cranmer raised his right arm and knocked again. It was more peremptory this time: three pounds on the door, *rat-tat-tat*.

Wally said, "Uhhhhhhhh."

I said, "Pull out your chair." When he'd wheeled it back, I crawled beneath the overhang of the console and pulled both chairs toward me. The room was kept dim to bring the screens to a greater apparent brightness, and it was fairly dark under the console, although nowhere near dark enough. Despite the chairs partly blocking me from view, anyone who took even a casual look would see me.

Cranmer knocked a third time. I pulled Wally's chair right up to the console, as close to mine as I could get it, and said, "Shut off the screens from Gabriel's. They'll still record, right?"

"Sure thing."

"Okay. When they're down, let him in, and then come back here and sit in your chair."

Wally said, "Oh, boy," not sounding at all enthusiastic.

A moment later I heard the door open, and Cranmer said, "Took you so long?"

"You were looking down?" Wally said with the interrogative lilt that said he was lying. "On that little screen up there, see it? I, uh, can't let anybody in 'less I see their face. Security, you know?"

"So," Cranmer said. "You sit here all day? Just watching from your hidey-hole?"

"It's not a hidey hole," Wally said defensively. "It says *Security* on the door, right?" He pulled his chair out, leaving me partially exposed, but a moment later he sat down and rolled it back into place.

"Listen, we need light down there," Cranmer said.

"I'm security," Wally said, sounding like someone whose feelings were hurt, "not electrical."

"Well, why's it so dark down there?"

"Like I was just saying," Wally said, and stopped.

"To who? Cranmer said. "You got an imaginary friend?"

"To my boss?" Wally said. "On my phone?"

He must have indicated the phone on his console, because Cranmer said, "I know what a fucking phone is, for Christ's sake."

"Shouldn't swear like that," Wally said. "It's almost Christmas. Like I was just saying to my *boss*, on the *phone*, it's because we been taking those fixtures out for the last year whenever we needed one in an active area."

"I haven't seen any active areas."

"Ha ha ha," Wally said. "Are you done? Any other unpleasant remarks you got saved up? Maybe something you wish you'd said to your wife?"

"What do you think about that guy? Bender?"

A pause. I have to admit I was interested in what Wally would say. "He seems okay."

"Yeah? Move over." Wally scooched his chair to his right, and then the one I'd been sitting in was pulled out. It squeaked as Cranmer lowered his weight into it, and I found myself looking at a pair of knees clad in stretch slacks that Vlad probably wouldn't have used to pick up the teeth that littered the ground all around that dented car. "Show me what you can do here."

"Stores," Wally said. I heard the buttons click. "Parking lot."

"Yeah, you said you saw him running across the lot? Can we see the car?"

"Hang on," Wally said. "I'll rewind."

A moment of silence, during which Cranmer crossed his legs, the tip of his size 12 shoe actually brushing my nose. He had a wad of gum on the sole, and I fought the urge to pick it off.

"That him?" Wally said.

"Who else dresses like that, the Penguin? Shit. You can't move the camera to follow him?"

"I could have," Wally said, "if it hadn't happened about an hour ago. This is tape."

"So what you're telling me is, you missed it."

"I didn't miss anything. No one told me to look at the lot. The lot footage is just for after, like if there's been an accident."

"Damn." Cranmer's foot jiggled up and down. "Useless. Hey, can you go to her store? The one who got killed?"

"It's up," Wally said. "Third from the left in the second row."

"Move it around—wait, this is real time, right?"

"Right."

There was a moment of silence. Cranmer broke into it to say, "Listen, if that guy Bender comes back, keep an eye on him. There's something wrong there. He's not in focus, you know what I mean."

Wally said, "No. That's not my job."

"Well," Cranmer said, sounding a little like he was sulking, "tell me if he comes back anyway."

Wally said, "Why would he come back?"

The jiggling foot stopped and the silence reasserted itself. Then Cranmer said, "Huh," he said.

"Look at 'em." He pushed back his chair and stood. "Just a bunch of women crying."

A moment later, the door closed behind him.

19
Unpredictable Diagonals

With Bonnie's death the entire landscape had changed, and with it the compass had reorganized itself so completely that north might as well have been next to south, and even up and down felt like unpredictable diagonals.

It made no sense at all.

Admittedly, Vlad probably left a trail of death the way Dwayne Wix down there in his Santa suit did with alcohol fumes. No question that Vlad had killed the poor schlub who'd rammed his car into me. I figured he'd had two reasons for that: first, to demonstrate that the guy had exceeded his assignment and unwisely acted on impulse; and second, to show me his cute little golf club in case I got impulses of my own.

But unless he intentionally hired people with no self-control, it didn't make any sense at all that Mini-me had tried to shoot me, not once but six times. Knowing how his boss rewarded initiative, he should have hidden from me all day and all night if necessary, after Vlad promised me there would be no more followers.

And Mini-me certainly hadn't killed Bonnie. There hadn't been time, even if I could conceive of a motive.

Was there any connection between Vlad and Bonnie's murder? None I could see. None even that I could imagine.

And now that I thought about it, I wasn't sure there was actually a connection between Vlad and Mini-me.

Wally was down in the security office where Cranmer had questioned me, talking to a new cop. I was sitting behind his console, half-watching the crime-scene cops on the second floor of Gabriel's. They'd set up some big lights so I could see most of what they were doing, and also see that Cranmer, the only cop who knew me by sight, was with them.

Mini-me. *Yes*, he'd been looking down at the ground floor, as Brando had been, when Vlad came in, but he hadn't left the mall when Brando did after I told Vlad to get rid of his watchers. In fact, ten or twelve minutes later, when I spotted Mini-me as Vlad was going down the escalator, it seemed to me, in retrospect, that he hadn't been looking at me at all, that he'd been looking down at *Vlad* before he felt my gaze.

So, a new possibility: he was watching Vlad for someone. And after Vlad left, that someone changed Mini-me's orders: watch whoever Vlad had met with. And whoever that someone giving the orders was, he would have been very, very unhappy if Mini-me had been caught because it would probably have brought Vlad's incisors right up against that someone's throat.

One of the unhappy co-owners?

So Mini-me tried to kill me?

It *almost* made sense, but to tell the truth, it didn't much interest me. I didn't particularly care about Mini-me or Vlad's problems or the shoplifting or a bunch of bullets that had missed me. What I cared about was the murder of a nice woman with a limitless tolerance for bric-a-brac, and who wished she had lived in the world of Mr. Pickwick.

Someone who'd had a real love of Christmas, or at least Charles Dickens's Christmas.

But, I suddenly remembered, there are really *two* Christmas stories in *Pickwick*, the gathering at Dingley Dell, conventionally full of good spirits, roaring fires, and lots of wine, and then there's the story of the bitter church sexton Gabriel Grub—*Gabriel*, I thought—who decides to cheer himself up on Christmas Eve by digging a grave and is set upon by goblins. He's dragged down, Gabriel is, through the dark, damp earth all the way to the goblins' hall, where he's beaten and shown visions of others who snarled at the happiness around them, and he awakes the next morning a changed man, as Scrooge would years later in *A Christmas Carol*. Unlike Scrooge, though, Grub doesn't stay and become a shining example of how Christmas should be celebrated. Instead he flees town and shows up unrecognized years later, an unshaven wanderer, a kind of Victorian tramp and, in my mind, a fictional anticlimax. "The Story of the Goblins Who Stole a Sexton" is a tale with a moral, but it's a confusing one. Of the two Christmas stories in *Pickwick* it probably wasn't the one Bonnie liked best, but it might have been the one that came into her mind as her goblin set upon her.

If the cops couldn't figure out—and pretty damn fast—who had killed her, I was going to do it. In fact, I was going to take a crack at it anyway. If I could solve Vlad's problem, too, fine, but Bonnie came first and second. And anyway, they *had* to be related. All I had to do in the meantime was figure everything out, keep Vlad from practicing his 300-yard drive on my teeth, and avoid running into Cranmer.

And Mini-me.

On an impulse, I located the picture I'd snapped of Mini-me off Wally's surveillance monitor and forwarded it to Louie with a message: I THINK THIS GUY MIGHT WORK FOR ONE OR

MORE OF VLAD'S PARTNERS. CAN YOU FIND OUT WHO HE'S ASSOCIATED WITH? MAYBE THE GUY IN JAIL CAN HELP, SEND IT IN THROUGH HIS LAWYER OR SOMETHING. Then I sat there, trying to think of all the things I'd missed.

Cranmer was still on Gabriel's second floor, and I was free to move around, within reason. I dialed Wally's cell.

"Uh," he said, and I could almost see him blush. "Yeah, boss?" To someone, certainly the new cop, he said, "It's my boss?" the interrogative flagging the fib like a handful of sparklers.

But the cop let it pass. I said, "How much longer do you think you'll be there?"

"Hold on, boss. Um, Lieutenant, how much longer—"

"We're done," a woman said. "You can get back to it."

"I heard her," I said. "Listen, I need you to come back up here and keep an eye on Cranmer. He's still in Gabriel's right now, but I need you to call me if he looks like he's leaving."

"Got it, boss," Wally said, and I admired the absolute lack of skill with which he lied. It was enough to wake up a part of myself I try to keep under control and make me want to ask him for a loan.

"Okay. I'll be around."

I hung up, checked the screen again, and saw that Cranmer had moved behind the counter and was looking down at what had to be Bonnie's body. My guess was that he'd be there for a while, so I let myself out of Wally's room.

Since I was on the third floor, I decided to stay on that level and go back to Sam's. That way I could at least avoid the escalators until Wally was back in place and keeping track of Cranmer.

Sam was wearing a ratty padded jacket and clearing things off the counters, obviously getting ready to shut the doors when I went in. It was about twenty to five. "Early to close down, isn't it?" I said.

"That lovely woman," he said, and his voice was shaking. "Terrible, terrible." He looked around the dim little shop and waved the back of his hands at it as though shooing it away. "I can't—I mean, I won't, I won't do *business* with her lying there. It's not fitting." He was blinking rapidly as though against tears. "And I need light, I want some light."

"You knew her."

"Everybody knew her. Lovely woman. Had a husband, just a piece of *ekskrementy*, you know, *kal*, just poop. She's here working her fingers off and he's home emptying the bank accounts, selling everything he can carry, and she goes home two, three months ago, and there's nothing worth anything in the house, and he's gone. Not even a note, he left. And she's losing money here, nobody buys her *tchotchkes*, her cute junk, nobody wants this stuff anymore. Now, if it doesn't plug in and light up, nobody wants it." He stood there, his back bent, flexing the strong, scarred hands. "I don't want to be here."

"Seems like no one does."

"It's terrible, isn't it? This rich country and no real happiness. And here in this place everyone hoping to get through Christmas, hoping to still have a business, a home in the new year."

"You?"

"Well," he said. "This is a kind of home, yes? But I've—" He swallowed, hard. "I have been chased out of home many times. In my heart, I always live in my first home, the one I told you about, but it's gone now. Gone a long, long time." He shrugged. "I have left so many homes, take my things, close the door, never come back."

"I'm sorry to hear that."

"Every time you lose a home," he said, "you lose a piece of your soul."

"Are you *going* to come back? Here, I mean?"

His lower lip popped out. "Where I can go?" he said. "You see saddlery in many malls? Everywhere you look, saddlery? Can I afford my own store? And to go out of here is, is difficult. A *lease* I have," he said, raising his eyebrows inquisitively, as though unsure I knew what a lease was. "A deposit I have. A *penalty* I have."

"Ah, well. Isn't that the shits? Sorry, *ekskrementy*."

He looked at me and his eyes changed, sharpened. "Why are you still here?"

"I'm the one who found her. I was chasing someone who stole something in the bazaar—the flea market—and he ran up the escalator."

"It was you," he said. He turned his head to the left a bit, keeping his eyes on me. "You run after people who steal things? This is something you do?"

"He didn't just *take* something," I said. "He pulled a table over, broke almost everything those people had for sale."

"When they tell me this," he said, "I think, maybe security, somebody working for the Russians—for the bosses here."

"Nope," I said. "Just old me."

"Just you," Sam said, still looking at me. He turned his back on me and went back to putting things away.

"So," I said. "What time did you eat lunch and where did you eat it?"

"Working for the bosses," Sam said without turning around. As far as he was concerned, I was no longer there.

Still on the second floor," Wally said on the phone. "They got some more lights. Looks like he'll be there for a while."

"How long are *you* going to be here?"

"Till closing. These are holiday hours, most everyone works time and a half."

"Hard on them, I'd think. Hard on you."

"Yeah," Wally said. "Well, you know, 'tis the season."

"Call me if he moves."

I'd spent the hour after I left Sam's Saddlery checking with the other businesses on the third floor, asking whether they'd had their employees clock out for lunchtime and looking at a surprising variety of ways to track that information, ranging from punch cards to on-screen spreadsheets to lists of names written on whiteboards or even on the backs of paper bags: schedules of meals and what used to be called cigarette breaks but which in several shops was now apparently called "personal time." At the end of the hour, I had two lists: those who had stayed in the shops between noon and one, the hour or so before Bonnie made her last sound, and the ones who had been either out to lunch or for some other reason out of sight of their coworkers during that critical period.

It wasn't much, but I've found that simple motion can relieve the kind of nervous frustration that I was feeling. At the very least, I was doing something I wouldn't have to do again.

A ping from my phone announced a text from Louie: AIN'T NO WAY HE'S WORKING FOR MORE THAN ONE OF THEM. THESE GUYS DON'T SHARE SECRETS OR EMPLOYEES. REMEMBER THE ITALIAN CITY-STATES, HOW THEY KILLED EACH OTHER ALL THE WAY THROUGH THE RENAISSANCE? I'D TAKE ITALIANS OVER RUSSIANS ANY DAY.

Vlad and his partners didn't trust one another. I'd already known that, but it was useful to be reminded.

The lunch break gave me hope because the nearest fast-food places outside the mall were a few miles away, and the break tended to be shorter during the Christmas season, so I figured that most of those who actually left their shops to *eat* rather than indulge in some other form of "personal time" would have fed themselves in the big room behind the food court where I'd talked with Shlomo. And that gave me a chance to check my list ("checking it twice" kept popping into my mind) from another perspective.

I took the stairs to the second level and headed down the NO ACCESS hallway to the employees' dining area. Once in there, I knocked on the door to Tito's, and a moment later it opened.

"Oh," she said. It was the woman from the day before. Her smile bloomed again. "Hi."

"Hey there. Ummm, what time did you come on today?"

Some of the wattage leaked out of the smile. "Why?"

"I was here—out front, I mean, not back here—about, I don't know, a little after ten-thirty, and there was a different—"

"Mercy," she said. "That's her *name*, I mean, Mercy. I'm not asking you to, you know, spare me or anything."

"I made a fool out of myself, giving her a big *Hi* before realizing she wasn't you."

"Well, hi *now*, then. Although I already said that, didn't I?"

"We both did."

We looked at each other for a count of three or four while I searched in vain for a transition. Abandoning the impulse, I said, "I need to talk some business," just as she said, "I got here about—"

We both stopped talking.

"Eleven-thirty," she finished. "Business? What kind of—"

"This is between you and me, okay? I've been asked to look into what happened today."

"You mean, with Bonnie?"

"Yes. One of the things I do is, well, figure things like that out."

"I knew you weren't really working in a store here," she said. "It was too much to hope for. What a *bunch*."

"And the first thing I need to do is figure out who among the people who work here couldn't have done it."

"How exciting," she said. She raised her right hand as though taking an oath. "I was here. Got here just around eleven-thirty, well, maybe eleven-forty, and didn't go anywhere. Promise."

"Don't feel left out," I said, "but you weren't real high on my list of suspects."

She squinted at me as though catching up to the conversation. "So you're, like, a cop?"

"Not much like a cop, but I *am* on a job, and I'm working for the good guys. Did you know her?"

"*Everybody* knew her. She was that kind of person, just walked up to you and said hello. I'll bet she knew the name of every single person who works in this dump." She looked back over her shoulder. "Mercy," she called, "I'm taking ten minutes. Be right back here."

"'Kay, hon," said someone who was presumably Mercy.

"Let's sit," she said. "This time of day I feel like I'm all feet. Yipes, I don't even know your name. I'm Amanda, *not* Mandy but Amanda."

"I'm Junior, and yes, that's my name."

"Bet there's a story behind that."

"Not anything you'd be tempted to write down." I'd followed her to an empty table near the condiments and plastic utensils station.

She surveyed the room as though looking for a better spot. "Is this okay?"

"It's scenic," I said. "All that stuff on the counter gives it a certain panache that the rest of the room lacks."

"I sit here all the time," Amanda said, pulling out a chair. "I like to think I shed a little light here, charm the corner up a bit."

"I have to admit that I sense a kind of, I don't know, *warmth*—"

"That's enough," she said. "Keep it up and you'll sweep me off my aching feet. So how am I supposed to help you?"

"Nobody really supervises this room, right?"

"Nope. People order from one of the stands, sometimes from back here, sometimes from out front. If he or she orders from our place, either Mercy or I bring the food back. Otherwise . . ." She shrugged. "We don't have any way of knowing."

"What I was afraid of. No cameras, either."

"Here and the johns, about the only place where old Wally isn't staring at you."

"Well," I said, pulling a tightly folded sheet of wrinkled paper out of my pocket, "what I need you to do is ask everybody who works in the food court to look at the names on this list and tell you which of the people on it were in here at lunch today between roughly noon and one. As soon as one of them says yes, cross that name off the list. If two or more people say yes, put a little check next to the name every time someone confirms it."

Her eyes were wide as she studied the page. "These are suspects? I *know* some of—"

"No, these are just people who were out of their stores, for lunch, mostly, around the time—the time it happened. I'm just trying to find someone who saw them while, you know."

"Got it." She was running a finger down the list, which had seventeen names on it. "Why nobody from the bazaar?"

"Haven't gotten to them yet."

"Oh, my God," she said. "The bazaar alone is, like, a million people."

"I'll deal with that tomorrow."

"Well, now that I've gone all dramatic, most of the bazaaros eat in their little tiny booths. One-person show, you know?" She bent over the list. "Here, here, and here," she said, indicating names with her forefinger. She reached into the pocket of her red apron and pulled out a little golf pencil about four inches long. "I waited on these guys myself."

"See how easy?"

"But you do realize," she said, checking the names, "that nobody, except maybe Bonnie, knows the name of everybody who works here. Most people think of the ones they don't know very well as, uhh, *Dina from Boots to Suits, the guy who always spills on his shirt, those two pregnant ladies who are always together, the guy who bites his nails and saves them in his shirt pocket,* and *that chick with the colored rubber bands on her braids who only eats ice cream.* The names aren't going to mean that much. And nobody's going to remember everybody they took care of." She looked around the room, which was about a quarter full, people getting an early dinner before the evening rush, if there was going to be an evening rush. "Noon to one? Is that when . . . when it happened?"

"Near as I can figure." I looked around the room again. "And ask the people who are eating in here now what time they ate lunch. If it was around that time, ask who they ate with, who they saw. Make me another list."

For a moment, I thought she was going to protest, but she said, "When they ask me why, what do I say?"

"Tell them the cops asked you to do it. They're just trying to figure out where everybody was."

"But *you're* not—"

"No," I said. "But I was a friend of Bonnie's."

"Everybody was."

"Not everybody."

"Well," she said. "Obviously. But come on, nobody hated her. She wasn't hateable. Whoever, you know, killed her, he was crazy. Or she knew something about him. Or, oh, I don't know. Okay, I'll try to make a list, but I don't know how it's going to help."

"I don't, either," I said. "But this is what you do when something like this happens. You start with the dull stuff and hope it leads you to the interesting stuff."

"Kind of like life," she said. She thought about it for a moment. "Right?"

20
Tumbling Tumbleweeds

When I rattled off that pap about a life told in Christmases, I skipped over a few of my own. I did it out of sheer cowardice.

My issues with Christmas go way back. In fact, the only seasonal present from my father that I've kept with me is an aversion to Christmas.

My father was a problem drinker, by which I mean something quite specific. He wasn't an alcoholic and he didn't drink often, but on the occasions when he *did* drink, he was a problem. At the center of his character, I think, was a radioactive core of resentment. He'd been a dweeb in high school ("Hey, *Merle,* no lipstick today?") and he was a dweeb as an adult. He was shorter, less successful, and, he thought, smarter than his two younger brothers, whom he always referred to as "Flash" and "Squeak." He'd settled in marriage for a woman who wasn't, by his standards, pretty enough and who had double-crossed him by getting older. He hated his job. My mother said he was a man who felt like life had given him a cheap hat and then trained birds to shit on it. All this festering injustice bubbled to the surface when he drank.

He dealt with being sober by wearing a tight, mean little smile most of the time—like someone who's got bad gas and can't bring up a burp—and by saying things he actually meant in a way that forced us to pretend they were jokes. When my mother had to take a job to help with the house payments, he'd survey the living room she hadn't straightened up before she left at eight A.M. for work and say, "Boy, if cleanliness is next to godliness, the Lord lives far, far away, huh, Junior?" Or, when my high school grades were in free fall because I was slipping out and breaking into houses at night, he'd say, "Guess we don't have to worry about paying big bills for college, huh, Ruthie?"

He despised his own father, whom he called Walt, as though calling him "Dad" would somehow legitimize the relationship. Walt had abandoned my father and his two younger brothers when my father was in his early teens. "Just packed up one fine day and took off," my father said maybe three hundred times in my presence, word for word, with the same intonation every time, a kind of involuntary mental tape loop. The moment he said, "Just packed . . ." my mother would close her eyes and sigh. My mother sighed a lot.

I met Walt exactly once, when I was ten, in a big, old Craftsman house in Pasadena where every blind and curtain in the place was drawn to create a permanent dusk. Walt had insisted on the meeting but when we got there he had nothing to say to either me or my dad. I had worn my cowboy hat to piss my father off, and Walt, grasping at straws, wound up sitting at a perfectly polished baby grand with keys yellowed by use, playing old cowboy songs for me: "Tumbling Tumbleweeds," "Don't Fence Me In," and a few others I never learned the names of while my father sat on the couch, cracking his knuckles.

Every now and then a thin, white-haired woman in a loose, pale gown with draping sleeves—a garment that could have been made any time since King Arthur—would float through the room without a glance at us, as though we were in a different dimension. For all the attention Walt and my father paid her, she might as well have been a draft.

The fourth or fifth time she solidified out of the shadows, my father stood up while Walt was in the middle of yet another song and said, "Okay, you've seen him. Come on, Junior." He'd preceded me to the front door, opened it for me, and stood aside to let me go first, something he didn't do even for my mother. It wasn't until I was almost to the car that I realized he'd done it just so he could leave the door standing open. He didn't say anything on the long ride home. I talked as much as he did.

And that was a day when he hadn't drunk *anything*.

But my father always drank on Christmas Eve. One Christmas, his next-to-last with us, marked in my mind the formal beginning of the end of my parents' marriage.

My mother's family had done Christmas the hard way, concentrating all the effort into the night before Christmas: decorating the tree, hanging up the stockings, and laying out the presents after my mother and her sisters were in bed. The one war my mother won during her marriage to my father was the Christmas Eve War. If my father had had his way, the tree would have stood in the living room shedding its needles all year around, just needing to be plugged in on Christmas morning, the presents would have been in their store boxes with the price tags still dangling from them, and my stocking would have hung permanently from the mantle, something for my mother to dust around.

So he would begin to drink as they hauled the tree in from where it had been hidden in the storage shed my father had built behind the garage, a room to which he incorrectly thought he had the only key. Generally by the time they were hanging the lights, he'd be three or four belts in and grumbling about her fancy family and their labor-intensive holidays, and she'd be doing variations on *They did it for the children, and you can do it for your son* and he'd be off on his eternal complaint about how *No son of mine wouldn't be able to climb a fucking rope in the fucking Cub Scouts* and then they'd start yelling at each other and, of course, I would've been awake all along.

When I was thirteen I went into the living room, dazzling in a thousand colors from the lights on the tree, and interrupted my father's seasonal rant with, "This is your idea of a silent night?"

"You're going to learn sooner or later, smart guy," he said, "that life isn't so fucking funny."

I said, "I'd choose funny over shitty any time."

And that's when he slapped me.

My mother responded by going to the Christmas tree, hung with the precious, hand-blown glass ornaments she'd inherited from her grandmother, and pulling the whole thing over. Glass had broken and the lights had flickered and gone out. On his way out of the house, my father stopped long enough to yank the screen door off its hinges. I heard his car door open and then the single word, "*Shit,*" and there he was again, even angrier at messing up his big exit. He stomped past us into the kitchen, and when he came back he had his keys in his hand. A moment later, we heard him leave parallel lines of rubber all the way down the block.

My mother and I stood there silently, looking at each other, and then I righted the tree and the two of us, like a couple of mimes, used wads of wet paper towels to pick up the shards of the broken ornaments. We never exchanged a word. When we were finished vacuuming up the slivers and the tree was shining again, I said, "Want to open the presents?"

"You know we don't do that until morning," my mother said, as though we were sipping high tea in Buckingham Palace rather than standing in a small house in Tarzana in the middle of the night with her husband gone, probably on his way to the woman whose existence she already suspected and whom he would eventually marry. She shook her head and said in all sincerity, "Do you want to *spoil Christmas*?" I was still laughing when I got into bed. My mother had her good moments, and that was one of my favorites.

So I had a lot to put behind me to get to the point where I could participate in those first miraculous Christmases with Rina, to get to the point at which jingling bells and *"Adeste Fidelis"* didn't make me pop anxiety sweat.

I'd just finished checking with Wally and learning that Cranmer was still at the murder scene, so I was adding to my lunch list in one of the second-level shops I'd missed when my phone rang. A little pink *Hello Kitty* heart announced that it was Ronnie. She'd never seen the sappy little heart, and if she had, she would have directed quantities of muscular scorn at it. I hurried to the stairs just in case Cranmer emerged unannounced through the doors to Gabriel's, and when I was five steps down and more or less out of sight I said, "Hi. How you doing?"

There was a lot of noise on the line, as though she were on a busy street. "I've been better."

I didn't like the sound of her voice. It seemed insubstantial and at the same time effortful, as though producing it at all took a lot of work. I cast around for something to say and settled on, "I'm really sorry to hear it. Is there anything I can do?"

"I don't know," she said. She paused. "It's not *about* you."

"Well, then," I said, and couldn't come up with anything that she might not reject as yet another probe into the sensitive areas she wasn't sharing with me, and took refuge in the neutrality of facts. I said, "Where are you?"

"Beverly Hills."

"Really. Um, see any movie stars?"

"They're all in disguise," she said. "As usual."

I was wandering back up the stairs, just moving, having forgotten all about Cranmer, I leaned on the handrail, looking up at nothing while my stomach cramped up. On the level above me, people streamed by. Business had picked up. When it was clear she had nothing to add, I said, "Why are you in Beverly Hills?"

"It's just where I *am*, Junior. I saw a parking space and pulled over to call you."

I was hating this conversation. Ronnie was a strong enough person for me to know that whatever was making her sound so hollowed out, it was serious. "Are you on your way somewhere?" There was no response, so I made a desperate snatch at something else to say. "Want to come out here, to the Valley? I can show you the worst mall on earth. Or want me to come to you?"

"I think," she said, and then she fell silent.

"I could introduce you to Shlomo Stempel, the world's best and skinniest Santa Claus." The anxiety in my voice was unmistakable. Even I could hear it.

"I think I'm going to the airport." Someone honked on the street where she was parked, and someone else shouted, probably at the person who had honked. "I think I need to be somewhere else for a while."

"What did I do?" I asked.

"It's not you," she said. "It's . . . it's everything. It's my life. Before I knew you. It's fucking Christmas."

"Let's skip it," I said. "We'll go straight to New Year. We'll go out tonight and buy stupid hats and champagne and those, those things that unroll and go *phweee* when you blow into them. Make resolutions. Sing that awful song about forgetting your old acquaintances. Just cut Christmas out of the calendar."

She waited until it was clear that I was finished.

"You would, too," she said. "Except for Rina."

I was rubbing my eyes with my free hand. "Well, yeah, Rina, sure, I mean, I've got to—listen, *please* don't go any—"

"I need time," she said.

"If this is, I don't know, the Christmas blues, or if you just need to be alone for a while—"

"Junior . . ."

"Then you can have the apartment. Okay? You like it there. I'll go back to motels, I've kind of *missed* the motels, to tell you the—"

"Christmas in a motel." she said.

"Then I'll stay in one of the storage units. Or the Bel Air Hotel. Hell, I'll go to the apartment and *you* can stay at the Bel—"

"Junior."

"The hell with Christmas. You can rattle around at the Wedgwood, get snubbed in Bel Air, work out whatever it is that's got you so—so damn sad, and I'll take care of myself, I won't even telephone."

Someone walking by at the top of the stairs with an armload of bags snagged at my attention but by the time I'd looked up, she was gone. "You can have all the space you want. Come on, nobody wants to get on a plane this close to Christmas. And it's cold back east."

"Back east," she said.

"You know," I said, using my free hand to punch myself on the jaw for sheer stupidity in bringing up the multiple towns where she'd said she'd been born. "Um, Trenton or Mount Airy or wherever it was."

"That's what I mean," she said. "It's not fair. I can't impose all this on you. You never asked for this."

"I asked for *you*," I said.

"But not my baggage."

I said, "Ronnie—"

"It's just Christmas," she said. "God rot ye merry, gentlemen, and all that."

"We can fix this."

"Men," she said. "It's like all you need is a pair of emotional pliers and suddenly the music will start again and everything will be *fixed*. The window won't stick, the toast will pop right up, like it's supposed to."

"Okay," I said. "How *should* I respond?"

"Just listen to me. Can you do that for a minute, just listen? I'm tired, I'm sad, and I can't handle Christmas right now. I can't put all my energy into acting like everything is fine, that all we need to do is find the mistletoe, and a kiss will magically make everything all right, okay?"

"I—"

"I won't be at the apartment tonight. I promise to think about it another day, and I promise if I decide to leave, that I'll call you and talk to you and try to—try to let you help me figure it out. Please? That's the best I can do right now."

"But where will you be?"

"I'll be fine," she said. "Take care of yourself. Get

something nice for Rina and Kathy. We'll talk tomorrow. Or the next day." She disconnected, and it felt like an especially personal disconnection.

"Well," I said to the stairs. *"Shit."*

I went up one step, back down, and then up again, trying to burn through an agitation so intense I felt as though my teeth were vibrating, a new and terrifically unpleasant blend of loss, centered on Ronnie, and rage about Bonnie's murder and my plodding attempts to figure out who killed her. Old Vlad was mixed up in there, too, somewhere. I did the up-and-down routine a couple more times, trying to work some of it off. The quadriceps are the body's biggest muscles, and it's well-documented that exercising them just floods the system with calming, mood-altering endorphins. I was getting short of breath before I consigned the quads-endorphins-mood-elevating phenomenon to the ever-lengthening list of exhaustively documented nonsense. Someone, I thought, should create an encyclopedia just for this kind of richly proven bullshit. Ants avoid marigolds. Eskimos can't sing bass. Cauliflower is edible. Optimistic people lose more weight. Anti-wrinkle creams work. Christmas is the happiest time of the year.

The phone was showing me the list of recent calls, and I pressed *dial* automatically and immediately hung up. Said again, "Shit." Called Wally instead. "Where is he?"

"Where he was. I told you I'd call you if—"

"What are they doing?"

"Looking all over the place. They brought in enough lights for the Rose Bowl."

"That's what they do," I said. "Have they gone up to the third floor?"

"Couple of guys with big old flashlights."

"Okay, thanks. Keep an eye on the ones on three, too, okay?"

"You all right?"

"I'm doing great," I said through my teeth. "What could *possibly* be wrong?"

"Jeez," he said and hung up.

I thought, *My goddamn lunch lists*, and went back up to the second level to ask more questions. Being useful was better than seething with undirected anxiety, so I focused on getting back to work, on doing something *productive*. I was so focused that I walked straight past the open doors of two stores I hadn't checked, and I didn't even register the tall, slender young woman coming toward me with an armload of shopping bags until she side-stepped in front of me and said, "*Here* you are." I had to look at her twice before I recognized Francie DuBois.

"So soon we forget," she said, but she was smiling.

"I, uh, I was a million miles away. What are you doing here?"

One eyebrow went up with an effortlessness that made it look natural. "What am I *doing* here? Remember *Hi?* Remember pretending to be happy to see someone?"

"Of course, I'm happy to see you." I looked down at the phone in my hand and put it into my pocket. It still had Ronnie on the other end, even if she'd hung up. "It's just that, well, there have been millions of people here the last day and a half, and none of them was you."

"Until now."

"Right," I said. "Right." It didn't seem to be enough, so I added, "I'm kind of distracted."

"And I can see why," she said. "There are a dozen police cars out there, all blinking away, and still smelling of donuts, and here's the burglar boy, right out in plain sight."

"No, it's—" I went completely blank, and then I saw

Bonnie on her back, her hand curving around the tinsel, and I said, "We've had a murder. Somebody I liked."

"Oh," she said. She hugged all the bags against her body with one arm and reached out with the other to put her free hand on my forearm. "I'm so sorry."

"I really am happy to see you." I looked down the length of the second level. One store in four or five was closed and dark. "This is a sad place."

Her hand was still on my arm. Even through the sleeve of my shirt it felt warmer than it should have. She said, "I know what you mean. All the glitter, all the people spending more than they have."

"All the desperation," I said. "Most of the people who do business here are on the verge of bankruptcy. The woman who died—who was killed—said this was her last year. She was failing. She, um, she served me hot punch with wine and spices and oranges."

"How was it?"

"Not so awful. She was a Dickens fan." I sounded even to myself like I was rambling. The "Jingle Bell Rock" loop began again, and I knew we were only four songs away from *PAH-rum-pum-pum-pum*. "And this *music*."

"I like Christmas music." I must have made a face, because she added, "But I promise not to sing along. *Oh*," she said, suddenly seeming to remember the bags jammed under her left arm. "Your question? *What am I doing here?* I was over at Louie's, and he said these were yours."

"Thanks," I said. "Let me." I got control of the three packages—the book, the bracelet and the *netsuke*. "We were shopping," I said. "I mean, thank you, and, and—Louie and I, we were shopping when things went wrong. The woman was killed while we were . . ."

"So I asked him," she said, leaning in to look at me more closely, "could I bring them to you."

"Thank you," I said again.

"It was an *excuse*," she said, as though speaking to an unusually slow learner. "He wanted to bring them over himself, but I said . . . are you okay? 'Cause you've got something, anxiety, confusion, *something,* just rolling off you in waves."

There was a moment of silence between us, blighted by "Here Comes Santa Claus."

I took a deep breath and was suddenly frozen where I stood, looking straight at that path diverging in the wood that Robert Frost wrote about, and I knew this was the moment when I had to turn either right or left. To one side, Ronnie and all her secrecy and her problems, to the other, Francie, possibly with equivalent problems but shimmering with the mystery of someone new. I saw the fork in the road so clearly it almost blotted out the mall and everyone in it, except Francie, and I chose a direction. "When I met you, I, um, I—last *night?* When I met you?"

She waited and then said, "I still remember last night. When, as you just reminded me, I met you."

There was nothing to do but plunge ahead. "You'd been, umm, Christmas shopping. Right?"

The way she was looking at me changed, became evaluative instead of just interested. She pursed her lips, so slightly she might just have been thinking about doing it. "Correct. Christmas, you know, it's the day after tomorrow."

"And I asked you who you'd been shopping for, and you said, like, Bluto the barber or something like that."

"Bluto," she said, nodding, and I had the impression she'd taken a step back, although she hadn't moved. "Always at the top of my list. Because of the way he does my sideburns."

"But you didn't tell me—"

She shook her head. "I knew this was coming."

"You didn't tell me who *else* you were—"

"This isn't really *about* me, is it?" She rubbed at a spot above her left eyebrow that didn't look any different from any other spot above her left eyebrow, but the gesture had the effect of covering one of her eyes. The one that remained was more than I could handle. "This is about you. What you're trying to say—"

"Hey there," someone said, and I turned to see first, Rina, wearing one of my old shirts, a bright red scarf, and a pair of shredded jeans, and second, Tyrone.

Both of them were a trifle bright-eyed with the kind of energy that comes when you're searching for a four-leaf clover and you find a two-carat diamond: diamonds are exciting, but what you *wanted* was a four-leaf clover. Rina's gaze bounced back and forth between Francie DuBois and me. Tyrone was regarding me with hooded eyes, and his expression was not one of unalloyed admiration.

I said, "Oh." It was obviously an insufficient greeting, so I made it worse. "Why are you guys here?"

"Seeing you," Rina said. "I was saying just twenty or thirty minutes ago, back home, how it was a shame about you being stuck *all alone* in this, this infected bubo of a mall—"

Tyrone said, "*Bubo*. She's been studying the bubonic plague." His eyes went back to Francie.

"—at Christmas time," Rina said as though Tyrone hadn't spoken. "But you're not alone at *all*, are you?" To Francie, she said, "Hi. I'm Rina. I'm his daughter."

"And I'm Francie," Francie said. She shot me a glance I couldn't read. "And this is Tyrone, right?"

This time both kids turned to me, and I felt a cold gust of judgment.

"Don't look so surprised," Francie said to Tyrone. "You and I, we have the same color eyes, and Junior mentioned it to me when we met each other. Said he'd never seen eyes your color before, until he saw mine."

"Well, what do you know?" Tyrone said, a rhetorical question if I ever heard one. Rina was chewing on her lower lip, regarding Francie in a way that could be charitably described as unwelcoming. Tyrone, with the ancient male impulse to smooth over an awkward moment, said, "Same color eyes. Huh."

"Well," Francie said, looking at each of us in turn, and then back at me. She gazed at me for what seemed like a long time. "Well, well, well. Nice to meet both of you. And since I can see that Junior here is a little uncomfortable, I'll take off. Your father, honey," she said to Rina, "he's crazy about you. Okay," she said, coming back to me. "I'll tell Louie I delivered your packages."

Rina said, "Louie the Lost?"

"The very Louie." She wiggled her fingers in my direction and said, "Bye-bye. And Junior? Be careful with how you throw yourself around, okay? Some people, you never know, they might believe you." And she turned and went back toward the escalators. Her back was very straight.

"That is a woman," Rina said, "who didn't know you have a girlfriend."

"I've barely met her."

"You discussed the color of her eyes, and you've barely met her? How *is* Ronnie, anyway?"

"I have no idea," I said. "And don't try to be subtle with me."

"Wow," Rina said. "I *like* Ronnie."

"Well, goddamn it," I said, "so do I."

Rina said, "The color of her *eyes?*"

"Listen," I said, feeling my face heat up. "Not so long ago, you thought Tyrone here—"

"I remember, Daddy. I thought he was seeing somebody behind my back."

"And you were wrong. So just slow down on unloading all that judgment. You of all people—"

"Rina was set up," Tyrone said.

"Yeah?" I said, and suddenly I was furious. "What's *my* excuse? Is that what you were going to ask me, Tyrone?"

"Well," Tyrone said, "yeah."

"I'm supposed to explain myself to you, is that it?"

Tyrone said, "Only if you care what we think."

Rina said, *"Tyrone,"* and I said, "Okay, okay, you're right. Give me a minute." I turned away and walked in a circle a couple of times as they watched me.

"I'm having a bad enough day to earn me a year of summer," I said when I'd worn out the circle. "Ronnie has left me, at least temporarily, and I'm worried about her. I don't like the way she sounds, and she won't talk about it. And a bunch of other things. But about Francie, I met her last night, when she probably saved my life." I held up a hand. "A guy was shooting at me and she interfered with him, very effectively, so I took her to dinner. We, we talked, and I—I didn't see the need to mention Ronnie." Rina started to say something, and I cut her off. "I know, I know, I *know*. But that's the whole story. And just to look at it from the other angle for a moment, for all I know, she belongs to a sect in which all the women have multiple husbands and she was trying to recruit me as number twelve or something."

"You just think that because *you* weren't being straight," Tyrone said. Rina took his hand, lifted it up, and kissed his knuckles.

"Am I lucky?" she said.

"You are," I said. "You both are."

"On the nose, Jose," Tyrone said.

I said, "I think it's pronounced Hozay."

"Who cares?" Tyrone said. "He's not here. So. Let's go shopping."

"I can't," I said. "I'm working."

Looking toward the escalator, Rina said, "She seemed like a nice woman."

"She *seemed* like she'd fallen from heaven," I said. "That's why I got into trouble."

PART THREE

KEEPING WATCH BY NIGHT

21

In Case the Knock Was Answered by Hermann Goering

An hour and a half later I had all the lunch information I was going to get from the remaining shops, and I was so hungry I almost forgot I was depressed. I gave the new lists to Amanda at Tito's, who regarded them with waning enthusiasm, so I reminded her how much we'd both liked Bonnie, which earned me a look that could accurately be described as *askance*. Then I asked for a burrito with everything and gave her my most persuasive smile, which felt frayed even to me, so I also gave her five hundred of Vlad's dollars. Then I went to pull out the chair next to Shlomo.

"Terrible thing," he said. He was about the fourth person to say precisely those words to me that day.

"It is," I said. "There's no shortage of terrible things right now."

He shook his head. He had another bowl of soup in front of him. "Never is."

"So here's the deal. I need a miracle."

"To me you come for a—"

"You told me you had a miracle, a Christmas miracle. I need it, and I need it now."

Shlomo looked regretfully down at his soup. "This is going

to get cold," he said. "I tell you this, my soup will get cold and I won't eat it, and when I don't eat my feet get all icy."

I said, "So wear socks. Does Santa stay home when his feet get cold?"

His attempt not to smile failed miserably. He put down his spoon, closed his eyes for a moment, opened them again to look at me more closely, pushed the soup aside, and began to tell me a story about his father, Morris Stempel.

Morris always said that the *first* worst thing was that he kept seeing the dead man's eyes.

The barn in which Morris was kneeling had slatted spaces in the roof where boards had fallen through, but the moon apparently hadn't risen yet, or even if it had, the clouds and fog were more than thick enough to absorb its light. Not an hour ago, as he, Keystone, and Sabathia were picking their way across a low, misty rise, with no idea of where they were, Sabathia had tripped and gone down with a percussive grunt. For a second, Morris had pulled out his angle-head flashlight, stinking from the wax that waterproofed it, and flicked it on.

"*Off,*" Keystone hissed, but in that brief moment the beam of light had bounced off the wide-open, glazed eyes of a fallen man, flaring into existence as suddenly and as brightly as the eyes of roadside wildlife at the edges of the long Canadian highways Morris had driven as a teenager. Morris had seen nothing but the eyes; they had commanded one hundred percent of his terrified attention, and he couldn't have said whether the dead man was American, German, or French.

Or maybe even Canadian, like Morris.

Keystone and Morris dropped in unison to their hands and knees. Sabathia, who had scrambled back from the man he'd stumbled over, was sitting up, swearing and rubbing at his right ankle. For a long, frozen, breath-holding moment, they all absorbed the presence of death and waited to see whether the light would draw a shot from whichever group of armed troops was within range.

Nothing. Either the fog was too thick or they had wandered farther than Morris thought they had. But the fog, Morris saw, was changing: instead of a featureless, muffling, all-concealing presence it had turned ropy and fragmented, closing them in, lifting, and then surrounding them again.

Sabathia whispered, "Sprained it."

"Well, then," Keystone said, "that means you didn't break it." He smiled, his teeth white in his dark face.

Morris said, "That's your Christmas present, Sabby."

"Not going to be able to run with my usual grace," Sabathia said. They were still whispering.

"Nope," Keystone said. "No Sabathia waddle for a few days. Can you get up?"

"That's really two questions," Sabathia said, "the first being, do I *want* to? Since we have no idea where we're going."

"We're going that way," Keystone said, nodding in the direction they'd been walking.

"Fine, then. For a destination that precise, sure, I can get up. Might need to lean on one of you for walking, though."

Down low and to their left, the sky flickered coldly, and they had all counted to four by the time they heard a hollow percussive sound, like someone hitting an empty barrel with a hammer. "Big Bertha," Morris said as the fog swept in again "Four thousand feet, give or take. Little less than a mile."

"See?" Keystone said. "The Krauts are to our left. So we'll limp to our right."

"It's all that military history you read," Morris said. "Having a complicated tactical decision like that right at your fingertips."

"Let's split it down the middle," Sabathia said, pulling himself up onto his hands and knees. "Forty-five-degree angle to the right."

"Why forty-five degrees?" Keystone said. He was, like the others, a private, but he was a year older and had almost three weeks' more battle time than they, so they tended to defer to him. He was also the first black man either of them had ever known personally.

"Why the fuck not?" Sabathia said, and all three men laughed, Morris into the sleeve of his coat and the others with their hands over their mouths. Sabathia began to cough and brought the bottom of his coat up to muffle the sound.

When he was laughed out, Keystone said, "Come on, it's Christmas Eve. What bad could happen?"

Ask the dead soldier back there, Morris thought, but what he said was, "Right ankle, Sabby?"

"Yeah." He jerked the leg back. "Don't you *dare*, don't you touch it, you sadist—" He started laughing again, lowering his head as far as possible and covering his mouth with the crook of his elbow.

"I'm a doctor, Sabby," Morris said. "Well, almost. Let me see whether it's broken."

"Fuck that," Sabathia said. "Whaddya gonna do if it's broken, amputate? One way or the other, I'll be limping. At least this way I won't be bleeding to death, too." Keystone laughed quietly.

"Okay," Morris said. "No miracle of modern medicine for you." The three of them crouched there, breathing hard and listening for anything that sounded closer than Bertha, anything that might help them find the direction back to their own lines.

First there was nothing, but then a static electricity crackle of small-arms fire erupted from the same direction as the boom from Bertha. "That settles it," Morris said. "Put your arm around my neck, Sabby."

"You have no idea how long I've been waiting for you to say that," Sabathia whispered. "I've always been drawn to male Hebrews."

"Well, this is probably as close as you'll ever get," Morris said. Sabathia draped his right arm around Morris's shoulders and Morris grasped the dangling wrist and said, "One, two, *three*." With a short, choked gasp from Sabathia, they were up.

"Here we go," Keystone said. "Forty-five degrees exactly." The fog swept past them, trailing *more* fog, enormous palaces of fog, so heavy and wet it drizzled icily on their faces. After the first few awkward steps, they moved in silence, Keystone and Morris passing Sabathia back and forth every ten minutes or so like the baton in a relay. They heard no more firing, and while it eased their nerves a bit, it also deprived them of their only dependable orientation. Up till now the firing had been to their left. Now that it was silent, whenever Keystone and Morris switched places, the free one followed their footprints back for a minute or two to make sure they were moving in a relatively straight line.

After thirty-five or forty endless minutes, at a time when Morris was once again supporting Sabathia, Keystone said, "Stop."

"What?" Sabathia whispered. His ankle had swollen badly, and they'd unlaced his boot and pulled it off with much between-the-teeth groaning from Sabby, and then they'd laced it around his forearm so he couldn't lose it.

"Somebody here," Keystone said. He dropped to one knee and lit a match.

On his back in the black, rich dirt, one arm upraised over his head as though waving to someone far, far away, was a black American private. His mouth was open in seeming surprise and his chest was soaked with the autumn brown of dried blood. As Keystone brought the match closer and leaned forward, obviously looking for something, a gold filling gleamed in the dead man's mouth.

"Nobody came back to get him," Sabathia said. "They must have been running for their lives."

"Or, you know, he's black," said Keystone. Morris could barely hear him.

"Oh, come on—" Sabathia said, but Keystone's eyes stopped him mid-word.

"Sorry about this, brother," Keystone said, and he blew out the match and threw it aside. Then he tugged the dead man's collar open, wrapped something around his fist, and pulled.

"What are you—" Sabathia said, and then he said, "Oh."

"Yeah, oh," Keystone said. "He's got other ID. It's not like no one will know who he is."

"Was," Morris said. "I can't wear those."

"But you will," Keystone said. "Because if you don't, I'll personally break your neck. You know, it's not good for us, either, we get caught out here with a Jew."

Neither Morris nor Sabathia said anything. They both knew that the Germans would probably kill a black soldier even faster than they'd kill a Jew.

"Willis," Keystone read, holding the dog tags up to his eyes. "Henry. Lee. Willis." He grabbed a lungful of air and blew it out. "Jesus *Christ*," he said. Then he handed the tags to Morris and said, "Come on, Henry Lee."

After another seven or eight minutes of following Keystone's lead, they hit a plowed field and began to stumble, swearing, over the frozen furrows. Sabby let out a low cry as he turned his bad ankle, and the cry was cut off as Keystone's hand covered Sabathia's mouth. At that moment, Morris saw the dark outline of a house and barn. One dim light, probably a kerosene lantern, burned in a window.

Keystone deputized Sabathia to knock. Poor, injured Sabby would serve as the point of the wedge, to get the folks inside to open the door. Keystone stood behind a tree a few yards off with his rifle pointed at the door in case the knock was answered by Hermann Goering or some gung ho SS officer. Instead, the door was tugged inward by a small, balding man in his fifties, stoop-shouldered and worried-looking, wearing baggy pants and suspenders.

"*Joyeux Noël,*" Sabby said in Chicago French as the man looked up at him.

There was a moment when Keystone, sighting down the barrel of his gun, thought the little man was going to close the door in Sabathia's face, but good manners won out, and he returned the holiday wishes. A moment later, Sabby was inside. Keystone counted to twenty and then went to the door and knocked.

Morris had chosen the barn because he needed to use his flashlight for what he had to do. He had it tucked beneath his left arm as he went through his things, finding everything that identified him as Morris Stempel and sorting it into a pile.

Every now and then, at the edge of his vision, the wide-open eyes of the first dead man, pulled from the darkness by the flashlight's beam, flowered into existence against the dark. The first three or four times, he looked over to where he thought the gleam had come from, but after that he ignored it, consigning it to the lengthening list of things that had made an adrenaline-charged imprint on his mind since he got to the front. He'd seen several of these imprints multiple times, mostly horrifying visual echoes, usually as he was trying to sleep.

The general knowledge in the ranks, probably no more or less dependable than general knowledge anywhere else, said that the Germans treated Jews like any other prisoners if they were taken in groups large enough to make it likely that non-Jewish POWs would survive to report that their Jewish comrades had been murdered in the field. If Jews were captured alone, though, or in small groups, it was said that they were often killed on the spot.

And every black soldier knew that there had been incidents in the African campaigns, especially now that the war was widely thought to be winding down to a German defeat, in where the Nazis had simply shot black troops from the French colonies where they stood rather than taking them prisoner.

So, not a good idea to be Morris Stempel—or, for that matter, Jerome Keystone—until they could figure out where they were and how to get back to their own lines. But Morris had never been anyone *except* Morris Stempel, and it felt as though something inside him was turning away in shame to avoid seeing what the rest of him was doing. Especially since nothing could be done for Keystone.

Henry Lee Willis, he thought. Who had he been?

Morris was cold. He felt like he'd been cold for a decade. He was so cold that he had to keep blowing into his hands to bring feeling back to his fingers; he needed his sense of touch because he was sorting pieces of paper, trying to get rid of evidence. The day they'd moved out to the front—what? Two days ago? Three?—there had been a mail call, and the stuff he'd been handed was still bundled, unread, with a tight elastic band. As he rolled it down to unwrap the papers, the band snapped and one end hit him on the back of his freezing hand.

The pain was so intense and so unexpected that Morris's vision was momentarily edged with red. He glared at the broken elastic band, a length of cheap, brown synthetic since all rubber was being rationed, and he picked it up in the stinging hand, rolled it into a ball, and threw it out of the small, yellowish circle created by his flashlight. "And *fuck* you, too," he said.

Morris had never sworn before the war.

On top of the sheaf of papers, now curled from having been rolled up for two days, was a letter from his mother. Instead of opening it, he decided to short-cut the act of getting rid of it so he wouldn't be tempted to change his mind after he read it. Using the semisharp edge of his entrenching tool, he hacked at the half-frozen earth beneath its wispy layer of straw, going up onto his knees to get a longer downstroke. A couple of minutes later, he had a sheen of sweat going ice cold on his forehead and a hole almost deep enough to bury one of his boots in.

It would have to do.

A scattering of small-arms fire, like hail on a tin roof. Closer than it had been.

So here come the Nazis, smelling blood, and here's the Jew, sitting in a barn having what Mr. Sartre would call an existential crisis. Not taking action, not even reading his mother's letter, just marinating in the oddness of having the entire weight, the cutting edge, of a global disaster, National

Socialism, pointed directly at his narrow chest, threatening to obliterate his second-rate (as his older brother, the physicist, liked to describe it) mind.

He opened the flimsy envelope, the thin airmail paper almost falling to pieces as his numb fingers wrestled with it. And there she was on the page, his mother, a woman who never talked about herself. In her version of life, she was the invisible narrator of the family's doings, the one holding the camera for all the snapshots. His father, she said, was feeling better, the indigestion that had plagued him all winter was on the wane. And here's something about Sophie Resnick, the young woman who, at thirteen, gave Morris his first-ever taste of bubble gum in someone else's mouth. The fruity smell of Sophie's breath, the rubbery smoothness of her well-chewed gum, and the warm, soft roughness of her tongue, was as fresh and new at that moment, sitting in that freezing barn, as it had been the first night he took the experience to bed with him. Sophie was getting married, to a Gentile, no less, a man who had (he could hear the condemnation in his mother's voice) *dodged the draft.* We're all thinking of you, worrying about you. Be careful whatever you do, it would (scratched-out words that he recognized as *kill me*) break my heart if anything happened to you. Love from us all.

He put the letter into the hole. Thanks, Mom. Bye, Sophie.

Sophie Resnick. He hadn't thought about her in years.

And here was something in a better-quality envelope, the envelope of someone spared the general privation of rationing, from, in fact, his insufferable physicist brother, sitting out the war in Washington with bad lungs and equations that were somehow vital to the national defense. Something from Jackie Morgenstern, a fraternity brother now adrift in the Pacific with the Navy, dated four months earlier.

Don't even open them. Put them in the hole.

An envelope from . . .

He sat there, feeling something rise up in him, the last thing he ever expected under these circumstances: he was going to laugh. It bubbled in his chest but lost its force on the way up and finally pushed his lips open three or four times to make a voiceless *phh, phh, phh*.

From the moment he, like so many other North American Jews, began to hear the rumors from Europe, from the people who had made it out in time, who had taken refuge in places like Prague and Vienna—safe for a time, for a *time*—the first shocked reports of *Kristallnacht*, the second- and third-hand rumors of the trains packed with Jews heading who knew where, that began to circulate among Jews around the globe in a long and long-ignored cry of anguish and stifled rage— from that moment, Morris had only one desire: to go to war as an American. To be in the front lines, in the very teeth of the machine that would chew Hitler's beasts like tender steak and spit them into the cities of Germany.

But he was born in Canada. He'd lived in the United States for fifteen years, he was finishing medical school at Columbia University in New York, he regarded himself as a New Yorker, but he wasn't a *citizen*. When America finally entered the war, he tried to enlist in the Army. He was turned down. He tried again and was turned down again. It got to the point where the people at the recruiting office would shake their heads and laugh when he came in. At last he took a train to Canada and enlisted, was accepted immediately, and was assigned to a theater of war in France and Belgium where he'd be fighting beside and with the Americans.

And there he was, eighteen months later, exhausted, filthy, freezing, huddled in a barn, trying to destroy his identity before the Germans arrived, opening an official US Government envelope to read, *Greetings from the President.* Forwarded to him through a succession of stateside addresses, redirected to Canada, and floated across the Atlantic to no-man's-land somewhere near the border between France and Belgium, here at last was his official notice to report for service in the American Army.

He wanted to laugh again, but the heaviness in his chest wouldn't let him. He let the letter fall into the hole, looking down at it while the impulse of laughter turned into something heavier and colder. He retrieved his mother's letter, folded it, and slipped it into his breast pocket. Then he reached up and took off Henry Lee Willis's dog tags, put them into the hole on top of his papers, and covered it up, sprinkling some straw on the patch of bare, soft dirt. He slipped his own tags over his head, feeling their cold weight on the back of his neck, and with a grunt of weariness got to his feet. He was Morris Stempel again, and as Morris Stempel, he thought, he'd face whatever was coming.

The air around his ears seemed to crackle with the sound of rifle fire, now even closer than before. Morris went to the door of the barn and peered out into the fog. It had a new feature: a shell-like, silvery paling to the east. The moon, beginning to show her face.

More firing from the left (*the east,* he corrected himself), closer still. The darkness had thinned enough for him to see the house, and, looking at it, he thought, *It'll be either shelled or searched. We'd be better off in a hole.*

But his friends were in there, so he picked his way over the frozen ground toward the light in the window.

22
The Coveted Serious Professional Size

I was thinking about the first part of Shlomo's story, up through Morris's decision to reclaim his identity, as I sat under the counter in the abandoned record store, waiting out the final security check before the two inside guards left for the night, abdicating security, such as it was, to the outdoor crew, who were supposed to cruise the parking lot and circle the building twice an hour. According to Wally, they were more likely to park at the far end of the lot and go to sleep in their car. Usually with a bottle of something.

Morris's journey across an unmarked and directionless no-man's-land with peril waiting in multiple directions was just too compelling a parallel to ignore. It was where we *all* lived, it seemed to me, deny it as much as we might, whatever theology or philosophy we armored ourselves in, and we're *out there* in that darkness whether we're alone or with someone. One of the cosmic jokes of being male is that we tend to think of those who are with us as being sheltered from that darkness under a sort of umbrella of our protection when many of them are probably more capable than we are. Might, in fact, protect *us*.

Ronnie, for example. Probably tougher than I was. Wherever the hell she was.

Acting under a literally irresistible compulsion, I dialed her number—and my certainty that she wouldn't answer proved to be justified. Just to leave no futile gesture unattempted, I called the landline in the apartment at the Wedgwood, a phone neither of us ever used, and listened to it ring until I couldn't listen to it anymore. Then I sat there among the dust rats, on linoleum so dirty I could hear the grit whenever I shifted my weight, and tried not to think about no-man's-land.

As dire as the circumstances were for Morris Stempel and his companions, they'd had an interval of grace, from one perspective, before they were shipped out. They'd had time to tie things off, to seal envelopes, to close doors gently, to say parting words that they knew might have to last for a while or forever. I wouldn't have traded places with them, but the opportunity they had to part well from those they loved isn't available to most of us as we blunder our way through the dark, never knowing when the rake will snap up and hit us in the face or when we'll step off the edge of the big one. Every time something important ends in my life, my first thought is for all the loose ends, all the sad incompletions, all the undelivered gifts. The young men of Morris's generation had a chance to take care of at least some of those things.

Things. There were things, I thought, I should have said to Herbie before he left us, things I could have done to keep my family together. Sacrifices I could have made to watch my daughter grow up as I shared fully in her life. *Something,* although I had no idea what it would have been, to make sure Ronnie knew that I loved her, whoever she was. And, if I'd had some kind of warning flag, some reminder that there are times we need to live on tiptoe, I never would have indulged my ego by flirting with Francie DuBois.

What a sad little list.

If Edgerton Mall had a drugstore, I thought, I'd break in and steal some antidepressants.

The grit beneath my left hand felt unpleasantly sharp. I lifted my hand in its thin food-service glove and looked down to see, in the light that penetrated the dirty window, a perfect handprint in the dust. Then I checked my bandage, still clean inside the glove, and looked again at the outline—the map—of my hand I'd left on the floor. A *map*. Almost automatically I drew the outline of the mall, not a rectangle but a big oval, straight on the long sides and rounded on the short ones.

The Christmas music stopped in mid-*Fa-la-la-la*. That meant that all the shoppers were out of the building. Without the music, I could just hear the voices of the people packing up, cashing out, and getting ready to go home. Since I was closest to the end with the bazaar, I heard the vendors in that area most clearly, calling out questions and answers, big-fish lies about how much they had or hadn't taken in, and for a moment I felt a pang for them, for everyone working here, selling their precious hours for small change, sealed away from daylight and moonlight, grubbing in a till, taking money from people who often couldn't afford to spend it, and running mental addition and subtraction all day on their own bank balances, the strength or weakness of their family ties, the holes in their lives, now that the holidays were upon them. 'Tis the season.

Maybe twenty, thirty minutes before I could start to move.

I looked down at the oval I'd drawn, just visible in the diluted light straining its way through the record shop's dirty window. I'd drawn it, I thought, for a reason, not just to put an outline around no-man's-land. What the hell had I been—

Right. I'd been down in the bazaar for twenty or thirty

minutes before I chased Mini-me up the escalator. The escalator had been in plain sight all the time, and no one but Mini-me had gone up while I was there. That big red cardboard ribbon had been intact until Mini-me rushed through it.

So how had *Bonnie* gotten up there?

I'd been so busy asking myself *why* she was there that I hadn't given much thought to how. But now that I was focused on it, I saw that answering the question might actually lead me to some other questions, and it was always good to have a lot of questions.

The oval drawn in the dust.

Here and *here*, bordering the curved walls on the north and south ends, were the anchor spaces. Only the anchor stores were multistory, only they opened onto all three floors. I drew spokes radiating from shops located along the long sides of the oval, and at the end of each line I wrote the name of the store. I found I could mentally locate and name about a third of the shops on the ground floor and a little better than half of the ones on the second floor, which wasn't because I remembered it more clearly, but because the food court took up so much space that there were fewer outlets there. The third floor I remembered least well, but was also the smallest and it had the biggest percentage of closed, vacant stores. So I got probably half of them more or less in the right place.

By then I'd drawn two more ovals, each about two feet long, one representing each floor, and I was well into indicating the stores where I remembered them. I drew in the escalators, and doing that brought more clearly to mind the stores in their immediate neighborhoods, so I labeled five or six more.

I drew a circle around Bonnie's store on the second floor and contemplated the whole thing.

She hadn't gone down to the ground floor and into the

bazaar and then up the broken escalator because I would have seen her. Lots of people would have seen her. That might mean that there were passageways I didn't know about, out of sight of the shoppers—and, for that matter, me—the same way the employees' eating area had been invisible until I'd been directed back there. Now that I thought about it, I realized I'd seen several doors marked EMPLOYEES ONLY or NOT FOR PUBLIC USE, and I did my best to indicate those on the diagrams, too.

And I thought, as I had for the fourth or fifth time that day, that she must have been picked up by Wally's damn cameras as she transited the public areas to whatever secret paths she might have used. I'd been in the back of the store, drinking her Charles Dickens punch with her, and there was no exit back there. So the cameras . . .

The *cameras*. I heard myself say to Cranmer, "Blah blah . . . the guy bursts through the second-floor doors out of the store into the mall—"

And Cranmer saying, "That wasn't on camera."

No, it wasn't. The doors leading from what used to be Gabriel's into the rest of the mall were not in sight of the cameras on any floor, nor was more than a fraction of the shops that shared a wall with the empty department store. Because, as Wally had told me, the department stores had their own cameras, they had their own whole security setup.

That very morning, which felt like a decade ago, I'd made Wally move some of the cameras focused on the second- and third-floor walkways so I could search for Vlad's watchers. Since most of the cameras were in the stores, looking out for shoplifters, there weren't a lot of cameras on the public walkways, although I remembered Wally saying the escalators and stairways were covered at least peripherally because that was the most fertile ground for personal injury lawyers. I studied the area of the second-floor oval where Bonnie's store was, and then with the edge of my hand I rubbed out the areas that the cameras in their normal positions couldn't see.

It was pretty interesting, from my perspective: there were limited but possibly very useful holes in the surveillance.

Male voices, shouting to each other over a distance. One of them called the other *Bud*. Practically everyone I'd ever known who was called Bud was a cop, but the cops had pulled up stakes and left, marking everything with the yellow crime scene tape I always thought was far too fragile for all the faith they invested in it. So let's say this Bud was a *private* cop, a security guard, and the reason the two of them were yelling to each other was that they were at opposite ends of the mall, about to close and lock the outer doors. And, sure enough, a couple of minutes later most of the overhead fixtures flickered off, leaving just a few ghostly fluorescents throwing a thin, chalky light tinged with red from the EXIT signs, like a drop of blood mixed into a quart of skim milk.

And then I heard the echoing racket of the big metal airplane doors being pulled down and locked, sealing the place off for the night.

And a long night it was going to be.

With the mall's overhead lights out, I took my little penlight out of my pocket and aimed it at the drawings in the dust, trying to figure out the most probable path from Bonnie's Bric-a-Brac to the doors leading into Gabriel's empty second floor. I had it worked out, one that would have called for an easy bit of moving camouflage: leaving her store with a little knot of customers and then falling in with some shoppers as she came in and out of the cameras' sightlines. Just as I finished tracing her theoretical route, my phone made the badgering little hum that was its way of demanding attention when the ringtone is turned off. The screen read *Unknown*, but I figured there was always a possibility that Ronnie was calling from a blocked phone, so I punched *Accept*—such a passive word for seizing at a hope—and said, "Hello."

"So," Vlad said, "you are in Tahiti? On the French Riviera maybe? Preparing maybe for *Dancing with the Stars*?"

I said, "This kind of sarcasm doesn't suit you."

"*Suggest* a way," he said, "for me to ask you why I have to be looking at the *fucking television news* to learn that there was a murder today in my—"

"Really?" I said. "Nobody called you? Gee, I would have thought a million people—"

"You would have *thought*?" he said. "I doubt that. Whatever your reaction is, I doubt it would have been thought."

"You want to talk to me? Take a deep breath, count to ten, change your tone, and call me back." I hung up and felt a hot flood of rage rise within me, almost closing my throat. But still, in some corner of my mind I was counting, because when the phone rang again I said aloud, "Seven," and then answered it.

"Who was killed?" he said. "They are saying something stupid on the television about next of kin before they—"

"A woman named Bonnie. Ran a shop on the second floor. Are you telling me that no one has reported this to you?"

"I am at a remove," he said. "No one talks to me personal. I am not the friendly landlord, yes? I am not always easy to find."

He stopped talking and I let him stew for a moment.

"The . . ." he said. "The police, they talked to you?"

"I *found* her," I said, "so sure, they talked to me."

"Why were you the one who—no, never mind. What did you tell them about why you were there?"

"Nothing. I told them I was shopping." I summarized the story I'd woven for Cranmer. "I'm not connected to you at all."

"Who else—who else asked you questions?"

His uneasiness pushed its way through the phone, and I remembered again the way he'd sat with his back to the camera in the food court. "No one."

"This is important," he said, producing a pretty good hiss on the "s" sounds in "this is." "*Nobody else* tried to get you to tell him—"

"Like who?"

"You do not question me."

"Okay, then," I said. "Goodbye."

"Wait."

I waited. Then I said, "You might as well tell me."

"Tell you what?" he said. Then he drew a breath deep enough for me to hear it.

"Who you're afraid of."

"I am afraid of no one. This is a mistake, I have let you forget who I am. Not your fault, mine, but you know what? It's my mistake, maybe, but *you're the one it will kill.*" His voice had gone muted and a little shaky, and I could see his eyes doing that fried-egg thing. "You find out who killed this woman, you find out who is stealing from me, and you *keep me out of it*, or you will celebrate Christmas dead. Is my English okay? Do you understand?" He hung up.

Friends to the right of me, friends to the left, friends in the rearview mirror.

I took my own advice and grabbed a deep enough breath to loosen the muscles in my chest, which were locked in fight-or-flight mode, and looked down at the second-floor diagram again, just checking it against my memory. Bonnie's entrance was in the range of a single camera, and there were only two stores between her and the edge of the lens's field of coverage, about a store and a half away from the locked doors to Gabriel's second floor, the place where she'd died. Not far at all, easy for her to negotiate without being seen if she'd wanted to. Of course, there were still the locks on the outside of Gabriel's doors to slow her down, and when I'd taken a look at them I'd found they were very fancy locks indeed. But no one knew better than I that locks are almost infinitely permeable. I stood up and mentally cleared the decks. Time to breathe ten or twelve times, in through the nose and out through the mouth, time to bring myself completely into the present tense, which, while the exercise had a New Age sound to it, was after all the tense that contained all the people who wanted to kill me.

All right, Junior. Move.

This marked the beginning of the formal burglary segment of the evening, so I pulled off the dirty gloves, stuffed them into my hip pocket, and tugged on two clean new ones. Nothing to interfere with my sense of touch.

I'd chosen the record store because it was out of camera range, and I had to assume that the video system ran all night long. From where I was, there was only one brief bit of camera-covered walkway between me and the stairway up to the third floor, which would be nice and dark at this point. If I could do what I hoped to do, though, it wouldn't matter if it were pitch black or as bright as the gates of Disneyland, because the cameras would eventually forget they'd ever seen me.

A couple of hours earlier, right after Shlomo had broken

off his story to call it quits for the night, I'd gone down to my car and climbed in. I'd driven it in circles for a few minutes to find a good residential street free from any pesky NO PARKING signs. That way, whoever reviewed the mall parking lot cameras in the morning, in the unlikely event that anyone actually did, wouldn't wonder why my little white Toyota had sat there all night long.

On my loop I hadn't been completely surprised to see a conspicuous eruption of gentrification in the middle of this firmly lower-middle-class neighborhood. Behind a conventional NO THROUGH STREET sign loomed three big white two-story houses all agleam in spotlights, obviously designed by a single architect who knew what he liked and stuck with it, no matter how often he was asked for minor variations. Big colorful flags said EQUESTRIAN ACRES and NOW ON SALE and MODEL HOMES. Behind the houses was a dark stretch of territory that turned out to be a street lined with modest houses, unlit and obviously unoccupied. I'd driven it out of basic curiosity until I realized that the new development, if it ever got built, would stretch practically to the parking lot of Edgerton Mall.

Equestrian Acres, I thought. Not a horse in sight, and the last ones that ever grazed there probably belonged to the funky little amusement park that had been sued out of existence. So the original Edgerton Mall owners had just been a quarter of a century too early. If they'd had the time and the capital to wait, the high-income neighborhood they had hoped would patronize Edgerton Mall would eventually have surrounded it.

Timing is everything.

I had parked the car on the abandoned street behind the model homes and changed into a dark, long-sleeved

T-shirt, dark pants, and my black burglary sneakers, plus a long-billed baseball cap that would hide my features if I kept my face down. As an afterthought, I balled up the shirt and pants I'd removed and stuffed them inside my dark shirt to give me a gut and some love handles—most of the data we collect in long-distance recognition is from the silhouette. I pulled my burglary penlight out of the dash compartment and grabbed my roll of very convincing yellow crime scene tape, bought several months ago from the obliging folks at Amazon. Then I'd hiked past the empty houses and across a narrow wooded strip to get to the Edgerton parking lot. I had slipped back into the mall along with the last-minute shoppers, and made my way up to the former record store.

And now the place was empty, and here I was, drawing bad schematics on a dirty floor.

I smoothed the gloves over my hands for the third or fourth time to minimize their interference with my sense of touch and used my foot to erase the three ovals in the dust, thinking it was probably a pointless precaution but hearing Herbie say in my ear, "You have no idea what will be pointless. Don't leave *anything,* not *ever.*" Then I pushed my hand through the roll of tape so I could wear it like a bracelet and keep both hands free, went to the door, opened it silently, and stood there, listening.

It was surprisingly noisy. The building was contracting as it cooled, so there were creaks and cracks and shuddering sounds. I identified a soft *whoooosshhhing* sound as the heat even though I knew it was turned off at night, so I guessed it operated on a timer. The ghosts of traffic sounds filtered in through the walls and ceilings; the elevated 101 freeway was only about half a mile away. The enormous open space took all that sound, wrapped it in a hollow echo, and bounced it back and forth.

I should have expected all this noise, but up until now the place had always been full of voices and that eternal satanic music, so this was the first time I'd experienced its ambient sound. I stayed where I was for four or five minutes, just trying to map out the regular patterns in the sound level, trying to identify its components, working to get myself to the point where anything out of the ordinary would leap out at me. When I thought I'd made a good beginning, I began to move.

Head down, face shielded by the bill of the cap, shoulder brushing the wall, I covered the short distance to the stairway. Almost no one used it, what with the escalators at both ends and the center of the building, and it surprised me when grit under my shoes made my first step sound like a giant match being struck. I climbed the rest of the way by putting my foot straight down on each stair, which is a lot more awkward than it sounds, but I managed to get to the third floor without making any more noise. Three steps from the top, I stopped and took advantage of the relative darkness of the stairwell to survey what I could see of the shops on the other side of the oval. They were all satisfactorily dark and still. The strings of Christmas lights, their colors gone with the electricity that had lit them up, were somehow depressing. More depressing than they should have been.

And then as I started to climb the last few steps, the despair in Ronnie's voice, the way she'd sounded on that last phone call, surfaced in my memory. I leaned against the wall, mouth-breathing shallowly, momentarily directionless, as though I'd been dragged forward by a string that was suddenly cut, and the question *What am I doing here?* filled my mind to the exclusion of everything else. *I should be looking for her,* I thought. *The way she sounded was* different. *I should have called and called and called until she picked up and then* . . . and then *what?* What she was going through—whatever it was—wasn't *about* me, she had said. Not everything is about me.

But I knew I hadn't tried hard enough to get through. I'd given up too easily. If she was really gone, what in the world would I do?

Some kind of noise—just a horn on the freeway—brought me back to myself, enough to realize that a small part of what I was feeling was plain, awful, squirm-inducing guilt. There had been something in the way Francie had looked at me in the restaurant, as though I was new and undented, with my weaknesses and my faults still hidden beneath an unblemished coat of paint, and I'd reacted partly to her charm and energy and partly to the bright, shiny picture of myself I saw in her eyes. And somewhere in me I'd weighed that against how well Ronnie knew me—and, to be honest, how little she'd allowed me to know *her*—and I'd angled away from her, in the direction of the new and the unknown. And I'd been dishonest about it. With no more than some conversation and a brief almost-kiss on the nose, I'd cheated on Ronnie, and I'd been dishonest with Francie.

This was new to me. I had never actually cheated on anyone I loved before, and while I hadn't committed the *physical* act of being unfaithful, I had been ready to. All I had to do to see the whole dreary, dishonest thing was to remember what I'd said and hadn't said to both of them. Rina had taken one look at Francie and me and seen it all.

I shook my head to break the train of thought. One of my father's favorite pieces of paternal advice to his sometimes troubled son was, "For Chrissake, get over it." I'd heard it a thousand times while he was with us, and here I was at last, twenty years later, at a juncture in my life when it was the precise counsel I needed.

Okay, all the stuff about Ronnie and Francie, the tone of Ronnie's voice on the phone, the extent to which most of it was my fault—all of that was for *later*. The thing now was to get through this night, to figure out how and why Bonnie had gone into that dark department store and who had killed her, and what those things had to do with whatever was going on in Edgerton Mall. What I needed to do was shift myself back into professional gear and get this job done. And collect the money Vlad was going to pay me (*sure*, he was), sever the connection between us (not so easy), and then find Ronnie (impossible if she didn't want me to) and put things back together.

There. A list.

Lists are so much more satisfying than emotions. An emotion is a cloud, but a list is a stairway. What I needed to do was finish climbing the stairway I was actually on and get back to work. Emotions could come later, maybe when I was drinking.

At the top of the stairs I made an immediate right, heading in the direction of Gabriel's. Two stores down, I stopped at the door to Wally Durskee's hideaway, pulled out my lock picks, and went to work.

Cheap lock. It yielded eagerly, as though it had been waiting breathlessly to be picked, as though it had made a bet with some other lock about how little time it would take me. I slipped into Wally's space and closed the door silently behind me.

It was brighter in there than I'd thought it would be. Even though the cameras were pointing into a shopping mall that was only intermittently illuminated, the thirty-two flat-screens still produced light, even if it was an ambiguous and shadowless light with no reassurance in it. I went to Wally's chair, sat down, shimmied it right and left for a second or two, and reassembled my recollection of how he'd handled the controls during the hours I'd spent with him, trying to memorize precisely what I was about to try to do.

On the wall in front of me, I located the monitors that covered the record store, the stairway, and the bit of walkway I'd traversed. The console contained thirty-two sets of switches and knobs, each corresponding to a different monitor. I found the set marked 29, for the screen that displayed the outside of the record store, and pushed the button that controlled the recording and playback mechanisms for that monitor. I twisted the knob to the left and the word *rewind* appeared on the screen. As I rewound I watched myself walk backward to the record store, pause a bit oafishly at the doorway, and step back in. My entire on-screen career on that monitor had taken a slow count of eight. When the door closed behind me, I pushed RECORD and counted to ten, then rewound and pushed PLAY again. I had vanished.

It took me about six minutes to erase all traces of my on-screen existence during the period of time between leaving the record store and picking Wally's lock. I rolled the chair back, laced my fingers behind my head, and thought. There was a time-strip at the bottom of each screen. If someone came in and decided to watch eight or ten hours of nothing happening on thirty-two screens at a time, and if he or she paid close attention to the time strips, he or she would notice that they'd been monkeyed with. On the other hand, if I could get through the next few hours without leaving any trace of anything, why on earth would anyone ever look at this tape? Was anyone in the world paid enough to review ten hours of nothing happening on thirty-two screens at once? It didn't seem any more probable to me now, sitting here with the screens in front of me, than it had when I'd been mulling it over earlier in the day. I figured what the hell, and hit the master switch to turn the whole system off.

The screens blinked out, and I was in absolute darkness except for a pale little rectangle over the door, the monitor for the camera that told Wally who was out there. I thought about it for a second and decided there was no reason that anyone would have attached that camera to a recording device; it was just a way for Wally to discern friend from potential foe. As I turned away, I heard Herbie cautioning me about assumptions, so I slowed down and checked both the camera and the little screen to see what they were hooked up to, and came up with a reassuring answer: each other. There were no lines running into the wall, where they might have joined up with the rest of the hardware. A single, fine wire connected them, taped to the top of the doorjamb, thin enough not to interfere with the upper edge of the door.

With my penlight on, I crossed the room to Wally's closet. Its lock was a first cousin to the one on the door, perhaps even easier. When it opened, it almost said *thank you*.

The closet contained four of Wally's *Security* shirts hanging in a straight military row; a hand vacuum, probably to keep potato chip pieces from getting inside the controls on the console—Wally ate a lot of potato chips; a bottle of some kind of high-tech liquid screen cleaner and a bunch of microfiber cloths; and a couple pair of spare shoes, size twelve. Gleaming brightly from a hook screwed into the wall on the left was Wally's ring of keys, in the coveted Serious Professional size.

So. Security man's ring of keys. No video to worry about. Empty mall. Lots of stores. Hours to go before I sleep. Burglar's paradise. Even if I wasn't going to take anything.

23
Slapstick Porn

I let myself out of Wally's room, once again pausing in the doorway and listening before closing the door. The creaking and groaning had subsided some, but in a shop below me a phone was ringing while outside some idiot motorcyclist stitched a long, jagged line of noise on the surface of the night. I waited without any expectation of satisfaction for him to hit a streetlight, but he just sped away, dragging his roar behind him. One pleasant surprise: after the darkness of Wally's office with the monitors turned off, the illumination cast by the mall's night lights looked relatively generous. I didn't even use the penlight as I worked my way around the key ring, trying to match keys to functions.

When you've spent as much time with keys as I have, they sort themselves effortlessly into types, and the types are usually a function of just how badly the owner of a lock wants it to *stay* locked against, well, people like me. We've come a long way from the old skeleton key of the 1800s, essentially a two-dimensional, metal stamp, just a clunky cluster of ninety-degree angles on a shaft, designed to defeat a mortise lock, a set of similarly uncomplicated rectangular tumblers that were designed to keep out the keyless. But skeleton locks were virtually made to be picked, easily defeated by hairpins or any length of wire, although they had to wait until 1899 and the invention of the paper clip to be vulnerable to almost anybody with a little time on her hands or a file to reshape her key with. In fact, the term "skeleton key" is used by burglars today to designate any key that's been filed down to eliminate anything designed to snag the lock while retaining the features necessary to move the tumblers around.

The first keys we know of were Sumerian and Egyptian, cumbersome things made of wood and then iron, designed to be levered (usually) upward to open large, wooden locking mechanisms. As metallurgical skills developed, iron and brass began to dominate, and keys grew smaller, more sophisticated, more intricate—and also more beautiful. I'm certain it's not solely because I'm a burglar that I find some keys so beautiful. And it was in part because they *were* beautiful that in Roman and medieval times, wealthy people—the only ones who owned anything worth locking up—took to wearing them as status symbols, similar to today's top-line designer logos, usually dangling prominently from belts. Since wealth and power are so often aligned, keys also found their way into the coats of arms of prominent families and institutions. The most famous of these is probably the two crossed keys in the coat of arms of the Holy See, representing the Pope's keys to heaven.

I know several burglars who have what I suppose you'd call a key fetish, expressed through collections of keys from all periods. Chrysanthemum Paige, one of Herbie's few female protégés, had a picturesque assemblage of tiny keys that opened diaries and dollhouses, including two in solid gold from Victorian birdcages. Most crooks, though, just collect in bulk; an up-and-coming kid (we have those in burglary, too) self-named Swifty Smith had almost a thousand, all of them the basic flat, serrated keys that dominated until a few decades ago, hanging densely on one wall of his living room like 3-D wallpaper. When I asked him what he liked about them, he told me that he also collected vinyl records, and that flat keys, like vinyl, were a technology that had faded into nostalgia.

Which, in this age of smart locks, keyless entry, and wireless remotes, is the truth. And that's why it was so easy for me to flip through the fifty or so keys on Wally's bracelet-size ring and pick the ones that opened something truly worth opening.

Most of the keys were the ordinary serrated kind that I was certain were for the shops, an assumption that was confirmed by the little square of white tape on each key, bearing a number from one to thirty-seven. The numbers undoubtedly referred to the slots rented by the stores, so if I could figure out which shop occupied space one, I could open virtually every door in the place that had an old-fashioned, conventional lock. That was good news, since exploring the shops had been a primary item on my agenda for the evening.

That left a couple of heavy clunkers, probably for the external locks on the big, sliding airplane doors; two small keys, serrated on both edges, that might have been for the control panels on the elevators; a jangle of mass-produced junk to open the restrooms and so forth; and three much lighter and more complicated items, delicate little masterpieces of obsessive-compulsive skill designed to conquer some truly hairy locks. They were made in Des Moines, Iowa, by a firm called Mul-T-Key and were impossible to duplicate unless you had so much money you could afford the cutting-edge stamping and industrial molding machinery necessary to the task, plus the programming software and its manufacturing interface, in which case it would be simpler for you just to buy the building the locks were keeping you out of. No serrations, just a pattern of dimples on one flat surface, plus a tiny blue button that sent an electronic signal to the lock that the key it was about to receive was the real thing and it should extend its little metal hand for a shake. Even if someone could replicate the dimples, if they didn't also have the key's unique remote signal, the lock would persist in denying entry even to the most skilled of us.

Looking at the external locks on Gabriel's doors, I'd expected something very much on that end of the difficulty scale, and here they were: three Mul-T-Keys, the *open sesame* to Gabriel's.

And then my heart slowed and the hair on my arms stood up. Something had *changed*. It was nothing I could identify, not an identifiable noise, which would have snagged my attention the instant I heard it, but an alteration in the mall's soundscape. My ears actually popped, as though the pressure had dropped. I went to my hands and knees and scrambled to the solid railing on the walkway, where I'd be invisible to anyone who wasn't up on the third level and coming straight at me, and then I held my breath, totally concentrated on listening. When I didn't hear anything new, anything that suggested movement, I began trying to summon up the components of the mix I'd heard the *first* time I listened, and when I had it, I relaxed. The forced-air heating had finally cut out.

Still, I waited. As far as I knew, I was the only person in the place, but being wrong about that could be disastrous. I gave it a count of twenty, heard nothing, and then, figuring discretion was the better part of valor, began to crawl toward the doors to Gabriel's.

I got there and then sat, my knees drawn up and my gloves filthy, breathing the way Herbie taught me, the quietest way. I wasn't particularly afraid of anyone hearing me in that vast space, but I didn't want the sound of my breathing to prevent *me* from hearing someone else.

Zero. Just the building's own sounds as it shivered in the cooling night air, the traffic from the 101—and beginning as I sat there—a pattering sound that I identified as rain falling on the roof about twenty-five feet above me. It wasn't helpful, but there wasn't anything I could do about it so I just focused again on establishing a new sonic "normal," and when I thought I had it, I pulled myself to my feet and looked down.

The mall looked different empty.

Below me and about twenty feet out was the red-and-green throne occupied during business hours by Dwayne Wix. It was centered at one end of a long, once-white carpet, now bisected by a grimy trail left by hundreds and hundreds of kids' shoes. The white, meant to suggest snow, frothed up around the sides and the back of the throne in a sorry attempt at snowdrifts. Even from here I recognized the not-very-special effect as puffed-up cotton from big rolls used for upholstery or padding. It was hard to believe it would fool anyone—it could have been mounds of mashed potatoes for all the cold it suggested—but the same treatment framed Shlomo's throne at the other end of the mall, and I'd seen kids look at it with the wide eyes you sometimes see in Flemish religious paintings on the faces of people who are witnessing a miracle. Maybe the snow was more convincing on Shlomo's end just because it was Shlomo who was sitting on that throne, and he had some of Santa's spirit.

As I searched for other interesting things to ponder, I had

to admit to myself that I really wasn't all that eager to reenter the dark, chilly murder scene that was Gabriel's second floor.

So I decided instead to take a slow circuit of the mall on the third level, committing the landscape to memory. When I got back to my starting point, I took the stairs down to the second level and did another circuit. Even empty, the place smelled of people: wet cloth, underarms, the stuff on the soles of their shoes. Smells of life, not particularly seductive, but nothing to turn up your nose at either.

I took a last sniff and turned to face the doors leading into Gabriel's. First, I took a picture of the left pair of doors with my cell phone so I could duplicate the way the cops had put up their crime scene tape when it was time to reseal the doors. Then I peeled the LAPD tape away, rolling it up with the adhesive on the inside so I wouldn't inadvertently leave it sticking to something, which had actually happened to the aforementioned Chrysanthemum Paige, she of the tiny keys: a big wad of crime scene tape stuck to the inside of the front door of the house she was in. She hadn't gone to jail for it, but it was squeaky there for a few hours because the cops had come back while she was still inside, and the first thing they saw when they went in, naturally, was that melon of tape right next to the indoor handle. She got out, but I don't want to slow things down by telling you how. Also, some day I might want to use it myself.

I pushed the little blue button on the first of the three keys and inserted it into the lock on the left-hand door, but there was no give. Since there were three keys and Gabriel's had originally occupied three floors, I had assumed that each key would open all four doors on its corresponding floor. My which-key, which-door theory was an assumption, however, and Herbie had always insisted that "assumption" was a synonym for "suicide," so I used the same key on the very next door, and it worked. As I pulled it open, just wide enough to slip through sideways, I wondered whether this was some kind of impenetrable subtlety or just old-fashioned sloppiness, installing the lock in the wrong place. If it was sloppiness, it was consistent with how overwhelmingly third-rate the rest of the place was.

It was as dark inside as the service entrance to hell. I eased the door closed behind me, one-handed to make sure it didn't slam, and heard it snick into place. From this side it opened with nothing more complicated than a hip-high pressure bar that would be hit by anyone trying to push his or her way out, as Mini-me had done. Ease of escape was, I remembered, a fire department requirement.

I had let in some light when I opened the door, and that would have attracted the attention of anyone who might possibly be inside, so I slowly edged six or eight feet to my right and then put both hands in front of me and took a few blind steps forward. My fingers hit the corner of a counter, so I moved farther right with my gloved hand on the glass, and then I waited again.

The rain was coming down a little harder, but other than that, the husk of Gabriel's department store was almost entirely quiet. I moved a few yards farther from the doorway, the last place that anyone inside could have seen me, and then I counted silently to a hundred. I used the time to listen and to orient myself.

The aisle in front of me ran all the way to the back of the store. Either it or its twin to the right was the one where I'd tripped Mini-me. That meant that the escalator was ahead of me and to the right, about two-thirds of the way to the far end of the store. I started to move, and when I'd gone just about the distance I'd calculated, I saw the faint nimbus of light coming up through the escalator opening from the all-night illumination in the bazaar down below. I kept sliding my feet over the carpet until I was about even with the escalator, and waited again.

Other than making sure I wasn't walking into the jaws of death, the thing that interested me most at that moment was the possibility that there was *another* way to get into Gabriel's, in addition to the doors and the escalator. Before I entered the mall for the first time, I'd driven three or four circles around it. This is always a good idea when it's possible to do it in advance of a job, because one thing you want to do is to locate all the possible exits before you're inside and you need one. I'd seen a loading dock at each end of the mall, which would make sense, since the two anchor outlets, the stores that had the most merchandise and were paying the most rent, were right there. And where there's a loading dock in a multistory structure, there's an elevator.

So I kept heading toward the rear of the store, but as the light from the escalator faded behind me, I asked myself whether I wanted to take a look at the third floor, which I'd never seen. I answered myself in the affirmative and hung a U toward the escalator that would take me up there. The night lights down in the bazaar were nowhere near as bright as they'd been during business hours, but they'd still pose a danger to any unfriendly presence whose eyes had grown accustomed to the darkness: they'd see a vague silhouette, a moving black cutout, when the light was behind me. So I turned left and went farther into the store, then made a right all the way to the wall behind the escalator so it would never be behind me. At the wall I stopped and waited and listened yet again, and again came up with nothing.

The escalator was still awkward because I couldn't see the variations in the height of the steps, and when I finally got to the top I felt a cool slickness on my face that meant I'd popped a sweat, either from exertion or tension. I mopped my face with my sleeve as I did the noise survey again, this time over the beating of my heart. The rain was louder up here, directly beneath the structure's roof, and it was augmented by some hollow plopping sounds that suggested leaks dripping onto carpet, so I adjusted for that. When I was comfortable with what I was and wasn't hearing, I headed to my right, toward the back of the store, in pitch darkness. It was clear sailing until I blundered noisily into something big and heavy with a sharp edge at shin level. I dropped to my knees, pressing my hand—which was already bandaged from cutting myself on the broken glass of the second-floor counter—to my shin in case it was bleeding, and waited to see what, if anything, the noise shook loose.

No bang, no flash of light, no bullet whizzing over my head. The response, in other words, was exactly what you'd expect from a large room full of inanimate objects. I pulled out the penlight and aimed it at my shin. It was bruised and already swelling, but not bleeding.

What I'd knocked over was a wheeled trolley on which clothing had once hung. I pointed the light at the floor and angled my way toward the rear wall.

To my left, the penlight's gleam brought into vivid relief the Christmas decorations of a year ago. Chains of red paper hung dustily over the counters. A couple of small, skeletal evergreens, now a forlorn, bare-branched brown and surrounded by the confetti of their fallen needles, gleamed with ornaments of red and green, the ancient colors of the holly and the pine that had been brought indoors in cold European

climates for hundreds of years—*before* the season was given
to Christmas—as part of an ancient celebration of light that
marked the shortening of the winter nights and the approach
of spring. Here and there, as I'd seen on the second floor,
hung color photos of Gabriel's employees, mostly women,
wearing Santa hats and even a few jokey beards, happy to
have a job and obviously unaware that the ax was already
in mid-fall.

I wondered where they were now.

This had been one of Gabriel's many clothing departments. Wall-mounted racks that had once held long coats
or dresses glinted in the light's beam, and more naked mannequins stood awkwardly wherever they'd been abandoned
in the aisles, looking plucked and cold. At some point after
the space was abandoned, someone with an unsophisticated
sense of humor and not much sexual experience had arranged
several of them in awkward, risqué tableaux, unintentionally
creating a new-to-me category: slapstick porn. It was especially ugly in the context of the smiling, open gazes in the
photographs, and I found it so offensive that I kicked one of
the sapphic threesomes over as I passed it. The mannequins
made more noise than I would have thought possible when
they racketed to the floor.

Acting on reflex, I snapped the penlight off. Just before
darkness reclaimed the space, I spotted the curtained
entrance to a fitting area where customers could try stuff on,
and I pushed the curtain aside and let it drop behind me, then
turned around and pulled it aside an inch or so to get a look
at nothing at all. I realized I was holding my breath and let
it out slowly.

As long as I was back here—a natural hiding place if I
ever saw one—I paced it off and found four changing rooms

containing nothing but bare benches and wall-mounted hooks. When I'd exhausted the scant possibilities, I went back out and passed the penlight over the back wall. It held a door in it marked NO ADMITTANCE, which seemed promising.

The entire doorknob had been removed, so all I had to do was push.

The opening door revealed a dreary, bare-bones space big enough to hold cartons of merchandise, extra display fixtures, two horrible little bathrooms with coffee-colored water in the toilet bowls, and, at the very back, a wall into which were set two double-wide freight elevators. Dead center between them was the conventional panel with call buttons. I looked longingly at them for a moment as I tried to feel secure in the certainty that I was alone in the mall, and then I thought what the hell; if the clatter of the mannequins hadn't brought anyone, there was probably no one to bring. I pushed the UP button and waited, and nothing happened. Either the power to the elevators had been cut or the buttons had been rendered inoperable. I tried the two elevator keys but neither of them would turn.

I pushed the buttons again. They felt stiff to the touch, as though they'd been monkeyed with, perhaps glued in position, which was probably the cheapest way to shut them down and keep Gabriel's from using them when the store skipped.

Okay. Barring any other access as yet undiscovered, that meant that both Bonnie and her killer had come in through the doors on the second or third floor—certainly the second in Bonnie's case, because that's where her store was and also where she'd been killed. I took a quick five minutes just moving around the big, dark interior without seeing anything that engaged my attention, so I returned to the escalator and walked back down to the second floor.

Here again, the back wall had a NO ADMITTANCE door with the knob assembly thoughtfully removed, and once again the buttons on the elevator didn't work. I blew it off and headed straight across the store toward the rest of mall, but didn't make it. As little as I wanted to revisit the spot where Bonnie had died, and as convinced as I was that the cops would have taken away anything that might have told the story of how it happened, I knew I had to take a look. When I was there, I turned the penlight back on. The cops had left a couple of unplugged standing lights, announcing their intention to come back tomorrow, and fingerprint powder had been scattered on the glass countertops. When I'd found her behind the counter, her body had absorbed all my attention. I hadn't looked at anything else.

The counters described a long, shallow U with a vertical display wall at its center and just enough room between the wall and the counters, maybe two and a half feet, for the employees to move easily. I'd seen Bonnie's feet first, extending from the end of the row of counters where I'd tripped Mini-me, and I hadn't even glanced at the countertop that defined the U. Now, though, I could see that it was *marked* somehow, an asymmetric scrawl of some kind, so I turned and took the long way around to get a look without having to walk over the place where Bonnie had lain.

The countertop had been written on, in shaky, irregular letters big enough to read from five feet away. I beamed the light on it directly, but it wasn't necessary: I'd already recognized the rusty brown of dried blood. The word scrawled on the counter was STOP.

24
So Oblique As to Be Formless

To get in, both Bonnie and her killer had needed a key to Gabriel's.

The issues that occupied my mind as I stood outside the doors and painstakingly matched Amazon's crime tape to the picture I'd taken with my phone were, in order: What were they doing in there? Where did they get these very specialized keys? And, obviously, who else had one?

These were not idle questions, even from what I presumed was Vlad's point of view. It seemed literally impossible to me that Bonnie's murder wasn't connected to the thefts I was being compelled to investigate.

And, of course, there was another issue: What did STOP mean? I was making the assumption that the person who killed Bonnie had meant the word to be read by whoever the message was aimed at, but it was his or her bad luck that a detail like a message scrawled in blood at a murder site is precisely the kind of thing cops keep to themselves.

Was it possible that the murder had essentially been intended as a sensational way to *get* someone to read the message? If so, whom?

I was getting a headache, which usually means *not enough information.*

So back to the keys. The killer had a key.

It took me all of three minutes, down on the ground floor, to figure out which retail slot was number one, a small space just beside the northern entrance, first on the right as the customers came in through that door. Its name was Interior Harmony and it sold stuff that wasn't as consequential as furniture or as trivial as bric-a-brac: throw pillows, huge vases with dry reeds and other weedy stuff sticking out of them, display bowls, "area rugs" (although it's hard to think of a use for a rug that doesn't involve an area), fancy table linens—the kind of merchandise Kathy used to bring home, as proudly as though she'd shot it in the wild, and for which I quickly learned to feign enthusiasm.

Under the counter: nothing. The cash register needed a code, but it was thoughtfully written on the front of the drawer, and there was no key inside the drawer. In a small metal box sitting beside the cash register but below the surface of the counter, making it an awkward reach for customers or shoplifters, I found keys on a ring smaller than Wally's, painstakingly labeled. *Bathroom (ladies)*, *Bathroom (gentlemen)*, *Locker*, and a few that were unidentified and had that dull, rejected look keys get when people have forgotten what they open but can't bring themselves to toss them out because they might someday open the door to the future. I pawed through all the keys on the ring, put it back and looked for more, but found nothing that would give the Interior Harmonizers access to Gabriel's.

Next to Interior Harmony was iShop, the store where I got the find-your-phone doodads for Rina, plus the brush-off about directions for using them from the kid named Wink, who had a teenager's face and a curly halo of grey hair. Wink's cash register was probably supposed to be ironic, one of the old mechanical ones with a bell that rings when you pop open the cash drawer, which had nothing in it, not even cash. Three keys hung on a hook beneath the counter, nothing dangling from it that raised my pulse rate. I'd had hopes for old Wink because these were high-tech keys, but no go.

So it went throughout the first floor: search, don't find, go away. A depressing sequence for a burglar, but even negative information is information. As I climbed the stairs, I said aloud, "Nobody on the ground floor." I've learned, in a long life of being puzzled, that the simple act of stating aloud the piece that seems odd will often send out a little mental golden retriever who may very well show up with a connected piece of data dangling from its jaws. In this case what the retriever fetched was so obvious I'd walked right around it. There were *no doors to Gabriel's* on the ground floor. They'd been pulled out to let people stream in and out of the bazaar.

I said aloud, "Hmmm."

I was in slot twenty-one, in one of the two stores bordering Gabriel's on the second floor, not far above Dwayne Wix's alcoholic sliver of the cottony North Pole, before I hit it. THE PAPER DOLLS, read the store's modest neon sign, and it sold stationery and other specialty papers, including gift wrap and those interesting, theoretically hand-cut Chinese stencils that look like physical therapy for the detail-obsessed. I'd shopped in there on my first day because Kathy had a soft spot for nice old-timey notebooks, and despite the plural in "Dolls," I'd seen only one woman working there, a notably short, unshakably perky, stylistic anachronism in her cheery sixties who favored sprayed, brutally curled hair from the 1960s and the kind of pantsuits that had disappeared for decades until Hillary Clinton strode onto the world stage. Even her name, Jackie, echoed the sixties, but her key ring featured the very latest in antitheft technology: a Mul-T-Key that was a perfect match to the three on Wally's big ring. Just to make sure, I went about fifteen feet from The Paper Dolls to the set of doors I'd used an hour or so ago to get into Gabriel's, and Jackie's key opened the first door I tried.

I must have been feeling more confident, because I said, out loud, "My, my, my."

As though on cue, the rain increased in volume.

I reversed direction and put Jackie's key back where I'd found it. It was impossible for me to imagine her stabbing anyone, so I kept searching, working my way around the remaining stores on the second floor, skipping Boots to Suits because they had lowered a slatted metal door across their open end. Untrusting bunch.

I'd already pretty much written off Boots to Suits anyway, because they had their own security, presumably more competent than Wally's operation, and they didn't share their internal shoplifting losses, whatever they were, with the crew that supplied Wally with his info. Therefore I had no idea whether they'd been hit as badly as the rest of Edgerton Mall and I couldn't honestly say I cared. When I went in to check on the lunch schedules of their workers, I'd been told, with a certain amount of attitude, that they did not share personal information about their employees. I'd pointed out that I wasn't looking for their prior drug convictions or their immigration papers, just what time they ate lunch on one lousy day, but rules, I'd been informed in a tone that was pure starch, were rules.

So the hell with them. I hoped they were getting the pants stolen off them daily.

The last shop I checked on the second floor—all the way around the oval, facing The Paper Dolls and bordering

Gabriel's—was called Hello, Dalí and the window said it sold large format "Art Prints." Rarely were quotation marks more advisable. In fact some little thug with a glass cutter had cut the letter "F" into the glass in front of the word "Art," and, delinquent or not, the kid had an eye. Lots of melting clocks, enervating Don Quixotes, super-realistic crucifixions, and a full line of the usual suspects: Wyeth's picture of the girl crawling endlessly toward the big house, Burne-Jones's Pre-Raphaelite redheads, even some Calvin and Hobbes, which slowed me down some. Nothing in the front part of the shop, but in the storeroom, just inside the door, a little box with the word KEYS obligingly printed on it was glued to the wall. It was locked, but it was a twee, semimicroscopic lock, and popping it took me less than ten seconds with a pick chosen at random. The Mul-T-Key was the only thing in the box.

I'd finished the second floor and found only two of the keys I sought, but there had been a few cash registers I couldn't open and a couple of safes. I've got some rote knowledge of safes, but get me away from the three or four models I know and I'm a duffer, so I didn't even try. I stood outside the door of Hello, Dalí, sighed heavily, and checked my watch. A little after midnight. I thought again about my decision to write off the bazaar. Since I had acres of time to fill before the cleaning crew came in, I shuffled back down the stairs and went into the area that had once been Gabriel's ground floor.

It was kind of spooky, to tell the truth. Most of the vendors who set up the booths—almost always one person per booth, as Amanda had said—closed up by the simple expedient of covering the goods for sale with a drop cloth, so the room looked like the Ghost of Retail Past, sale table after sale table decked out in pale sheets or cheap blankets.

Probably half the objects in the room had passed through

the hands of dead people, people who had died on every continent and over a considerable period of time. And here were their spirits, linked in uneasy assemblage by delicate filaments extending from the things they'd owned, an unlikely group of folks from every walk of life, most of whom would probably have nothing to say to the others even if they'd all spoken the same language. A dud party. I've often thought that people with genuine spiritual powers must be gobsmacked—once they finesse their way through all the ectoplasmic woo-woo and make contact with the silent majority—by how prosaic, how just plain *dull*, most of the dead probably are. Why should people become more interesting when they die than they'd been when they were alive? *Visit the haunted house,* the sign outside the theme park ride should say, *but bring a good book because you'll be bored half to death.*

At the table where the kid had sold me the signed copy of *At Play in the Fields of the Lord,* I peeled back the sheet and found a really clean first edition/first printing of *The Wapshot Chronicles,* signed by John Cheever, in its original dust jacket, looking quite sprightly for its sixty-plus years, and worth quite a bit. The signed copies you see most often are a fancy-shmancy reprinted, leather-bound "Franklin Center" edition from the late 1970s, which I think Cheever signed in exchange for a fat stack of dough. These days copies of that edition, published by the same Franklin Mint people who usually specialized in "collectable" commemorative coins, plates ornamented with pictures of recently dead movie star "icons," Princess Diana with songbirds perched on her fingers, and other kitsch, went for multiple hundreds. An actual first like this one, signed, was worth a *lot* more. So Cheever was somewhere in the room, too, probably with a drink in one hand and a cigarette in the other, looking for a

corner where he could be alone with a potted plant. I stood
there paging through the book, finding the telltales that said
it was the real thing and thinking about just toting it away
with me, but at the last moment, I put it back.

Didn't seem right to steal it, what with Christmas right
around the corner. I gave myself an A for virtue and another
one for guile because I'd probably get it cheap out of Gramps's
house before New Year's.

Okay, back to the keys.

Up on the third level, smaller and with fewer shops because
the building tapered as it rose, I found no Mul-T-Keys behind
any of the counters in the first six shops I went into. But then,
in the cash register of Time Remembered, a teensy stall that
sold cheap knockoff watches plus a few very nice old ones,
I found a third key beneath a litter of quarters in the cash
register. I trotted next door to the doors into Gabriel's, and
the first door I tried opened as easily as if I'd been a djinn
with the magic password. The owner of Time Remembered, I
recalled, was a very thin, very nervous guy in his mid-forties
named Milt who wore enormously thick glasses and whom I
had seen in the food court chewing alternately on his lunch
and his cuticles.

Nothing else on that side of the third floor.

My eyes were beginning to feel sandy, and I caught myself
in the middle of a huge yawn that probably could have been
heard in the parking lot. One forty-seven, so I'd lost a little
time in the bazaar. The cleaning crew arrived, I'd been told,
at seven or seven-thirty every morning, although it wasn't
easy to find anything that looked like it had been tidied up
lately.

The other reason the third level offered fewer hiding places
than the others was that Boots to Suits, which must have

been doing well *somewhere*, if not actually here, had conquered and occupied four more stores, two on each side, and had moved their slatted metal barrier outward to demarcate and defend their new border. This was the cheapest floor, in keeping with the mathematical formula that priced square feet mainly on how close they were to the entrances and the food, and also on whether they were on the way to or from a big attraction that would build foot traffic. This level had several abandoned shops with windows displaying dead flies rather than merchandise.

The rain was really slamming down by now, and without the carpets that Gabriel's had put down, the sound was magnified. I'd dismissed any thought that I might have company in here, but the sheer volume of the rain made me nervous enough to hurry things along so I could get someplace where I wasn't so exposed.

A shoe store called Ankles Away, nothing. Nautical junk shop called Ships Ahoy! that catered to people who either owned boats or wanted other people to think they did, nothing. Nothing in the shuttered storefront where the lettering had been scraped off the window, but not well enough to conceal the words Different Smokes for Different Folks, probably once an all-tobacco emporium, maybe with an ancillary line in chewing tobacco and spittoons, all now a fading memory in the culture's rearview mirror. A future anthropologist, I decided—since I had nothing much else to think about—would be able to assess cross sections of buried shopping malls the way biologists did with redwood trees, to trace the ebb and flow of cultural variables like permissiveness, health-consciousness, conspicuous consumption, the global exchange of goods, and so forth.

It made me yawn again.

But it also woke me up a little, because when I begin to drift off like that, wandering toward the foothills of irrelevance, it often means that another part of my brain is actually working on something and is trying to divert me from paying attention while it does its stuff. Whole areas of my mind, I have come to realize, distrust other areas.

So leave it alone. Don't bother it. Be mechanical. Open doors. Look for keys.

The last three stores on the floor were a former Sunglass Shack, now empty; an off-brand makeup store called KissyFace; and, bordering Gabriel's, Sam's Saddlery. The Sunglass Shack smelled of dust and mice. In welcome contrast, KissyFace smelled of every cut-rate fragrance molecule on the planet, and, for a brief moment after I went in, I imagined bringing Stinky here to see which molecules he could identify. This thought, both improbable and uninteresting, was a dead giveaway that searching a bunch of shops for keys was not quite enough to keep the mind alive, but just as I reached that conclusion I realized that if I gave the drawer of KissyFace's cash register a sharp tug upward when it was wide open, I could pull it all the way out. So I did, and there was another Mul-T-Key, its metal dimples gleaming coyly at me.

"Well, you little dickens," I said to the key, and the name brought back the taste of Bonnie's hot spiced wine, lifted straight out of *The Pickwick Papers*, and the sense I'd had of someone who, when she looked around at the shop and the life she'd created, knew perfectly well that it would all vanish as though they'd always really been smoke.

I had liked her quite a lot.

I walked past Sam's Saddlery and tried the Mul-T-Key in the right-hand door into Gabriel's. It worked its magic, so I went back and returned it to its fragrant hiding place at Kis-syFace, slotted the drawer, and closed it again. Then I stood there, staring down at the counter feeling as limp and unen-gaged as a flag on a windless day. I was so distracted that I closed the door of KissyFace and then realized I'd left Wally's keys in there on the counter, so I picked the lock, trudged back inside, and got them.

I went next door to Sam's and, barely registering what I was doing, shoved the next key on Wally's keychain into the lock. It didn't work. Distracted as I was, I concluded that I'd grabbed the wrong key. I pulled it out of the lock, looked at it—right number—and inserted it again. It went in without a hitch or a snag, but when I tried to turn it, it wouldn't budge

I did the whole thing again with the same result. Then I reread the number scrawled on the square of tape, recounted the stores on this level, and came out even. This should be slot thirty-seven. The key was marked 37. So far, so good. But.

So Sam had changed his lock, and Wally hadn't gotten the new—

When I thought the name *Wally*, I felt a tug on a line I didn't even know I'd been holding, as though a very small fish had just taken its first experimental sniff at the bait.

I realized I was at the elevator. Not even knowing whether it was on, I pushed the call button and got a reassuring hum from below.

I leaned against the wall beside the elevator doors, inten-tionally putting my mind on idle and waiting for the rest of the thought to show up, whatever it was. Then I went over to the railing and stared down at the lower levels, and at that very moment the rain stopped. The silence was almost startling. I gazed down, trying to remember anything I'd seen that would make possible, or even be consistent with, the idea that seemed to be going through my mind. I heard the elevator doors open behind me.

An uneventful ride took me to the ground floor, dim without most of the overheads, and growing cool and damp. The warmest place to sit, it seemed to me, was Shlomo's throne, so I climbed up the two steps and lowered myself into it. For a bony guy, he didn't demand much padding from a chair.

When something hits me like this, so oblique as to be formless, the best thing is to leave it alone. Look in the other direction, so to speak. So I leaned back in Shlomo's lumpy Santa throne and listened in my mind to act two of his story.

25
The Badge *Rouge*

As he eased the barn door closed, Morris heard laughter. It was muffled, but it was laughter. It seemed like a long time since he'd heard anyone laugh without a hushed or bitter edge on it.

The laughter had come from the little house, twenty or thirty foggy yards from the barn. The yellow light in the window drew him even as he realized that the smartest thing to do would be to put the lamp out. As he took the one step up onto the porch, the laughter rumbled and crested again, but when he knocked, it stopped instantly. He heard movement inside.

A full minute passed before the door cracked open to reveal a stooped man in suspenders and a loose linen shirt. Even through an opening no more than six inches wide, Morris could smell food cooking. Morris said, *"Bonsoir,"* and then, in the French he had heard spoken his entire life in Canada, *"Joyeux Noël."*

The little man's eyes dropped to Morris's uniform and he nodded and backed away, opening the door farther. It hit something solid, and Keystone stepped out from behind it, holstering the Remington Rand .45 caliber automatic they all carried. "Done?" Keystone said.

"As you see," Morris said. His dog tags were out of sight beneath his tunic, which he'd buttoned almost to the throat. "Guess what? I finally got my induction notice." Keystone, who knew the story of Morris's multiple attempts to enlist, gave him a grin.

The room was obviously the center of the farm's domestic life. On the small rectangular table in front of the window burned the kerosene lantern. There was a small divan, its two cushions shedding stuffing material, against the wall, with a single upholstered chair between it and the table. Beyond that, in the far-right corner, was a kitchen with a wood-burning stove as well as a counter that contained basins for washing dishes, a rack for drying them, several stacks of heavy plates and bowls, and a tin box full of cutlery.

The place smelled like heaven: steam rose from a big pot on the stove, carrying with it the scents of herbs and garlic. The left side of the room was largely taken up by an unfinished round wooden table with three candles burning on it and six cane-seated chairs drawn up to it. Keystone's and Sabathia's rifles stood sentry duty behind the table, leaning against a rough-plastered wall. Sabby came in from somewhere to the left, so apparently there was a hallway there. He was using a crude cane, too short for him, but it let him ease the weight on the sprained ankle. "You made it," he said.

"It wasn't that far."

"This is Claude," Sabby said, nodding at the man who had opened the door. "And the wizard of the stove, who is down the hallway, doing something—"

"She is make dress for dinner," said Claude from the kitchen. He had picked up a broad wooden spoon and was stirring whatever was in the pot.

Keystone said, "What kind of M-units you got?"

Morris didn't even have to check. "Ham and lima beans, mystery meat and noodles."

"Chocolate?"

"Got some."

"Put it all on the table with ours. They have in the oven—hold onto something so your knees don't buckle—a chicken, can you believe that? An actual goddamn chicken."

"Is a *coq*," Claude, tasting the liquid in the spoon.

Keystone, pulling up the chair beside Sabathia, said, "Don't have a heart attack. It just means—"

"I know what it means," Morris said. At the stove, Claude was laughing.

"*Madame* Loiseau," Sabby said, "is going to make something, something *French*, out of this canned crap we been hauling around. We're gonna have a real, honest-to-Christ Christmas dinner, can you believe that?"

Claude—or, rather, Morris thought, M. Loiseau—put the spoon down and turned to face them. "If come the *Boche*—mmm, *les allemandes*—"

"The Krauts," Sabby said.

"Yes, *merci*, if come the Krauts, you must all point the guns at us, at Hélène and me, yes?"

"Yes," Sabby said. "We busted in and took you prisoner. Nothing you could do about it . . ."

"I am sorry," M. Loiseau said. "For Christmas, we should not . . ." He let his voice taper off, and then he shrugged.

"It's a war," Keystone said. He had a deep, resonant voice that after all that time on the battlefield seemed too big to be brought indoors. Keystone evidently heard it, because he grimaced and said much more quietly, "We thank you."

"I think," Morris said, "that we should take the lamp out of the window."

"Yes, yes, yes." M. Loiseau put down the spoon and replaced the lid on the pot. "This is a good idea." On the way to the table, he caught his toe on a small oval hand-braided rug halfway between the kitchen area and the front door. "Always," he said, with a quick glance down at it, "always I am making myself trip here."

"Want me to move it?" Morris asked.

"*Non, non,*" M. Loiseau said, picking up the lantern. "Under we have . . ." He put the lantern back on the table and used his right hand to mime hammering a nail. Then he held up his thumb and forefinger half an inch apart and said, "Stick up."

From the unseen part of the house, which Morris guessed comprised a short hallway leading to a small bedroom, came a tiny woman carrying a thick towel. She was making a straight line for the kitchen, but she threw a quick, bright-eyed look at Morris and then faltered for a moment when she registered where her husband was standing. "Claude," she said and followed it with a short sentence in French that was very much in the imperative, too fast for Morris to follow, and her husband nodded quickly, placed the lantern on the table, and said to Morris and the others, "More wood." He went outside, disappearing almost instantly in a thick wreath of fog.

"*Bonsoir*, Madame Loiseau," Morris said. "*Joyeux Noël.*"

"Yes," the tiny woman said. She forced a smile, but her eyes darted to her left, in the direction she had come from, before they returned to him. She wore a formless parchment-colored dress, probably yellow many years ago, and a violet shawl with fringe from which the dye had been leached unevenly, turning bits of it an unappealing pink. Covering her hands with the towel, she picked up the simmering pot and moved it to the back of the stove and then turned to face him. "This," she said, pointing imperiously at the canned rations on the table. "This is food?"

"Manner of speaking," Keystone said, and Mme. Loiseau said, *"Pardon?"*

"Sorry," Keystone said. "Yes, ma'am, it's food."

Since Morris hadn't sat down yet, he said, "I'll bring it over," and stacked the three tins so he could lift them all at once. Mme. Loiseau squinted dubiously at the tins as he approached, then stepped aside and indicated a relatively empty area on the scarred wooden counter. "Here's how you open it," he said, and when he'd snapped off the little key and unwound the strip of tin that sealed the can, Mme. Loiseau picked it up between thumb and forefinger, her other fingers spread wide as though to avoid contact with the tin, and took a halfhearted sniff. Instantly, her entire face screwed up and she straightened the arm with the tin in it to get it as far from her as she could without actually throwing it. Her other hand came up to her mouth. All three men burst into laughter, and they were still laughing when the door opened and M. Loiseau came in with an armload of wood, shushing them even as he himself began to laugh at the expression on his wife's face.

"Eating this," Mme. Loiseau said, "you can *win*, eating this?"

"We can try," Keystone said, and then he started laughing again.

"Well." Mme. Loiseau put it down and stood, hands on hips, staring down at the tins of rations. "If I can cook turnips twelve nights in a row, I can cook this." She undid another tin, sniffing it this time from eight or ten inches away. "I have onions," she said. "I have garlic. I have rosemary." She put the tin down and said to the soldiers, "I promise you. You will *not* smell this."

They'd eaten a few bites of *almost* everything—the mystery meat, which Mme. Loiseau had identified as *"la viande de cheval"* and Morris had translated as "horse meat"—defied improvement, but the chicken, which they'd just cut into, was perfect (if tough) and the other M-rations had gone into Mme. Loiseau's stew without, as she said, *absolutely* destroying it. Mme. Loiseau was once again in the back bedroom, which she'd visited several times, always coming back wiping her hands on the white dress and looking worried.

M. Loiseau had pulled the cork from an unlabeled bottle of earthy-tasting red wine and was raising his glass and saluting the holiday again when the front door flew open, just missing Morris in his chair. Four German troops pushed their way in, rifles pointing directly at Morris, Keystone, Sabathia, and M. Loiseau.

"All hands on the table," said the heavyset, red-faced soldier in the lead, whose left sleeve bore the single green stripe of an *Unteroffizier,* the German Army's lowest-ranking sergeant. He registerd the empty hands and jerked his gun toward the ceiling. "Up," he said in English. "Everyone up." He stepped farther into the room, the others crowding behind him. "Put the bottle down, old man." His English was accented but serviceable.

They all rose, hands uplifted. One of the German privates, a boy still in his teens, pulled the door partway closed, saw the rifles standing against the wall, and said something in German to the sergeant.

The sergeant's reply was also in German, but the meaning was clear: he motioned the young private to take the weapons out onto the porch. As the boy complied, the sergeant said, "Hands on heads. *Now.* Not you, old man. Who else is here?"

"My wife," M. Loiseau said. "My daughter. She is ill, my daughter. Are you hungry?"

"We will eat," the sergeant said, "in a few minutes." He waved the other two soldiers, one heavy and balding prematurely, the other thin and sharp-featured, toward the hallway. Both men, rifles still extended, took their first steps, then stopped simultaneously.

"Oh," Mme. Loiseau said, coming into the room. She stopped, took in the two armed men in front of her, and said, "More guests. *Joyeux Noël.*" There was a quaver in her voice that brought home to Morris the fact that they could all die in this room: he, Sabby, Keystone, and the Loiseaus.

"Stay there," the sergeant said to Mme. Loiseau. "My men will check the rest of the house. Who else is here?"

"Our daughter," Mme. Loiseau said. "She is, she is ill."

The sergeant motioned the two waiting privates forward, and Mme. Loiseau watched them go with her fingertips pressed to her mouth. The young German private who had taken the rifles out onto the porch was just coming back in, and the sergeant said to him, "Schmidt. Take their sidearms." Schmidt, looking slightly panicked, approached them as though they were mined.

There were noises from the back of the house. "Please," Mme. Loiseau said, "it is only my daughter. She is not well."

"Schmidt," the sergeant snapped. *"Get their guns."* They all kept their hands on their heads as Schmidt relieved them of their sidearms. The boy's uniform was too big for him. His cheeks were pink with either cold or embarrassment, and up close, Morris could see that he wasn't yet shaving.

More noise from the hallway announced the reemergence

of the two soldiers, looking more relaxed. One of them said, "*Ein Mädchen,*" and the sergeant nodded as the young soldier, Schmidt, took Keystone's automatic.

Morris breathed in the aroma of the food and felt the room's warmth, which until then he hadn't really noticed. He thought, *We probably won't live through dinner,* and, feeling a gaze, looked up to see the sergeant regarding him, his mouth pulled slightly to the left.

Morris said, "We were—" and his voice broke. He swallowed and said, "about to eat, we were about to—"

"I can see that," the sergeant said. At that moment, Schmidt, who was trying to carry three automatics, dropped one with a bang and emitted a little sound that sounded to Morris like the German version of *eeek.* Everybody jumped a little. Schmidt threw an anxious glance at the sergeant, bent with a grunt to pick up the dropped weapon, and then stopped at the door, since he had no free hands. The sergeant shook his head slowly and pulled the door open, and Schmidt, going through it, apparently forgot about the step down because he dropped about six inches and landed with a thump and an "Ooof." The sergeant let the door swing closed on the boy, blew out some air, and said in a half-whisper, "*Scheisskopf.*" One of his men, the plump one, smothered a laugh.

"My wife," M. Loiseau said, with courage that flooded Morris with shame, "wished you a merry Christmas."

"Yes, yes," the sergeant said. "*Frohe Weihnachten,* merry Christmas, *joyeux Noël,* however you want to say it. Now be still until Schmidt gets back."

"If he doesn't get lost," Keystone said, and the plump soldier laughed again and the sharp-featured one followed suit and then looked up quickly to see the sergeant glaring at him, but then the sergeant laughed, too, and at that moment it seemed to Morris that the flames on the candles, which had been flickering in the draft from the door, were suddenly burning straighter and brighter. And then Sabathia began to laugh as well, and M. Loiseau said, "Please, *Unteroffizier*, send one of your men back to the kitchen with me so he can guard me while I can get some more glasses and another bottle of wine."

The sergeant took a slow look around the room, his eyes slowing when they reached Morris, and then he said to the plump soldier, "Go with him."

Twenty minutes later they were all sitting around the table and some German rations had been scrambled together, heavily seasoned, doused with wine, and left to simmer on the stove. Since there were only six dining chairs for nine people, M. and Mme. Loiseau shared one, the sharp-featured private was jammed very uncomfortably next to Morris on a chair with one short leg that rocked every time either man shifted his weight, and the *Unteroffizier*, whose uniform announced his name as Autenburg, had pulled up the upholstered chair that had previously been at the table in front of the window. It was the most comfortable but it was also lower than the others, which would have had a slightly comic effect—Autenburg's blunt, bright red, mercilessly shaved face at a child's height above the food—if it hadn't been for the sight of his gun on the table next to his plate. It was the sole weapon in sight, although the German privates all still had their sidearms in their holsters. All the Americans' weapons were outside on the porch, but Morris knew that Keystone kept a little two-shot Derringer .38 in his boot.

Autenburg drained his second glass of wine and put it down. "We were winning," he said in his deep voice, almost as deep as Keystone's. His left hand held a fork, from which dangled a piece of chicken. Now that he'd lowered his glass, he returned his right hand to the neighborhood of his gun. He wagged his head side to side, an equivocal gesture. "Winning for the moment, at any rate, and they sent us on a flanking maneuver to take out one of your guns, and the fog came in, and we were cut off."

"*Lost.*" Keystone said. "Repeat after me, *lost.*"

"We were *not* lost," Autenburg snapped. "We knew where our troops were. I know exactly where we are now. But there remained the problem of returning to our lines without getting the *Scheisse*—excuse me, Madame—shot out of us. Our men don't like the fog any more than yours do."

"I am getting up now," Mme. Loiseau said, "to check on my daughter and to stir some more seasoning into your horrible food."

"Helmut," Autenburg said. The sharp-featured soldier got up quickly, sending Morris and the chair he'd been sharing with Helmut toppling sideways. Morris hit the floor, hearing the laughter around the table, and brought his eyes up to register that he was inches from a holstered German automatic. He darted a glance upward to meet the eyes of the boy Schmidt, who shook his head urgently, shifted the chair back a few inches, extended a hand, yanked it back, and then held it out again.

"*Danke schön,*" Morris said, getting up.

Autenburg raised his eyebrows in acknowledgment of the German as Mme. Loiseau and Helmut disappeared into the hallway, and Keystone asked him, "Are we in France or Belgium?"

"Belgium is nine or eight kilometers away, and we are in German-occupied France," Autenburg said. His eyes flicked to M. Loiseau, who was staring at the tabletop, his neck stiff and his mouth a straight line. "But it probably will not be so for long."

M. Loiseau sighed, and the heavier of the German privates sighed with him. Werner, his name was, although Morris didn't know whether it was a first or last name.

"You are from where?" Autenburg asked Morris.

"Canada."

Autenburg squinted at something only he could see. "In the north."

M. Loiseau rose, and Autenburg flicked a finger at Werner, who followed. M. Loiseau went into the kitchen, where he bent down and out of sight and, from the sound of it, began to rummage through a cabinet. Werner looked questioningly over the counter at Autenburg and got a peremptory nod in response.

"He's only getting more wine," Sabathia said. He had spoken rarely since the Germans barged in, even as the atmosphere around the table lightened, although he had laughed once or twice. "He's got half a dozen bottles down there."

Autenburg nodded at Sabathia's foot. "Shot?"

Sabathia made a snorting sound. "Sprained. Tripped over a dead guy in the dark."

"Yours or ours?"

Sabathia grimaced, and suddenly Morris could visualize the uniform on the fallen solder who had until then been, to him, only a pair of eyes. Sabathia licked his lips.

"German," Morris said, since no one else volunteered, and for the first time the dead man's face came into focus. "Very young."

Autenburg continued to stare at Sabathia, who was almost squirming, and then brought his eyes slowly to Morris. He wiped his mouth with an open palm as though he'd tasted something bitter. "Yes," he said, with a glance at Schmidt, who was pretending not to listen. "They are sending very young ones now."

From the other side of the counter, where M. Loiseau was struggling with another cork, Werner, who was probably no more than twenty himself said, "Children. They are sending children."

Morris said, without thinking, "*All Quiet on the Western Front.*"

"Yes," Autenburg said. He pushed his plate away with some uneaten chicken on it. Schmidt looked at the remaining bit—most of a wing—longingly. Autenburg pushed the plate over to him. "You have read Remarque?"

"I have," Morris said. "In English."

"A great book," Autenburg said. "Like his soldiers, like Remarque's hero, after the Great War we will have to return home." He touched the barrel of the automatic beside his plate with his forefinger and then pulled his hand back. "If we live through the defeat, we will have to return home. Seeing what we have seen."

From the kitchen, Werner said, "Doing what we have done."

Autenburg blinked heavily in Werner's direction. "This is worse than Remarque's war, the Great War," he said. "I have soldiers who are fifteen, sixteen." He blinked again. "Some maybe younger, but this is what they have been told to say. Fifteen, sixteen."

"Sixteen," Schmidt said with his mouth full, then threw a quick glance at Autenburg and blushed scarlet.

"All war is dreadful," Morris said.

Autenburg said, "And yet you are here. You are Canadian, you did not have to come. Your country did not draft anyone until, what? A month ago? You have read Remarque. You have read—" He paused, evidently searching his mind for something. "The badge, the badge *rouge*—"

"*The Red Badge of Courage.* Yes, I've read it."

"And still you are here. Why?"

Morris had the sensation that the entire room, which seemed to him somehow to have been holding its breath, suddenly rushed at him from all directions until he was alone in a very bright pinpoint of light from a single candle, and there was a sustained note, as though from a violin, in his ears. Swallowing, he tasted Sophie Resnick's bubble gum again and remembered the big table, completely covered by the food for the holiday, and the two of them knotted together in the secret space beneath it. He blinked it all away, heard his heart drumming in his ears, and felt the weight of the dog tags hanging around his neck. It had seemed so simple in the stable to remain who he was, not to accept the disguise Keystone had offered him. But here it was, far too soon, the moment he'd thought wouldn't come. He met Autenburg's eyes and said, "I'm a Jew."

Keystone groaned and Sabby's head snapped around, his mouth open. Autenburg and Morris held each other's eyes as though they were alone in the room, and then Autenburg brought his right hand up to the top of the table and put it on his automatic.

Morris swallowed and said, "You asked." He tapped the pocket of his tunic to show there was nothing hard inside it and then, very deliberately, inserted two fingers and came up with his pack of cigarettes. Feeling Autenburg's gaze, he shook out one for himself and then extended the pack across the table at Autenburg. "Would you like a Jewish cigarette?"

For a moment it seemed as though Autenburg might laugh and accept it, but there was an abrupt jabber in French from the hallway, a woman's voice, some panicked-sounding questions in German, and then a low female wail that scaled up into a shriek. Instantly, all the Germans had their guns in their hands and Autenburg said to the others, "Wait here," and disappeared into the hallway.

Where he was standing, M. Loiseau clasped his hands together at his chest and began to pray aloud.

26
Directly Beneath *Mom*

It was a long way from that French farmhouse in a free-fire zone to Shlomo's vacated Santa throne in the empty Edgerton Mall in the middle of the night.

Shlomo hadn't had time to tell me the third part of the story, the one that, I guessed, would contain the miracle. In its absence, I was too weary and too dispirited to resist seeing the vacant mall as a big, brightly decorated gift box with nothing inside it. Christmas has always seemed to me to be an empty box, a broken promise, to so many people. I see the trees gleaming in people's windows and the commercials designed to make children demand things they don't need, and all I can think of is the other side of the holiday, Christmas as it must seem to the old and the lonely, the disappointed and the displaced, the people whose connections to the world of love and friendship have been cut or worn away, people who lived alone or in loveless relationships or in poverty with young children who would be disappointed by the things the holiday wouldn't or couldn't bring them. Christmas hung in the line of vision of our mind's eye all year long, glittering bright and often empty, way back there in the final pages of the calendar: the last letdown before the theoretically happy New Year, even at the best of times a holiday with a stiff dose of regret. The two of them, the one-two punch at year's end, just when we look back to see how we're doing. Even Scrooge, I thought, had been old and lonely.

My yawn seemed to come all the way from my toes, and it prompted me to look at my watch. Almost three-thirty. Four hours before the cleaners showed up. Time, I thought, to get the video running again so there would be a few hours of nothing happening in case Wally was inclined to start his day with a few minutes' worth of high-speed rewind.

And there it was again: *Wally.*

This time, I knew what the tug was, although I still couldn't see how it could fit in with what I thought I'd seen on my first and second day, or, for that matter, how the whole thing could even be possible. Or how Bonnie's death fit into it. Still, there was one aspect of the situation that pointed obviously and exclusively at Wally, unless someone was doing an extremely sophisticated frame, and nothing about anything that was happening in the little bubble of Edgerton Mall felt very sophisticated.

And I knew one other thing: at 3:30 A.M., Ronnie wasn't doing anything that would keep her from answering the phone, if it was somewhere she could hear it. She might be grumpy about being awakened, but I thought I could endure that without permanent damage, so I dialed her.

I let it ring until her voice mail picked up, and then I hung up and dialed again. This time her voice mail picked up on the second ring. She still wasn't talking to me. If she was even still in Los Angeles.

I tried the landline at the Wedgwood again, just to be thorough, and got a ring that would probably continue until the sun exploded, since I'd never activated any of the answering service options. After twenty-two rings I hung up. There was a cold, leaden lump low in my gut. I had a very bad feeling about this.

But there was nothing I could do about it right then. I was trapped in the mall until morning. On the other hand, I had plenty to do while I was here.

So I got up off Shlomo's throne feeling heavy, eye-scratchingly tired, and sore in spots that were usually immune to soreness, and speculating, as I limped toward the elevator, that Shlomo's Santa suit probably gave him enough padding to sleep comfortably on a bed of nails. Maybe what I needed right now was emotional padding of some kind. Or a radically different kind of life where I had no reason to leave people and they had no reason to leave me.

I glanced at the stairs and thought, the hell with it. I had a brief Brad Pitt moment as I pushed the elevator button and the doors opened for me instantly, the way they only do for the star of a movie. One of the few advantages of being alone in a large, multilevel structure is that the elevators stay where you left them.

On the second level, I made a detour to the employees' dining area and opened the lower door in the condiments station, which housed a large plastic trash can into which people threw their disposable utensils and crumpled paper plates. I tilted the can back a few inches, reached beneath it, and pulled out a few wrinkled pieces of paper: the list Amanda had created to tell me who'd been in the lunchroom while Bonnie was getting stabbed in Gabriel's, plus the notes I'd made about where and when people had *said* they went to lunch. I'd hidden it all there a few hours before closing, when the room was empty, because I didn't want it on me when and if Cranmer returned and he and I bumped into each other, and also because that room, free from

cameras, was one of the few places I could do something fur-
tive without being beneath the gaze of Wally's electric eyes.

Thinking again, *Wally*, I took the stairs to the third level,
my joints still aching, and hiked on down to Wally's surveillance room.

The first thing I did after pulling Wally's chair up to the
console was to restart the video system. The monitors blinked
on in no particular order, the room getting lighter as they
did, and as vista after vista popped on-screen reassuringly
empty, I felt a slight easing of the tension I'd accumulated
during the evening. I'd had occasional *Phantom of the Opera*
moments when it seemed inescapably obvious that the mall
would by now have spawned its own disfigured specter, perhaps someone who was scarred for life and driven mad after
being trampled by Black Friday crowds and had lurked here
in the shadows, probably on the third floor of Gabriel's, ever
since. But if he was out there, he wasn't in camera range.

I pulled open the little cupboard under Wally's end of the
console and shone my light into it. I don't know exactly what
I was hoping to find, but what was there exceeded all reason-
able expectations: a zigzag of perforated graph paper from
an old printer and a little wire-bound appointment book. The
graph paper was what Wally had promised me, a graphic rep-
resentation of the dates the stores were especially crowded
and the shoplifting levels they'd reported each week during
the month just past. I put the graphs aside for the moment
and focused on the appointment book.

It was for 2013, so Wally didn't have a lot of appoint-
ments, but then, neither did I. And I found exactly what I
needed in the section for phone numbers and email addresses.
It was the second entry (directly beneath *Mom*) on the page
reserved for those whose names began with M: *Mul-T-Key,*

it read. *Wendy Straub*. And a phone number, complete with extension. The corner of the page had been folded down to make it easier to locate. But that didn't necessarily mean anything. Maybe he just called his mom a lot.

Close to four A.M. now. Des Moines, where Mul-T-Key was housed, was on Central time, so if the business opened at nine, I could put in a call a little after seven.

I squeezed my eyes closed and rubbed them with my palms, producing a nice display of retinal fireworks, and then, for a change of pace, I rubbed at the bridge of my nose while I looked at the factors in play. One dead woman. One locked and empty department store, open only on the ground floor via a dead escalator that was in plain view of eighty to a hundred people during business hours. Sealed off on the second and third floors behind very exotic locks that opened only with very exotic keys.

Expensive exotic keys.

And I'd found four of them tucked away into odd corners of four shops, little shops with nothing either to distinguish them or to lump them together: a paper goods store, a bad prints store, a watch store—little more than a booth, really—and a place where teenage girls went to economize on second-rate cosmetics. Of the four shops, I'd met three proprietors: Jackie (paper), her personal TARDIS stuck in the 1960s; Milt (watches), chewing his cuticles; and LaShawn, the owner and sole employee of KissyFace. I'd briefly seen LaShawn do makeovers on a couple of her customers, and she was the Michelangelo of makeup as far as I was concerned. Four small shopkeepers, and in each I'd found an unusual, expensive, impossible-to-duplicate key.

And, of course, there could have been even more of them, in the safes or cash registers I didn't (all right, *couldn't*) open, or hidden in places I didn't think to look in, and there were people who might have taken the keys home, and there were the eighty or ninety vendors in the bazaar, and then there was old Sam of Sam's Saddlery, who had changed his lock—

Oh, for Christ's sake. I'd been so absorbed in the mechanics of *find the key, open the lock*, that I hadn't even—

I shut down the cameras again, went back out into the mall, climbed the stairs—I didn't feel like I deserved the elevator after being such a bonehead—*used my picks* on Sam's new lock, and went in.

And found nothing.

Well, not quite nothing. Just nothing interesting. A bundle of mail addressed to a PO Box. He'd probably picked it up on his way to work and then forgotten to take it home. There were three penciled notes, each more insistent than the last, demanding the rent from, I supposed, whoever owned the place where he lived, a couple of redlined notices from his bank about his checking account being overdrawn, and some other snipes from creditors, but after two full days at Edgerton Mall, I figured Sam wasn't the only one who was getting goosed by the banks. The curtain behind the counter slid aside to reveal a storeroom, three rows of shelves neatly stacked with leather-smelling merchandise. I played the penlight over it without going in, and gave up out of sheer discouragement. The whole place, not just Sam's but the entire mall, had the distinctive funk of bounced checks, unpaid bills, and debt accruing on the doorstep.

With things so generally dire, why was Vlad in such a swivet about some shoplifting?

I needed to get the cameras going again, so I closed up Sam's store and went back down to Wally's place, turned the record function back on, and tore three unused appointment sheets from his book. I took the lists Amanda and I had drawn up and started making comparisons. I'd asked shopkeepers when they and their employees took lunch, and Amanda had asked the workers in the food court whom they had seen in the staff dining area while Bonnie was meeting her maker up in Gabriel's. And now I had a third line of data: people who had a Mul-T-Key and were careless enough to leave it where I could find it. I added a fourth data point: discrepancies between Amanda's list and mine—someone who said he or she had eaten in the food court at the right time but who hadn't been seen there.

This was not the world's most interesting task, and I kept slipping off the edge of the page into a nod that, unresisted, would have led straight to sleep, so the lists took a long time to reconcile. I was only about 60 percent of the way through when I sensed movement on the video monitors and looked up to see the cleaning crew trailing in downstairs with push brooms, waste cans, and the other tools of the trade. I checked my phone, and it was almost seven-forty. Nine-forty in Des Moines.

I opened Wally's appointment book, picked up the phone on his console, and dialed. Eyes closed, I listened to the ring on the other end, punched up the extension when it was requested, and said, "Wendy Straub, please."

"It's *me*, Wally," the woman on the other end said cheerfully. "I know your number by sight now. Are you telling me you need *another* one? What are you doing with them, eating them?"

27
Never

I finished collating the data from my lists and Amanda's while keeping one eye on the screens so I could pick my exit time. I wanted to get out of Wally's at a point when I'd be less conspicuous because the cleaning crews were on multiple screens. But I also needed to avoid bumping into any of them as I exited Wally's lair. Over the hours I'd spent squinting down at my checklist, hard to read in the light from the monitors, it had slowly become apparent that virtually no one met all four criteria. Either they were in the dining area during the window of time I was checking or they weren't but they'd gone somewhere else, with someone who would substantiate their story, or they had told me in the first place that they hadn't gone to lunch, that they'd eaten in their shop because there was no one else to cover. And, of course, almost none of them had a Mul-T-Key.

Exactly one person, LaShawn of KissyFace, had a key, hadn't been in the dining area, and had told me that she had been.

LaShawn was a happy, even giggly, permanent post-teen who would still be a post-teen in her seventies, who wore more cosmetics than Nefertiti, and lost business all day long because she just loved to putter with her customers' makeup.

Give her one customer who was willing to sit at the counter and let LaShawn redo her eyes, and anyone else in the store not being beautified could wait for attention until they qualified for Social Security without being served or, if they were feeling larcenous, could have emptied the shop. They probably could have taken the brush from her fingers without her noticing. I'd watched her for about ten minutes back on the first day, when I was gathering impressions, and no matter what the collated data said, LaShawn was too big-hearted, too spontaneous, too damn *nice* to have had anything to do with Bonnie's death. I know people can hide their real natures, but LaShawn was as clear as a glass of water—she was a little girl who had loved to play with makeup and had grown into a *big* little girl who still loved to play with makeup and had found a way to do it for a living, although it couldn't have been much of a living.

Also, she was pretty in a heavily made-up kind of way and she looked like a huge amount of fun, and twice I'd seen one of the guys from Boots to Suits sitting in the shop, apparently waiting for her before she went on a break. Maybe she'd *said* she was eating lunch because what she was really doing was none of my business.

I blew out a lungful of frustration, looked up, and saw cleaning-crew movement on six screens, none of them depicting areas near me. That would have to do. I put everything except the graphs back where I'd found it, hung the keys from their hook, rechecked Wally's closet door to make sure it was locked, lined up the chairs at the console so they were exactly as he'd left them, and then went to the door with the graphs and the pages torn from Wally's appointment book tucked under my arm. A seventh screen showed movement, and I figured that was enough camouflage so I wouldn't stand out, especially to someone who was watching all the screens at once in high-speed reverse. I put the baseball cap on again—three members of the cleaning crew shared my taste in headgear—opened the door, and went out.

And found myself squinting because the crew had turned on some of the overhead illumination, but then I ducked into the stairway to the second level, where it was dimmer, and I waited there a moment until my eyes had adjusted. When the glare had subsided I went on down to level two, took a quick look around, and took the NO ADMITTANCE hallway to the employees' eating area. Since I had it to myself, I sat where Shlomo usually sat.

I knew instinctively that LaShawn wasn't the person I was looking for, but out of curiosity I checked the graph to see how much stuff she'd reported as stolen, and it was about as high as I would have expected. I'd actually watched her get ripped off, I'd seen a couple of teenagers palm a puff or a tube or a spritzer, and beat it.

So since I had yet another data point available, Wally's graph, I thought I'd check to see how often LaShawn's heavy losses occurred in a week during which there had been unusually large crowds in her store.

Someone came in behind me, and I turned to see one of the cap-wearers, broom in hand. I said, "Good morning. Tell me when you need me to move," and he nodded and started sweeping the perimeter of the room.

Never.

Never?

I looked at the graph again because I thought I'd misread it. I still got *never*. There was no week when she was especially crowded that LaShawn reported heavier theft than usual.

I became aware that I was hearing furniture being moved, and I looked up and saw the guy in the cap sliding the tables toward the walls, onto the area he'd swept, so he could do the rest of the room. My head was ringing with what I'd just seen on the chart, but I must have gotten up and helped him move the tables because the next time I realized where I was, I was sitting at a table at the edge of the room and studying the printout as a whole.

The conclusion was inescapable. Thanks to Wally's thoughtfulness in plotting the graphs, it was impossible to miss. The correlation between crowds and higher losses was essentially zero, which is to say it was low enough to be random, maybe six to nine percent. There was no actual relationship between hordes of customers and a rise in shop-lifting.

It wouldn't be accurate to say that I'd had a good idea of what was happening in Edgerton, but whatever wispy inklings I had were related to those odd crowds, the atypical movement I thought I'd caught sight of once or twice when looking down at the ground floor. I had erected a rickety bamboo structure of suppositions that was based in part on the assumption that there was something nonrandom, some-thing *intentional*, about the movement of some of the people in the holiday crowds who had chosen Edgerton.

And, apparently, there wasn't. I supposed Wally's graph could have been intended to mislead, but I doubted it. The surveillance footage was still available, so the contradictions would have been spotted in minutes by anyone who could count.

So my airy, improbable bamboo structure collapsed into an unsorted collection of sticks, and I sat there in that brightly lit room, a little before 8:00 A.M., having been up for more than twenty-four hours straight, and a line from Sherlock Holmes popped into my mind: "How often have I said to you that when you have eliminated the impossible, whatever remains, however improbable, must be the truth?"

Okay, my bamboo structure hadn't been impossible, but it had been wildly improbable, and now even *that* was consigned to the reject pile. And I was about twelve hours away from the deadline by which I was supposed to report my findings to Vlad. I got up, stretched, and made a rapid, almost involuntary, internal decision to give up. Instantly, a huge weight was lifted from my shoulders and I drew what felt like my first deep breath in two days. The whole world was waiting outside, flawed though it might be, and it was Christmas Eve day. I could actually leave Edgerton. I shrugged off the residual tension in my neck and shoulders and figured I'd exit with the cleaning crew. I waved at a couple of them, one baseball cap to another, as I went down the stairs, since the escalator was still off, and then I stood on the ground floor, looking up at Edgerton Mall in all its empty melancholy. Saying an unfond goodbye.

Now that I had a little distance, it presented itself as a sort of closed ecosystem, a walled-in environment, a psychological and moral Galápagos, where certain kinds of behavioral mutations had been encouraged until they produced a place in which pretty much everyone acted differently here than they did in the outside world: here it was all about selling and buying in all its variations, and other human beings were divided into subspecies: customers or vendors or competitors or obstructions. At the end of the day, you rated the progress of your life in dollars and cents. And the ones who couldn't adapt left their lifeless fossils behind.

The North Pacific Gyre unexpectedly presented itself to

me as an equally accurate parallel: out in the middle of the largest body of water on earth, currents from all over the globe had brought together millions and millions of objects, fragments of objects, bits and pieces of everything that floats. It had all entered the water for different reasons and in different parts of the world, but the currents that had swept it away led inexorably to the Gyre, and once something arrived there, it could never leave. Here in this mall the fragments were people, and the currents that brought them here were need or sustenance or ambition or even aesthetics, like Bonnie's love of bric-a-brac; or delight, like LaShawn's relationship to makeup; or even death, like the grandfather whose books were being sold so inexpertly in the bazaar. And, not to stretch a point, Edgerton, like the Gyre, was a dying region, its vitality sapped by refuse and entropy, its remaining vitality slowly draining as people like Bonnie faced up to the long decline they were sharing and prepared for the inevitable end of their reason for being here.

Nothing can leave the Gyre.

Something cold ran up my back. I straightened, not so much a movement as a spasm, and I thought I saw the *however improbable,* as Holmes put it, sail into view.

What Sam had said to me: "A deposit I have. A *penalty* I have."

For once, I knew where to look.

When Cranmer had led Wally and me to the security office to question us the previous day, we'd passed a door that said SITE MANAGEMENT in tarnished, dusty, fake brass letters. Wally told me later that the Edgerton Partnership, or whatever it was called, had fired the last site manager a year and a half ago, but he hadn't said anything about whether they'd taken the files with them.

The hallway leading to the security office and the site manager's space, another EMPLOYEES ONLY domain, was at the south end of the structure. Keeping an eye open for the single security guard who had raised the airplane door at the north end to let the cleaning crew in, I silently opened the door to the hallway. The door at the far end, which belonged to the security office where Cranmer had interviewed me, was closed, and between me and it was a thin, dark-skinned, tired-looking Hispanic kid, maybe seventeen, another member of the baseball cap league, with a big, triple-wide push broom. This was probably his last chore of the morning, since the second guard would arrive right about then to open the other airplane door to admit early-bird employees. The kid returned my nod but still launched a rill of dirt at my shoes and socks, and then meticulously swept around me to the door and out through it, letting it close behind him. If our positions had been reversed and I'd been a seventeen-year-old who swept decaying malls all night, I'd have aimed for the shoes, too.

I didn't have much time. The second security guy was due any minute. He'd probably join up with the other one and make an immediate beeline for their office. That would take them past the site manager's empty room, so it didn't seem like a good plan to be picking the lock to that room when they came by. And in fact, as I began to mess around with my picks, I heard the second of the big doors groan creakingly upward.

The site manager had not been shortchanged with the kind of lock they'd slapped onto Wally's door. This was a lock with muscles. I was making slow progress when I heard the airplane door slam into its housing—all the way up—and I knew without even thinking about it that it was the guard who looked like he bench-pressed school buses.

The image of his huge shoulders and small, shaved head fueled a burst of inspired improvisation with the picks, and just as I caught the sound of the two of them chatting as they approached the corridor, the lock yielded with a sullen, resentful *click,* and I was in.

I closed that door as they opened the one at the end of the corridor, one sound covering the other, and then I froze. The floor in here hadn't been swept since the last site manager rode off into the sunset, and it was gritty, even under the soles of my sneakers. And, since there were no windows, it was also pitch black.

Well, *almost* pitch black. The thin strip of light beneath the door, once my eyes had adjusted, was enough to tell me that, even if they'd removed the files, they'd left the filing cabinets. Since moving a filing cabinet is by several orders of magnitude the easiest way to move files, the little serpent of anxiety that had coiled in my chest uncoiled, blew me an aggrieved raspberry, and slithered off to find someone else to frighten. I pulled out the penlight and went to take a look.

Correspondence, invoices, construction junk, licenses, office supplies, sponges, rubber gloves, hair tonic—who still used hair tonic?—paperback books, mail to and from the city and the county. And then, in a drawer by themselves, the documents I was seeking: contracts.

I flipped through a couple of the ones that were filled out and then reached past them, to the very back of the drawer, for the blanks: a lawyer's opium dream, unclouded by details and people and negotiation, of what the relationship between the mall and its "commercial lessees" should be. I grabbed one and scanned straight down to the pertinent section.

And there it was, the legal equivalent of the little key Morris Stempel had used to open that sealed can of M-rations for Madame Loiseau. There it was in literal black and white, what the whole damn thing was about, even if I couldn't quite put all the pieces together in the right order yet. It was the Christmas gift that kept on giving. I would have been happy just to have so many things finally made clear—the shoplifting, for example—but it also did me the vast favor of eliminating from the pool of people who might have killed Bonnie all the vendors in the bazaar, all the employees of Boots to Suits, and all the people who worked in the few outlets that belonged to chain operations.

It was the *however improbable* old Sherlock talked about, just waiting for me to figure out where to look for it. And now I'd found it.

28
Christmas Gifts for People We Hate

"What *time* is it?" Anime Wong said on the phone, cranky as a hibernating bear whose alarm clock had gone off in January.

"Almost nine. Come on, it's a brand-new day. Get up, stretch, run in place, open your clear young eyes to the wonder of—"

"Wait, wait, wait, *wait*," she said. "I'm doing subtraction. I've been asleep two hours and . . . jeez, what's twenty-nine from sixty?"

"Thirty-one. Are you telling me you know the minute you go to sleep?"

"I know the minute I put my head on the pillow, and if this is nine, that was two hours and thirty-one minutes ago."

"Come on," I said. "You're a kid. You've got your whole adult life to feel tired."

"Gee, what a rosy glimpse of the future. What?"

I said, "What what?"

"What do you *want*?"

"You and Lilli."

"Why?"

"Expertise."

A muffled sound that might have been her actually saying, "Grrrrrrrrr," just like it's spelled. Then she said, "When?"

"Around noon."

"Where?"

"Edgerton Mall."

"Ohmigod," she said. "What's the name of this chapter, 'Christmas Gifts for People We Hate'? I thought they turned Edgerton into an animal shelter."

"Will you be there?"

"Grrrrrrrr," she said again. I could hear her sitting up in bed, or on a couch, or wherever the hell she and Lilli had gone to sleep. She yawned in my ear. "Have you ever heard anybody actually say, 'What the—'?"

"Not without a few words following it, no. What the *heck*? What—"

"What I thought," she said. "It's all over the place in comic books and graphic novels. Usually with an apostrophe or one of those other squiggles after the *h* in *the*. Like 'What th'?' You can't even say it out loud."

"Well," I said, "not meaning to disrupt your belief system, given how much thought you've put into this, but graphic novels are not real life."

"I guess that's one of the things I'll understand when I get older, right?" Anime was going on fifteen.

"None of the things you're supposed to understand when you get older are worth understanding," I said. "Take it from me. You already know everything you'll ever need to know. You'll pick up some extra facts, sure, but you've already got the world down cold."

She paused, probably in replay mode. "Is that a compliment?"

"Up to you."

"So Edgerton at noon, right? Where?"

"At Santa's throne," I said, and as Anime hung up I heard her say, "Yeah, sure, where else?"

Motel 7 was one of those ideas that had probably sounded great at first. I chose it because I had neither the time nor the inclination to go to the Wedgwood and listen to the echoes in the empty apartment, and also because Motel 7 was only a few miles from Edgerton and I knew it to be relatively vermin-free. The one time I'd stayed there, back during the grey stretch of gloom I think of as The Motel Period, the guy who owned the place gave me a very compressed ten minutes on how he'd gone back and forth between naming it Motel 5 and Motel 7—5 suggesting extra savings and 7 clearly indicating higher quality. He'd had a global franchise in mind but it never happened, and he'd been bitter ever since for not having gone with Motel 5.

It wasn't a story I wanted to hear again, so I was a little short with him as I checked in. The rooms, he insisted on telling me, wouldn't be cleaned until after eleven, but when I cross-examined him he admitted that only two of them had been slept in this week and the others had been made up for days. I literally plucked the key from his hand while he was enlightening me on the difficulty of managing a cloud of maids when you never knew how many rooms there would be to clean. He'd branched off into a plan to spice the place up with French maids' uniforms when I let the glass door close mercifully between us.

Nine-eighteen as I pulled my overnight kit out of my trunk and realized I didn't have a new razor. I get a little crazy if I don't shave. Well, I thought, maybe being a little crazy would be an improvement. Being sane hadn't gotten me anywhere until about an hour ago. I had one errand, a two-stopper, to run before going back to Edgerton, and I figured that it would either take an hour or be completely impossible, so I set my phone to erupt at ten-thirty and play "Satisfy Me" by Anderson East, since I didn't have any actual Stax/Volt on my music list. Then I dialed Ronnie again, listened to it ring, disconnected, and went to sleep with my shoes on.

At quarter to eleven, I was squinting into the morning sunshine of a bright blue Southern California Christmas Eve day. My quick shower had been more successful at getting me wet than at clearing my head, but a Venti or a Gulperino or whatever Starbucks persists in calling its biggest cup of coffee had taken me from weary and fuddled to jumpy and fuddled. It felt like an improvement. And for what seemed like the first time in months, I had a plan of sorts.

One of Shlomo's kids, he'd said, had become a lawyer, and the other was in real estate. Since I figured real estate was at the heart of the problem anyway, that was the one I picked.

One of the most frequently bemoaned aspects of the age of social media is the loss of personal privacy. People in my line of work take a different view, which is that it's not being lost anywhere near fast enough. Still, it took me less than two minutes on my phone to find Stempel Estates Realty (the "estates" was a nice nose-in-the-air touch); the full name of its owner, Philip Harold Stempel; and Philip Harold Stempel's office and home addresses, plus a picture of his Woodland Hills house from the street. Two minutes, and I was *groggy*. If this trend keeps up, people might just as well put their stuff out on the lawn every night.

I'd been feeling for a while that I was overdue for a wish

come true, so it was pleasant to see the bright, cheap-looking little pennants hanging limply in front of Stempel Estates Realty, indicating that it was open for business for at least a few hours on Christmas Eve. Shlomo had said that both of his kids had essentially gold-plated themselves, and that was certainly consistent with the approach Philip Harold had taken to the building that housed Stempel Estates Realty. A basic stucco box, it had been fitted out in front with a grand portico, complete with columns that might have been salvaged from Tara. If you drove around to the side, as I did, looking to see how many cars were parked there, you were looking at the back of the original, unadorned cube with its cheap aluminum track windows. The fancy front wasn't even the same color as the rest of it.

The winter sun glinted off two cars parked in back, one a highly polished black Cadillac SUV sporting the plates *PHIL RE*, undoubtedly standing for real estate, and the other a dusty, bird-spattered Kia. As long as I was idling back there, I called the business number and got a woman who had majored in perky, who identified herself as Rhonda, and who said that Mr. Stempel was in a meeting and the place would be open until one.

So. Straight south to Ventura, across the boulevard into the high-rent district, and a couple of blocks northwest to Woodland Hills. I figured I was four or five miles and four or five hundred thousand dollars away from Shlomo's house or, as his sons called it, the teardown. But the teardowns on *these* blocks had been reduced to kindling some time ago, and what we had now was the architectural equivalent of a pocket yanked inside out: big, mostly new, mostly ugly structures that had been inflated to cover every legal square foot of the lots on which they stood and which gave off (to me, anyway) the sad miasma of striving and dissatisfaction. One after another, they seemed to say, *This is everything in the world I have now, and I'm not sure I can hang onto it.*

Philip Stemple owned, or at least was making payments on, a Mediterranean fever dream, an apricot-colored assemblage of arches topped off with a slightly crooked tile roof that put me in mind of a slipped toupee. As I slowed, a little black Mercedes convertible backed out of the driveway at a high rate of speed, did a quick three-point turn, and zipped past me, giving me a glimpse of a dissatisfied-looking woman whose skin had been stretched as taut as a tom-tom and whose expression suggested that she had long ago stopped expecting moments of grace that didn't have a price attached to them.

I kept on going, all the way around the block, and then eased back up Philip Stempel's street, which was lined spottily with tall eucalyptus trees, where they hadn't been cut for construction. I parked two houses down and went up Stempel's driveway, walking as though I held the title to the property. The gate was set back from the front of the house, probably to let more than one car park in the drive, which is always a mistake. Here's a tip: if you're thinking about building or remodeling, put the gate *flush with the front of the house.* Otherwise, you locate one of the property's most vulnerable spots in a cul-de-sac, out of sight from most of the street, creating an ideally secluded entry point for someone to whom you would refuse entrance, if you had a choice in the matter.

It took me about five seconds and a short running start to go over the gate and roughly three minutes to get in through the back door. It was 11:22 A.M., and I was due at the Edgerton to meet Anime and Lilli in less than forty minutes.

Still, I stood there and listened. There might be a maid,

there might be a cousin visiting from Cleveland, there might be (there had once been) another burglar, so I gave those possibilities the long, careful moments they deserved, and then I went straight to it. I'd had some time to think about the theft of Morris Stempel's dog tags, and it seemed almost certain to me that the act had something to do with the pressure Shlomo's sons were exerting on him to sell the house, and that the tags had been stolen so close to Christmas so that they could be either held for ransom or, more plausibly, returned to him as a gift in some persuasive fashion.

What those assumptions suggested to me was that the dog tags, which had no intrinsic value, wouldn't be locked in a safe or hidden away. They'd be somewhere close at hand, ready to be used as a bargaining chip or a present with strings as thick as ropes attached to it. I went through the house quickly—it had an airless quality, as though they never opened the windows, and there was plastic sheeting on the living room couch, adding a petroleum pong to the stuffiness. I didn't look at anything except tables with chairs pulled up to them, where someone could do paperwork. In the upstairs room that I presumed was Philip's office, I found them, but I'm half-ashamed to admit that what drew my attention wasn't the shape of the tags but the distinctive gleam of gold.

He'd had them gold-plated.

There were two of them, identical. *Stempel, Morris L.* said the first line, followed by a line of numbers that I presumed comprised his serial number and then *T44*, which I thought indicated the year he'd been inoculated against Tetanus, and the letter O, probably his blood type. Down in the lower right corner was the lethal letter *J*, for Jewish. The letter that could have gotten him killed.

The tags had been worn down, dented, and scratched, and

all that wear showed through the gold plating. When I picked them up, the weight took me by surprise, and I took a closer look at the chain, which was also gold.

They were resting on top of a Hanukkah card depicting a stylized menorah. I opened the card to find the words, "Dear Dad," followed by a blank expanse of paper, a prayer for inspiration if I ever saw one, and obviously an unanswered prayer since Hanukkah had ended on December 14 and the card was still undelivered. I set aside the card and dog tags so I could look at the document beneath them. It was an offer for a house at an address in Tarzana, and it was for $1,820,000, a lot of zeroes.

So Philip had been doing client drive-bys on the house without telling his father—the house, Shlomo had said, that sat on *two lots*—and he'd gotten an offer he simply couldn't resist, and this whole charade—borrowing his grandfather's dog tags, which he probably thought his father wouldn't notice, gold-plating them, and hanging them on a heavy gold chain—was his way of presenting the offer.

I sat in Philip's chair and tried to see it from his point of view. He was obviously morally tone-deaf. He had no idea what kind of person his father actually was, probably projecting his own values on Shlomo to come up with an offer that he thought would represent an irresistible windfall to his parents. He'd been uncertain enough, though, to dress it up with the presentation of the gold-plated dog tags, a little schmear of sentiment to mask the dryness of the underlying business transaction. I wondered whether Philip had even considered turning his commission over to his parents, too, and then I decided that there wasn't a chance. Anyway the issue at hand was what to do with the dog tags. Take them or leave them?

The tags gave off a kind of emotional sizzle, the intangible aura that Herbie had trained me to spot, even at a distance: *Look for the one thing they can't bear to lose*, he'd said in various ways over the years, *and then don't take it*. In the end, I went with his advice, as I had so often, and trusted Philip to return them. I used my phone to take a few pictures of the whole setup—tags, card, offer—to show to Shlomo later. At least he'd know where the tags were.

As I got up, I heard a car and looked out the window to see the little black Mercedes pulling in. I was halfway down the stairs when the motor that opened the gate began to grind, which meant she was coming in through the back, so I went out the front. I was most of the way to my car before I heard the house's rear door swing shut.

29
Foreshortening

Noon on Christmas Eve day, and the place was as full as I'd ever seen it. The music was back on, the colored lights were blinking in obsessive-compulsive fashion, and a group of what looked like high school kids in white choir robes was being herded up onto a temporary platform that had been laid down over the dirty water in the reflecting pool. Fortunately, the fountain had been turned off. The kids shuffled aimlessly, apparently waiting for someone to kill the PA system so they could sing. Most of them seemed nervous, and I wanted to go tell them that they looked great and everyone would love them, but I knew they'd disregard it as the nattering of some weird old guy, and also, it wasn't true. After the first thirty seconds, no one would listen to them.

But I was, happily, wrong. The overhead recording of "I Saw Mommy Kissing Santa Claus" came to an abrupt end—not quite abrupt enough for me—and a middle-aged woman in a matching robe, augmented by a bright red-and-green scarf that hung to her waist, lifted both hands and waited, eyebrows raised, surveying the kids until they were all facing her attentively. Then she marked the downbeat and the kids' faces changed somehow and they all began to resemble one another, mouths open, eyes on the woman with the scarf, and with a fluid movement of her hands, she brought them together to the breath that supported the first note, and as it rang out, the kids looked like people somehow sharing a dream. By the end of the first long, slow lines—

The first Noel
the Angel did say . . .

—the sounds of chatter and movement began to die away, and all over the mall people turned to look. And in the absence of noise, the great hollowness of the mall took the sound of the kids' voices and purified it, deepened it, gave it the resonance of a cathedral, and the kids heard it, too, and some of them closed their eyes.

Was to certain poor shepherds
in fields as they lay,
In fields where they
lay, keeping their sheep . . .

The line of children waiting to see Shlomo had fallen silent, many of them turning, having forgotten they were holding a parent's hand, to see the choir. One of them, I was surprised to see, was the kid with the Frida Kahlo unibrow, so this was his second pass at Shlomo. Beyond the children I saw Shlomo lift a four-year-old onto his lap and turn her toward the singers, whispering some Christmas promise in her ear, and she burst into a delighted smile and a couple of the kids in the choir smiled back at her.

I was smiling, too.

"You didn't say there were two Santas," someone said beside me. I turned to see Anime, and beside her, looking like she'd spent the night in a wind tunnel, her girlfriend and partner in larceny, Lilli. Anime was, as usual, as slick as an otter, her straight, black hair pulled back and meticulously smoothed into place except where it had been blunt-cut directly across the middle of her left ear, a mirror-image of Lilli's haircut, and her face had been scrubbed until it shone. Lilli looked as though every rumple that had fled Anime had taken refuge on her and that she resented every one of them.

On a cold winter's night
that was so deep.

"This is the only carol I like," Lilli said grudgingly.

"It's an old one," I said, almost whispering. "More than two hundred years. It's from Luke."

"Luke who?" Lilli said.

"She's being intentionally obtuse," Anime said. "She was up all night."

"God, this place is a dump," Lilli said.

I said, "Ssshhhhhhhh," and we listened to the rest of the carol.

For a moment, as the final chord died away, the place was almost as silent as it had been the previous night when I'd had it to myself, but then people began to move, conversations were resumed, interrupted complaints were aired, and by the time the choir accepted the downbeat for "Jingle Bells," the moment had passed.

"You guys want to meet Santa?"

"A lifelong dream," Lilli said, trying to smooth her wheat-colored hair and looking enviously at Anime.

"Well, then, wait for me a minute." I pulled my phone

from my pocket and brought up the picture of the dog tags, and waited until the four-year-old slid off Shlomo's lap. Then I held up the phone and wiggled it back and forth so he could see I had something to show him, and moved up the line of kids, saying to Shlomo's elf, "This will just take a second of Santa's time."

Shlomo looked at me and then down at the phone, and then he closed his eyes and used his left hand to massage the bridge of his nose. "Gold-plated?"

"Yeah."

"My kids run true to type. Which one?"

"Philip."

"You went into his house?"

"Well, yeah."

"Did you take anything?"

"Just pictures."

"The good thief," he said, shaking his head. "What am I supposed to do with this?"

"Enlarge the document under the card."

He did, and then he shook his head. "One point eight." Then he looked past me. "And who's this?"

"This is—" I turned to check. "This is Anime Wong. She wants to say hi to Santa."

"Hi," Anime said, blushing furiously.

Shlomo gave her all his attention. "Have you been good?"

"Oh," she said. She fidgeted. "Um, not very."

"She's been fine," I said. "Better than fine."

"I can see that in her eyes," Shlomo said. "What are you going to give for Christmas?"

Anime's eyes widened. "*Give?* Oh, right, *thank you* for asking. Umm—" Anime glanced behind her to make sure that Lilli wasn't within earshot. "I'm going to give my girlfriend a, um, a poem I wrote." She looked at him and then up at me. "Is that corny?"

"It is not," Shlomo said. "I know a lot about presents, and I promise you it'll be one of the best she's ever gotten."

Anime was grinning like her face would split, and when she felt my gaze she turned and punched me on the arm. "He's my friend," she said to Shlomo, a bit fiercely. "Junior is. Thanks, Santa."

"And merry Christmas," Shlomo said.

"Same to you, as silly as that sounds," Anime said, and to the child who was already on her way to Shlomo's lap, she said, "Merry Christmas, kid."

"Are we done yet?" Lilli said. "Did you ask for your sled?"

"Just had to tell him where to hang your lump of coal," Anime said. "Let's get going."

"The place is being looted," I said to the girls as we climbed the stairs to the second level.

"What kind of stuff?" Anime, who was in the lead, asked the question. Lilli, behind her, yawned.

"Everything, you name it. But only from the smaller stores."

"*Tumblr,*" Lilli said as though it were the most obvious thing in the world and she couldn't believe that neither of us had said it yet. "There's whole *communities* of lifters, mostly teenage girls, or twists who like to think of themselves as teenage girls. Handles like prettylifter, toocutetopay, sweetydeeppockets, kleptokutie. There's a couple of hangouts where they swap ideas. The big one is called Winona Ryder University, you know, 'cause she got snagged trying to—"

"We get it," Anime said.

I blew out a bunch of air.

"I'd think you'd be interested in this," Anime said. "Considering what you do for a—"

"I have mixed emotions about it, okay? And it's going to take me longer than ninety seconds, which is how long I've known about it, to sort them out." Anime and Lilli, still in their early teens, were computer-age thieves. Working under the supervision of a heavily tattooed human equation who called himself Monty Cristo, they looted the infrequently audited funds that states set up for the money they seize from abandoned safe deposit boxes. The girls' long-term objectives were doctoral degrees in computer science for both of them from Carnegie Mellon, Harvard, or MIT, and a completely debt-free graduation, throughout which they'd be holding hands.

"They've got moral codes and everything," Anime said. "No lifting on the really big sales days, like Black Friday, because that's the only time poor people can afford stuff, so you're stealing from the poor, which is uncool, no low-end food for the same reason, no lifting from mom-and-pop stores because—"

"Well, that leaves Edgerton out," I said. "As I said, the mom-and-pop stores are the ones getting looted."

The choir launched into "Do You Hear What I Hear?" and Lilli covered her ears and said, "Take me *away*, somebody. This is the most *guy* carol of them all."

I said, "What's so guy—"

"Here's a little kid," Lilli said as Anime rolled her eyes, "just been born, right? Probably still *wet*, and he's freezing to death, shivering in the cold, like it says, and what are these lunkheads going to give him? Silver and gold. Come on, any woman in the world would say, 'Hey, take your silver and gold to the damn store and buy the kid some *blankets*.'"

"She wasted that on me yesterday," Anime said, "and she's been dying to trot it out for someone smart enough to appreciate it."

"Well," I said, "it's certainly changed *my* life. Listen, to tell you the truth, I don't really care who's specifically doing the lifting. I already know, pretty much, what's going on. What I want to know is *how* it's being done. On the macro scale, the big picture."

"The big picture," Lilli said in a deep radio-announcer voice. She'd gone to the railing to look down. "Clear away, little people, make room for the mental giant."

"You didn't like her insight," Anime said, following her girlfriend. "She gets grumpy when—"

Lilli did a brusque little hula move to the left and hip-checked Anime hard enough to send her a step sideways, then licked the tip of her index finger and made an imaginary vertical mark in the air. "Twenty-nine to three," she said. "You gotta keep your eyes open."

"So," Anime said, rubbing her hip and looking down at the ground floor. "*What's* the question?"

"I don't want to suggest an answer," I said. "My first day here I noticed—I *thought* I noticed—something odd about the crowd, about the way they move. I want you to—"

"Next level," Lilli said, heading for the stairs. "The higher the better."

We climbed the stairs, the girls bouncing despite their lack of sleep and me feeling like I should be using both hands to lift my legs. At the top, Lilli chose a corner for, she said, *perspective*. Something, she said, about *foreshortening*, and Anime said something about the *angle of approach* when there were too many *individual data points*, and Lilli high-fived her and then the two of them shut up and just looked down for a while.

"Jesus," Lilli said after a few minutes. "This is like binge-watching fungi." Then she yawned again.

I yawned, too. Then Anime yawned. We passed the yawn among us like a talking stick and I said, "I'm going to bet that among the three of us we didn't get a total of nine hours' sleep."

"No takers," Lilli said, and yawned again, but then her spine straightened and Anime and she craned down at the crowd below with a new energy.

"Could be," Anime said, pushing her aside.

"Is," Lilli said. She did the hip thing again but Anime stepped back and Lilli grabbed her lower back and said, "*Ow.*"

"But then on the other—" Anime dropped the sentence and instead pointed across the diagonal of the mall at the far corner.

"*I* see it," Lilli said, sounding cranky. She was rubbing the small of her back. "I'm not an ashtray, you know."

"See what?" I said.

"Wait," Lilli said, as though speaking to a member of a lower species. "Five . . . four . . . three . . . two . . . one . . ."

"Smartass," Anime said. "Nothing."

Lilli said, "Oh, *yeah?*" and pointed in the direction of Dwayne Wix's throne. "Three of them," she said. "All in different directions." To me, she said, "Take a look."

I was already looking, but now I looked harder. The throng of people on the ground level were milling around, except that they weren't *all* milling around. From everywhere in the crowd, individuals, or in some cases families, began to move, detaching themselves from the larger patterns and filtering purposefully through the throng. First it seemed to me that they were going to the escalators, and then they seemed to be going toward the stores in the center of the west side of the mall, and then they seemed to be moving toward the stairs, except, as they kept moving, I realized that the crowd was slowly producing three smaller groups, little rivers of people, each headed in a different direction. Many of those who were on the move were looking at their phones.

"What's your guess?" I asked Lilli and Anime. "What percentage of the crowd is on the move?"

"About a fifth," Anime said. She could pick a fraction like that and be right. "The others are still just wandering."

The Choir began to sing "O Little Town of Bethlehem." Many of the idlers looked toward them or stopped to listen for a second, but as far as the three streams of people were concerned, the choir wasn't even there.

"Flash mobs," Lilli said. "Three at the same time."

"Actually," I said with my eyes closed, visualizing what I'd seen, "about five, ten seconds apart."

"One source," Anime said.

"What do you think?" I said. "Is it live or is it on some memory chip somewhere, set to dial at this time?"

"Live," Anime said. "Too many variables for it to be programmed. Somebody's running it in real time. Where's the nearest geek with a view?"

"Down there," I said, pointing at the second level. Standing at the railing, looking down at the ground floor, conspicuous because of the gleam of his prematurely grey hair, was Wink, the guy who owned iShop. He was focused on the screen of his phone, but he seemed to sense our attention because he looked up and around, but by the time his eyes passed over us, Anime and Lilli and I were facing one another, pretending to be in conversation.

"Don't look at him," I said. "But as soon as he looks away,

I want you to video the crowd movement on your phones, okay?"

"Why don't *you*—" Anime began, and said, "Never mind." Lilli snickered.

"You'll do it better than I could," I said. "Twenty-five, thirty seconds at least, a single take so no one can suspect editing, and you both send them to me."

"Okay." Anime already had her phone out.

"And when the geek down there goes to his shop on the first level, you guys go in a moment or two later."

"And?"

"Keep an eye on where he puts his phone when you come in," I said. "And then, right in front of him, steal something. And when we're finished with that, I need your help with some shopping. Okay?"

"It's Christmas," Anime said. "How could we say no?"

30
The Second Question

At least my shopping was done. I was surrounded by seven shopping bags full of presents I never would have picked out in a million years. But in the forty whirlwind minutes since I'd followed Anime and Lilli into Wink's shop, they'd demonstrated almost terrifying shopping skills. The moment either of them had pointed at something, I'd known who it was for and why she'd like it. They'd even led me back to *Will o' the Wisp* to buy my mother two saucers, *sans* cups, to replace the ones she'd broken years ago. She loves that pattern.

So here I was in Wally's gloomy lookout post, all Christmas-presented up at last and ready to test my assumptions about what had been happening at Edgerton.

I didn't have a script, but I had enough, I thought, to find my way through the conversation and get what I needed. I felt like I was at a slight disadvantage because I'd allowed Wally—old Honest Abe, can't-tell-a-lie Wally—to mislead me so badly, but for the first time since I'd met him, he and I were in a room together and I knew something he didn't.

Wally was sitting behind his console. Usually when a male feels threatened, he'll stand up to increase his size, the way a bear will raise its paws above its head or a blowfish will swell up or some canine species will make their fur bristle. But for

Wally, the console was the extension that gave him the power he had exercised so skillfully over the past few months, and he was staying put.

I was leaning with my back to Wally's door, blocking the only exit. Wink was standing uncomfortably where I'd put him, in front of the rows of monitors so he couldn't even lean against the wall. They couldn't exchange a glance without me seeing it.

"Here's where we stand," I said, focused on Wally. "Until about forty minutes ago I had two questions."

"Only two?" Wally asked. He wasn't the people pleaser today.

"At that moment, yes, two. The first question was, how the crowds were coordinated. So that's taken care of. It was old Wink here, sending text messages to mailing groups, people who were mostly down on the first level." Wink raised his head to say something, but I turned toward him, and he took a step sideways away from me. "As he'll tell you, I had a couple of young ladies distract him, and then I went in and picked up his phone, and here we are." I held up Wink's Samsung. "Three texts sent in about a minute and a half, to three groups of twenty to thirty each. Each message is just two or three words, the name of a store." I looked up at the display of screens, three of which were packed with people. "Do you want to guess which three stores?"

Wally said, "So Wink is behind—"

Wink said, *"Hey."*

I said, "Not exactly *behind* it. As you know perfectly well, Wally. An adjunct, maybe. A functionary. What he was doing—it was essentially a clerical job. Just part of the enterprise. There are dozens of these texts on his phone, each the name of a store in this mall," I said, "going back for weeks."

Wink said, "Nothing illegal about flash mobs." He didn't sound as scornful as he had when I'd asked him about the directions on the things I'd bought for Rina and Ronnie.

"No," I said. "As long as they're not stealing anything. I suppose, if they *were* stealing stuff, you could be nailed as an accessory or even, if the prosecutors wanted to get inventive, on criminal conspiracy charges."

"But," Wally said. And then he stopped and regarded me with the abstracted air of someone who sees something wrong with his chess position. Then he plunged back in. "But you saw the graphs."

"That's right, I saw the graphs. And let me tell you, it made me completely crazy when I did. Listen. There's a science to how crowds move. One or two anomalies, well, that's to be expected, but *repeated* anomalies, in a *single location*, over a *period* of time—" I'd been ticking off the points on my fingers, and now I held up all five and wiggled them. "Well, that means someone is fucking with the rules of movement. So the flash mobs were for a purpose, but guess what? They didn't really have anything to do with the shoplifting." I looked from Wink to Wally. "Did they?"

Wink licked his lips, and Wally immediately cleared his throat. Wink's tongue disappeared.

"Well, of *course* they did," I said. "They had *everything* to do with the shoplifting, in one regard at least. But here we are, with this big, fancy video system."

"Not so fan—" Wally began, but I said over him, "Fancy enough to record the crowds once they assembled in the stores. You were *stuck* with that, with the crowds in the stores; there was nothing you could do about it. You needed the crowds because they let you coordinate the shoplifting: the store owners were scheduled for crowds on certain days because it was all divided up, wasn't it, and they had to *prepare*, didn't they? So the crowds were on the surveillance tape, and anyone who reviewed the tapes would see them. But, of course, no single camera covered the movement of the whole crowd down on the first floor. Bits and pieces of the floor are covered, but there's no master shot, so to speak, nothing that would pick them up as they organized themselves and headed for their assigned destinations. I know, you told me that most of the coverage is where the merchandise is, and who needs a shot of the entire floor? All makes perfect sense."

Wally said, "And?"

"And also, no coverage of the doors into or out of Gabriel's. And yes, I remember, Gabriel's had its own system of cameras, another perfectly good reason for the lack of coverage. So no one could say that the camera coverage was contrived to hide the mechanism through which the shoplifters were sent into the right stores at the right time, or any of the ancillary activities. But that pattern of video coverage, which you know better than anyone, Wally, it was *taken advantage of* when all this was being mapped out. It shaped the whole plan."

"*What* plan?" Wally said. "You saw the reports. High rates of theft. You saw the graphs. No correlation between the crowds and the rate of theft."

"Which just poses the inevitable question, doesn't it?"

"Um," Wally said. "What question?"

I said, "Who's lying?"

Wally looked down at his console.

"I'm assuming we can leave out the off-site security people who chart the losses. They're independent contractors, not answerable to you. So that leaves us with *you*, Wally, and the people who own the stores. And look, here we are, with one person from each group: you, representing you, and Wink here, representing the shop owners. Has iShop been stolen from, Wink?"

"Well," he said.

"It's on the *record*," I said. "The amount you've reported as stolen."

"Since you put it that way."

"But you didn't report the thefts in the weeks in which they took place, in the weeks the crowds filled your stores, did you? You waited until—"

My phone began to ring, and I pulled it out and looked down at it. "Guess who," I said to Wally. "Mr. Poindexter is going *crazy* to learn what I've figured out. In fact, my deadline to tell him is tonight. Christmas Eve, of all nights. Does he strike you—or you, Wink, if you know him—does he strike *you* as a particularly forgiving person?"

"He, ummmmm," Wink said. To Wally, he said, "Can I have a chair?"

Wally didn't even glance at him. He cleared his throat. "I represent his interests," he said to me. "Mr. Poindexter's."

"Really," I said, "I doubt he'll share that view. I mean, there's no one else in this place who knows exactly where the holes in the camera coverage are, is there?"

His face was expressionless but once again, I could hear him swallow.

"Well," I said, "Christmas is coming, so let's get it all on the table. I'm not particularly interested in handing you to him." I looked over at Wink. "Neither of you, actually. So maybe you can help me figure out how not to."

Wally said, "You don't know enough to—"

"Oh, but I do." I felt like I had a weight on my chest, and I sighed to loosen it. "In fact, I know almost everything except

the thing I want to know most, the *second* of the two questions I mentioned, which is who killed poor, sweet Bonnie.
Listen, why don't we all sit down? Roll that chair over here,
would you?"

My phone began to ring again: Louie. I hit *reject* and said.
"Mr. Poindexter is *assertive*, isn't he?" Wally got up and
pushed his chair to me. He sat in the one I'd used, and Wink
gave me a resentful glance and perched on the edge of the
console.

"Okay. Once there was a mall, right? Not a very nice mall,
not a very successful mall. Malls are failing all over the place
anyway, and the ones that stay in business all have something
special. The one I'm talking about . . . well, it doesn't."

Wink said, "No kidding."

"It lost its anchor stores and replaced them with a discount
outlet and a flea market. Neither of those attractions is particularly appealing to people with a lot of disposable income,
who are the customers malls need. Some of the mall's shops
went under, and when they did, they were just allowed to sit
empty because who's dumb enough to move in? Empty stores
are not attractive. They're the ruins of failure, not conducive
to the kind of suspension of reality that makes people in a
good mall forget things like bank balances and rising mortgage
rates, so they can get in the spirit to spend. And spend."

Wally was watching me as though I weighed three hundred pounds, had eight legs, and was flexing all of them at
the same time. Wink was biting his nails.

"And now, if you don't count Boots to Suits, all the mall
has left is small businesses, and they're all—or at least most
of them—in trouble. Given half a chance to escape with their
tail feathers intact, most of them would close up, go home
for good."

After a moment, Wink said, "But?"

"But two things. First, everyone knows that the guys who own this place are not gentlemen. Everybody knows they'd take every last penny they could get, if they were in a position to do so. And second, as soon as someone tries to pull out, those owners will be in a position to do so. Right?"

Wink said, "It's your story."

"They'd be in a position to take everything, practically down to your socks, Wink, because you all signed the *same contract*. You can't get out without giving two years' notice, and if you try to go anyway, you owe the mall a major pre-set financial penalty, in addition to—what was the phrase? *Whatever other demonstrable damages the management may see fit to assess*. We saw what happened to Gabriel's, didn't we? In addition to however much they were sued for, they had to leave behind hundreds of thousands of dollars' worth of fixtures, display units, counters, changing booths, even business machines."

Wink said, "Assholes," and I didn't think he meant Gabriel's.

"So the merchants can't make any money and they can't shut down without leaving everything behind and then being at the mercy of *management* who, as we've said, are not nice guys." My phone rang again, and I said, "Hold that thought," and answered it, holding it away from my ear. All three of us could hear Vlad screaming.

I covered the speaker outlet and said, "Nine-thirty tonight." He stopped so suddenly he might have been corked, and then, when I moved my finger aside, he was saying "—that late?"

"Because that's how long it'll take me to finish," I said.

"Finish what?"

"For Christ's sake," I said, and Wally unconsciously rolled

his chair back a few inches, "you want it right or you want it sloppy?"

I had the phone at my ear again, and Vlad said, "What can you tell me now?"

"I know how the stuff is being stolen," I said. "I know by whom. But I don't know all of it, so leave me alone and meet me at nine-thirty, when I will."

"Where?"

"This place closes tonight at eight," I said. "It's Christmas Eve, so everyone should be gone by nine. Why not give the slowpokes an extra half hour to get out of here, and meet me in the parking lot. It'll save me a drive, and I can show you a couple of things here."

Wally began to swivel back and forth in his chair as though he had to go to the bathroom.

Into the phone, I said, "Nine-thirty. North end, okay? Oh, and hey, it's not that I don't trust you, but you're going to be bringing me a wad of money and I don't want to see anyone with you who might encourage you to change your mind about paying me."

"Satisfy me," Vlad said, "and I will pay you."

"If I'm right," I said, "you will be satisfied in every regard." I disconnected. They were both looking at me wide-eyed, and Wink had a sheen of sweat on his forehead even though the room was, as always, cool.

"I can see why none of you wants to rely on the better angels of his nature, as Lincoln put it," I said, "because he doesn't have any."

"Get to the point," Wally said.

"So there *is* a way to avoid being ruined, isn't there? See, in return for your rent and for observing the terms of your lease, the owners guarantee you—"

I was interrupted by Wally's sigh. He was kneading his face with the knuckles of both hands.

"In exchange for all that, *et cetera*, they make you a few guarantees of their own, don't they? They guarantee you that they'll do a certain amount of advertising on the lessees' behalf, including that big, ugly sign out there; and they'll pay for, publicize, and supervise a number of seasonal promotions like Shlomo and what's-his-name, Dwayne. They also guarantee that they'll keep the building in acceptable condition, that there will always be adequate parking, and they guarantee a certain level of *security*. Security against what, Wally?"

It took him about twenty seconds, but then he said, "Theft." He was watching the screens on the wall.

"Right," I said. "And the failure to prevent that theft has what effect?"

Wink said, as though the words were being dragged from him by pincers, "It invalidates the lease."

"There we are," I said. "An escape clause."

Still watching his screens, Wally said, "So that's why I'm in this conversation? You think I've been lax in security? I'm *surveillance*, I don't control the guards. They're a different company. I don't install or maintain the alarm systems." He dragged his eyes away from the screens as though I were interrupting the last at-bat of a perfect game. "So how am I—"

"Don't disappoint me," I said. "You're in this conversation because this whole dodge was planned around your damn cameras."

He said, "Anyone who's been here long enough—"

"And also because Wendy Straub says hi," I said. Wally was motionless, his face frozen. I said, "You know, Des Moines? Mul-T-Key? *That* Wendy Straub?"

Wally began to chew on his lower lip.

"Keys," I said, "that are interesting if for no other reason than that they open a murder scene. But that's *not* the only reason they're interesting, is it?"

"You tell me," Wally said.

"Well, let's frame it this way. Would you want old Vlad to know about them?"

"Who?"

"Sorry. Mr. Poindexter or whatever he calls himself. Because, come on, Wally. You have a *role* in all this."

The room was so silent I found myself wishing the monitor screens had sound. My phone chimed and then chimed again, and I saw that Aphex Twin 1 and Aphex Twin 2, aka Anime and Lilli, had sent me attachments, almost certainly the iPhone movies of the crowd in motion. Now all I needed was a chance to put them to use.

"Okay, let's cut to it," I said. "Everybody's guilty."

Wally raised a hand. "Everybody who? And of what?"

"Wally," I said. "You're not spotting the shoplifters on your screens in here. I suppose you could say it's because of the crowds. But Wally—*Wally*, why haven't any of the shop owners snagged some of these thieves? There's really only one logical answer to that, isn't there? They don't *want* to catch anybody, they're in on it, they're the ones with the *motive*, right? What do you say to that, Wink?"

Instead of answering, Wink nodded at Wally, a silent *go ahead*. Wally drew in most of the air in the room and said, "First of all, it's not everybody, okay? It's sixteen shop owners." He closed his eyes. "Fifteen now that Bonnie's gone. And second, all they're doing is *stealing from themselves*. Last I heard, stealing from yourself wasn't a crime. And the crowds? Okay, all the owners nominate eight or ten people each, friend, family, neighbors, every day we pull the scam. Relatives, girlfriends, and boyfriends, I don't know. Sometimes different people, sometimes the same people."

The kid with the Frida Kahlo unibrow popped into my mind's eye.

"But jeez, it's not hard to get them; they *want* to come back. They get to hit three or four stores a day, and in every store they're told to hit they get a freebie they're allowed to keep. Helps with the Christmas shopping."

"And those things have already been separated from their alarm tags."

"Well, sure. So the crowd shows up in, say, Wink's place."

Wink emitted a barely audible moan.

"They buy something for cash," Wally said. "Wink messes around in the register because he's on camera, remember? And it's his store because, like everyone else in this deal, he's the owner and the operator. So he hands their money back to them as change. If they give him a card, he slides it along the terminal, but he keeps it just under the slot. And then he slips whatever they've 'bought' into a bag, which already has two or three extra things in it, already in a little bag. That's the other reason for the crowd, the shops need to be ready on the days they're scheduled. They have to have the extras all bagged up and ready to go. So the people in the crowd, they get to keep the item they chose, and before they leave at the end of their day, they drop off the bags containing the other stuff at a different store. Sounds complicated, but it's not. They're told which day to show up, they get three or four texts telling them which stores to go to for free stuff, and the only thing they have to remember is which four stores they can drop the extras in. Because it was all explained to them when they were asked if they wanted a bunch of free stuff.

And not that week, but a week or so later, all of it, the things they kept and the things we slipped to them, get reported as stolen."

"And the stores where they drop the extras off are all next to Gabriel's," I said.

Wally looked at his screens again, as though he'd never seen them before. For a long moment I didn't think he'd reply, but then he said, "Yes." He glanced at Wink, and then back to me. "What tipped you off?"

"First, the minute I arrived, on my first day, the crowds were bigger than I thought they should be. In this neighborhood, I mean, in this mall. Even Shlomo noticed. More kids, more people. Second, the, ummm, vigilance against shoplifting seemed way down. I've never shoplifted in my life, I'm a rank amateur, but I was waltzing into stores with empty pockets and out with full ones. Not in all the stores, but most of them. Third, the patterns of movement on the ground floor. And, finally, when I found those fancy keys last night, they were all, except for KissyFace, in shops next to Gabriel's. So, as you were saying, everyone, all the fake shoplifters, they drop off the stuff when they leave."

"Sure," Wally said. "That way, they go home with all the stuff they picked for themselves, and the other stuff gets left where we can get to it later."

"So just as I thought, that's the stuff that gets dropped at the stores that are next to Gabriel's. Those are everybody's last stop. And at the end of the day, the owners of those shops use their Mul-T-Key to open the doors, which are out of camera range, and take all the stuff someplace inside. My guess is that it all winds up in the loading dock that's been closed off since Gabriel's split, down below the ground floor. The one with the broken elevators. The cops haven't turned the stuff up yet—*but*."

"Cops are back." Wally was looking at a screen. "They've got lights up on the third floor now."

"What *about* those elevators?"

"So you're *not* so smart, are you?"

"They've been monkeyed with," I said. "*How* is just a detail."

"It's a fake plate," he said, sulking slightly. "It's snapped over the real plate with the real buttons. You pop the plate off with a screwdriver, use the buttons underneath, and then push it back when you're finished."

"So at the end of the day," I said, "no actual loss. I mean, the shopkeepers are out a few bucks for the stuff people took home, but that's still the cheapest way they'll ever get out of their leases. And they get the other stuff back."

Neither of them spoke for a moment, although they locked eyes, and then Wally said, "If you say so." Wink looked at the ceiling.

"Fine, okay, so there are still a few things I don't know," I said. "But the important thing is that *I will know,* and soon. And the reason I'm going to figure it all out has fuck-all to do with you and this scam. It's about learning who killed Bonnie."

Both of them were squinting at me like tourists face-to-face with a native in the Valley of the Liars.

"That's it," I said. "That's all of it. I don't really care about the dodge people like Wink here are doing to get out of their leases. In fact, I salute their ingenuity. But I *am* going to find out who killed Bonnie."

Wink started to say something, stopped and thought about it, and then said, "So you're on *our* side?"

"He was hired by—" Wally began.

"If there are *sides* in this nonsense," I said, "I suppose

I'm on yours. Unless you had something to do with Bonnie's murder."

"I was crazy about Bonnie," he said, and Wally said, "We all were."

"So back to Gabriel's. What was Bonnie doing up there?"

"Nobody knows why she was there," Wally said. "Or at least nobody admits that they know."

"I was here all night," I said. "I went over Gabriel's pretty well except for the only part of it I couldn't reach, which is to say, the loading dock. Do you know about the word that was written upstairs?"

My phone rang again, and it was, once again, Louie. This seemed like a good time to let them think for a moment, so I said, "Yes, Mr. Poindexter?"

"And merry Christmas to you, too," Louie said. "Lavrenty Barkov."

"That's the guy?"

"No, that's the *boss* of the idiot who shot at you upstairs in that store. I found two people who do business with the Russkies and they both recognized the idiot's picture and placed him with Barkov."

I looked at Wally and mimed a gun to my head. "Barkov is a member of the Edgerton Partnership, right?"

"Yeah, and according to Rodion, up in the pen, he's got the most weight. He's also the one who is least happy with Poindexter."

"I need to talk to him."

"You'll have to do that yourself. I'm not getting near him. I got a number for you, but you didn't get it from me. You never *heard* of me. You never met anybody named Louie in your life."

"Do you have a name for the one who shot at me?"

"You mean the squirt?"

"Yes."

"Domnin, D-O-M-N-I-N, first name Vassili."

"Great. What's the number for Barkov?"

He gave it to me and I wrote it on the little pad in my wallet as Wally and Wink whispered together. Wink glanced at me, and I pointed at the phone and shook my head helplessly. "He's furious," I said.

"So," Louie said, "you coming for dinner?"

"Boy," I said, "that's a tough one. We'll have to talk about it later. When I'm alone." I disconnected and said, "Whew."

"You said, 'Barkov,'" Wally said. He wiped his brow.

"Yeah, Poindexter is so mad he's bringing his partners in."

Wally said, "Oh, Jesus."

Wink got up and said, "I'm outta here."

"Not until we're finished. Just hold on a minute." I took a moment to think about what I needed to say while Wink and Wally fidgeted. Then I sent Barkov a text message that said, I KNOW YOU HAVE VASSILI DOMNIN WATCHING POINDEXTER. AND I KNOW SOMETHING YOU AND VASSILI HAVEN'T FIGURED OUT YET. I attached the photo of Domnin I'd sent Louie and pressed *send*. "Who thought all this up?"

"Bonnie," Wally said. "Or at least, she's the one who told me about it. She suggested it for the first time last November or so and got a couple of other shop owners to sign on, but she couldn't get enough, so she tried again this year."

"I wouldn't have thought she was so devious."

"We were all surprised," Wally said. "But she really wanted out, and she knew everyone else did, too. So, like, necessity is the mother—"

I put up a hand. "She personally recruited everybody?"

"Far as I know."

"So that means she's the keystone. Pull her out, and the arch collapses."

"What word?" Wally said. "You asked if we knew about the word."

"Better you don't know. Okay, so Bonnie's running this con, and she lined up the people who are participating. They could all identify her under pressure. Wink, has anyone asked you who set up—"

"Just you," he said. "Just today."

"There's been no pressure," Wally said. "Till now."

"Got it," I said. "Okay, then let's look at it this way. There must have been people she talked to who said no."

"There were, I think," Wally said. "But they got in on it, mostly, after the first three, four days. They could see it was going to work. I don't know for sure that they *all* changed their minds, but—"

"What are you doing in the middle of this, Wally? Wink, I understand, but not you."

"I hate those guys," Wally said. "And I have friends here. Bonnie took a chance on me, talked to me about the cameras, and I thought about it and signed on. These people are my friends, and they're being treated like slaves, and it's not like they're actually breaking the law. I was going to quit after Christmas anyway. *What* word?"

"Something written upstairs, near where she was killed. Well, listen, if you don't know for sure who turned her down, maybe there's another way to approach it. There are four stores that border Gabriel's, meaning that their owners could slip out at the end of the day, unlock those doors, and put stuff in there without being on camera. I'm leaving out the ground floor because the bazaar is down there, lots of light and some camera coverage of anyone who goes in or out. Of the four stores that border Gabriel's, three had a hidden Mul-T-Key, and I had to pick the lock to get into the fourth. My guess is that's a shop owner who might have passed on the whole idea."

Wally said, "Oh." He looked like he'd been hit on the head with a rock. "The only one who's next to Gabriel's who didn't get a key was Sam, and he—" He rubbed at his chin with the palm of his hand, and I could hear his whiskers bristle. "I don't know whether she talked to Sam, but . . ."

"But she *didn't* ask you to get him a key," I said.

"Umm, no."

"Sam hated the whole thing," Wink said. "He went kind of crazy, Bonnie said, talked about losing another home and, and having to live on a border, just nutso—"

I said to Wally, "Did you know he'd changed his locks? Your key won't open his door now."

"It's a *fire code* rule," Wally began, and then he got up to follow me because I was already halfway through the door. "He hasn't come in today," he said. "He never misses a day, but he hasn't come in." We were out on the walkway, headed toward Sam's. "And it's *Christmas*," he said.

The moment I made the right toward Sam's, my phone pinged to indicate a text. It was from Barkov, and it contained nothing but an address.

31
Reindeer in the Snow

By the time we got to Sam's Saddlery, Wally and I were both running, with Wink lagging behind. I let Wally go first and then stood there impatiently as he riffled through his big ring of keys just as I had, but with more swearing. When he'd tried one in the lock and failed, I said, "Hang on," took off my long-sleeved shirt, wrapped it around my fist, and punched a hole in the shop window just to the right of the door. Then I reached inside and opened it. I could almost see Herbie planting a hand over his face in disappointment.

"He is going to be *pissed off*," Wally said.

I said, "I think I can live with that."

I was through first, the smell of leather assailing my nostrils. Last time I'd seen the place, I'd been using my penlight. Now, with light streaming through the windows and with the merchandise cleared from the tables and out of the display counters, the room looked bigger than I remembered, grimier and colder. Behind me, Wally said, "Look here," and I stopped and turned to see him holding the door away from the wall it closed against. At the juncture of the wall and the floor, where the open door would hide it, was a Mul-T-Key.

I said, "Don't touch it," and reached into my pocket for my food service gloves. Wally was backing away from the doorway as though the key had hissed at him. "Put your hands in your pockets and keep them there." He did, but he also kept backing up until he hit the edge of the doorjamb.

"It's hers," he said. "Bonnie's."

"How can you tell?"

"It was the first one I gave to anybody, and I thought I should track them. I took a nail file and put a single groove into the edge of the plastic."

"Did you mark them all?"

"No. The others got theirs all together, so I just handed them out. He must have been with her, I mean, they must have gone into the store together. Listen, I think we should get the cops in here."

"Give me one minute." I leaned down and used my plastic-covered index finger to slide the key about an inch. The floor beneath it was discolored, the rust of dried blood. I heard Wink, looking through the broken window, gasp. I said, "Wally, why don't you go out there and wait for a minute or two? You and Wink can keep people out while I take a quick look."

"Just a minute or two," Wally said. There was a lot of stress in his voice.

"Time me," I said, "and then you can go call the cops."

The rest of the shop's display space had been cleared off and—minus the beautifully crafted leather goods—was roughly made, mostly cheap plywood with strips of veneer on the edges. Behind the counter was the loose stack of bills and warning notices I'd glanced at the night before. Everything was as I'd left it. I closed my eyes and counted to ten, wanting to curse myself for my carelessness the previous night, no matter how tired I'd been, and then I turned and once again slid aside the curtain, just a neutral-colored drape of cheap cloth hanging on rings from a length of unpainted doweling. Behind it was the storeroom I'd barely glanced at, just three lines of shelves running to the back wall, stacked with the goods that had been on the tables and beneath the counter.

I went farther in. The three shelf units created two corridors no more than a yard wide and six or eight feet deep. At the end of the second corridor, the one farther from the curtain, a wooden workman's bench was butted against the wall. It was about five feet long, scarred and gouged with a lifetime of labor, squared on one end but narrow and rounded at the other to provide a place for the workman to sit, straddling it like a saddle. A sheet of heavy canvas with many pockets sewed to it, something like the thing Kathy used to hang on the closet door to store her shoes in, but thicker and plainer, dangled from the shelf on the right. Tools of every description bristled from the pockets, but the tool that mattered, a wood-handled knife with a four-inch blade, stood upright in the wood of the bench, holding in place a piece of paper.

It was a Christmas card, a winter scene with a couple of caribou—or, I corrected myself, taking the context into account—*reindeer* in the snow. Behind the reindeer was a dark, far-northern wood, and the snow leading to the wood had been grooved in parallel lines by the runners of a sleigh. Floating above the wood was a single brilliant star. I used a gloved hand to pull the knife straight up, slid the card down over the dried blood on the surface of the blade, and opened it.

On the right half was a printed message in what looked like Polish, and a signature: Eva. On the left, written with a ballpoint pen that had been pressed so heavily it had torn several triangular holes in the thick card stock, was Sam's own Christmas message.

I could not, it said, and then the line terminated in one of the torn spots.

Could not lose home again.

I lose every home . . . Another rip.

Cannot.

I am sorry.

I am sorry.

She was nice woman.

I refolded the card and carefully put the knife through the hole Sam had made when he pierced it the first time and stuck the point back into the wooden bench. When it was done I stood there, breathing deeply and counting each breath until the spots in front of my eyes finally went away, and then I went back out into the store and rejoined Wink and Wally.

"The word written on the counter," I said, "was *STOP*." By the time Wally was calling the police. I was out of there, out of Cranmer's way, out of the massive dead end that was Edgerton.

The address Barkov had given me, to my surprise, turned out to be same glass-and-granite office building on Ventura that once housed one of the Valley's more successful executive crooks, a facilitator named Wattles, who could and had set up anything from vandalism in a supermarket parking lot to a triple hit. One of his schemes had turned its head to bite him not so long ago, and he was now a fading memory. I parked in a spot that ended in a wall on which were stenciled the pale words *Reserved for Wattles & Co.* They'd been sharp-edged and pitch black the last time I was here, when the old man was still presiding over his ratty, occasionally bloodstained empire, but now they were a ghostly grey beneath a budget mixture of whitewash.

When I got out of my car and turned around, Mini-me was about five feet away with his fingers wrapped around a snub-nose revolver, the gun nestled so easily it could have been there for years.

"Whoa," I said. "People don't usually get that close without me knowing it."

"Is only open parking space on this level," he said a bit proudly. "Reserved for Mr. Dead from upstair. So you take space, and I wait *there*." He indicated the cars parked directly behind me.

"Pretty good," I said. "Shall we go?"

"I am not errand boy," he said. "Open trunk."

"I don't care what you say, I'm not climbing in."

"Ha. Ha. Ha." It sounded like he'd practiced but still had a way to go. "I need to see. You open, you step back."

"There's a gun in here," I said, and there was because I'd made a stop at one of my storage units.

"Don't care," he said, "just don't touch." So I opened the trunk and stepped aside.

He angled around to the other side of the car and looked at all the bright Christmas bags in the trunk and then, still pointing his gun dead center at my chest, he peered through the windows at the backseat. I identified the squeaky sound he was making as sucking his teeth. Up close, he wore his hair plastered down, Rudolf Valentino style, possibly in an attempt to trap his dandruff and keep it off his gunmetal grey lapels, which folded back from a short jacket with a nipped waist. He looked like the doll Mattel hadn't designed yet: Barbie's Untrustworthy Suitor.

When he was done, he said, "What will you tell Mr. Barkov?"

"That I think you have remarkable fashion sense."

He waved the gun back and forth, I suppose to remind me that we weren't just chatting. "About the *mall*."

"That's for him," I said. "And don't threaten me because I can't imagine the conversation you'd have after you tell him you shot me in the garage."

"No, no. No. What you will tell him about *me*. About, you know, up in the dark. And before."

"Well," I said, "what would you like me to say?"

His eyes rose to a point over my shoulder, and he squinted. "I was following you where were the little shops, and you saw me . . . because you stopped at a, at a place selling . . . mirror—"

"There's no booth that sells mirrors."

"Oh," he said, and some of the confidence in his face waned.

"The glassware," I suggested. "I saw you reflected in all the glasses and stuff, and your very individual clothes—"

"Not my clothes," he said quickly. "Mr. Barkov is not liking my clothes. But glasses is okay. You would not see me except for the glasses, okay?"

"Fine. And then?"

"And then I run up the electric stairs to the dark store and I see the dead lady."

"Did you?"

"Of course," he said. "Why you think I am *shooting* at you?"

"Yeah, I'd been wondering about that."

"I run in, I hide behind glass thing—"

"Counter."

"Counter, and there is dead lady. I hear you coming, but I am not seeing anything, I don't know where is front of store. You understand?"

"So far, so good."

"And I run to back of store. Is mistake. And then you are making noise, tripping on things, and I realize you are *between* me and front of store. And I think about dead lady, and I get frightened—"

"No," I said. "You make a *strategic decision* that the best way out is to frighten *me* into running—"

He was already nodding his head. "Yes, this is what I do. Strategery. Yes, you running. Running where?"

"You wanted me to run back down the escalator," I said, "so you could leave without anyone seeing you. So you fired your gun, but I got scared and confused and went in the wrong direction because I thought you were one of Vlad's men—"

"Vlad?"

"Sorry, Mr., uh, Mr. Poindexter, so I was all frightened and running away, making little high noises, but I was between you and the doors and you couldn't get past me, so you shot in one direction to make me run in the other, setting me up in a place where you could ambush me, and then you hit me on the head and, um, made a skillful escape."

"I see dead lady," he said. "But I don't get scared. I trick you. I ambush you." He nodded. "Is good."

"Done," I said, and I held out my hand. He transferred the gun into his left and shook, and I was thinking, *I'm glad I'm not this guy's life insurance agent*, and he clapped me on the back and said, "We go."

Barkov was in his mean early fifties, squat and square, and looked like he was made out of iron scrap. He had little black eyes partly overhung by thick, bristling brows that made it hard to tell where he was looking, a short nose with nostrils that flared dramatically, as though he were following a scent toward something he didn't want to find, and a decisively downturned mouth. He sat behind a relatively high desk, a little interior design intimidation, and I couldn't tell how tall he was at first because he didn't get up from the desk when Mini-me and I went in, but after I sat I saw that his feet, in brilliantly polished wingtips, didn't quite reach the floor.

The moment I sat on a hard wooden guest chair, he said, "You have five minutes. Why are you here?"

"Why am I *there* first," I said. "At Edgerton. That's going to take a couple of minutes on its own."

"Vasya," Barkov said. "Out."

Domnin began to protest in Russian. Barkov lifted his head far enough for Domnin to see the eyes beneath the black hedge of eyebrows, and Mini-me backed out of the room.

When the door was closed, I said, "Vasya?"

"Nickname for Vassili," he said. "Also, in Russian, popular name for kitty cat."

"Poindexter—"

"Pffffff," Barkov said. "*Poindexter. Tip.* Name for fairy boy in ballet."

I couldn't see any margin in advocating political correctness, so I let it go by. "He went to Trey Annunziato—"

His eyebrows met in the middle and wrestled for a moment. "You know her?"

"I helped her out once. People like her hire me to solve problems."

"One more name," he said. "One more person you have worked for."

I mentally crossed my fingers for luck and said, "Irwin Dressler."

Barkov had been looking into my eyes, but now he seemed

to be focusing through me at the wall behind my head. "You are telling me that Mr. Dressler, Mr. *Dressler* has—has talked to you."

"Many times. I've been to his house."

"Yes?" Barkov said, and there was a note of *gotcha* in it. "*Where* is house?" Very few people knew where Dressler lived.

"Bel Air," I said, "but I'm not suicidal enough to give you the address. From the street you can see that the driveway curves to the right and there's a fence so the house isn't visible, but it's grey stone."

He raised a hand. "All right, all right."

I figured *what the hell* and added, "Last time I was there I ran into Jack Nicholson."

Barkov leaned forward and put his elbows on the desk. His sleeves were rolled up and his forearms had so much hair on them you probably could have used his skin as a potholder. "How tall he is? Jack Nicholson?"

"Maybe five ten. About your size." Barkov was probably five seven.

"Yes," he said with a pleased nod. "Jack Nicholson."

That seemed to be the end of the thought, so I said, "So Poindexter called Trey to ask for someone who could handle a problem, and Trey sent me."

"Problem is?"

"Stealing at Edgerton. You know about this?"

"I see spreadsheets. But you know, small money for me. Not worth stomachache."

"Small money for Vlad—sorry, Mr. Poindexter, too. Small enough to make me wonder why he hired me."

"How much he paying you?"

"Fifty thousand."

His heavy eyebrows had gone up at the number. "And you know who is stealing?"

"I do."

He seemed to be considering his next question, and when it came, it wasn't "Who?" It was, "When will you tell him?"

"Never," I said. I had to stop and take a breath, because this was the cue to start my pitch. It had sounded pretty good when I thought it over as I drove, but now I'd have to say it out loud.

I'd never known what it meant when someone was said to *bristle*, but now I wouldn't have to ask anyone. "Why?" he demanded. "Why you say never?"

"Because he'd kill me in a minute if he knew I'd figured it out. He hired me in the first place to see whether anyone *could* figure it out."

Barkov's gaze had dropped to the surface of his desk, which was empty except for an appointment calendar in Cyrillic and a crystal wine goblet full of Tootsie Pops. He didn't say anything, so I added, "In fact, that's why I'm here. I'm going to tell you instead."

He leaned back in his chair and put one foot on the desk. The sole of his shoe looked like it had never been walked on. "Why?"

"Well, when you learn you have an enemy, one course of action is to go to your enemy's other enemy."

"Why you are thinking we are enemies, Tip and Me? We are partners, we are friends. We are brothers."

"Then I'm in the wrong office," I said, starting to get up.

"No, please," he said patting the air with his palm to indicate that I should remain seated. "This is habit of mine. When I do not understand other person's train of thought, I wonder who is stupid, him or me, and I ask question to find out." He bent his ankle to get a new perspective on his shoe and regarded it approvingly for a moment. "Usually is him. Why would you think—"

"The Italian city-states," I said, "they were allies sometimes but they always fought—"

"Yes," he said, a bit wearily. "Much can be learned from history. So we are here, we have some time, tell me what you think I should know."

The iron band that had begun to squeeze my chest when he finally asked me "Why?" began to loosen. "I'm going to start," I said, "by reaching into this shirt pocket"—I tugged on the fabric first to show him what I was going to do—"and pulling out my phone. I have a picture to show you." He nodded, so I took it out, powered it up, and went to the picture I had taken just after I left Edgerton about thirty minutes earlier. I handed him the phone.

He pushed back from the desk and let his foot drop. It swung back and forth an inch from the floor. "Yes?"

"That is Equestrian Acres. It's a new development. It borders your mall."

He looked up at me, and I could practically see his ears prick up.

"It's ambitious," I said, "but it doesn't make sense. Big houses, but hardly any land, considering the startup costs—buying a bunch of houses, demolishing them, clearing it away, building the new ones. Hard to see how they'll make much money. Can I have the phone back for a minute?"

He gave it to me, and I went into Chrome, to the site where I'd parked the browser. "There you go, the sales site for the development." I gave it to him. "Gated community, blah blah blah. Quarter-acre lots, so that's four houses per acre. Asking prices go from eight hundred thousand through a million three. So figure a million one as a median, that's four point four million per acre."

"And?" he said.

"And it's only six acres."

Barkov was looking at me, and he could have been made out of wood.

"But right next door to it, Poindexter is emptying *your* *mall*. On purpose. Your contract has this Draconian exit clause, so he's giving most of the small merchants two big presents. First, he's handing them this Christmas season, which is when they make most of their money for the year. And second, he's giving them a free out on that exit clause."

He looked down at the phone again, then to the wall, then back to me. "The shoplifting," he said. His voice had deepened half a tone.

"Exactly. He went to one of your merchants, one everybody liked and listened to, and he told her that the vendors could invite people they liked to come in and get some free stuff, and he's turned those invited guests into an organized plague of shoplifters who come in and empty the shelves on schedule. He's got it all worked out, letting the merchants each bring in twenty, twenty-five people and having them wander around until—do you know what a flash mob is?"

"Humor me."

"Give me the phone again." I brought up the footage Anime had taken, which was better than Lilli's, and handed it to him. "See? At first you just see a crowd, a mass of individuals or small groups. They're essentially milling, which is what you get when every individual is doing what he or she wants. But look what's—"

"I see it. Three, yes? Three direction."

"They're getting texts from someone Poindexter stationed

on the second floor. If you look at the security footage for today, you'll see that when stores were crowded, *three* were always more crowded than the others."

"Why? Why would he do it this way?"

"You have one guy at the mall looking at thirty-two monitors at the same time. Hard enough to spot anything, but with three stores crowded he'd need extra eyes."

Barkov's gaze was not friendly. "But *he* does see the crowds."

"Yes," I said. "He does."

"And he knows they are not natural."

"Yes."

Barkov said, "His name."

"That's not going to do you any good," I said. "There isn't one person or two who are responsible. Almost the whole place is in on it. Poindexter talked to one store owner, one who was in a *lot* of trouble, one whom the others all liked. He promised her that they'd all have legal grounds to break their leases after Christmas, and he paid her five thousand bucks to talk to the others, which she did. He only talked personally to that one person."

"Who? Who is she?"

I said, "She's the woman who was murdered yesterday."

I could almost hear the key snap in the lock. He got up, which involved a two- or three-inch drop, said something under his breath, and climbed up again. Then he said, "He kill her?"

"Well, she was the only one in the world who could say he was behind it all, so yeah. But probably not personally. He got someone else to do it."

"Maybe you kill her."

"Oh, come on," I said. "Let's at least try not to be silly.

She was still alive—dying, but alive—when your boy in the other office, Vasya, found her, and I chased *him* up there. Look, there are two clinchers, as far as I'm concerned. First, I went after Vasya, because Vlad—sorry, Poindexter—said he needed to talk to him. Said his partners were spying on him and Vasya could confirm that. Why else would I have gone after him? He didn't have anything to do with the shoplifting, he was just watching Poindexter, and then after Poindexter left he was watching me, because he saw me meeting with Poindexter. And Poindexter was scared. I don't know whether you've seen the tape of the meeting, whether there's another feed off those cameras that you can get to—"

"Is."

"Then you saw. He sat with his back to the camera so that I was the one who was facing it. I'm telling you, the whole time he was there, he was looking over his shoulder."

"Vasya agrees with you. And the other—what was the word?"

"Clincher," I said. "You know he's a developer, you've probably gone in with him on a few projects."

"A toll road, maybe some houses."

"Right. He told me how he scared all the homeowners away to clear the route for the road. He was laughing about it, about how he had to be the one to do the heavy job. Well, behind the model houses of Equestrian Acres there are twelve deserted houses just as empty as the ones on your road, then a little strip maybe ten feet wide, and then your parking lot. So what I think he's going to do is let the mall get stolen blind, let the vendors exercise their option to scram when we all know it's going to be impossible to replace them, and then he's going to come to you and beat his breast and tear his hair and say the mall's a bust and he failed, and he'll offer to make everything good, to pay you off, give you what you shelled out for it, plus a tidy little something extra out of his own pocket to prove how sorry he is. He told me how cheaply you put it together, twelve, thirteen million, so let's say he pays you double that, even more, and when you're gone he'll own two acres where the mall building is now, fifty-one acres of parking space, and an acre, give or take, of miscellaneous access space. Plus the six he's building on now. So that's sixty acres at, what did we say? Right, four houses per acre, average one point one per house makes four point four million per acre, times sixty, makes two hundred sixty-four million dollars. And he'll have paid you twenty-five, thirty million. Oh, yeah, and he already owns the land, because you bought it for him."

The silence stretched out for almost a minute. Then Barkov said, in an unsteady voice, "And one more time, you are telling me why?"

"You know why I'm telling you. I already said it. The only reason I'm alive now is that he doesn't know that I've put it together. But I'll tell you, it won't to be long until he starts to worry about me."

"No," Barkov said. "Not long."

"And when he does, I figure I'll be able to measure my life expectancy in hours."

"So," Barkov said, and he crinkled his eyes without bothering to produce the friendly smile that would have made it a little less terrifying. "You come to me. Better the devil you don't know."

"The devil I don't know," I said. "Not bad. But I'll tell you something I *do* know."

"Yes? What?"

"I know *exactly* where he'll be at nine-thirty tonight."

PART FOUR

GOOD WILL TO MEN

32
Do Not Sound a Trumpet Before Thee

When you have to lie, it's always a good idea to mix in as much truth as possible. That way, if the people you were fibbing to find out that it wasn't *all* gospel, there's a better chance of them thinking the part that was a lie was just a mistake.

Also, as much as it pains me to admit it, truth is usually more convincing than fiction.

On the whole, I thought, as I drove back toward the Edgerton, I'd sold Barkov a pretty good blend. I had no idea, obviously, whether Vlad had been the one who put the whole idea into Bonnie's head, but it made more sense to me than the notion that she came up with it herself and then, acting totally independently, trotted it out to all the others. On the whole, I thought it was about 70/30 in Vlad's favor.

Of course, poor old Sam had killed Bonnie, but even when the news broke this evening, as it certainly would, there would be nothing in it that contradicted anything I'd told Barkov. Someone other than Tip had killed her; it might as well be Sam.

And then there was the big one. Did Vlad *really* own Equestrian Acres? I hadn't had time to dig up the owner's name, which would in any event be hiding behind some uninformative corporate shell or other, but it seemed to me about 70 percent certain, yet again, that he did. Getting the families who had lived in those empty houses to abandon them had undoubtedly required a distinctive and now-familiar force of personality, and that name—*Equestrian Acres?* How wanna-be Anglo-Saxon *nouveau riche* can you be? Vlad all the way to his slender gold bracelet.

No. On the whole I would have bet good money that Vlad owned 100 percent of Equestrian Acres and that he planned to make about a hundred million clear, after expenses, out of repurposing, as people like to say these days, those empty houses—formerly *homes*, where people *lived*—and the acreage on which the mall sat. It would not only make him permanently rich, it would also be the lever to dissolve his partnership with a troika of Russian thugs and establish himself once and for all as Tip Poindexter, gentleman developer. If I was right, he wasn't just double-crossing his partners. He was abandoning his past.

And if he wasn't already planning to have me killed, he would be in the near future.

The thing I *didn't* know was just how pissed at him Barkov and the rest of the group actually were. In their shoes, I would have been thinking: get rid of him—he'd led them into a terrible investment and he was planning to cheat them. If they just turned down his offer to take the mall off their hands, they'd all still be stuck with a money-losing mall, and Vlad would be left to struggle with a small and not-very-profitable housing project. While that would probably offer Barkov some tiny level of satisfaction, it couldn't begin to compare to the potential of knocking Edgerton down and building their own development, and it would be even sweeter to grab control of Equestrian Acres by erasing Vlad from the picture entirely. Two hundred forty million dollars outweighs a little frayed loyalty.

I yawned for the fiftieth time since I'd gotten behind the wheel. Despite the two-hour nap at Motel 7, this felt like the longest day of my life. I hadn't eaten since the previous evening, but I wasn't hungry. I was still worried about Ronnie, I felt powerless in the situation with Vlad—I hate having to depend on other people—and I was mourning Bonnie.

And, I supposed, I was also mourning the too-frequently dispossessed Sam. I wondered for a moment who Eva was, and then someone honked at me and I realized I was lane-drifting, so I pulled to the right and took it more slowly for a few miles. This was a part of the Valley I'd had little reason to explore. A couple of miles northwest of Edgerton lay a stretch of cramped stucco houses, smaller and more modest than the ones that had been emptied to make way for Equestrian Acres. They'd been built in the post WWII boom of the 1950s, a dozen at a time, and sold for $7,500 to $10,000. Now they went in the low hundreds of thousands and a great many of them were rentals, often to large families, or even several families, sleeping in shifts and packed inside with a density that rivaled Mumbai.

But still, their Christmas lights were up and beginning to flicker on in the early December gloom, and Styrofoam Santas stood on brown lawns here and there, accompanied by reindeer formed from wire and thickly outlined in lights. In those little houses, people were wrapping packages, decorating their trees, putting up stockings, making, or even eating, Christmas Eve dinner.

I made a wrong turn into a little circle and found it filled with rambunctious kids, all juiced on the energy of Christmas, so I crept around it at about two miles an hour, returning the kids' waves like someone in the Rose Parade, and then made a right and coasted another block to the correct street, the street, according to Wally, on which Sam lived.

Or rather, *had* lived. There were people gathered on both sides of a particularly squat little bungalow with a chain-link fence surrounding its backyard. The gate in the fence was standing open to make room for a fire department emergency medical truck and an ambulance, and people in various uniforms went back and forth from the vehicles to the open door of what was obviously a rebuilt garage with a sagging roof, tricked out as an illegal rental. Sam's final home in what he had called *this rich, rich world* had been a garage, and he was being threatened with eviction even here. Involuntarily I saw in my mind's eye the dark, snowy European forest on the card Eva had sent him.

I parked the car and joined the onlookers, waiting fifteen or twenty minutes until a little knot of people emerged through the garage door wheeling a gurney. The person on it was covered head to foot. The young woman next to me must have seen my expression, because she said, "Did you know him?"

"A little," I said.

She said, "Maybe I shouldn't tell you this, if you were his friend."

"An acquaintance, really."

"Well, one of the cops said he shot himself."

I said, "Sad as that is, it's not a surprise." His confession had been the first step in his suicide.

The first eager stars had popped out directly overhead, although the sky above the hills to the west was still washed with magenta. I was parked on a narrow street south of

Ventura, about two miles from the house I once shared with Kathy and Rina. The breeze was quite cool—chilly, even—but the hood of my car was warm, and that was where I was reclining with my back against the angle of the windshield. I was looking at the little points of fire burning in the broad cold emptiness of the heavens.

Must have been something to have been a shepherd, seeing that star. The angels, I remembered, were in Luke and the star was in Matthew. Dividing up the miracles, I supposed. I wondered how it felt to believe fully and unquestioningly in all that extravagant divinity. I took my own divinity where I could find it, and most of the time it was measured in small sips, usually delivered through natural beauty and acts of unprovoked kindness. Divinity, I thought, should have its roots in mystery. Mine was distressingly everyday.

There were a hundred things I could have done, but I didn't have the will to do any of them. The edge of sorrow is especially sharp in what's supposed to be a season of joy. I was exhausted, which meant that my emotional immune system was tissue thin, my eyes were heavy, and my body seemed to weigh four hundred pounds. I felt adrift, and none of the lighthouses toward which I usually steered—Rina and Kathy, Ronnie, even the occasional joy of solitary freedom—burned brightly enough to draw me. I envied those shepherds that brilliantly unfamiliar star.

If I'd felt any lower, decomposition would have set in and I would have been found in that exact spot on Christmas morning, the biggest and ugliest hood ornament in the history of Tarzana. Just as I reached the deep end of my pool of self-pity, my phone rang.

"Where are you?" a male voice said.

"Depends on who this is."

"Really? You must live an interesting life. Your location is variable according to who's asking? Sounds like quantum physics. I'm where I am, no matter who's calling."

"Hi, Shlomo."

"Come on," he said. "Get over here. You're missing it."

"Over where?"

"Edgerton."

"Shlomo," I said, "I personally like you quite a bit, but there is nothing happening at Edgerton I wouldn't much rather miss. My life plan, while it might look wobbly and weak-willed to others, definitely does not include Edgerton."

"How about this?" he said. "How about I absolutely guarantee you a good time?"

"At *Edgerton*?"

"We're only starting at Edgerton, and then we're off. Come on, get your heinie in gear. It's after six already. We'll be leaving in about twenty minutes."

"For where?"

"Those who come," he said, "learn. Meet us at the loading dock behind Gabriel's."

"Who's us?"

"Did you hear me? I said, *the loading dock behind Gabriel's.*"

I was sitting bolt upright. "Ten minutes," I said.

I almost missed them.

The parking lot was emptying, leaving only the lonely shoppers who didn't want to go home to no one, the terminally indecisive, or the procrastinators like me. If it hadn't been for the shopping skills of Anime and Lilli, I thought, I'd probably be in there myself.

Most of the remaining cars were parked close in, and the

vast majority of them were on the western side, where the entrances were, but even so, I drove past the activity at the loading dock without seeing anything except a couple of straggler cars and a small, nondescript van. A light being waved back and forth in my rearview mirror slowed me down and turned me around, and at the other end of the beam I found Shlomo, still in his Santa suit but with his beard pulled to one side, the way some businessmen tuck their neckties over their shoulders when they eat lunch.

"It's Mister Mystery," Shlomo said when I pulled up next to him.

"Do you actually own any clothes?"

"Corduroy," he said, "I got corduroy. Retired teachers wear corduroy. Get out of the car and lend a hand."

Behind him, the darkness of the mall's outer wall framed a darker rectangle above the dock—an airplane door—and in that darkness, with the imprint of Shlomo's flashlight still ping-ponging off my retina, I could just see people moving around. There seemed to be eight or nine of them.

By the time I'd parked the car, I had my night vision back, and the figures inside the open loading dock had resolved themselves into people I recognized: LaShawn from Kissy-Face, Wink from iShop, and eight or nine others whose shops I could identify but whose names I couldn't recall offhand. Many of the people, in short, who had been playing roles in Bonnie's scheme—or, as I hoped Barkov now believed—Vlad's.

But what I was seeing wasn't part of any plan I'd suspected. A jumble of goods was piled at the end of the dock, on a sheet taken from the stock of (I guessed) Interior Harmony. Heaped up there I saw clothes, gadgets, toys, blankets, food baskets, small items of (I supposed) bric-a-brac that had to have come from Bonnie's. Still in his green polo shirt despite the cold, Wally was taking items from the dock and putting them into the back of the van.

"Give me a hand," he said. "Got to try to keep the stuff in categories. We can't go searching through it at every stop."

"What are your categories? And where are you stopping?"

"*We,*" he said. "You're with us, right?" Without waiting for an answer, he pointed at the piles he'd made in the back of the van. "Clothes for women, clothes for men, clothes for kids, extra-warm clothes for, you know, everybody. Shoes, toys—we don't got enough toys in the mall, so we bought some extra—electrical gizmos from Wink, baskets of all kinds of stuff that LaShawn made up. She makes really pretty baskets, maybe a little heavy on the makeup, but you'd be surprised at how much women want the makeup. Then we got blankets, pillows, and little whatzits, mostly Bonnie's. People like whatzits, too." He stopped for a moment, and for the third time since I'd met him I heard him swallow, and then he said, "Let's get to it."

We got to it. About fifteen minutes later, when the van was loaded, LaShawn, Jackie—mistress of The Paper Dolls—and Wink clambered into it, with LaShawn at the wheel. It was apparently her van. Five others jammed into a dark sedan with Wally driving, and Shlomo said, "I'll ride with you."

"So," I said as I followed the other vehicles out of the lot, "where are we going?"

"Studio City first, and I don't know the address, so don't lose them." He settled back and switched his beard from the shoulder on my side of the car to the other one, probably so it wouldn't tickle his face when he looked over at me. "This is my third year of this. This is why I was worried when they decided not to use me this year, just to go with poor Dwayne, before it got crowded. I wouldn't miss it for the world."

"You knew about Bonnie's plan?"

"No, not the shoplifting part. But these people have been setting aside some of their stuff every Christmas, and I guess one of the effects of Bonnie's idea of having them all steal from themselves is that it increased the number of gifts that got stored away in Gabriel's."

I said, "Oh," and spent a moment getting used to the notion that I wasn't actually so smart.

I had to step on it to squeeze through a yellow light— LaShawn, in the lead, had an enviably aristocratic attitude toward things like lane lines and stoplights—and when we'd made it, Shlomo said, "I wonder where all these people will go."

"I've been thinking about that myself."

"This has to be the end for Edgerton," he said. "Not that anybody will miss it very much. But I think there's going to be a hole in these people's lives. Even if it's just the *community* that happened there. There are a lot of friends there."

"So we're giving all these things away."

"Very perceptive. Maybe you *are* a detective."

"It's a shame that they probably won't be able to do this anymore. People should have known about it."

"*When thou dost give thine alms, do not sound a trumpet before thee,*" Shlomo said. "That's from your part of the Bible. No, I think they've done just fine without publicity. And you know what? It's probably made their time at Edgerton much better than it would have been. I just wish Bonnie had been here to see this."

"And Sam," I said. "Don't forget Sam."

o o o

The first stop was a family shelter in Studio City, where we were obviously expected. Everyone was seated at long tables, eating a Christmas dinner, but the moment the door opened in front of us, half a dozen kids jumped to their feet for a ragged but enthusiastic version of "Here Comes Santa Claus." A cheer went up when Shlomo Ho-Ho'd his way into the room with his sack over his shoulder, and I was surprised to see that the people in the van and those who had been jammed into Wally's car had somehow divided among them bright green bits and pieces of the Edgerton elves' costumes. A cap here, a cape there, green gloves, a pair of tights, a bracelet of bells: they were patchwork fragments, but everyone who came in with Shlomo was identifiably of the elven persuasion. When we left, about fifty people crowded through the door to watch us go. Shlomo pointed to me and said to a couple of kids, "He's taking me to my sleigh. This is a no-reindeer zone," and we pulled out.

Wally had been right: they *were* thin on toys. After a quick stop at an almost empty Toy Palace, where I let people shop for a few hundred bucks' worth of toys that would be my contribution, we went to a shelter on Van Nuys Boulevard for kids who had been rescued from the sex trade, and then a refuge for battered women, always working our way back toward Edgerton. After the fourth stop, a care facility for the aged, Shlomo said, "I owe you the rest of the story," and he told it to me in between the incandescent pauses to deliver Christmas.

33
Noëlle

In the wake of the scream from down the hallway, the room seemed to Morris to have come alive in some way; the flames on the candles flickered erratically in the wake of Autenburg's departure, and shadows danced everywhere. When the cry of pain was repeated, Autenburg called for Werner, and the soldier took off at a trot, heading for the back of the house, gun in hand. As he crossed the bit of carpet Werner caught the toe of his boot on something—*a nail*, Morris remembered—and when he pitched forward his automatic went off, a deafening noise in the small room, and from the direction in which Mme. Loiseau had disappeared, the moan of pain scaled up into a scream of terror, and then a male voice, either Helmut's or Autenburg's, was shouting panicked instructions. Werner disappeared into the hall.

The smell of the fired gun was overpowering. Looking self-conscious, Schmidt brought his automatic up and pointed it in the general direction of the Americans, but his eyes kept flicking toward the hallway.

Morris saw Jerome Keystone cross his legs and begin to slide his hand toward the boot with the two-shot in it. As Morris was estimating the length of the jump to the front door, on the other side of which their weapons were stored, Autenburg came back in, his face even redder than before.

He nodded approval at Schmidt's vigilance and turned to the kitchen, but M. Loiseau rose from his chair quickly, ignoring the spasmodic jerk of Schmidt's gun as it followed his movement, and shouted a burst of furious French at the sergeant. Morris caught only one word: *Enciente*.

"Yes," Autenburg said. He stopped, looking at M. Loiseau. "This is what I am believing," he said. "She is—" He shaped a belly with his arms.

"It is now, I think," M. Loiseau said. "She is many days late."

The cry was repeated, but higher in pitch, and over it they could hear Mme. Loiseau, trying to calm her daughter and then calling, "*Claude*. The water, the *water*."

Autenburg called out in German and got a shaky reply from, it sounded like, Werner. He nodded and waved M. Loiseau ahead, following him down the corridor.

Schmidt, his gun pointed in the general directions of the Americans, blinked several times and licked his lips.

"What a world," Keystone said, slipping his fingertips into his boot, "to bring a baby into."

Sabathia said, "She needs a doctor."

Schmidt said, "My sister . . . has baby, three month before."

"Everything go okay for her?" Keystone asked. He shifted to put the boot with the gun in it out of sight below the tabletop.

"It went good, good," Schmidt said. His eyes drifted to the hallway. Keystone bent his head so he could see what he was doing.

Watching Keystone inching down toward his gun, Morris could almost see the sequence his friend was running in his mind: the only German gun in the room being wielded by a distracted teenager, the disorientation the kid would experience seeing the derringer in Keystone's hand, the rush through the door to grab the weapons and disappear into the fog. The possibility that Schmidt would fire. The possibility that Schmidt would be bleeding to death on this farmhouse floor in a moment or two.

The young woman in the other room.

Morris said, to Keystone, *"Jerome."* Keystone's head came up, his eyes wide at the betrayal, but Morris said to him, "Jerome. I'm a doctor."

Schmidt's mouth dropped open, and Autenburg burst into the room and went straight into the kitchen. *"Ihr Fruchtblase,"* he said, moving things around on the stove. *"Ihr Fruchtblase . . .* is, is *geplatzt—"*

"Yes, her water has broken," Morris said. "Let me see her. I'm a doctor."

Autenburg said, "Yes? This is true?"

"I have my degree," Morris said. *"Ich habe—"* His German, sketchy at best, had flown out of his head. "I have my, my—*meinem Medizinstudium."*

"You have had baby—" Autenburg shook his head impatiently. "No, no, you have helped *woman* to—to bring baby before?"

"No," Morris said. "But I know what needs to be done." He felt compelled to add, "Unless things go really wrong. I mean, I'd hate to attempt a cesarean section, but—"

The girl at the end of the hall cried out again.

Autenburg's gaze was so intense Morris could almost feel it blow straight through him. The German sergeant nodded once, brusquely, and said, "You tell us what to do." Then he looked over at Sabathia and Keystone. *"You.* You stay sitting here, yes? *Schmidt—"*

Schmidt swiveled to point his gun back at the table where Sabathia and Keystone sat. Keystone lifted both hands above the table, fingers spread, and made the little back-and-forth movement that meant *I'm not up to anything* all over the world.

"I need soap, hot water, towels," Morris said. "*Now.* I need to go in there."

"Yes, yes, *yes*," Autenburg said in a tone that suggested he'd given the order several times already. "You go." Then he called down the hall, something to Helmut and Werner, and stepped aside to make room for Morris. Over his shoulder he called out, "*Schmidt*, you stay here. You are too young."

He repeatedly called for more light, and by the time Morris brought the baby, tiny and shining and perfect, into the lantern's hard yellow gleam, the bedroom was almost as bright as day. The young woman on the wet mattress was undernourished and terrified, but the moment her mother used the word *docteur*, she put herself and her child unquestioningly into his hands. When she cried out during the delivery, it was because of pain rather than fear, and Morris encouraged her in his unstudied French to make noise, make all the noise she wanted. Once he added, idiotically, that she wouldn't wake anyone up, and she smiled at him and the rigid doctor-face he had adopted to mask his terror dissolved into a smile of his own, and from then on they worked together.

The windows were defining themselves as pale grey rectangles by the time he had the child firmly in his grip and smacked its bottom, and when the child cried, the girl on the bed said, "*Ohhhhhhh*," and tried to sit up so she could see it better, but her mother snapped a caution and she settled back. As Morris wiped the baby clean with damp cloths that had been boiled in the kitchen, Mme. Loiseau got extra pillows and lifted her daughter's shoulders to slip the pillows behind her. From the time she caught sight of the baby, the girl never took her eyes off it.

"A daughter," Morris said, wrapping the baby in a blanket. "*Une fille.*" He put the infant on her mother's breast, and the mother curved her arms around the bundle, which chose that moment to begin to cry again.

"*Une chanteuse,*" the girl said, "a singer. *Maman, elle s'appelle Noëlle.*"

"Noëlle," her mother said nodding. Then she came up to Morris and took both his hands in hers. "*Merci, merci, merci.* Thank you."

Behind her the doorway darkened, and Autenburg stood there. He surveyed the room, his eyes pausing on the mother and child, and he said, "We heard the crying." He cleared his throat. "Everybody wants to see the baby."

"Her name is Noëlle," Morris said. He felt light enough to drift away.

"Madame?" Autenburg said. "Can the men see Noëlle?"

Mme. Loiseau turned to her daughter, and her daughter said, "Yes. They have been so quiet."

Autenburg made a brusque military bow and said, "Thank you," and half a minute later the men were at the foot of the bed. There were no guns in the room. In the grey dawn of Christmas day, they all gazed down at the child, and Morris had to look away from Schmidt, whose face was as clear and transparent as water.

The three German privates and Keystone used two of M. Loiseau's overcoats to make a kind of gurney and they cheered the mother into sliding across the bed and onto it as her mother held Noëlle, and then, with much cautioning in two languages, they carried mother and child to the dry bed in the other room, where M. and Mme Loiseau usually slept.

Morris was spared gurney duty, and when he went back into the front room he found Autenburg bent over a piece of paper. Autenburg said nothing while Morris, suddenly exhausted, collapsed into a chair and buried his face in his hands. He sat that way for a few minutes, hearing men making cooing sounds from down the hall as well as the scratch of pencil on paper.

He might have dozed off because when he opened his eyes, Keystone was sitting beside him and, in the next chair, Sabathia. Helmut and Werner were in the kitchen, washing things, and Autenburg was sitting back, regarding him. Morris looked around for Schmidt, and Autenburg said, "He's in the room with the baby."

"The *other* baby," said Sabathia.

Keystone nudged Morris and nodded in Autenburg's direction. When Morris turned, Autenburg slid across the table the piece of paper he'd been drawing on.

"The house is the rectangle on the right," Autenburg said. "The curving line over to the left is the road, which you want to stay away from because we planted mines there. Not many, but you only need to step on one, yes? Try to stay at least ten meters from the road. The terrain slopes down toward it a little, so you can see it."

He waited, and Morris said, "I understand."

"The lines up here," Autenburg said, tapping on the top of the page, "are us. Germans. Down there, in the bottom, this is you." He frowned at the page. "Maybe, maybe farther east. If you keep this house behind, you should find them. The big square here"—he leaned over and circled it—"is a church, now—now *vernichtet*, destroyed. When you see it you will be going correctly." He looked up at Morris. In the kitchen, Werner and Helmut were still and listening. "Any questions?"

"Yes," Morris said. "What's your first name?"

"Günther. And yours?"

"Morris. I'm Morris Stempel."

Autenburg rose and stretched, his hands knotted into fists. When he was finished, he pushed the candle on the table, seeming dimmer now in the grey dawn, toward Morris. "We will wait," he said, "until this candle has burned out."

Morris leaned forward and blew out the candle. Then he stepped back and opened his arms. He said, "Merry Christmas, Günther."

Autenburg looked at Morris's outspread arms, shook his head, and said, "Hurry." Then, as Morris turned away, he said, "*Fröhliche Weihnachten*. Merry Christmas."

Their rifles were where they'd left them, with the pistols Schmidt had carried out right beside them, and all the guns were cold to the touch and wet with condensation. They armed themselves in silence, and then Keystone, the map-reader among them, looked at Autenburg's drawing and set off, Morris and Sabathia trailing behind. Sabathia was limping, but not as badly as the previous night.

None of them spoke.

Four or five minutes later, Morris looked back, but the house was lost in the pearly grey fog. He said, "Slow down a little, Jerome," and Keystone stopped and turned to watch them come. "Do you need to lean on me, Sabby?"

"I'll walk in on my own two feet, thanks," Sabathia said.

For a quarter of an hour or so, they moved silently. The road was to their right, but they couldn't see it through the fog, and Keystone, checking the map occasionally, kept shading them a little left as they went. Just as Morris was about to say he thought they were heading *too* far to the left, the great dark bulk of the ruined church loomed in front of them. Out of the corner of his eye, Morris saw Sabathia cross himself.

It was growing lighter, and the fog was thinning. From time to time, coming from in front of them, Morris heard little drifts of noise: metal on metal, the occasional murmur of speech, in English. As the three of them slogged toward the sounds, Morris found himself thinking about the ground they were walking over. Men had died there by the hundreds, by the thousands, in 1917 and 1918 and again now, in 1944. Young men with lives in front of them, with people who loved them, with unborn children, unborn ideas and ambitions.

French, German, Russian, British, American, Italian, he thought, they fought here, and then, suddenly neutral in death, they fell here and let their blood soak the soil. It seemed to Morris, as he followed Keystone away from the house where no soldiers had died and a child was born, toward the muted sounds of the American lines, that he could feel the fingers of the dead plucking enviously at his boots, trying to slow him, trying to keep him with them a little longer on this killing ground, to keep him here on the fields where they lay.

34
What Is *Nickels?*

Nine-fifteen on Christmas Eve with Santa well on his way, and Shlomo's story was still echoing in my mind as I dropped him at his car at the far border of Edgerton Mall's dark, empty parking lot and prepared myself for whatever was going to happen. I was early, I thought.

But no, as I rounded the north end of the mall, a big black SUV blinked its lights at me, and I realized, with a jolt of panic that brought me suddenly upright, that my gun was still in my trunk. Whatever happened next would be up to Vlad.

Figuring it was a *much* better idea to be in a car than on foot, I pulled up on the driver's side of the SUV. When the tinted front window slid down I was looking at Barkov.

He said, "Nice houses over there."

"I thought you'd like them."

"Very nice," he said. He raised the bushy eyebrows. "You are right: is Yevginy. I have debt for you."

"Forget it," I said.

"I don't forget." He raised his hand, thumb out, and stubbed it toward the highway. "Go away."

I said, "But I'm supp—"

"We are taking the meeting," Barkov said. "This is what they say in Hollywood, right? *Taking the meeting?*" Beyond him, in the passenger seat, was someone whom I couldn't see clearly but who was almost certainly Mini-me.

"Well," I said. "As they also say in Hollywood, don't take any wooden nickels."

"What is *nickels*?" Barkov said. "No, never mind. You go."

I went.

But not far. I pulled into Equestrian Acres, past the model homes, opened the garage of one of the Vlad-cleared houses, and drove in. Then I lowered the door quietly, hunched over and bent my knees to change my silhouette, and walked on the balls of my feet into the thin scrim of trees that bordered the parking lot.

Barkov had moved the van so it was all alone in the center of the lot. Because of the distance and because of the sound absorbed by the trees, what happened next felt like a silent film.

A second dark SUV pulled into the lot, took a slow loop around the perimeter as though making sure there weren't people in other cars waiting on the far side of the building, and then drove slowly toward Barkov's SUV, dimming its lights thoughtfully. When the vehicles were about fifteen yards apart, the new car stopped. For twenty or thirty seconds the two vehicles stood motionless, facing each other. Then the driver's door of the second SUV opened and someone got out. He was in the headlights of both vans for a moment, until they were switched off almost simultaneously, so I was able to recognize the muscle boy I'd thought of as Brando the morning Vlad had come to the mall to give me my money. The fact that he was here tonight, when I'd told Vlad to come alone, made it fairly clear that I was not actually in line for that second $25,000.

Brando's arms were loose and relaxed, curved slightly at the elbows; he was showing them empty hands and widespread fingers but not making a big deal about it. He moved slowly at first but then picked up the pace. From my perspective he seemed to be heading for the passenger side, but the left turn signal came on in Barkov's vehicle. Brando slowed and changed direction to the driver's side. Barkov's window went down.

I heard nothing, but from Brando's body language it was a spirited discussion. Three minutes passed, and then four, and then the headlights in Vlad's car flashed its high beams once, then twice. So Vlad had slipped over to the driver's side.

Small things crawled on me. A clutch of crickets began to fiddle away on all sides, as though I were in the center of an insect orchestra.

Brando lifted a hand in Vlad's direction, universal sign language for *hold on a minute*, and then he nodded at Barkov a couple of times, straightened up, and ambled back toward Vlad's SUV. He went to the driver's side, and once he had the door open something in his right hand flamed red four, then five times, and I heard a spatter of sounds like paper bags being popped, and the crickets fell silent.

They remained silent as Brando went around to the passenger door and made a big show of tugging something heavy and hard to move onto the empty seat. Then he closed the door quietly and went back around the SUV, got in behind the wheel, closed the driver's door behind him, and waited.

The crickets began to tune up again.

Barkov's vehicle started to move, almost magisterially, like a galleon slowly catching the wind, and the SUV containing what remained of Vlad after his encounter with the Ghost of Christmas Future followed it at a deliberate, presidential-candidate speed out of the parking lot.

I stayed right where I was for a few minutes, remaining perfectly still and listening to the crickets.

I like crickets.

35
It's Christmas in Denver

Some of the lights were out in the enormous underground area parking beneath the Wedgwood and its sister apartment buildings, the Royal Doulton and the Lenox, now known in the neighborhood—thanks to some burned-out neon—as *The Royal Doult* and *The nox*. A few of the garage lights were *always* out, another strategy to discourage people who didn't know about the place from getting out of their cars and going into the buildings, but tonight there were more out than usual, and the huge space stretched away to darkness on three of its four sides, so even if I'd been on the lookout there wouldn't have been much to see.

I'd been mildly careful all the way home, just out of habit, and now I sat in the car for a few minutes, listening to the engine tick as it cooled, waiting for movement that I wouldn't be able to see anyway.

It was all exactly as automatic as it sounds. First, I wasn't actually worried about a threat; the only person on whose hate list I was guaranteed a place was Vlad, and wherever he was, I was certain that his body temperature was plummeting. Second, I didn't really give a damn if someone took a crack at me. I probably would have welcomed it: *Look, a diversion. Something to do.*

The muted pops of Brando's gun as he dispatched Vlad were still echoing in my skull, driving away the afterglow both of Morris Stempel's miracle and the light in the faces I'd seen in the shelters where the Edgerton thieves had shared their holiday loot. It all seemed like years ago.

As vile a specimen as Vlad had been, being shot into hamburger in a parking lot on Christmas Eve was, I thought, a little stiff. And I'd been a participant, whether I pulled the trigger or not. It felt to me like I lived in a toxic zone where such things could and did happen, that I was responsible for choosing the life that put me there, and that some of the spiritual mud from Vlad's execution had inevitably splashed on me and stained me. *Again.* When I could have been in a warm, well-lighted room, decorating a tree. With a family.

I thought briefly about counting my blessings, usually my go-to spirit raiser, but it seemed like too much effort. What I *really* wanted was to be a bear in a warm, dry cave with a lot of cozy leaves on top of me and pounds of fat beneath my skin to live on while I waited out the winter, dreaming bear dreams of blackberries and unguarded apple trees and really slow deer.

The bear thing comes on me from time to time. It's never a good sign.

My sigh was heavy enough to fog my windshield. Seeing my malaise condense on the glass in front of me was more than I could take, so I got out of the car and popped the trunk.

There they were, all the presents I'd bought with Louie and, later, with Anime and Lilli. None of them was wrapped, of course, and I had forgotten to buy more paper and ribbon, so I'd either have to go back out to an all-night drug store and pay through the nose for being such a schlump or improvise some kind of wrapping. I wouldn't have gone back out again to be blessed personally by the Pope, so improvisation it was.

In California, the war against shopping bags has trained all of us to drive around with a trunk full of empty bags, so at least I didn't have to juggle all the stuff. I jammed it into a Trader Joe's bag and a big old leather tote, and some of the good feelings that had gone into finding and buying that stuff rubbed off on me. As I handled each one I remembered why I'd chosen it, or why Anime and Lilli had, and how I felt about the person for whom I'd bought it. I was especially pleased with the two willowware saucers for my mother; she's never cared much about material things, and this was the kind of gift she appreciated most, one that couldn't have been bought for anyone else. Getting them had also given me a chance to make an oblique apology to poor old Will, who was, after all, just another harmless con man who'd found an edge he could use against the world. I'd been feeling a little guilty about the way I'd flattened him.

By the time I pushed the button to bring the creaking elevator, my spirits had lifted to the point where I'd mentally selected half a dozen shirts I could cut up to wrap the smaller gifts. I stopped on the lobby floor to give the Korean security guards a couple hundred bucks to divide up with the guys on the day shift and then rode the rest of the way up, my spirits ascending as I did. And then I got off on the third floor, and the reality of the empty apartment hit me across the face with a wet fish. Up and down, up and down. Maybe, I thought, I should give up the apartment and live in the elevator.

It usually takes three keys to open the door, but when I got to the third, the deadlock, it was already open. I paused for a moment, feeling a little prickle on the back of my neck.

I never forget to lock it. But then I remembered that Ronnie had been the last person to leave, and she sometimes *did* forget, so I opened the door and went in.

I had reached for the light switch before I registered the pale light coming from the living room.

Carrying the tote bags as quietly as I could, I crossed the entryway into the hall, past the library, which was dark, and into the living room, my favorite, with its angular art deco windows and the view of downtown.

And there she was.

She was looking up at me, her head down and her fine gold hair hanging over her brow and framing her face. The coffee table had been pushed aside to let her sit on the floor with her back against the couch. A wobbly candle flame emitted shivers of light on the table beside her, where I also saw a bottle of white wine. No glass. Scattered in front of her were several small presents in various stages of being wrapped. None was finished, and they had an air that suggested they'd been abandoned. She leaned forward and swept them aside with her forearm and then kicked one halfway across the room.

I said, "How are you?"

"Almost drunk," she said. "On the *way* to drunk."

"Want company?"

She pushed her lower lip out and drew it in again. Then she rubbed her face with an open hand, refocused on me, and said, "I thought you'd never ask." Then, with no apparent transition, she began to cry.

"Oh, no, no, no," I said, dropping the bags of gifts, and by the time I was on the fifth or sixth *no* I was on my knees in front of her, and she put her arms around my neck and made deep, heartbroken whuffing sounds, interspersed with the sniffs of someone who needs badly to blow her nose. I hugged her again, got up, and said, "Hang on," and when I came back I had a whole roll of toilet paper in my hand. She took it even before I'd finished kneeling, spooled about a yard's worth around her hand, and scrubbed at her face. Then she blew her nose hard enough to turn herself inside out, wadded the paper up, and tossed it over her shoulder onto the couch. She said, "Surprise."

"It is a surprise. I'd say I'm happy, but it's hard for me to be happy when you're not."

"Gimme the wine," she said, and I handed her the bottle, which was about three-quarters empty. She upended it into her mouth, knocked back a couple of inches, and put it on the table, which, judging from the force with which the bottle hit it, was about an inch higher than she'd thought it was. She looked past me at the room and then back at me. She said, "Trenton."

"Trenton," I said, and I could feel the pulse bumping away at the side of my throat.

"Open one of them," she said fiercely. "Any one. They're not really wrapped anyway."

I took the nearest one. When I picked it up the paper fell away, and I was holding a box that said *First Steps* on the side. I opened it to see a tiny pair of shoes.

"I don't even know," she said, and then she stopped and blinked a couple of times, cleared her throat, and said, "how big his feet are now. I don't know how tall he is now. I don't know"—she was blinking again, rapidly—"whether his hair is still blond." She closed her eyes for a long moment, and I watched a tear track its way down her left cheek. "I don't know what color my own baby's hair is." And then she was sobbing full out and I had her in my arms although she barely seemed to register it until she finally rested her forehead, hotter than I'd expected it to be, against my neck.

I waited until it passed and said, "What's his name?"

"Eric. *Eric.* He's almost two."

"His father has him?"

"Yes. And he told me I'd never see him, never see my own baby, again."

"Who is he?"

"Eric Rossi. *Doctor* Eric Rossi. You'll enjoy this. My baby is a junior."

It was easy to identify the black thing blooming inside of me as homicide. "What's he got? I mean, to keep you from taking the child and telling him to go fuck himself?"

"The Jersey mob," she said. "The whole bunch of them. And don't suggest anything silly or heroic because all you'll do is get yourself killed."

"He's a doctor? Like a medical doctor?"

"He's *their* doctor. He's the *man*, as they say, for all of it. From a bullet to a childbirth."

"And."

"I was going to go back. When I phoned you, I was going to go back, just to drop off these, these presents. Just to see— just to see him. And he said, he said if I ever came through his gates no one would see *me* again." She looked down at her lap and nodded twice, decisively. "And he could do it. There are a dozen people who'd kill me for him. *Pop*, no problem, and I'm in the foundation of some building in Atlantic City."

"Okay," I said. "Not now, nothing now, all right? But in the next few months, Ronnie, I'll bring you your child."

"You can't."

"I can."

"How?"

"I'll steal him. That's what I do, I steal things. Does he know you're in California?"

"No. He . . . he, umm." She shook her head and fell silent. Reached for the bottle.

I intercepted her hand and put it against my cheek. She didn't pull away. I said, "We don't need to talk about this now. We've got lots of time to talk about it. But I promise you, here and now, a Christmas promise: I will bring you your baby."

"You can't," she said again.

"Here's what *I* want for Christmas," I said. "I want you to stop saying I can't. I won't do anything that you don't know about, but I'm telling you, if I can find a way to get that child out of the house, even for five minutes, even in someone else's charge, I can make him disappear forever, as far as your ex is concerned."

"How?"

"I know someone," I said. "I met her recently. A specialist. I think you'd like her."

"It's not going to work."

"Here's the deal," I said. "It won't be next week or the week after that, or maybe even in the first six months of the new year, but I promise you that every day that passes, you'll be one day closer to seeing him again. To being with him."

She was looking past me, at the hallway I'd come in through, but after a long moment, she nodded. "We won't talk about it."

"Not until it starts to happen." A few seconds slipped by without making any noise. I said, "We're invited to Louie's for Christmas dinner."

Ronnie said, "That's sweet. But we'll have to live through Christmas Day first."

"We'll survive it together," I said

She brought both hands up to the sides of her face and pressed so hard that her hands shook. Then she interlaced her fingers and let her hands drop into her lap. "I have a present for you."

"And I have one, no, two for you."

"In that pile over there?" She lifted her chin in the direction of the spill of bags on the floor.

"That's where they are."

She nodded, looking at the bags, and rolled her shoulders. Then she shook her head, as though to clear it. "Not wrapped," she said.

"No. I'm not very good at this."

"I have paper," she said. "I have lots of paper."

"Well, then. Looks like we're in business."

"Partners," she said. "What time is it?"

"A little after eleven."

"My, my." She put her arms around my neck. "That means it's Christmas in Denver. Let's get to work on this stuff."

Afterword

If you've come this far it probably won't surprise you when I say that my view of Christmas as we celebrate it today is equivocal. I agree with Junior when he muses in one of his (many) internal dialogues that the soundtrack for the modern celebration is a duet for sleigh bells and cash registers. And I do believe that the unremitting barrage of bright, pricey material objects—*merchandise*—is, on the one hand, cruel to those who can't afford it (and to their children) and light years away, spiritually, from the event the holiday is supposed to commemorate.

I'm not conventionally religious, by which I mean I don't subscribe wholeheartedly to any of the world's widely held belief systems. I see them, in a way, as beaches, some facing East and some facing West, each bordering an enormous sea from which a great many interesting things wash up. Some of these things I've picked up and carried with me for life. Others I've given a wide berth. But I'm profoundly grateful to the Christmas story for its impact on Western visual art: nativities, mother and child, halos of gold, hands upraised in blessing. The rapture in the eyes of the ragged, unshaved shepherd in Van der Goes *Adoration of the Shepherds*; Fra Angelico, painting on his knees; the guttering candle and fanning pages in Van Eyck's *Annunciation*, blown by the word of God. Some of the most beautiful images I know.

And many of the first serious paintings of women in the Western artistic tradition. Whenever I see a really individualistic painting of the annunciation I wonder what young woman served as the model for Mary and what impact the experience might have had on her. There's probably a book there, although I'm not the person who could write it.

The writing soundtrack for *Fields Where They Lay* was all over the map. A reader who works in a bookstore that's part of a mall in the Great Lakes area somehow stole and sent me a huge mp3 file of Christmas shopping music that she says she hears from mid-November through December 25. I tried, I really tried, but in the end I practically pulled my hair out trying to get my earphones off.

From then on, it was mainly classical, a lot of Mozart and Vivaldi, with some old Solomon Burke (God, he could sing), Arcade Fire, Anderson East, and a *lot* of the Phil Spector Christmas album, which is blessedly heavy on Darlene Love. Also an Emmylou Harris mix I made, slanted toward her stellar Christmas album, *Light of the Stable* (from which I deleted "Little Drummer Boy"). But a lot of Emmylou's music has holiness in it, to my ears, so there was quite a bit of her.

As always, if you want to broaden my musical horizons (or try to adjust my attitude toward the modern Christmas), feel free to contact me at www.timothyhallinan.com.

Acknowledgments

Thanks to the usual Santas—I mean suspects—for their contributions: to Bronwen Hruska for publishing it, Juliet Grames for editing it, Jennifer Ambrose for copyediting it, Rudy Martinez for that amazing cover, Rachel Kowal for shepherding it through the process, and Paul Oliver for telling the world about it. And thanks to Everett Kaser for reviewing it under a lot of pressure.

And merry Christmas to you and yours, whenever you read this.